DIANNE MARSHALL

THE SPEAR of DESTINY

The Journey Begins

The Spear of Destiny
Copyright © 2013 by Dianne Marshall. All rights reserved.
Reprinted 2020
ISBN 978-1-7361278-2-7

Published by Marshall Enterprises
USA
Marshall Enterprises is committed to freedom of expression in the publishing industry.

Book design copyright © 2020 by Dianne Marshall.   All rights reserved.
Cover design by
Dianne Marshall
Interior design by
Lee Marshall

Published in the United States of America

ISBN: 978-1-62902-143-0

SECOND PRINTING ISBN: 978-1-7361278-2-7

1. Fiction / General

2. Fiction / Christian / General

31.12.20

DEDICATION

The battle between good versus evil has raged throughout history and continues to this very day. This book is dedicated to all who fight the good fight and come to the aid of those who suffer needlessly at the hands of others. Those who take a stand for what is right are truly the heroes of the day.

ACKNOWLEDGEMENTS

A special and heartfelt thanks to Bonnie Mendez, Patty Cummings, and film director Douglas Green whose encouragement, support, and input was a vital part in completing this novel.

TABLE OF CONTENTS

PREFACE

Now when the Centurion, and they that were with him watching Jesus, saw the earthquake and those things that were done, they feared greatly saying, "Truly this was the Son of God.

Matthew 27:54 (KJV)

Throughout the ages, kings and men seeking power have sought to find and possess the spear that pierced the side of Christ. Why? According to legend, he who holds the spear will hold the power to control the world for either good or evil purposes.

In my quest to find why men believed this spear held a power so great, it became clear that there was no actual documentation leading up to the historic hunt that continues to this very day. Given to reason one must acknowledge that some chain of events must have taken place at the time of the centurion who originally possessed it in order for kings and Roman Caesars to covet it so.

Therefore the question- *What took place at the time of Longinus the centurion to give the spear its magical illusion?*

This book is a biblically themed, fictional concept of what may have taken place to bring such fame to a simple Roman hasta. The fact seems to be that it is not the spear itself, but the blood upon the spear that has the power to overcome all darkness and set up a kingdom that can never be destroyed. Perhaps the very mystery of the Lord's own words and his promise to return to do this very thing is what started the quest to find the spear? We may never know.

This story provides a look into the man who originally held the spear and what struggles he might have faced. It also portrays what might have happened in the lives of Mary Magdalene and other disciples at the time. It is a bold look into the very first ones who sought the power of the spear and how the reputation surrounding its mystery may have actually started. The missing years are both intriguing and mysterious, leaving one's imagination to fill in the blanks.

When I began writing, it became evident that there were lessons to be learned in the quest for the spear of destiny. One: the battle between good versus evil is one that continues to this day and is as ancient as mankind. Two: the true power lies within the blood and not an artifact. Three: the power of the blood is truly as alive and well today as it was the day it was first spilled on the cross.

Please enjoy this compelling saga full of emotionally charged, action-packed twists and turns as the forces of good and evil work their intrigue to bring the man Longinus to his knowledge of truth. A truth that leads him to understand principalities and powers, free will, and how to serve a master other than Rome.

It is my hope that the reader will travel back in time and enjoy the journey as much as I enjoyed researching and writing it. The destiny awaits.

Dianne Marshall, Author

INTRODUCTION

Our story opens in the year 33 A.D. early Imperial Rome was at its height as the most powerful empire on earth. Its emperor held supreme power. Legions of men with the strength of iron followed the commands of their officers, living, breathing, fighting and dying for the cause of Rome. Now all of Jerusalem and Judaea were subject to their dictates, yet, they were granted permission to use their laws to judge their people.

The Jews' mighty fortress palace built by King Herod the Great to guard the great temple situated on the north side of Jerusalem between the temple and the moat was now the garrison and headquarters of the Tenth Roman Legion and filled with Roman soldiers guarding over Jerusalem. The high towers of massive stone now loomed over the city as an ominous sign of Imperial Rome's dominance that signaled their mastery over all of Judea, let alone Jerusalem. But for Longinus, whose only home was allegiance to Rome, it was merely a place to bed.

WHAT WILL THE GODS GIVE US

ROMAN PALESTINE, IT IS THE LAST DAY OF THE 7 DAY PASSOVER FEAST DAYS OF THE JEWS – JERUSALEM 33 A.D. It is now late into the night. Centurion Longinus and his soldiers are positioned along the Colonnade that connects the Temple to Antonia Fortress. There is a great multitude inside the city.

Longinus, a Roman Centurion, stood guard with his men at the colonnade that attached to Antonia Fortress to the Temple. It had been a tiring week of controlling skirmishes among temple goers, a task Longinus felt was beneath his rank and that of his men.

Longinus looked over and saw a new group of soldiers approaching. "Good." He said out loud under his breath. The approaching Legionnaire shouted, "Take leave."

The soldiers didn't have to be asked twice as they quickly made their way through the colonnade heading for their barracks in Antonio Fortress which was once where the High Priests held their quarters, but now had become a compound for the Roman Governor and the garrison for the Roman guard.

It had been a long week and the last day of the seven Passover feast days of the Jews in Jerusalem. A great multitude throughout Judea and all Palestine had come to attend the Passover Feast and worship in the Temple. Tension among the Jews and the followers of a Nazarene named Jesus were already high but to make it worse, the Nazarene had disrupted the marketplace inside the temple making a scene overturning merchant tables and releasing their animal sacrifices. The high priest Caiaphas and his key confidants on the Sanhedrin were outraged and the Roman guard was on high alert for trouble.

There was always some unrest during the gathering of so many people, but tonight was especially risky, the soldiers stopped any misbehavior immediately, and arrests were made even for little squabbles. Rome was taking no chances at having uproar.

As Longinus marched along the colonnade into the garrison his Centurion helmet made him look nearly a foot taller than his 6'4" build. He towered above the height of his soldiers with a muscular body of stone with strength to match that of a bull. He was loyal to Rome and had the scars to prove it. His left eye had been wounded in battle, leaving him blind and scared, serving as a constant reminder to never take your eye off the enemy.

Longinus could taste his bed as he reached the garrison at Antonia Fortress.

"There is little time to sleep before the cock crows," he hollered as he stepped into the barracks.

"Hail to that!" cheered several of the men.

"What will the gods give us for all we do?" shouted one of the soldiers.

Longinus reached his bed and dropped his weapons and started dismantling his armor. "They'll not grant you rest!"

"A day of grace with the gods and all the favor of Mars," A soldier called out.

"I say, may the gods send me Diana to comfort me in all my desires," hailed another.

Laughter and requests to the gods filled the air, but were quickly silenced as a senior centurion entered the barracks. The men immediately stopped their clamor and stood at attention. The room fell silent.

It was Octavian Sullius, whose reputation for vain arrogance and harsh punishment instilled fear in both soldier, and civilian alike. It was only his officer's rank as Primus Pilus, marked by the transverse crest on his helmet that extended from side to side, that elicited him respect. With a height of merely five feet six, and a soft chunky build, his helmet towered another foot, giving him the appearance of a much taller man. Whenever he was seen without his uniform and helmet, he appeared so insignificant that no one knew who he was. He made certain he never went anywhere without both.

As Primus Pilus, Octavian Sullius was one of the most powerful heads of the Roman army. He held the command of a powerful cohort made up of ten centuries consisting of 800 men. He exercised the power of Rome and was the senior centurion of the legion and commander of the first cohort. Longinus's century was under the command of Octavian.

Octavian Sullius peered at the detachment of century and announced, "The Jewish Festival of Feasts is over, but there are still multitudes of people in the city. You will be expected to get some rest and then report to your posts at dawn."

"Yes, sir," answered Longinus.

Octavian gave a haughty stare at the men, and then he turned and left.

"You heard the order," shouted Longinus as he made his way to the water trough.

At the trough, Longinus splashed his face with the cool water. As the water settled, he peered into it and looked closely at the scar over his left eye.

Longinus slowly raised his hand and gently felt it. Suddenly he was triggered with the memory of the day it happened…

Parthian scoundrels were attacking Roman soldiers and pilfering the village square. He was in the midst of battle when he heard the painful cry for help from his beloved Sabena.

"Longinus – Longinus!" He quickly looked over and saw Sabena being dragged from her house into the street.

"Sabena!" he shouted.

"Longinus help me!" She cried out.

Longinus was encircled by savages and could not break free without battling through them. "Sabena fight!" he shouted.

Longinus quickly cleared his way to run to her, while at the same time she had struggled free from the Parthian. They ran toward each other when from out of nowhere, another Parthian rode past and brutally swung his sword at Sabena. Longinus watched in horror as her head soared through the air and hit the ground rolling. He stood frozen in shock.

The same Parthian rode up fast and slashed his sword at Longinus striking him. It happened so fast, he did not realize he had been slashed until his eye was clouded over with blood.

Suddenly he felt the pain, but it was the pain of Sabena's death that gave him the strength to pursue and kill his savage assailant, for as the savage circled back with his sword raised, Longinus threw his dagger slicing off his hand.

The Parthian's hand still clutched to his sword hurled through the air as Longinus swung his sword sending his head rolling with it. He slaughtered him and a great number of Parthians using their own savage war tactics - slicing them limb from limb into many pieces. Something a Roman soldier didn't do in battle.

Ever since that day, Longinus had sworn to avenge Sabena's death on every man he killed. Anyone who went against Rome was his worst enemy.

Longinus stood up and wiped his face with a dry rag. He felt a tear roll down his cheek from his clouded blind eye.

"Memories, damned memories," he snarled. "Rome has no use for such things and no use for those who have them." He quickly disregarded any sentiment he was feeling and made his way back to the barracks to get some shut-eye.

No sooner had Longinus bedded down to get a few hours of shuteye, and he was haunted by the sounds of revelry from the off-duty soldiers in the common area who were reveling and drinking from jugs of wine. He tossed and turned but could not ignore the sounds. He had to get up and partake in at least a few cups of the wine. Or so he thought and more than thinking he desired to do so. He quickly dressed and left for the common area.

Gods Don't Exist

Upon entering the festive area, Longinus looked around but was only interested in going straight to the barkeep. Ignoring the others he marched straight to the bar.

"Wine, your best," he ordered.

Chugging the first cup down as quickly as it was served, he hollered out, "More wine, your best."

Longinus repeated this several times. Now feeling the effects of the wine in his blood, he drank slower.

As he looked about, he noticed his trusted legionnaire named Marius. He was placing a burning stick of incense in the figurine of an owl, as a sacrifice to his gods.

Longinus, now given to much wine, was triggered by Marius's actions for he had a deep distrust of the gods due to the loss of his beloved Sabena who was innocent and worshipped them. The gods did not help her in her time of peril, and since that day, Longinus had no faith in them. He approached Marius.

"You're wasting time and incense, Marius."

"I am petitioning Mars for protection."

"Gods don't exist!" exclaimed Longinus. "The men in this room are your protection."

A soldier who had also partaken in too much wine, approached Longinus and interrupted, "You distrust the gods?"

Longinus turned and said, "Your gods are but ornaments to keep silversmiths in coins."

The soldier angry at the audacity of Longinus to mock his gods shouted, "You offend Rome when you offend the gods. They are the only things worth fighting for."

"Then we fight," shouted Longinus as he gulped down another

cup of wine and slammed it on the table.

Marius cautioned, "Longinus, sir, you've drunk a lot of wine."

"So what if I have?"

Marius took a position across from the soldier with his hands out barring him to come any closer. The soldier laughed and handed a cup of wine to Longinus. He turned, addressing Marius, "He is too drunk to fight. May as well have another cup."

Longinus took the cup and drank it down, and then he threw it across the room. "You think another cup of wine will make me purr for you like a kitten?"

At that, the soldiers all broke out in laughter. Longinus motioned to the others to stand back and took his stance with his arms out ready to fight.

The soldier readied himself, and Longinus gave him a hard fist to the face then picked him up by his waist and threw him against the table, breaking it into pieces.

At the same time, the senior centurion, Octavian Sullius, entered the room from the back. He stopped and secretly watched.

Marius shouted, "Longinus, sir, stop, you have won."

"Anyone else wish to challenge me?" Longinus shouted." I did not think so." He went to the barkeep and demanded a jug of wine. The barkeep handed him a jug, and Longinus took it to his table and poured another cup. He lifted it to his mouth and finished it off then threw his empty cup at Marius and shouted, "More wine!" He laughed and lifted the jug and took another swig.

Amidst the rivalry a soldier noticed Octavian and jumped to his feet and stood at attention. He shouted, "Senior centurion present! On your feet!"

At that all the soldiers stood at attention. Octavian smirked arrogantly in the doorway. He relished the sudden silence and then mockingly mimicked Longinus, "More wine!"

He stepped further into the room and looked down at the soldier on the floor and the broken table then over to Longinus.

"It appears that is all you know how to say these days." Octavian purposely walked up and down the men, intimidating them by his presence. After he eyed each one he announced most arrogantly, "This night's festivities are finished. Quarters now!"

The soldiers quickly began to move out of the room and to their quarters. As they moved out Octavian stated, "Except for you, Longinus."

Octavian walked up to Longinus who was weaving back and forth a bit but still standing at attention. He looked him up and down and spoke in a stern and direct manner, "It seems where there is a brawl there is Longinus and a wine jug."

"With respect, sir, wine clears my head."

"It will soon clear you of your centurion rank if you continue as you are," shouted Octavian.

"Yes sir," mumbled Longinus.

"Louder."

"Yes sir!"

"I'll overlook your stupidity and blame it on the wine but I never want to see this reckless exhibition again. Understood?"

"Yes sir."

Octavian looked at the table where Longinus's wine jug lay. He arrogantly walked over and picked up the jug.

He slowly poured it out onto the floor as he spoke, "A centurion should never be entertainment for his century. He can have a drink with them, but you seem to not know how to do that. If you took pride in yourself and your duty to Rome, you would shun the wine jug. The gods have protected you in battle and favored you."

"The gods? Or my skill?"

"You will go to your quarters and sleep off the wine," ordered Octavian as he placed the empty jug back onto the table.

Longinus continued to stand at attention as Octavian walked to the door. He stopped and turned looking directly at Longinus.

"I never want to see this reckless exhibition again. Is that understood?"

"Yes sir."

After he left, Longinus banged the table with his fist then returned to his quarters and slept.

The next day…

In the morning, Octavian sent word to Longinus that he was not to return to his post in the Colonnade, but instead he was to bring his detachment to the streets of Jerusalem and oversee an angry mob.

Longinus shouted, "Where is Octavian? This job is not fitting for a centurion, it is a duty for an auxiliary! It is beneath my salt!"

Marius cautioned, "Longinus, you are in no position to question Octavian today. After last night you are lucky he hasn't stripped you of your century."

"I see what that fox is up to," said Longinus, "He punishes me by sending me on simple errands like a slave boy."

"Nonetheless, we have our orders," said Marius." You must follow them as we all must do."

Longinus fumed and girded his armor about him and said, "An angry mob? They have not seen an angry centurion. I will show no pity on any of this angry mob that causes me this duty. I will have my sport with them."

Marius cautioned, "Longinus, don't do anything that will anger Octavian further. Do the duty and be done."

Longinus gave Marius a hard look, then shouted out, "Soldiers, fall in. We go and gather eggs from chickens this day."

CRUCIFIXION AT GOLGOTHA - CALVARY

When Longinus arrived in the streets of Jerusalem he quickly understood why Octavian ordered the finest in his century of men to oversee the angry mob. This was not an ordinary unrest. It looked more like a revolt. He had never seen such hatred and madness over a Jew. His disdain for the people of Jerusalem was kindled even more. Not for their injustice, but for their superiority and foolish beliefs.

"Why do we even allow these people to exist?" asked Longinus to a legionnaire standing next to him.

"Tiberius gets a lot of taxes, nothing more," he answered.

The soldiers poked and prodded the people, having sport with whomever they desired as they exercised their superiority with the crowd. It came to be about the sixth hour and Longinus was addressed by Octavian.

"Get your detachment to the pavement now. Pilate has ordered the zealot to crucifixion on Golgotha."

"Yes sir."

"You will escort the Nazarene and the others to the hill to be executed."

"Yes sir."

"Don't allow this execution get any uglier than it already is. Understand?"

"Yes sir."

Longinus ordered his detachment to the pavement at the Tower of Antonia and took charge of the Nazarene to escort him to the place of the skull, Golgotha, also known as Calvary. It was only 500 yards to the Gate of Ephraim and 60 yards past that to Calvary where the Nazarene would be crucified. It was not far, but it was a tedious task to get there. The city streets were narrow and downhill through the town. They were very rugged with cobblestones jutting up, with deep gaps between. Just past the town, the road sloped upward and was very winding. It would normally take a good thirty minutes to go from the Tower of Antonia to Calvary because of the terrain itself. But today, with an angry mob and all the havoc, Longinus knew it would take much longer.

"Move back!" shouted Longinus as he readied his spear at the mob. "Back you swine!"

Longinus and his detachment enjoyed cracking whips at the angry crowds and prodding them with their spears.

"Cattle!" shouted a soldier. "Pigs and cattle!"

As they made their way, Longinus noticed a woman trying to help the Nazarene and motioned to a soldier to get her back. The soldier raised his whip to flog her, but latched eyes with the Nazarene. For some strange reason he lowered his whip and gently pulled her back instead.

"Back, woman," stated the soldier. "Back."

Longinus kept his eye on the crowd and the Nazarene. He longed for rebels to take advantage of the confusion and foolishly fight.

"Make haste!" he shouted to his detachment. "Get this over with!"

Shouts of mocking taunt and accusations ran together sounding like a roar of confusion.

"He is a blasphemer. Death is not good enough for him!"

"Kill him, kill him!"

Some spat in his eyes, others reached out and smote his cheeks. Many threw stones, vegetables, and sticks at the Nazarene. Some missed their target hitting the soldiers and were met with retaliation.

"I'll teach you to aim right!" shouted a soldier as he cracked his whip, slicing through the jeering mob.

The taunting and mocking continued all the way to Golgotha.

The soldiers reveled in flogging the crowd. Some made it more of a sport lashing out at anyone among the horde. Tempers flared from both the angry Jews and enraged soldiers. It was a laborious climb to the gate without the furious mob but with them swarming it made it even harder.

At the top of the hill Longinus stood erect as he watched his fellow soldiers strip the garments from the Nazarene exposing his battered and slashed body. Blood was drenching from his ripped flesh. The soldiers delighted in playing to the angry crowd and mocked him as they pressed his crown of thorns deeper into his bleeding head. They seemed to be as much out of control as the mob that followed him to the execution.

The jeering and shouting continued unceasing as more and more people made their way to the top of the rocky skull-shaped hill just outside the walls of the city Jerusalem.

Nailing the condemned man's hands and feet onto the wooden cross added to the frenzy of the crowd. It brought sheer delight to the high priests of the temple as they shouted out their railing accusations.

"Death to the blasphemer!"

"He calls himself the son of God, well, look at him now!"

Longinus had never witnessed anything like this at a public execution. He watched as the bitter mocking of the soldiers excited the onlookers, causing them to push and shove, trampling one another to get a closer look.

"So this is what they do with zealots in Judea," stated Longinus.

The cross was raised, and with a terrible jolt, it was dropped into a hole in the ground. The force was so great it vibrated the Nazarene's body like a shaken reed. With the cross in place, the soldiers divided the Nazarene's garments and cast lots to see who would win them. Meanwhile, the people and the chief priests continued to mock him.

"He saved others, let him save himself now if he can!"

"If he be the son of God, then let him now come down from the cross!"

The soldiers added to the shouting, "If you are king of the Jews, deliver yourself!"

In the midst of this chaos, Longinus watched from the hill onto the city as merchants continued to sell their wares. He looked over to the roads and watched others continue to travel with donkey and with camels. It was as though they did not see any of the chaos, or if they did, they wanted no part of it. They seemed content to stay busy with their own affairs.

Longinus turned and saw three women approaching the Nazarene's cross. They came weeping and lamenting. The soldiers told them to stand back, but they pleaded and moved closer. Longinus wondered at the lack of obedience to the soldiers' command. He wondered even more at the way his soldiers allowed them to disobey their orders.

"How dare they allow three women to defy orders!" snarled Longinus to the sentry next to him. "I will address this myself!"

Longinus made haste to approach the women, and as he did, the Nazarene on the cross looked upward toward the heavens and spoke out in a powerful voice, "My Father forgive them for they know not what they do."

The delivery of those words stopped Longinus in his tracks. The manner in which he interceded was more powerful than Octavian. He spoke with the authority of Tiberius Caesar. It was not at all what Longinus would expect a condemned man to say. He wondered as he stared at the women.

Longinus approached the cross and looked directly into the eyes of the Nazarene. He felt a warming in his veins and had to break the stare. Longinus looked above the dying man's head and read the title Pilate had commanded to be placed on his cross. It was written in Hebrew, Latin, and Greek letters so all could read it.

Longinus read the Greek words, "This is the King of the Jews."

Longinus, now very somber and alert, wondered at this. He didn't understand why he stopped. He only knew he had too. He could only stand there in silent awe as the air around him seemed to dissipate. Suddenly an evil foreboding filled his heart and soul.

As the sixth hour of the day (noon) began to pass, the sky suddenly darkened to pitch-black and the sun eclipsed. The ground began to shake and a succession of rolling thunder roared unceasing, deafening the ears of the onlookers. Many in the multitude became frightened.

The more Longinus watched, the more he could not reason this. He wondered at the darkness, at the ground trembling, and the rolling thunder. Why were the three women the only ones that dared come close to the Nazarene on the cross, and why were they not afraid? This did not make sense. Why were they so brave to defy Roman soldiers and come close to the cross of the Nazarene? They could be stoned, beaten, or arrested for being blasphemers as well. Yet no one dared to lay a hand on them.

The women continued to cry and lament, tormenting the ears of Longinus. "How long must they go on?" he muttered as he turned his eyes away from the cross. He kept looking at the mob and prodding at them with his spear to make sure no one came any closer.

The darkness continued to hover like a foreboding omen and the ground continued to tremor from the sixth hour to the ninth. Jerusalem was shaking, and the mob that came to watch the death of the Zealot began to fear. Many left because of all the strange and evil forebodings.

Longinus turned and saw Octavian approaching on horseback. As Octavian reigned in his horse, the glazed-over whites of a spooked animal's eyes was all he could see. Longinus grabbed hold of the bridle and wrestled with the steed. It took all of his strength to steady him.

"Whoa, whoa…easy there."

Octavian gave a look of disgust and pulled the bridle bit up till it cut. He spoke in a hurried manner, "I have an order from Pilate. It seems these eager Jews that want to kill want these deaths to be over before their sacred Sabbath begins at sundown. Break their legs and hasten their death."

"Yes sir."

At that moment, a bolt of lightning crackled across the sky, followed by a bellowing roar of thunder. It began to rain. Octavian's horse reared and almost knocked him out of the saddle.

"Cursed horse!" he shouted and rode off.

Destiny's Curse

"Grab iron bars and break their legs!" ordered Longinus.

Longinus watched a soldier break the legs of the thief on the cross to the left and cringed, watching him unable to push his broken legs up to gasp for another breath. He looked at the thief on the right hanging limp, legs broken, turning blue and gasping.

A soldier headed to the middle cross ready to hit the Zealot's legs with the cold heavy iron bar, and for some unknown reason, Longinus shouted, "Leave the Nazarene to me."

Grabbing an iron bar in one hand and his spear in the other, he walked over and looked up at the Zealot. Something inside him made him stop. *He's dead,* he thought. *I must make sure.*

He took a short stare at the sign, "This is the King of the Jews," and scoffed. Dropping the iron bar, he grabbed his spear with both hands and thrust it into the man's side. Instantly, water and blood gushed forth, splashing into his eyes and onto his face.

"Yuck!" he shouted and shook his head, sending the fluids whisking into the air. Groping for something to wipe his face, he felt for a cloth, grabbed it up, and wiped. Instantly, his eye burned intensely and he shrieked out in pain. "Arghhh!"

The cloth happened to be the very one that had been dipped in gall, causing a burning sensation in his clouded eye. Or was it something else that caused his eye to burn?

Simultaneously, the air crackled and a blinding white light flashed. Longinus winced and shielded his eyes. His ears were deafened by a crashing peal of thunder, and the ground beneath him quaked like it was about to open up, causing him to stumble.

Longinus rubbed his good eye in an effort to see clearly. He gazed toward the city and tried to focus, but his vision remained mottled. Through the rain and blur, he watched as the walls surrounding

Jerusalem rocked back and forth. He heard distant screams of terror among the continuous reverberation of rolling thunder.

He looked out toward Antonio Fortress and witnessed massive stones falling from the Jewish Temple as it shook and heaved back and forth. The earth quaked and split open, creating jagged chasms. The tall tower of Antonia was vibrating fiercely.

Truly, the gods are angry at the killing of this man, He thought. *Those who condemned him are chastised by the hand of fate.*

The soldiers exclaimed, "Truly this was the Son of God!"

Longinus yelled, "Truly, this was!"

Fearful in knowing he pierced the Nazarene's side, he began to feel cursed. He shrugged it off and quickly focused back on the task at hand. He shouted, "Make sure the thieves are dead!"

Longinus turned and found himself face-to-face with one of the women. Even in tearful sorrow, her face was beautiful. She looked deep into Longinus's eyes with pity.

"Your name?" he asked as the rain poured down upon them.

"Mary of Magdalene."

A soldier, holding an iron bar, stepped between them. He shoved the woman out of the way with such force, she fell to the ground in the mud.

"Legs are broken," he reported.

Longinus was angered by the soldier's actions. He shouted, "Leave my face before I strike you!"

With the rain pouring down, Longinus extended his hand and

helped the woman up. Mary humbly bowed her head in thanks and hurried over to the foot of the cross.

Longinus watched as she mourned in deep sorrow and grasped the bloody feet of the dead Nazarene and kissed them.

Mesmerized with the woman, Longinus stood there in deep thought, Her voice is so much like… he quickly shook off the memory of his beloved Sabena as he spotted Octavian galloping on horseback rapidly toward him. He noticed he had a new steed, one that seemed oblivious to all the ominous horror. Longinus stood at attention.

"Remove the bodies from the crosses," he ordered as he dismounted.

"But him," Octavian pointed to the man on the middle cross. "The Nazarene is to be released to a man named Joseph of Arimathea by order of Pilate. He will be here with some help to assist with the body. Get him down."

"Remove the nails," ordered Longinus. "Raise the ladders!"

"Make sure he shows Pilate's seal and order. Don't give the body to anyone without that!"

"Yes sir."

Longinus turned to see the woman named Mary of Magdalene waiting and grieving with the other women. He had a fleeting moment of pity then got back to the duty at hand.

"Get this dead man down!" he shouted.

Soldiers quickly leaned a ladder against the horizontal beam of the Nazarene's cross. Longinus watched as a soldier climbed to the top and began pounding out the nails. The body was carefully lowered down with ropes.

As Longinus watched the soldier descend the ladder, a man named Joseph of Arimathea approached him with an order with Pilate's seal upon it. Longinus opened the seal and read the order. He looked close at the man's face.

"Go quickly," ordered Longinus.

He observed closely as the followers wrapped the body in linen, but his eye was more focused on the woman named Mary.

Longinus ordered an escort of soldiers to oversee the burial to ensure they did exactly what the orders from Pilate stated and nothing more.

As the followers carried the body to a sepulcher in the garden by the hill, Mary glanced back toward Longinus. There is something about that woman, he thought. He stared for a moment, then suddenly focused his attention back to the task at hand.

"Fall in!" ordered Longinus.

The soldiers all gathered. Longinus took one last look toward the garden and watched as a large boulder was rolled in front of the tomb.

"Clean up and detach to the barracks."

"Yes, sir," shouted the soldiers.

THE FIRST VISION

Upon returning from Golgotha Longinus heard wailing and lamenting from the Jews and moaning about the veil in their temple being torn from the top to the bottom. The entire city looked like a war zone. He looked at the destruction and mumbled, "What power could have done such devastation?"

As he reached Antonia Fortress, the once invincible stronghold had now been weakened. Many of the great stones had cracked and some had fallen. The once iron-clad fortress was in need of great repair. Soldiers were busy moving debris and salvaging what they could.

For Longinus it had been a long, exhausting day with little sleep the night before and none in sight for now. The quake had left the barracks in a total shamble and no one was going to have the privilege of rest. Upon entering his quarters Longinus found it filled with dust and debris from portions of stones of the walls that had been damaged. Weapons were strewn about in disarray along with beddings and soldiers belongings.

"I don't want to hear any clamor!" declared Longinus. "Clean this up!"

As he dismantled his armor, he looked at the dishevelment of his private quarters. Shaking his head, he made his way out to the barracks to a barrel of water. Grabbing the metal cup that was chained to the wall, he scooped some water. As he lifted it to his mouth to drink, he paused. Staring at the cup, he moved it closer, then farther away. He repeated this several times, back and forth.

Marius watched as Longinus peered at the side of the cup.

"What are you doing?" asked Marius.

"Marius, I never realized how many scratches are in this cup."

"Now you hallucinate. The wine jug has made you mad."

Longinus uncertain, answered, "Yes that must be it."

"I've heard of such things. Next your skin will crawl with

leeches," stated Marius as he began to remove his armor.

Longinus took a drink of water from the cup, and then carried his spear directly to the water trough. He placed the bloodstained spearhead under the water then pulled it out and rubbed it with a cloth. The blood still remained. He submerged it again, this time rubbing it harder underwater with his cloth. He rapidly repeated this process several times. The stain remained. He held it up close to his eyes and noticed three red blood crosses were formed on the spear's head. He fiercely tried to rub them off in vain.

Suddenly, he stopped, as though in a trance, and gazed at them. As he peered into the blood-stained crosses, he began to see a vision as the bloody red crosses on the spear's head began to glow.

Instantly, the bloody face of the dying Nazarene on the cross was seen, the image began to zoom out into the distance, and the crown of thorns were visible.

The image continued to zoom out until the entire man on the cross was shown. His blood and water gushed forth from his side. He hung on the cross limp and lifeless.

Then he saw a golden bronze city bursting upward out of the ground; it had layers and layers of the most stately buildings one could ever imagine. He watched until a magnificent entry gate formed; it had upon it the majestic face of a bronzed lion. It appeared to be a most fantastic kingdom, one of an architecture he had never seen nor could have ever imagined.

Then the image zoomed further out into the distance, exposing a most barren and ugly wilderness in front of the fantastic kingdom.

The ground broke open, and coming up in the front of the most beautiful kingdom was fire and molten lava, and from the fire was seen the most horrid-looking place. It was full of darkness and had multiple layers of dungeon like prisons, guarded by the most hideous of creatures. They had black, leathery, tar-like bodies with sharp fangs that hung down past their jaws like stalactites from a cave. Their teeth chattered hauntingly. On their backs were blackened and torn leathery wings, full of jagged rips and slashes.

He looked and saw inside the dark dungeon-like prisons. They were empty, all but one that bound a horrid and pitiful looking serpent who was wailing out all manner of evil vengeance in tormenting shouts. He could not understand the language this hideous beast was shouting, but he knew it meant that these dark horrid prisons must be filled up.

Suddenly, the smell of putrefactive pools of evil pus filled his nostrils; he dropped the spear.

So real, he thought. *So hauntingly real, but how?*

"I am tired, that is all," he mumbled. "That was nothing more than a self-hypnotic trance, like the sorcerers do. I need food, wine, and rest. In that order."

Reaching down, he picked up his spear. Then he dipped it in the water one last time. He rubbed it fiercely with the cloth. Suddenly, Longinus felt his eye begin to twitch. The skin above and below his socket felt like it was moving.

"Leeches?" he thought. Then his eye began to burn. He dropped the spear and frantically flushed his eye with water, over and over again. Finally the burning subsided. Longinus peered into the water as it settled and he could see his reflection as clear as day with his blind eye.

He saw the skin. The scar was gone. He quickly felt his face with both hands. All around his eye it was smooth. "How could this be?"

He said to himself, "What has happened?" He trembled inside as he tried to understand this thing. He reasoned in his thoughts.

"Is it from the blood of the Nazarene on my spear? Does it have a power. Or was it from the fluids that splashed in my eyes and on my face when I...I...speared him?"

At that moment he feared and at the same time he was joyful. Yet, for some reason he felt very guilty and anxious about what he had done. *I was…I was…obeying orders,* he thought, in an attempt to comfort himself.

Longinus thought back and relived the moment at the cross. He recalled the powerful words he had heard the Nazarene speak with authority, *"My Father, forgive them, for they know not what they do."*

Longinus starred at his reflection in the water and wondered. He continued to try and remember, *"What else did he say? He said other things, what were they?"*

Then, Longinus heard in his mind's eye, the words the soldiers had exclaimed at the cross of the Nazarene when the ground quaked, *"Indeed, this was the son of God,"* and how at that moment, he had agreed. He thought hard trying to make sense of all of this. *What was it that made me agree? Was I under a spell?* Then suddenly, he heard a shout from Marius.

"Longinus, are you all right?"

"I'm fine Marius!"

Longinus was unsure as to what or how his eye was totally healed; he only knew he wasn't ready to answer questions as to its miraculous healing. If he told that the spear had a power, it would be seized from him and taken to Caesar. If he told that the body fluids of the Nazarene healed him, they would say he had the curse of a sorcerer. He only knew that he had to find out what the three red crosses of blood on the spear meant for him and the meaning of his vision. How did the spear glow? The only thing he knew for sure was that he pierced the side of the Nazarene, and now, he could see from his blind eye and its color was no longer cloudy, instead it was as blue as blue could be. The skin around his eye was now smooth and the scar was gone.

He grabbed a cloth and wrapped it carefully around his head, covering his once blind eye and the skin that was once scarred, but now very smooth. He checked his reflection in the water. Satisfied that no one could see he had been healed, he picked up his spear and covered its head with the cloth he tried to clean it with.

Satisfied that no one would know anything, he went back into the barrack.

Marius noticed that Longinus had wrapped his eye.

"What is that?" queried Marius.

"Damn eye burns from the light now. I need to shield it. Must have been the lightning flash."

Marius looked at Longinus strangely, "They say a sober man feels the pain once the wine has left, but," he added as he laughed, "The rag improves your looks."

Longinus looked at Marius and retorted, "Clean the barracks, Marius! Clean the barracks!"

GUARDING THE TOMB

The next day the high priests, Elders, Scribes, and Pharisees were afraid of all that had taken place and talked among themselves of what to do. The veil of the temple had been torn from the top to the bottom, and the followers were declaring that Jesus was the true Messiah.

Caiaphas, the high priest, and Annas convinced the Court of the Sanhedrin that they must petition Pilate to place a guard at the tomb or else the people may steal the body. They went before Pilate.

Pilate, arrayed in his finest royal attire, sat dignified on his palace throne, yet he was wearied at all that had taken place.

"Your king is dead. Now what do you want from Rome?" he demanded sternly. The Chief Priest Caiaphas stepped forward and boldly approached Pilate.

"Give us soldiers that we may guard the tomb for three days, lest his disciples come and steal his body away and the people suppose that he is risen from the dead and do us evil."

Pilate answered, "His followers have run and hid. You have nothing to fear but your own actions. Rome has nothing to do with that."

Caiaphas pleaded, "Sir, we remember while he was still alive, how that deceiver said after three days I will rise."

Pilot was quickly annoyed at their superstitions and interrupted, "The man is dead Caiaphas. Might I remind you that I have already washed my hands of this."

A Pharisee spoke up, "Indeed, but, if his followers steal his body from the tomb and say to the people, 'He has risen from the dead.' The last deception will be worse than the first."

Caiaphas added, "There will be a rebellion against not only us but against Rome."

Pilot fumed, "If, If, If. No facts, nothing but ifs!"

Caiaphas argued back, "It is a fact that his followers believe he will rise and rebels will stop at nothing to make this be true."

Pilate contemplated for a moment then answered, "You will have a guard; if for no other purpose than to stop your incessant pleading."

He then turned to Octavian, the senior centurion, "Post a guard at the tomb of the Nazarene until these rumors are laid to rest, and I want you to personally oversee this watch."

Octavian bowed, "Yes, prefect."

"Secure it and place a seal upon it. If it is broken, we shall know it was done by grave robbers," added Pilate.

He then looked at Caiaphas. "Go with the guard and make the tomb as impenetrable as you know how."

At that, the elders and priests bowed and left with Octavian.

Outside, Octavian addressed his sentry to go with haste and send word to Longinus to bring a detachment to the gate to meet with Caiaphas and go with them to secure the tomb and guard it.

The sentry went straightway to the barracks.

In a little while the sentry arrived and addressed Longinus.

"Octavian has sent orders for you to bring your detachment to the gate of Antonia Fortress with haste. Pilate has ordered to secure the tomb and a guard be posted to secure the body of the Nazarene Zealot."

"This is not a job for a centurion, he needs to place the temple zealots at the tomb," snapped Longinus.

Several soldiers snickered.

The sentry looked at Longinus and in a very serious tone said, "You and a detachment are to meet Octavian at the gate. He is waiting now."

"You heard the sentry," shouted Longinus. "Fall in."

As the sentry left, the soldiers began to ready their armor and weapons with great speed. Longinus pulled his sword, checked it, looked at his reflection, and placed it back in its sheath. Looking down at the spear on the floor by his cot, he remembered his vision. He picked up the spear and carefully removed the cloth wrapping he had placed on it the night before. Instantly, the three red crosses glowed for the time length of a blink of an eye.

Longinus dropped it from his hands. He looked around. Fortunately, no one saw it glow but him. But Marius heard it fall.

"Pull it together Longinus or Octavian will have your head!"

"Mind your own matters Marius or I'll have yours!"

Securing the Tomb

Longinus and his detachment arrived at the gate of Antonia Fortress. There, waiting for him was Octavian, along with the High Priest Caiaphas, a group of elders, scribes, and Pharisees. As he and his detachment approached, he overheard them speaking of the veil of the temple being torn from its top to its bottom and the fear that this had raised among the people.

Caiaphas was speaking to Octavian, "This deed was only from the eclipse and the quake. Nothing more. Yet the people fear it was done by the wrath of God."

"I agree," Answered Octavian.

Caiaphas continued, "We must secure the tomb and make sure none of his followers deceive us and take away his body and say he has risen from the dead."

"Reporting for duty, sir," stated Longinus.

Octavian motioned with his hand and ordered Longinus, "This way. Make haste."

The Jews followed with Octavian, Longinus, and the soldiers out of the gate and down the steps. As they walked, Octavian briefed Longinus.

"You will escort these men to the tomb, in the garden, by the place of the skull. You will help them secure the tomb. Then you will stand guard until the end of the first day of the week. I will meet you there shortly."

"Yes, sir," answered Longinus.

As they marched off Octavian mumbled under his breath, "If I were Governor, Caiaphas would be guarding that tomb, not Rome!"

The soldiers made their way through the city and up the long twisting incline to the top of Golgotha with Caiaphas and his men complaining about the followers and their deception every minute of the walk.

When they arrived at the tomb, Longinus had not remembered how ornate it looked, nor how the entrance was so well carved with precision. It gave the appearance of an eloquent entryway carved right into the stone.

The men and the soldiers removed the smaller boulder from the tomb's entrance, and began to roll a greater, heavier one in its place. It took wedges, ropes, and the strength of all the soldiers and all the Jews to move it. They were having a hard time getting it into place.

Octavian approached the soldiers and saw the men heaving at the boulder. He dismounted and moved over to the boulder and began to heave it with the men. With the extra strength of Octavian, the boulder finally slipped into place.

"Now seal it!" ordered Octavian, "By order of Pilate!"

As he proudly dust slapped his hands as though he, alone, had positioned the great stone. Octavian arrogantly addressed Longinus, "I trust all things are in order and will be carried out."

"No one will move that boulder!" proclaimed Longinus as he looked and noticed it now hid all of the ornate entryway. "It will take a foolish legion of men to dare even try to budge it, let alone get past the best of Rome's Ironclad Tenth!"

Octavian noticed the wrap around Longinus's eye. He pointed to it and asked, "Why that?"

"It burns from the light now. Must have been the lightning flash."

"Or too much wine," scoffed Octavian.

Octavian stared at Longinus for a moment, then turned to Caiaphas and asked, "To your satisfaction?"

"Indeed. Indeed," said Caiaphas.

"My men and I will pitch camp. We shall stand guard until the third day is over."

Caiaphas nodded in agreement.

Octavian arrogantly looked up and down at all the Jews and stated, "I trust when you return, you will immediately let Pilate know that I am overseeing this."

Caiaphas answered, "It shall be done."

"Go then."

Being satisfied, Caiaphas and the Jews nodded and left.

As soon as they were out of sight, Octavian mounted his horse, turned it around, and addressed Longinus.

"I will be watching you."

"Yes sir."

"Like a hawk!" he glared. "Like a hawk sighting his prey."

"Yes sir."

"Oh, and by the way, pitch a tent for me. The gods shall reside there in my absence until I return to check on you."

At that, Octavian rode away.

Longinus shook his head and stomped the ground. "Damn that Octavian!" He then ordered the tent to be pitched and posted the guard.

The First Day of the Week, at the Third Hour of Night

Longinus wondered as he looked over at the empty tent they had pitched for Octavian. He looked at Marius and mocked the voice of Octavian, "The gods shall reside there in my absence until I return to check on you." Marius snickered. "He's watching you like a hawk's prey Longinus. From above in the sky."

Longinus grinned and said, "Is that why we haven't seen the sight of him during this entire watch?"

Marius broke out in laughter. Regaining his composure, he smiled and said, "It's almost over, Longinus."

Longinus sneered mockingly, "Thank the gods. When it's over, I'm sure Octavian will appear like a dove before the throne of Pilate to let him know all about his three-day watch at the tomb."

Marius snickered, then snorted as he laughed.

"Senior centurion approaching," shouted a soldier.

"Well…speaking of doves and hawks," mocked Longinus under his breath as he stood at attention.

Octavian dismounted and commanded, "As you were."

Forthright, he approached Longinus. "I expect that all is well?"

"Well, indeed, sir. It's been as quiet as a dove."

Marius fought hard to hold back a grin and managed to do so.

"Very good, very good," smiled Octavian as he looked around.

"This duty is about to be wrapped up. If all continues to go well, you and the men will get a two-day leave."

Longinus was pleased at that, "Yes, sir! Thank you, Sir."

Suddenly, the ground began to tremble in the same manner it did at Golgotha. But there was one big difference. The dark night was no longer filled with stars, for the sun burst forth, illuminating the sky brighter than it had ever shone.

A rolling thunderous roar vibrated through the air, piercing the ears of the men. It was so deafening, it hurt. The soldiers held their ears and staggered blindly as the ground shook beneath them. Longinus looked down and shielded his eye from the sun.

Feeling the earth quake under his feet, he watched as the ground began to liquefy and fluidly roll like a wave of water. Suddenly, the ground ominously began to split open beneath him. With great fear, he leaped in the air, thrusting his body as far as he could thrust it, away from the opening chasm. He landed on his side, rolling and tumbling on the quaking ground.

Fearful, beyond words to describe, he knew he had barely escaped the hand of death that reached out to pull him into the deep recess of Hades. The sun was so blinding no one could see. All the soldiers, including the arrogant Octavian, cowered on the ground and sightlessly groped for something to hold on to. Fear seized every soldier.

Bloodcurdling screams were heard from people in the city as they were pummeled by falling stones. Many fell into deep fissures, disappearing in the dark abyss. Their cries for help made the sounds of the earth splitting open even more chilling. All of Jerusalem reeled to and fro. Many of the synagogues and houses were swallowed up into deep and jagged chasms as the earth continued to quake and split.

Suddenly, there was a great shout from above, and they saw the heavens open. Two men descended from the sky with great light and approached the tomb. As they came closer, the stone that was blocking the entrance rolled away on its own as though it were alive and obeying a command. Both of the men entered in.

The ground finally ceased to tremble and quake. The sun remained bright in the sky, but was no longer blinding.

"Sir, did you see—"

"I did," interrupted Octavian.

"It is the Nazarene," Longinus said, trembling. "A curse has befallen all of us because of his death."

"It is a sorcerer's trick," snapped Octavian. "Nothing more!"

As the soldiers marveled and exchanged an account of what they had just witnessed, they froze in silence when they saw three men come out of the tomb. Two supported the one in the middle and a cross followed them.

"You see!" exclaimed Octavian. "Sorcery!"

The soldiers watched as the heads of the two reached into the heaven, but the head of him who was led by the two overpassed the heavens. A deep resonating voice was heard from above.

"Thou hast preached to them that sleep, and a response was heard from the cross. Yea."

"What manner of sorcery is this?" asked Longinus.

"Cheap magic," Octavian answered, yet with less conviction than he had held before.

"What report shall you give to Pilate? One of sorcery, magic?" queried a fearful Longinus.

Octavian quipped back, "Of both, and a full account. Let him make of it what he will!" Looking over to the city, he added, "I'm certain he has his hands full right now."

As Octavian and Longinus considered how to tell Pilate of this account, the heavens opened again and they saw a man descend. His countenance was like lightning and his garment was white as snow. He entered the tomb.

The soldiers trembled at the sight of this one and fainted like dead men. No one was left standing. Longinus laid there, trying to move but was as though he were frozen. He could see and hear, but could not lift even a finger.

As he lay paralyzed on the ground, he heard footsteps and saw a figure hurriedly coming up the hillside. As the figure drew closer and went past him, he saw it was a woman. Soon he saw her run past him again and heard her weeping.

A length of time passed, and Longinus still could not move. He heard footsteps again, this time it was several people running. He tried to lift his head, but he could not. He saw a woman's feet and the feet of a man. It wasn't long, and the feet of the man ran past him again, this time, away from the tomb.

Longinus heard the voice of a woman weeping. Then he heard another voice of a man say, "Woman, why do you weep? Whom do you seek?"

The woman answered, "If you know, tell me where you have laid him and I will take him away."

The voice was familiar to Longinus. It sounded like the woman at the cross.

The other voice spoke again, "Mary."

"Rabboni!" came the voice of the woman.

The man's voice was again heard, "Touch me not, for I am not yet ascended to my Father, but go to my brethren and say to them, I ascend unto my Father and your Father and to my God and your God."

Longinus lay and wondered. He heard footsteps leaving very quickly. As more time passed, Longinus had given up trying to move and slept. After a while, he awoke and was able to move. He wondered if all that had taken place was nothing more than a dream.

He looked around and Octavian was waking as well.

"A sorcerer!" Octavian declared. "They can do great damage. And make the unreal appear real. I will return to Pilate and give an account. You stand guard and let no one near this tomb."

"Yes sir."

Octavian returned to the city and was astounded by the devastation and ruin throughout. He swore he saw apparitions of illuminated bodies walking about in the streets.

Strange... he thought. *This has to be the work of a sorcerer.*

He made his way to Pilate and stood before his throne. Looking very concerned and a bit disheveled, Pilate asked, "What is your account?"

Octavian was very serious and gave an account of all he saw. At the end of his account, he declared to Pilate, "This has to be the work of sorcerers. Only dark magic could do such a thing. Roman gods would not care to avenge a Jew for their folly."

Pilate asked, "Why would a sorcerer do such a deed?"

Octavian thought a moment, then answered, "To offend Rome and stir conflict? Or perhaps to lessen the power of Zeus? Doing such things would weaken the pride of Rome."

Pilate listened, but did not respond. He sat in deep thought.

THE SPEAR OF DESTINY

Octavian added more account, "Perhaps the rebels hired such a sorcerer to make it appear as though the Nazarene was a form of god? Bring life to the myth of the followers? And perhaps they sought to overcome the High Priests as well as Caesar in order to control the region? Bring about a new order?"

In hearing all of the account, Pilate made a decision.

"You will say nothing, Octavian."

"Yes Prefect."

"Keep the guard at the tomb."

Octavian nodded in agreement.

Pilate added, "I will look into the matter. Go now."

Octavian bowed and began to leave.

"One more thing Octavian."

Octavian turned and stood at attention.

"Stay close. I may need you."

"Yes Prefect.

HE HAS RISEN

At the opened tomb, Longinus sat on a stone by the men who had fainted.

"I don't know if I am guarding the tomb or the soldiers from thieves," he grumbled.

All of the events of the day left a surreal omen hanging over his very being. He clutched his spear to steady himself and carefully touched the cloth covering the left side of his face. In his mind's eye, he replayed all the unexplained happenings. For the first time, he was thankful for his life. The memory of the ground opening up to swallow him was haunting. He wondered if the man that descended from the heavens and entered the cave was an apparition or real. Was he/ it still there? Was it nothing more than a cheap sorcerer's trick?

As Longinus replayed his memories, he was distracted by a figure hurriedly coming up the hillside. As the figure drew closer, he saw it was a woman.

Longinus hollered, "You must leave this place! No one is allowed!"

The woman hurried past him and ran into the tomb.

"Crazy woman," mumbled Longinus. He no sooner got up to start after her when his eye caught a glimpse of an image on the side of the great boulder that rolled itself away. He stopped and took a close look. He saw three burnt crosses in the stone. Immediately, he held his spear up beside them.

As he compared the two sets of crosses, he gasped. What he saw was a mirror image. The crosses on the stone were exactly the same as those on the head of the spear. What could this possibly mean? Chance? Fate? A sorcerer's trick? Or the sign of a true God?

As Longinus studied the crosses, he felt himself being pulled into a trance. He fought against it and focused back on the woman

THE SPEAR OF DESTINY

who ran into the tomb. He quickly moved to the narrow entrance and bent slightly over, entered and walked down several steps.

The sun peered through the opening and illuminated some areas well, yet other spots were dim. It took a few moments for Longinus to focus his eyesight in the tomb.

He saw the woman's face. It was the woman from the crucifixion, Mary of Magdalene. Her face seemed to glow. She was standing very serene by the burial linen that was neatly folded. Longinus noticed that the neatly folded cloth had appeared to be purposely placed, on the end of the burial slab.

She smiled at Longinus and said, "He has risen."

"Did you do this?" asked Longinus as he pointed to the folded burial linens with his spear.

Mary calmly looked at Longinus and said, "An angel told me, he is not here for he has risen. Come. See the place where he lay. And he showed me these as they are. He told me to go and tell the others he has risen. I have not touched a thing. I came back to see this one more time."

Longinus leaned his spear against the wall of the tomb and picked up the linens. He carefully held them toward the light shining through the tomb's entrance and examined them. A warm chill surged through the blood in his veins. He quickly laid them back down on the burial slab.

"How do you know that it was not a sorcerer that told you such things?"

Mary answered, "I saw him. He spoke to me. He has risen."

"You saw him?" asked Longinus." I don't understand?"

"I saw him. I thought he was the gardener. Then he asked why I was weeping and it was him."

"Sounds to me like you have the magic of a sorcerer."

"No magic. I have the blessing from the Son of the one true living God, who has risen from the dead and is alive." Longinus looked around the cave as Mary continued to speak, "When he was alive, he said he would rise from the grave in three days. I must go now and tell many others." Mary turned and ran out of the tomb.

Longinus called out, "Wait…"

Mary quickly ran down the hill and did not look back.

Longinus turned his eye back to the slab and stared at the neatly folded linens. In his mind's eye, he recalled the moment that he pierced the side of the Nazarene. He relived the internal fluids pouring out onto his face. The memory was so vivid, he could even feel the wetness as they splashed onto his face. He recalled the burning sensation from the cloth.

Touching the cloth covering his eye, he thought, It was at that time…or was it the spear? Suddenly his thoughts were interrupted as Octavian Sullius entered the cave.

"The body? Where is it?" he demanded.

"It has vanished, sir."

Octavian peered around throughout the cave and spied the spear of Longinus. He grabbed it up and arrogantly poked it into the neatly folded linens.

"The woman said he has risen," answered Longinus.

"What woman?"

"The woman who was with him at the cross."

"Dead is dead. Men do not rise from the grave," Octavian boasted. He then turned locking eyes with Longinus and asked angrily,

"Are you telling me that you allowed a follower to enter this tomb? And that you allowed her to leave?"

Longinus said nothing.

Octavian was livid at the situation and grit his teeth. He growled, "Bring her back here. I will make her speak."

"Yes sir," answered Longinus as he reached out his hand to receive his spear.

Octavian did not hand it to him.

"You will get your spear when I get the woman."

"But sir, what if I encounter rebels?"

"You have your sword. Now go."

"Yes sir."

"Report to me upon your return."

"Yes sir."

"I trust that a little woman is not too much to ask of a centurion to find?" taunted Octavian.

"Yes sir."

Longinus hesitated. He did not want to leave the spear in the hand of Octavian.

"I gave you an order."

Longinus tried not to let his reluctance show and answered,

"Yes sir." At that, he left the tomb and ran in the direction he saw Mary go.

Octavian wondered at the reluctance of Longinus to give up such a common Roman hasta. He examined the shaft, finding nothing on it. Then he continued to examine it down to the blade where he saw the strange crosses. "Interesting," He said out loud to himself. He took one last look around the cave then proceeded to walked out, glancing at every nook and cranny on his way.

Outside the cave, he recalled how the great boulder had just rolled itself aside. Approaching it, he noticed three crosses branded in the great stone.

Strange, he thought as he looked at it closer. Curious, he reached out his hand and felt the three red crosses. He lifted the spear blade up next to it and wondered, "Sorcery?"

Spreading the Good News

Longinus continued down the hill in the direction he saw Mary go. He decided to stay on the path, thinking that a woman returning to tell others would not veer off of it. He ran a short distance and saw Mary speaking to others on the path. Longinus suddenly stopped and hid himself behind a bush.

I will let her be for now and continue to follow her, she will lead me to others, he thought. A bigger prize for Rome. He positioned himself to get a better view and watched as Mary joyfully talked with them. She quickly left and Longinus continued to follow at a distance. Mary hurried through the streets, winding around a few side alleys, and came to a humble-looking building. She pounded fiercely on the door.

"Open up, it is I, Mary!" she exclaimed, "He has risen, he has risen!"

The door opened and she hurried in. Longinus came closer to look as the door was shut.

"I have found a great prize for Rome." He smiled. "A perfect exchange for my spear."

He continued to watch the house and waited for Mary or any others to leave it.

After a long while, the door opened and several men come out. Mary followed behind them last. But the men ran in one direction and Mary ran in another. Longinus took a good look at the men to identify them later and followed after Mary.

The streets were buckled and in disarray from the quake. Great stones had fallen from the buildings, some were completely destroyed. Jagged fissures split through the streets, some with deep open chasms. Moaning and wailing filled the air.

As he followed, he listened as rumors of the dead rising were being exclaimed among the people.

"My dead father stood in body and told me he was alive," claimed an old man.

"I saw Moses himself!" another announced to a group of people. "I bore witness to Elijah and Jeremiah!" he heard a woman say.

Longinus noticed the peaceful countenance and joy on the faces of the ones who said these things.

He wondered, "Had Mary really been talking to a dead man at the tomb?"

Longinus continued to follow her . As she ran she would turn to others and exclaim her good news.

"He has risen as he said he would do! I saw him, he spoke to me! Go and tell the others!"

Mary ran through the rumble in the temple gateway and showed no sign of distress at the devastation. Her countenance was one of extreme joy.

"Is she blind?" thought Longinus, "Can she not see this is a day of woe for Jerusalem? Perhaps she herself is a sorcerer."

As Mary entered the inner gate of the temple, a Jewish priest stepped in front of her. "Women are not allowed to enter the temple."

Mary ran on past the priest and into the temple.

Longinus secretly followed her and hid behind a column.

Caiaphas who was conferring with the elders of the Sanhedrin was distracted by Mary as she yelled with joy, "He has risen on the third day as he said he would!"

Outraged, Caiaphas shouted, "A follower of the Nazarene! And now she openly disrespects the law of the temple! Seize her!"

Overruling Caiaphas, a Pharisee held up his hand and shouted, "Let her speak!"

Mary approached the men and bowed her head in respect. She then proclaimed, "He has risen."

"Who, woman?" asked an elder.

"Jesus, the one you crucified."

Caiaphas and the Jewish Priests, Scribes, Pharisees, and Elders that were present looked at each other and exchanged a fearful glance.

Mary declared, "I must tell the others." She turned and made her way quickly out the door.

Longinus watched a few moments and heard Caiaphas speak. "We must offer payment to soldiers to swear for us that his followers stole the body in the night's confusion."

Longinus snuck out while the men of the temple plotted. He

THE SPEAR OF DESTINY

continued to follow Mary. He watched as Mary stopped to speak to two men. The men clasped their hands in joyful prayer after hearing her speak.

Longinus was baffled at all he saw as he continued to follow her. Touching the cloth covering his eye, he contemplated whether to seize Mary now or wait. He had many questions he wanted her to answer. He decided to continue to follow her.

THE MYSTERIOUS OLD MAN

Meanwhile, Octavian wasted no time in trying to find out what the strange markings on the spear meant. As he pompously walked through the open-air marketplace, he ignored the rubble and fallen debris from the earthquake. The wails and lamenting from the people meant nothing to him. He held only bitter disgust for Jerusalem. To him, Rome had endured nothing but chaos due to their superstitious beliefs and pious attitudes.

He found his way to a half-standing shanty, where an Old Man could be seen inside of it adding spices to a fire.

He snidely remarked, "Surprising that you have any wood left standing."

The Old Man paid no attention to Octavian despite his centurion crest.

"I was told you are a practitioner of sorcery?"

The Old Man did not answer.

"No need to fear me, old man. I am alone. We must speak in private."

The old man reached over and motioned for Octavian to come closer. Octavian walked up to him and the Old Man reached over and lowered a canvas flap over the opening of the shanty closing it off. The room darkened and the Old Man lit a candle. He sat at a small table and motioned Octavian to have a seat.

Octavian leaned over and placed the spear cross side up on the table.

The Old Man's eyes widened, then winced.

"Get it out of here."

Octavian picked it up and shoved it closer to the old man. The Old Man raised his hands in front of his face and refused to look upon it.

"It has a power I have never encountered!" the Old Man trembled.

"What is this power you speak of?"

"I do not know. You must leave! Now!"

Octavian pulled the spear back from the Old Man.

"I will leave when you answer my questions."

The Old Man shouted, "Then put that away!"

Octavian lowered it under the table. Then asked, "How do I use this power?"

The Old Man stood up and lifted up the canvas flap, flooding the shanty with light.

"Your mind cannot understand what your eyes have seen."

"How do you know what my eyes have seen?"

"I saw a vision in the spear. The same as you. That is why you came."

"I have not seen any vision from this spear. Tell me what you saw, Old Man."

"You must go."

Octavian grabbed the old man by his throat and in a threatening tone, whispered,

"If you want to live to throw more spice at the fire, you will answer me now."

The Old Man, choking, tried to nod his head yes. Octavian loosened his grip, but kept his hand on the old man's throat

"Speak!"

"It has the power to overcome all dark magic. Too overthrow the world. Too raise up a kingdom that will never be destroyed."

Octavian was awe struck at what he was hearing. His eyes glazed over with the sheer thought of such power.

"How do I use this power? Answer me now."

"That, I do not know. I swear on my life."

Octavian let loose of the man's throat and pounded the table with his fist. He railed, "You lie!"

The Old Man trembled and pleaded his case, "I told you all I know. I am an Old Man with little power. Find a greater sorcerer than I. He may be able to tell you more."

Octavian thought a moment.

"Yes. How foolish for me to think that an Old Man with a tin of spice could answer such secret things."

He glared at the old man, and as he left he turned and said, "Old Man, if you have lied to me, it will be the last lie you will ever live to tell."

The Old Man sat and trembled until he saw Octavian move out of sight. He slowly stood up and feebly went to the opening of his shanty. He looked and saw no sign of Octavian. Reaching up, he closed the canvas opening. As he turned around, his countenance changed. It became youthful, tall, straight, and sinister.

"Foolish Old Man," he mocked, "We shall see, we shall see."

He grabbed a tin of spice and threw it on the fire. A burst of purple flame plumed the air. He muttered:

"Oh, Prince of Hell who answers to evil masters, the potentates of the earth are subject to thy power. It was you who sharpened the spear for his suffering. The one who mixed the gall and vinegar and commanded that he should drink.

You prepared the cross to crucify him and the nails to pierce through his hands and feet, and now his death has brought him hither, subject now are both thee and me, to replace the captives released from hell. Keep the power that lies in the spear, a secret forever, lest we lose a war that from the beginning was ours to win. I adjure by the powers of Sheol that belong to me, that no mortal dare to bring the power of the spear close to thee."

THE DECISION

As Mary returned to her home, Longinus caught up to her before she reached the door.

"Woman."

Mary stepped back in fear as he approached.

"Where is the body?"

Mary answered, "You will not find a body."

Longinus very impatient asked, "Is this deceit worth your life? My superiors will make you tell them. I have seen what they do."

Frightened, Mary hurried away and went into the house.

Longinus was not sure whether to storm the house or to wait. Something inside of him told him to wait. He thought, The woman believes so much in what she says it will only anger Octavian. The torture he will place on her will be great. She has not wavered from her story one time in this entire day. Even to Caiaphas, she boldly spoke the same. I must find someone among her friends who will speak the answers Octavian seeks. I will wait. I will follow her again tomorrow.

Touching the cloth that covered his eye, he thought, There are many questions I must ask her, but how shall I ask them? He left and returned to his barracks. Upon returning, Longinus observed all of the new damage had been done from the recent quake.

"Is there no end to this madness?" he mumbled.

He was beginning to doubt his Roman duty. He wanted no harm to come to the innocent woman who claimed her master had risen. She had done nothing wrong except believe her own crazy ideas. Whether it was the way she reminded him of his beloved, or whether it was the haunting that emanated from his spear, he did not know why he was reluctant. He only knew that now, his allegiance to Octavian had grown cold. For the first time, he was not willing to obey his centurion's order. He wanted his spear, but not at the price of an innocent woman. He desired to have both, but arrogant Octavian stood in his way.

Longinus dropped his armor and grabbed a wine flask. He filled his cup and gulped it down. Then, he filled it again. He lay down on his bed and closed his eyes.

Rest, he thought. *I need rest.*

Suddenly, Longinus had another vision.

In the vision he saw the tomb and the blinding light, but this time, he could see a faint figure in the midst of the light. It was the figure of a man, glowing, with a beautiful white robe.

Then once again, the bloody red crosses on the spear's head began to glow. Suddenly, the bloody face of the dying Nazarene on the cross was seen, the image began to zoom out into the distance and the crown of thorns were visible, the image continue to zoom out until the entire man on the cross was shown. His blood and water came gushing forth from his side. He hung on the cross limp and lifeless.

Then he saw a golden bronze city bursting upward out of the ground; it had layers and layers of the most stately buildings one could ever imagine. He watched until a magnificent entry gate formed; it had upon it the majestic face of a bronzed lion. It appeared to be a most fantastic kingdom, one of an architecture he had never seen nor could have ever imagined.

Then the image zoomed farther out into the distance, exposing a most barren and ugly wilderness in front of the fantastic kingdom.

The ground broke open and coming up in the front of the most beautiful kingdom was fire and molten lava; from the fire was seen the most horrid looking place. It was full of darkness and had multiple layers of dungeon-like prisons, guarded by the most hideous of creatures. They had black, leathery, tar-like bodies with sharp fangs that hung down past their jaws like stalactites from a cave. Their teeth chattered hauntingly. On their backs were blackened and torn leathery wings, full of jagged rips and slashes.

He looked and saw inside the dark, dungeon-like prisons. They were empty, all but one that bound a horrid and pitiful-looking serpent who was wailing out all manner of evil vengeance in tormenting shouts. He could not understand the language this hideous beast was shouting, but he knew it meant that these dark horrid prisons must be filled up.

Suddenly, the smell of putrefactive pools of evil pus filled his nostrils. Then the vision faded out.

Longinus gasped for breath. He sat up trembling. He began to sweat profusely. Wine, he thought as he filled his cup. More wine.

He lifted the cup to his lips, then hesitated." No!" he shouted and threw the cup against the wall. He watched as three red streaks of wine slithered ominously down the rugged masonry, bleeding together, forming a jagged cross.

"My spear", he thought, " I must retrieve my spear."

Longinus moved to the weapons rack. Searching through the rack, he found the best spear among them and checked it.

"This will do," he said out loud to himself.

MAD WITH POWER

The cunning Octavian had returned to his private quarters. There was only one thing on his mind: to find a sorcerer that would show him how to use the power in the spear.

Mesmerized by the power he now knew lay within the spear, he stood caressing it as though it were the most beautiful lover.

"A power with the force of ten cohorts! A power to rule the world and build a kingdom without end. And it is now in my possession." He whispered as he stroked it gently. A cold chill shot up his veins and into his blood. He was obsessed with unleashing its power. For the moment, he could not put it down.

"I will find a sorcerer who can tell me how to use your power," he whispered lovingly to the spear. "I will pay the one who knows in gold. That always gets an answer fast. But who is the one that can tell me?"

A loud bang on the door broke Octavian's trance.

"Who goes there!" he shouted.

"Sentry, Sir."

"Speak," shouted Octavian through the closed door as he clutched the spear.

"Sir, Pilate has summoned for your presence."

Octavian hesitated for a moment, disgusted at the untimely interruption.

The soldier persistently shouted through the door, "Sir, I'm sorry but the prefect is waiting."

Octavian took a hard look at the spear and then answered, "I will be there without delay."

Octavian quickly looked about his private quarters for a place to hide the spear. He moved about quickly, trying several places, then turned to his bed and placed it beneath the beddings cushion.

"I will be back for you," he spoke to the spear as though it were alive.

Arriving at the palace of Pilate, Octavian approached as Caiaphas was speaking to the prefect.

"The missing body will now become the symbol for a movement."

Octavian ignored the fact that Caiaphas was speaking and bowed before Pilate.

Pilate made a stern glare at Octavian and also ignored Caiaphas as he began to reprimand, "I assigned a simple task to you, Octavian, and you have failed me."

Octavian answered, "Not so, my Prefect."

Pilate asked, "Explain."

Octavian created a false scenario to save disfavor from Pilate,

"Oh Prefect, remember how I told you the events were a sorcerer's trick?"

"Go on," nodded Pilate.

"The rebels hired such a one. An old man in the open air market. He has a shanty there. His magic is limited, but it was enough to create a blinding light while the rebels entered in and stole the body. The soldiers all fell down in a faint like dead men under this spell. Only I and the Centurion Longinus remained with our wits about us. Yet the spell blinded our eyes."

Listening closely, Pilot wondered at what was said then he spoke, "Strange account. So what then will be done to retrieve the body of the dead Nazarene?"

"Oh great Prefect, let me rid Rome of the old man that did this deed for the rebels by whatever means necessary. For he is a Roman citizen and as a citizen of Rome, he is deserving of a trial. Rome cannot afford to allow him time to cast more sorcery and do more harm, due to lengthy Roman judicial processes. Perhaps in my report, he shall have met his demise by a terrible accident?"

Caiaphas pleaded with Pilate, "You see, we speak the truth. Rebellious followers stole the body from the tomb."

Octavian continued, "Then after I rid Rome of the old man who cast this spell, grant me permission to seek out a greater sorcerer who can cast a spell on the rebels so they will show us where they have taken the body. For as you know my Prefect, a sorcerer's magic can only be countered by a sorcerer of greater power."

Pilate thought for a moment, then gave his decision.

"Permission granted. Do whatever must be done to retrieve the body."

Octavian nodded and kept a stern look on his face, all the while fighting back the urge to smile with delight.

Then, Pilate turned to Caiaphas and stated, "I want to have a full account of every rumor of every deed the dead Nazarene has ever been said to perform."

Caiaphas nervously bowed and answered, "His deeds were done by the power of demons."

"I will decide what is what," ordered Pilate.

Caiaphas bowed.

Pilate added, "And I want access to all your foolish prophecies."

Caiaphas looked astonished and answered, "They are within the Temple. But of what good will they serve you, they are the history of our people?"

"I will decide of what good they are. Prepare for me to see this history."

Caiaphas bowed and Pilate announced, "Go now all of you and do as I have said."

At that, Octavian bowed and left. Smiling within himself at his cleverness, he thought, "Now, to find that old man again."

As Octavian walked out from the palace of Pilate, a shadowy figure secretly followed out behind him. "We shall see, we shall see," the shadowy figure said softly, under his breath.

Stealing Back the Spear

Meanwhile, when Octavian was at the Palace Longinus had made his way with great stealth to Octavian's private quarters. He spied a guard on watch outside his door. Longinus thought a moment, then boldly approached him.

"Octavian is expecting me."

The guard looked suspiciously at Longinus and answered, "How can he be expecting you when he is not here?"

In a flash, Longinus grabbed the soldier by his helmet and slammed the soldier's face into his knee, then pummeled the back of his neck with all the force of his fist, knocking the guard out cold.

He opened the door of the quarters and pulled the fallen guard inside the room. Shutting the door behind them, Longinus began to search the quarters for his spear. Finding nothing, he wondered if Octavian had taken it with him.

Shaking his head, Longinus began to leave, then hesitating, he turned and pulled apart the cushions of the centurion's bed. There it was. His eye caught hold of three blood-red crosses as he grabbed it up. Longinus placed his other spear between the cushions and straightened up the bedding. He opened the door and pulled the guard back out into the corridor. After closing the door to the quarters, he dragged the guard down the long corridor and outside. Spying a hay bin, Longinus threw the guard inside it. Then he ran like lightning back to his quarters.

As Longinus ran, he realized that what he had just done had officially stripped him of his life as a Roman centurion. Octavian and all the cohorts under his command would be after him. Yet, somehow it didn't matter to him. His only thought was to find Mary and have her answer his questions.

IN SEARCH OF
THE OLD MAN

Pleased with having permission granted to do what he will with the old man, Octavian promptly returned to the open-air market. Foremost on his mind was to find a sorcerer who could tell him how to use the power of the spear.

He thought as he made his way through the streets, "I will have the Old Man tell me the name of the greatest sorcerer that lives. Then, I will make him beg for his life as I take it from him."

Eager to get this done, Octavian made his way to the shanty. He looked and saw that the canvas flap was down. He quietly grabbed hold of it and thrust it back. He peered into the shanty to seize the Old Man, but to his surprise, there was no one there. He looked around and all of the old man's tins of spices and rickety furniture were gone. Octavian wondered at this as he felt the ashes in the fire. They were as cold as if they had laid there for a week.

Strange, he thought, *I was just here a few hours ago.*

He sensed someone watching and turned to see a man standing back from the shanty's entrance on the street. He was definitely watching Octavian.

"The Old Man," commanded Octavian. "Where is he?"

"Old man?" questioned the stranger.

"The Old Man that was in this shanty!" shouted Octavian. "I spoke with him a few hours ago. Where is he now?"

"You mean the greatest sorcerer that ever lived?" replied the stranger.

"What?"

"I trust you parted him on good terms."

"We parted on terms," Octavian arrogantly announced. "I am returning to complete those terms."

The stranger turned to leave and Octavian grabbed his shoulder and pulled him around.

"You said, 'the greatest sorcerer that ever lived,' explain now."

"There is no need to explain. He is what I said. It was common knowledge among all practitioners of black magic."

"He told me he was an Old Man with little power. Why would he tell me such a lie?"

"May I suggest that you find the Old Man and ask him yourself."

"You know where he is, don't you?" accused Octavian.

"Perhaps…for a price," answered the stranger.

"The price you will pay for not telling me is your life."

"What price will you pay me if I tell you. That is my question," grinned the stranger.

Octavian, believing the stranger knew, answered, "I pay in gold if your answer pleases me."

"Tempting. Very tempting. How much gold?"

"One gold coin if I am pleased, and five gold coins if you show me a greater sorcerer than he."

"Well, well. Indeed, a tempting offer," smiled the stranger. He graciously bowed and said, "At your service, Centurion. At your service."

"Now, tell me where he is," Demanded Octavian.

The stranger looked around to make sure no one was listening. He motioned with his finger for Octavian to come closer. Octavian drew closer and the stranger whispered in his ear, "The question to ask is not where is he now, the question to ask is what is he now."

Octavian shouted, "I have no time for riddles!"

The stranger glared his eyes and retorted back, "And I have no time for a centurion fool and his gold."

"You dare call me a fool." Octavian pulled his sword. "Why I'll have your head for that!"

"And then you'll never find the Old Man to find the secret of the spear."

Octavian stopped and put his sword back in his sheath. "How do you know of the spear?"

"The Old Man told me. He said you were a fool who knew nothing of secret powers, only of brawn. Brawn has limitations as you well know. But the spear has none for the one who knows how to wield its power."

"Why would the old man tell you such things? Who are you to him?"

The stranger squinted his eyes and in a slithering voice answered,

"I am his Apprentice."

Octavian looked the stranger in the eye and said in a snide voice,

"Then you do know where he is."

The stranger pointed his finger upward to a hawk soaring above in the sky and said,

"I know what he is." He then lowered his finger down until it pointed directly into Octavian's face. He sneered as he spoke, "You need me more than I need your gold. You will do as I direct, or you will never learn the secret of the power that you seek."

Octavian was caught off guard at the stranger's words. He bit his lower lip and asked, "And that is?"

"You will go and get the spear. Return to the shanty with it. I shall wait. Then I will take you to the sorcerer you seek. Or as you call him, the Old Man."

Octavian had no choice but to agree.

"As you say. I trust you will wait as you said."

The stranger nodded his head yes, and Octavian turned and left.

The stranger watched until Octavian got out of sight. He grinned and whispered under his breath, "I will wait, oh yes, I will. When that fool returns, the spear will be mine."

CHOSEN

Longinus could feel his heart pounding as he ran to the barracks. The price he paid to regain his spear was just beginning to hit him. He knew that by hurting the guard to break into Octavian's private quarters and steal back his spear, Octavian would strip him of his rank and pronounce him a deserter of Rome. There would be a bounty on his neck, and he would not be safe in all of Judea. He knew he had to flee.

He searched through his belongings, grabbing only the things he might need to survive a long journey. There was no time to waste.

He quickly left the barracks and went directly to the house where he last saw Mary of Magdalene enter. If his destiny had changed by spearing the side of the Nazarene, she would have the answers he sought. Or so he hoped.

Longinus made his way to the door of the house where Mary stayed. As he approached the door, he remembered their conversation in the tomb and all the things he saw her do and heard her say as he followed her. How all the people in the street greeted her with warm welcome. The only one that showed disdain against her was the High Priest Caiaphas. He recalled the evil plot Caiaphas planned to use against the testimony of Mary. He somehow knew in his heart that she had the answers he sought. He trusted that she would not tell a lie.

Longinus knocked on the door.

He saw it open slightly and saw the corner of her face.

"I must speak with you."

Mary answered, "Please, Roman, leave this house in peace."

Then, she closed the door.

Longinus persisted, "The Nazarene on the cross, who was he?"

Mary opened the door just a crack and answered, "He was Jesus of Nazareth, the son of the living God."

"He has cursed me with visions."

"Cursed?" asked Mary as she opened the door a little more.

"I have had visions that I cannot explain."

At that point, Mary and Longinus locked eyes. Longinus spoke as though he were pleading, "I only followed my orders. I meant him no harm."

"Perhaps that is why he has chosen you," answered Mary.

"Chosen? I don't understand? I only want the visions to stop."

"Then do what he asks of you."

Longinus shook his head in confusion. "I don't see him, I see visions of things, places, other horrid things. He asks me nothing in these visions."

"He must have done something to let you know he has chosen you."

Longinus looked directly at Mary while lifting the cloth from his left eye and said, "Like this?"

Mary was not startled; she looked very serene and lifted her hand to touch the area that she remembered had been scarred.

"I remember seeing your eye. It was blind. And the scar."

The touch from Mary's hand felt so soft and comforting. Mary removed her hand and said very assuredly, "He has chosen you."

"I don't understand what you mean by chosen?"

"Come inside. Hurry. We shall talk."

Longinus entered the house.

IN SEARCH OF
THE SPEAR

Octavian returned to his barracks and noticed the guard was not at his door.

"Guard! Guard!"

There was no answer. Thinking something was not right he drew his sword and cautiously entered his private quarters. Everything looked the same as when he had left. He moved to his bed and looked beneath his cushion, there was the spear. He sighed in relief and picked it up.

"There you are," he said as he carefully held it. He peered at the spearhead and noticed the three blood crosses were gone. He turned it over and over, looking intensely at it.

"Longinus", He thought. He threw the spear down and left.

Suddenly, a figure appeared in the shadows of the corridor. It was the stranger from the marketplace. He had followed Octavian. He went over to the spear on the floor. He looked down at it, then around the room.

"This may be a little harder than I had thought," he said under his breath.

Outside, Octavian addressed a group of soldiers.

"Where is Longinus?"

"I saw him go into the barracks not long ago, sir."

Octavian mounted his horse and ordered the soldiers, "All of you follow me to the barracks."

The stranger watched from the shadows.

Octavian stormed into the barracks with the soldiers but found no Longinus.

"Search his belongings for weapons."

The soldiers rifled through all the possessions of Longinus but found only a dagger and a blunt-edged sword.

"Find him!" Octavian shouted. "He isn't far, all his things are still here."

The soldiers all scurried out to search for him.

Octavian stood with his hands on his hips, very angry.

"Damn you, Longinus, you've taken it for yourself."

As Octavian turned to leave, a sentry entered the room.

"Sir, Pilate has summoned for you."

Octavian glared, then regained his composure and said, "I will be there."

The sentry left and Octavian kicked the pile of Longinus's ransacked belongings, and blared out, "Dam You!"

Octavian at the Palace with Pilate

Octavian entered the palace of Pilate and Caiaphas was speaking.

"The gullible people believe lies spread by the followers of the dead Nazarene. They continue to run through the streets, claiming to others the body rose from the dead, this is an outrage. They must be arrested or the lies will spread. There will be much unrest."

Pilate responded, "Or does the unrest lie upon your shoulders and that is what you fear? The Roman legion is not a bodyguard for temple priests."

Caiaphas continued to plead, "Sir, I tell you in concern for Rome, this act of stealing the body away has created much division among all of Jerusalem and Judea. The people now question the authority of the temple."

Pilot was very disgusted at the entire fiasco and losing his patience, "A division among your people is none of Rome's concern."

"A division among our people will give fuel to those who lead bands of rebels against the authority of Rome. We of the temple have led the people to obey the governance of Caesar. Surely, you do not want the followers to lure others to rebel through the false hope of such a lie as this? Please grant that they be arrested."

"And if I grant this wish of yours today, tomorrow you will come to me with another one to arrest, and the next day another. This chaos is of your own making!" Shouted Pilot. "You can't arrest all your people for not believing what you want them to."

"But Governor I deplore you these have always been the trouble makers," Urged Caiaphas.

"You have a point," stated Pilate as he looked up and acknowledged Octavian.

Octavian bowed to Pilate, "You summoned me, Prefect."

"I assigned a simple task to you and you have failed me and instead of hunting for the body of the dead Nazarene you pleaded to hunt down an old man and some nonsense about a greater sorcerer. Moreover, as you just heard, dissent against Rome is growing."

"Prefect, I have sent two detachments to search for the body."

Pilate went up from his chair and approached Octavian.

"You send out two detachments? Only two? Why did you not summon all of your soldiers? And why were you not with your men to do a duty I assigned for you to personally oversee?"

Octavian's eyes widened and he turned pale.

"If you were not such a decorated officer, I would have you flogged. I still may."

Octavian defended his stance, "Prefect, I could not be in two places at once.

I sought to find the sorcerer that performed the evil magic that led rise to these great rumors. In so doing I learned it was Longinus, my centurion who conspired with the followers to perpetrate this hoax."

"How do you know this to be true?" queried Pilot, "Why would a centurion conspire with the followers?"

"Because he desired a woman, Prefect."

"Of course," answered Pilate as he pondered. "What else could it be."

Caiaphas interrupted, "There was a woman follower in the Temple today. One of the elders spied a Roman Centurion following her."

"Who was the woman?" Pilate questioned.

"It was Mary of Magdalene. She was a close disciple of the Nazarene," answered Caiaphas.

Octavian continued to defend his stance, "When he told me she had been inside the tomb and got away, I ordered him to find her at once and bring her to me. There was no reason to believe he would disobey my order. I had just discovered he had other plans in mind and was preparing to go after him when you summoned my presence."

A guard entered the room and announced, "Prefect, the bounty hunter has arrived."

"Let him enter," answered Pilate.

Octavian looked at Pilate and wondered why he summoned a bounty hunter, but said nothing.

A tall, six foot six, rugged-looking man of Syrian descent, entered the room with a wild-looking dog the size of a lion. The man's hair was disheveled and shaggy with a crooked part in the middle. The front and sides raggedly stopped at his shoulders, while in the back, there was a long, bushy, dreadlocked braid that hung past his waist.

His armor was dirty and looked well worn, yet it was well suited to his rocky build. Weapons of all sort hung from leather harnesses strategically arrayed on his torso. He smelled like a wild animal and looked as haggard as one.

Pilate addressed the man, "You are the bounty hunter?"

"The name is Khalid. You desire my services, Prefect?"

"I summoned you here due to your reputation for finding those who seem to slip through the hands of Roman soldiers. I want you to use your methods to assist my senior centurion."

Octavian looked at Pilate and said, "Sir, I can find the deserter

THE SPEAR OF DESTINY

and the woman without this man."

Khalid looked at Octavian and remarked, "It is said in the streets that you faint at guarding tombs. You need me."

Octavian drew his sword and raised it at Khalid; at the same time, Pilate raised his hand for Octavian to stop.

"I will pay you twenty pieces of silver to capture the deserter," offered Pilate.

"I accept, with one request," answered Khalid.

Pilate motioned to his personal assistant to give him a parchment and writing instrument.

"And what is that?" he answered as he began to write.

"Vitali gets paid twenty pieces of silver as well."

"Vitali?" asked Pilate.

Khalid pointed to his dog. "Vitali. She has methods too."

Pilate took a puzzled look at the dog, then at Khalid.

"Ten denarius and not a bit more."

"Agreed," answered Khalid.

Pilate finished writing and handed the parchment to Octavian.

"These orders give you full authority to arrest any followers and act as you see fit." He added, "You will follow all methods of Khalid."

"Yes Prefect."

"Now I trust you shall lay to rest any myth of a dead body having more power than Caesar himself. The next time you come before me, I expect you to bring the deserter, the woman, and the dead body of the Nazarene."

"Yes Prefect."

"If not, you will be stripped of your rank and beg to have Vitali's job."

Seething inside, Octavian answered, "Yes, Prefect."

"Now go, all of you."

Preparing for the Hunt

Outside of the palace, Khalid wasted no time in getting started. In a demanding voice, he addressed Octavian, "Take me to the deserter's quarters."

"There is nothing there for you."

"Do not question my methods. Take me there."

Reluctantly, Octavian did as Khalid asked. They made their way to the barracks, and Octavian stood in the doorway and pointed, "Over there." He watched impatiently as though Khalid were wasting his time.

Khalid went over to the ransacked area of Longinus and looked over at Octavian. "Either he's the messiest Centurion in the Roman Legion, or someone's already went through his stuff."

He reached down inside a very rummaged through trunk and pulled out a dirty tunic. "I trust this is his."

He tore a piece from it and shoved it under Vitali's nose. Vitali sniffed the torn fabric and growled, showing her teeth. Khalid tied the fabric around Vitali's collar, then turned to Octavian and said, "Now, I want some food for me and for Vitali."

"I am not your slave. You waste my time."

"We do not work on an empty stomach."

Octavian scowled and pointed in the direction of the dinner hall. "Food is that way."

They made their way into the common area, and Khalid heaped two plates full of meat and bread. Octavian gave a nasty glare as he watched Khalid place a big plate full of meat in front of Vitali.

Octavian shook his head, "Disgusting," he said and then ordered a soldier to prepare him a haversack of supplies.

Vitali finished her plate and was licking it clean. Khalid looked down at her and said, "You are finished, Vitali?" Vitali barked.

Khalid reached his hand down and pulled a piece of meat, hanging from the hair on Vitali's chin. He grabbed hold of it and picked it off, then put it in his mouth and chewed. He swallowed and gave out a deep belch.

"Swine have more manners," mumbled Octavian as he cringed

at the barbaric display.

Khalid looked at Vitali and said, "First, we find the woman. She will tell us where the deserter is hiding. Then we find the dead body."

Octavian shook his head, "He will not be that easy to capture. And I doubt it can be done in that order."

"He is no different from any other deserter," said Khalid as he let out another belch.

Octavian rolled his eyes and asked, "And just how do you plan to do this? Especially when no followers are talking?"

"The solution is simple," said Khalid as he grabbed a fly from the air with his hand. He placed his hand in front of his dog and opened it a little way. His dog licked the fly up with his tongue and ate it. Khalid looked at Octavian and stated, "Vitali!"

CHOSEN OR CURSED

Meanwhile, back at the home of Mary of Magdalene, Longinus was eager to have his questions answered. Yet, for some odd reason he suddenly felt awkward like a young lad full of foolish questions.

He thought, How does a centurion ask a woman he knows not, such questions that I have to ask? What if she laughs at me? Scoffs me? He abruptly caught hold of his thoughts and said to himself,

"I am a man of war, I don't feel emotion, I follow commands and slay whomever Rome tells me to slay. Now ask her what you must."

He turned to Mary, "In the tomb, you said the Nazarene told you that he would rise from the dead after three days."

Mary nodded her head yes.

"You said an angel appeared to you and told you he had risen from the tomb."

Again, Mary nodded her head.

"I heard you talking to your Rabboni. I must know, was he a sorcerer?"

Mary looked at him for a moment. She smiled as she answered, "It was my Master."

"Your Master?"

"It was him, the one whom you speared. He has risen."

Longinus felt his eye and turned away from Mary as he spoke, "And now I am cursed as low as a runaway slave."

Mary responded quickly," You have been chosen."

Longinus turned back around, "Chosen! Chosen for what? To die for my action, under the direction of the Roman legion? To regain my sight, just to see my death with both eyes?"

Mary shook her head. "You do not believe."

"Woman, believe? Nothing makes sense," he argued.

"You must ask him to help your nonbelief."

"Ask a dead apparition that appeared to you like a ghost for belief?"

Mary stood silent.

Longinus raised his spear up to Mary's face broadsided. Not knowing what he intended, she drew back frightened.

"Do not fear," Longinus said. "Look at the three red crosses of blood and tell me what you see." Mary looked at the head of the spear. "This is the one you thrust into my Master's side."

Longinus nodded.

Mary kept looking at the spear. She reached out her hand and touched it. "It has the power of his blood."

Longinus feared and asked, "What power is that?"

"The power to have redemption, healing, protection and a life of victory over evil."

"How does one use this power?"

"You must believe," answered Mary.

"How do I believe?"

"You must ask him."

"How do I address a dead man!" shouted Longinus.

"He is alive," corrected Mary.

"Woman, you speak like you have gone mad from the death of the one you loved. You make no sense."

Mary was silent for a moment and then spoke, "You must go now. I have told you all I can. Seek him and you shall find him."

Longinus shook his head in disgust and left.

"Seek him," he scoffed as he mounted his horse. "Seek the dead man's ghost." He rode off and looked for a place to hide for a while.

"I must think of what I am to do, where am I to go now?" Lost and confused, Longinus rode out of the city.

Brawn versus Words

A few days had passed and Octavian and Khalid had not found any sign of the deserter or the woman. Octavian continued to hunt his way venturing through the streets of Jerusalem, stopping people, asking for the whereabouts of the woman. They came upon a small room where a half-dozen men sat on a dirt floor having a conversation.

"Where do I find the woman follower named Mary of Magdalene?" shouted Octavian. The men did not answer.

"Surely, one of you would like to return home to your family this night?" he bullied.

Khalid shook his head, now very weary of Octavian's approach and so-called authoritarian methods.

"You are too patient." He looked down at his dog and ordered, "Attack, Vitali!"

Vitali leaped in the air and attacked one of the men on the floor, tearing into his arm, and the man screamed, "She lives on the eastern outskirts of the city!"

Khalid smiled and looked at Octavian, and as he mounted his horse, he said, "We now go find the woman."

Suddenly, from the shadows, a figure appeared. He called out, "Centurion."

Octavian looked; it was the stranger from the shanty, the Old Man's Apprentice.

"Did you forget our agreement?"

Octavian motioned for Khalid and the others to wait for him up ahead, and as he approached the stranger, he reprimanded in a harsh whisper.

"Can you not see I have my hands full at the moment?"

"Can you not see that I am not happy with deception?"

"There is no deception here."

"No deception? Then answer me, where is the spear? Should I be waiting for you to bring it to me at the old man's shanty, like a fool?"

Octavian thought a moment and mocked, "You are the apprentice. You tell me where it is."

The stranger looked deep into the eyes of Octavian as though he were reading his mind, "Find the centurion and you will find the spear. Go with haste. Each moment he has it in his possession, he increases his knowledge of its power."

Octavian felt a chill go up his spine. The thought of anyone, but himself, increasing the knowledge of the power of the spear was horrid to even think of. He mounted his horse and took one last look at the stranger. He turned his horse around and readied himself to catch up with the others. Without warning, the stranger grabbed hold of the bridle of Octavian's horse, preventing Octavian from leaving. He locked eyes with Octavian and spoke,

"He is with a woman. The men go in the wrong direction." He pointed in the opposite direction, westward. "It is that way."

Octavian nodded, and the stranger let go of the horse's bridle and lurked away in the shadowy street.

Octavian shouted at Khalid, "We go this way, the man told me the way to the woman's house."

Khalid continued to journey east. He looked over at Octavian and shook his head.

"I listen to Vitali," he hollered out. "Not strangers in the shadows. We go this way."

Octavian was not used to following any man's orders but Pilate. He seethed at having to be subordinate to a filthy, mangy dog and its filthy mangy owner. He was sure the old man's apprentice had told him right, and he believed Khalid was leading them in the wrong direction. But his orders from Pilate were to follow the advisement of Khalid. They made their way eastward to the outskirts of the city. All the while Octavian was fuming inside and thinking only of finding the spear.

LONGINUS AND MARY FLEE

It had been a few days and Longinus was still haunted by his visions and unsure what to do now that he was being hunted down by Romans. He kept asking himself why he allowed the spear to become more important to him than his allegiance to Rome? He couldn't understand his obsession with the spear and the man he pierced on the cross? He had a strong urge to flee but for some reason he chose to stay in hiding and struggle as though time would make everything go away and his life would somehow return to normal.

Alone and desperate Longinus believed that the only one who could offer any help in understanding these things was the woman named Mary. He pulled up his camp and mounted his horse and headed out to return to her house. He rode hard and fast and arrived quickly.

As Longinus knocked on Mary's door, his heart began to pound. He feared she may not answer, or worse that she would answer and refuse to talk with him. He stood holding his spear sideways in front of him as if to steady himself as he anxiously anticipated for Mary to answer the door. He knocked again, this time a bit louder.

Mary answered the door. He lowered the spear and looked at her and humbly said, "I need your help."

"Come in," she said softly.

Longinus was relieved that she let come inside.

"Woman, I am trying to do as you say. I am just a hard-headed Centurion. Forgive my loud outburst from the other day."

Mary nodded in compassion.

Longinus began to relax a bit and said, "I do not know how to do the thing you asked. How to seek him, I have asked, but I have found no answers."

"How have you asked?" she asked him.

"I shout at the spear. Who are you? Where are you, show yourself. Nothing happens."

"What else do you do?"

"I demand that if he exists, show himself to me."

"I see," answered Mary. "This is all in vain. This is how you order people as a soldier. Not how you seek the Son of God. It is best to begin with some humility."

"Humility? Isn't it enough that I seek him?"

"You must first desire to seek him for the right reasons. What are your reasons?"

"To have him lift this curse from me. And to…to…I do not know any other reason?"

"What is your curse?"

"My eye. My visions."

"A healing to see when you were blind and to see in more ways than in the flesh as he has given to you through a spear is a gift. It is not a curse," said Mary.

"A gift? To run and be hunted down by Roman soldiers is a gift?"

"I do not understand," asked Mary.

"I was supposed to capture you to receive my spear back from my senior centurion. Instead, I let you go and I stole it back. Now I am hunted. This is a curse."

Mary looked at Longinus very bewildered.

Suddenly, Longinus heard men approaching on horseback. He went to the door and opened it a hair's breadth. He saw the transverse crest of his senior centurion, Octavian, leading a group of soldiers. He shut the door tight and bolted it. He turned to Mary and asked, "Is there another way out?"

"There is." She pointed through the room into a room in the back. "There is a door in the back. Go, I will be fine. I have done nothing wrong."

Longinus grabbed Mary by the arm and pulled her along with him as he said, "They will torture you and then kill you! "

Longinus ran with Mary to the back door. He opened it a little way and peeked out. He heard soldiers talking. He watched as they left to return to the front of the house. He whispered to Mary, "Come. They are looking for both you and me. They will kill us both."

"Why do they seek me?" she whispered back.

"They seek you because you were in the tomb. They believe you stole the Nazarene's body. At least, they will blame it on you and torture you until you claim that you did."

Mary and Longinus waited until the soldiers were all in the front of the house. They opened the door and ran outside as fast as they could. They made their way swiftly down a narrow path and past many streets.

Back at the house, Octavian dismounted and shouted for the two soldiers to go and stay guard behind the house. Khalid was holding Vitali as she was barking ferociously at the house. Khalid looked at the house cautiously and, in a very low voice, replied, "He's here." He turned Vitali loose from his grip and said,
"Get him!" Vitali ran fiercely into the house, barking and snarling her huge teeth.

Octavian and his soldiers searched the house inside and outside. They found no one.

Vitali continued barking and snarling her nose at the spot where Longinus was standing minutes before.

Khalid stood with both hands out as though he was ready to grab someone. He looked to the left and to the right and stated, "They couldn't have gone far."

Octavian shouted to the soldiers, "Search the entire area!" He turned and there in the dark was a shadowy figure.

"You there, halt!" shouted Octavian. Then he ordered his soldiers,

"Seize him!"

The figure turned and was holding a spear. "Oh, there you are, Centurion. I thought you might want this." He held it out.

Octavian shouted to his soldiers, "Let him go, I'll handle this. Find the woman and Longinus!"

Octavian reached out and received the spear. He looked at the spear's head and saw three blood red streaks. His heart began to pound rapidly as he held it, "Where did you get this?"

"I told you, they were on the Western side of the city, not here. I seized it when he was in bed with the woman. I saw you had no command of your men and decided to take matters into my own hands."

For the moment, Octavian was mesmerized with the spear and very happy with the apprentice. "You did a fine job." The Apprentice smiled, "Now for the other part of the bargain. I will tell you where the old man is, for my price." He held out his hand as if he expected to be paid.

"I have no gold on me now, but tell me and I will see to it you are rewarded."

"The Old Man went to Joppa and set sail on a seafaring ship. His destination is Rome. You will find him set up in the marketplace, just past the Augusta Archway. Go now and you will find him. Now where shall I pick up my reward in your absence?"

Octavian was delighted in regaining the spear and in knowing the whereabouts of the old man. Now, he no longer had need for the apprentice, but he wasn't ready to tell him. Instead, he lied.

"When I am done here, I shall go to Rome. When I return, I shall deliver the gold to you myself."

The Apprentice gave a very sinister look and winced his eyes, "We had a deal. I deliver the spear that you couldn't hold on to and tell you where the old man has gone, and now, you play me like a fool?"

Octavian thought a moment, remembering he was dealing with a sorcerer's apprentice. He relented. "Very well, you will be paid. Go to the Fortress Antonia in the morning. Ask for Senior Centurion Octavian. I will have an escort bring you to my quarters for payment."

The Apprentice smiled, "Indeed. Indeed." He started to leave, then stopped. He turned and shook his head, "These men go on a fool's hunt. Send them to the western side. They will have better luck there if they hurry."

Octavian looked at the spear and smiled. He turned to the detachment of soldiers and shouted, "Follow me to the western side of the city. They are there." Then he turned to a sentry, "You there. Go tell Khalid, that when he is done having his dog chase a dirty cloth, he can join us on the western side of the city. Longinus and the woman are there. I have his spear as proof."

The soldier answered, "Yes, sir."

Octavian left with most of the detachment, leaving behind only those who were searching in the area with Khalid and his dog, Vitali. None of them knew that Octavian had left, breaking Pilate's order to follow under Khalid's methods. It would be a while before the soldier would find and alert them all, for they had scattered throughout the eastern outskirts.

The Chase

Longinus and Mary stopped to catch their breath in an alley. The ferocious barking of Vitali caused them both fear. Longinus leaned over and held his knees to stretch his back and catch his breath. "I don't know what kind of dog that is, but it has the haunting sounds of a jackal."

Mary held her body against a wall in the alleyway. She stood very still and listened. "A horse is coming."

"Back," whispered Longinus as he pulled Mary into the recession of a doorway. The sound of running horse hooves began to taper off, changing to a slow clopping sound. The silhouette of a horse and a rider with the front to back crest of a Roman soldiers' helmet were visible on the adjacent wall. Longinus waited for the rider to come near.

Just as the horse moved past, Longinus reached out and pulled the rider off. He quickly grabbed the rider in a headlock, knocking his Roman helmet to the ground in the struggle. Longinus recognized the soldier. "Marius," he exclaimed in a very low voice.

Marius gasped for air as his neck was being squeezed by the arm of Longinus. He spoke in a choked voice, "Longinus, what are you doing?"

"Marius, what are you doing? Talk now!"

"We were detached here with Octavian to find you and a woman follower of the zealot we killed at Golgotha. Orders are to arrest you both on sight."

"Arrest us or kill us?"

"Arrest and bring you to Pilate. Eventually, they will kill you, I'm certain," choked Marius.

Longinus said softly, "I hate to do this Marius, but"—he knocked him out with a blow to the back of his neck—"I have no choice."

He quickly mounted the horse of Marius and reached out his hand for Mary. Mary grabbed hold of his hand and he lifted her up onto the back of the horse. The threatening howls and barking from the dog were heard much louder, along with the sound of a galloping horse's hooves. They were definitely gaining on them fast approaching their direction.

Longinus shouted, "Yaah!" As he gave his horse a kick, and they bolted through the alley and out into the open field.

Shortly after, Khalid galloped to where Marius's body lay. He reared his horse up and took a look around. Vitali was barking fiercely toward the open field.

The sentry sent by Octavian appeared, galloping fast toward Khalid. He hollered out, "Octavian has ordered everyone to go to the western outskirts. He knows where they are!"

Khalid shook his head and growled in disgust. "I don't follow damn blind fools!"

He turned to Vitali. "After them!" Vitali ran into the open field and Khalid galloped behind him.

A shadowy figure appeared. He walked over and looked down at Marius laying on the ground. He lifted his head and turned toward the long alley. He gazed outward into the open field and muttered under his breath, "A runaway centurion, and yet a man who is not afraid of death? We shall soon see what you fear more; to live or to die."

AN EVIL PLAN

Octavian led the soldiers to the western outskirts of the city, believing that he would find Longinus and the woman. With the spear now in his possession, he believed he was unstoppable.

"I will seize Longinus and the woman and return them to Pilate myself. I will show him that the barbaric bounty hunter was no more than a hungry fool with a mangy dog. I will be rewarded graciously by Pilate."

Octavian and the soldiers arrived on the western outskirts going house to house ransacking each and every one of them. No Longinus was found. Octavian began to fear he had been lied to by the Apprentice. There was only one more house to search. The thought of returning to Pilate empty-handed had him worried. Especially since he took his detachment and left the bounty hunter. He thought quickly and devised an evil plan.

Octavian called out to his soldiers, "If there is a woman follower in the house, arrest her and bring her to me."

"Yes, sir," they answered.

"I will make her admit many things," he muttered under his breath.

The Roman soldiers barged into the house, pushing a man to the floor. A woman screamed out, "Don't hurt him!"

A soldier grabbed the woman by the arm and dragged her out of the house as she cried out, "Where are you taking me, I have done nothing wrong!"

The man got up and ran after the soldier, but another soldier slashed him with his sword. The woman shrieked in horror at the sight of it. The soldier slapped the woman and dragged her to the feet of Octavian's horse. He threw her to the ground in front of him. She lay there wailing and sobbing.

"Well done," said Octavian as he dismounted his horse. He walked over and looked at the woman then kicked her in the side.

"If you must wail, I will give you something to wail about," he hatefully boasted. Grabbing her by the hair, he pulled her head back and looked into her face. "You are a follower of the dead Nazarene Zealot, aren't you!" he growled.

The woman did not answer; Octavian pulled his dagger and held it to her cheek, "You will answer me, woman." She remained silent.

Octavian slowly penetrated his dagger into her flesh, cutting down about an inch, and the woman yelled, "I am!" Octavian pulled his dagger away and said, "I thought so," as he let go of her and pushed her to the ground.

"Take her to the stocks," he shouted to the soldier. "Torture her until she admits her dead husband was among the thieves that stole the Nazarene's dead body."

"Yes sir."

Octavian mounted his horse then ordered the sentry, "I will be in my quarters. Report to me as soon as this is done."

"Yes sir." Answered the Sentry as he turned to the soldiers and shouted, "Take her to the stocks and make her confess her husband stole the dead body!"

Meanwhile Khalid and Vitali Are Still In Pursuit

Longinus ran his horse hard through the open field and into the woods. As he weaved his way through the trees, the blood curdling bark of Vitali continued to bellow in the distance.

"We must throw the dog off our scent," he said to Mary while he led his horse around in circles.

"In my pocket I have some spices. Will that help?"

Longinus held out his hand. "Give them to me."

Mary reached in her pocket and pulled out a pouch and handed it to Longinus as he dismounted the horse. He broke off a piece of brush and ran over to the circle of horse tracks he had just made. Bending over with the brush he began to erase the tracks that led to his horse. He was careful not to erase any from the circle. Going backward, he continued to erase all the hoof prints until he came to his horse. He walked the horse back a bit further behind a cluster of trees, carefully erasing the new tracks in the same manner.

Taking the spices he quickly dusted his entire body with them from head to toe, adding extra to his armor and tunic. Longinus picked up each hoof from his horse and dusted them carefully with the spice. He continued to dust the entire horse's body, saddle, bridle, and the haversack.

Returning the pouch to Mary, he mounted the horse and said, "My scent is on you. Rub the spice on your clothes and body."

Mary did as told, then placed the pouch back in her pocket. Longinus turned the horse and galloped deeper into the woods.

Longinus and Mary no sooner rode out of sight, and Vitali approached the circle of hoof prints. He stood barking and growling as Khalid approached on horseback.

Khalid looked down at the array of hoof prints, leading up to the circle and then weaving around trees and back to the circle.

"You stop, Vitali?"

Vitali kept barking at the circle of hoof prints.

"Girl, what are you telling me?" Vitali looked bewildered and let out a whimpering whine.

Khalid wondered at this and said to himself, "She has never lost the scent of anyone."

Uncertain of which direction to proceed, Khalid trotted his horse east, Vitali followed. "Anything girl?" Vitali looked up at Khalid as if to answer no. Khalid trotted his horse to the north and repeated, "Anything?" Again, Vitali looked up to Khalid as if to answer no. Khalid trotted west, then south, and Vitali could not find the scent. Khalid sniffed the air. He could only detect a floral scent, like a hint of jasmine.

"He got away," muttered Khalid. He turned his horse around and headed back to Fortress Antonia. Vitali ran close behind.

A Toast to Khalid

Thinking he had everything perfectly planned, Octavian returned to his private quarters and locked his door. He couldn't wait to look over the spear and test its powers.

Walking over to a lit oil lamp, he held the spear up to the light. He smiled and peered at the three blood red crosses.

"And so you return to me, your rightful owner," he said to the spear as he gazed at it longingly. "Soon, I will know how to use your power."

Octavian thought back at the apprentice and wondered how he really got the spear from Longinus. Had his men overlooked something on the western side, or did the sorcerer obtain it by other means? Either way, Octavian had no more use for him.

He carefully placed the spear by his bedpost and began to think of what to do with the apprentice when he came for his pay.

"When the apprentice comes for his pay, I will give him his due reward, less the amount of gold it cost me to come back emptyhanded to Pilate. One gold coin should be enough, if that. Perhaps I will reward him in another way."

Suddenly, there was a knock on his door. Octavian walked over and opened it. There stood Khalid, with Vitali at his side.

"I hear you returned empty-handed, no Longinus," stated Khalid.

"I see you have no Longinus as well. Or did your dog eat him?" Octavian bantered back.

"I want to know about that stranger in the street. The one that gave you the spear."

"You mean that worthless stick," Octavian sneered, looking over at the bedpost.

Khalid looked at the spear, then back at Octavian. "Why did you listen to the stranger and not stay with me like Pilate ordered?"

"A Primus Pilus doesn't explain his actions to a dirty bounty hunter." Snarled Octavian.

Khalid snapped back, "A bounty hunter cares little what a centurion's actions are. But when things are not as they should be, a bounty hunter asks questions."

"None of this is as it should be. Do you just now see this?" retorted Octavian. "Now leave."

"Very well, I will leave and tell Pilate all that has transpired."

"Wait," said Octavian as he reconsidered. "We are both emptyhanded. Pilate will be displeased with us both. We must conspire to a new plan. Come inside, but leave that outside," he said as he pointed to Vitali.

"Vitali goes where I go."

Octavian rolled his eyes and reluctantly said, "Very well, but she stays at the door."

Khalid and Vitali entered, and Octavian looked down the corridor then over to the guard and spoke, "I do not want to be interrupted."

"Yes, sir," said the guard.

"Except for news from my sentry about my prisoner," added Octavian.

"Yes sir."

Octavian shut the door and walked over to the table. He picked up a flask and began to fill two cups. "Wine for my new comrade."

Khalid looked at him. "And some for Vitali as well."

Octavian cringed and took a deep breath. "And some for Vitali."

He handed the two cups to Khalid and poured another cup while Khalid took the wine and placed it on the floor in front of Vitali.

Octavian raised his cup, "Now, a toast to our efforts in finding Longinus. I trust we will both agree on what is best to tell Pilate." Khalid raised his cup in agreement and drank. At the same time, Vitali lapped her wine from the cup on the floor.

THE BONDING

Longinus and Mary had gone through the woods and were now at a barren stretch of land in the outskirts of Judea. The eerie sound of a ferocious dog's bark had long left them. Their efforts to throw the dog off their scent were successful.

Resting the horse from his long run, Longinus and Mary were now on foot, with Longinus leading the horse by his bridle rein.

"What is your name?" asked Mary.

"Longinus."

Longinus stopped the horse and handed Mary the bridle rein. He walked to the rear of the horse and dug around in his haversack. Pulling out a jerky of beef, he bit off a bite. He pulled at it while he chewed and ripped off a small piece. He handed it to Mary. She took a bite, then spit it out. Making a bitter face, and handed the remaining piece back to Longinus.

Longinus shook his head and handed it back to her, "Save it, you will eat it when you are hungry."

Mary took the jerky and placed it in her pocket.

Longinus looked at the sky, then over to the horizon. "We stop here for a while."

Mary moved over to a patch of dried grass and sat on the ground. She lifted up her tunic, just enough to see above her sandals, and began to massage her ankles.

Longinus noticed the soft skin above her feet had become a bit swollen.

"It's been hard for you," he said softly." All of this."

She did not answer.

Longinus thought about his many questions as he watched her rub her ankles. He looked at the three blood-red crosses on the head of his spear, "I do not understand what I witnessed at the tomb. My senior centurion said it was sorcery."

Mary looked up. "That was not sorcery you witnessed. It was the Son of the Living God rising from the dead."

"Which God?" inquired Longinus, "Mars, Jupiter, or an unknown God?"

"Your mockery is cruel. But I would expect no less from a Roman centurion."

Longinus was silent as he realized he was now being hunted down by the same Ironclad Tenth he once vowed his life and the honor of Rome to defend.

"I have only unanswered questions," he gruffed as he bit off another bite of jerky.

"You have a stubborn heart," answered Mary as she stood up. Longinus looked at Mary as she turned and looked back toward the way of Jerusalem.

"You long to go back, don't you," garbled Longinus with his mouth full of jerky.

"I go where my Lord leads me. He has led me here for some reason. A reason, I do not understand."

"Now, you speak some sense. You admit you don't understand any more than I. You are waking up, woman."

Mary closed her eyes and prayed softly, "My Lord help his nonbelief."

Suddenly, the spearhead glowed. Longinus dropped it. "Sorcery!"

Mary now witnessed the glow of the spear. She was struck with a great discernment and spoke, "The power is in his blood. Not in the spear."

Longinus fearing, looked at Mary. "How do you know this?"

"It is written in our books that by his stripes, we are healed. The power of his blood is one of atonement."

"Atonement?" asked Longinus.

"A blood sacrifice of the greatest atonement to life everlasting," Mary answered.

"Are you saying the spear has the power for one to live forever?"

"The power to live forever is in his blood. Not in the spear."

"If he had such power in his blood, why did he die? I saw him dead. I speared his side to make sure."

"You did not kill him. He gave his life that all who believe might live. Just as he promised he would do."

"Woman, you speak like you have gone mad. Enough of this talk."

Mary walked over and picked up the spear. She looked at it and handed it back to Longinus and said, "He has chosen you."

Longinus reached out and took the spear. Looking at it, he said,

"Then he has chosen a dead man, for there is a bounty on my head and the armies of Rome at my heels."

A VISIT FROM
THE APPRENTICE

Back in his private quarters, Octavian was having a very serious conversation with Khalid. As always, his lies were being artfully crafted into various scenarios and filtered here and there with truth. The cunning Octavian was a master at manipulating any situation to serve his purpose.

As he filled his and Khalid's cup with more wine, he made his closing pitch, "So you see, Khalid, we can accomplish this task better by working together. We find the old man that performed the sorcery for the rebels and then we kill him. Bring the dead sorcerer back to Pilate and then you will receive your bounty." He then went over and put a bit more wine in Vitali's cup.

"Indeed," answered Khalid. "Vitali can chomp a sorcerer just as quick as he can a thief."

"So we are in agreement?" asked Octavian.

"Agreement," Khalid answered.

"Very good. Now, if the woman prisoner does as I expect, she will bear witness to Pilate that her husband took part in stealing the dead man's body. Pilate will be satisfied that thieves and sorcery were the cause of the strange events. I will request permission to stop any further dissension by whatever means I see fitting. Pilate will have no reason not to grant permission. I will send soldiers throughout Judea and abroad to arrest the followers of the dead Nazarene. It will be then, that we go to Rome and find the old man. And you and Vitali will take care of that matter."

"This should take no more effort than batting flies," bragged Khalid.

Octavian smiled and said, "As for the deserter, I will place detachments up and down the entire Mediterranean coast. He knows he can't hide in Palestine. The soldiers will take care of him. You, Khalid, will start earning your silver by getting rid of the double- talking Apprentice. Agreed?"

"Agreed."

A knock at the door was heard. Octavian looked at Khalid, then shouted through the closed door, "Speak."

A voice from the sentry was heard, "Sir, the prisoner is ready to bear witness."

Octavian grinned. "Assign a guard and bring her to the prison gate. I will meet you there."

"Yes, sir."

He then looked at Khalid and raised his cup. "Just as I planned," and he gulped the last bit of wine.

Octavian and Khalid left the private quarters and headed to the prison gate of Fortress Antonia. There waiting for them was the sentry, holding a battered woman who could hardly stand on her feet. Octavian looked deep into her eyes and said, "Woman, state your guilt."

With her head bent, she answered, "My husband helped to steal the body from the tomb."

"When?"

"At the same hour a sorcerer cast a spell to cause chaos."

"And why were you beaten?"

"Because I lied to protect my husband."

"Are you a follower of the dead zealot?"

"Yes."

"Do you now know that to lie to a Roman soldier is worthy of death?"

"Yes."

"Very well." He turned to the sentry guard and ordered, "Take her to the palace of Pilate. You are to wait with her outside until I call for you."

"Yes, sir."

Octavian turned to Khalid and said, "Batting flies was a very good comparison." Khalid nodded in agreement.

Suddenly, Octavian felt a presence as though someone were watching him. He looked and saw a shadowy figure. The figure walked forward, making himself seen. It was the Apprentice. He moved toward the Apprentice and said, "I imagine you have come early to get your reward?"

The Apprentice smiled and answered, "You have imagined correctly."

He turned his palm upward and extended it as though he expected to receive something.

Octavian turned to Khalid and said, "Pay him his due, then meet me at the palace."

Khalid nodded his head as he watched Octavian leave. He turned to Vitali and shouted, "Get him!"

Vitali growled, showing his giant canine teeth, and ominously moved toward the apprentice. Quickly, the Apprentice shouted, "Wait!" and pulled out a coin pouch from beneath his cloak.

Khalid spied the pouch and commanded Vitali to halt.

"You are a shrewd bounty hunter, are you not?"

"I am," answered Khalid.

"What if you could gain more bounty for your efforts?"

"I always listen to such ideas."

"I had believed so," said the Apprentice. "There is a spear that belongs to the centurion. I will give you five gold coins now, merely for your effort. Bring it to me and I will reward you with ten more."

He then threw the pouch to Khalid. Khalid opened it and found five gold coins.

Khalid grinned. "This spear, describe it to me."

"It is a typical Roman hasta, but it has three identifiable blood red crosses on its head."

Khalid remembered these markings on the spear at Octavian's bedpost. "You want me to steal back the spear you gave to Octavian?"

Surprised at Khalid's knowledge of the spear he had given to Octavian, he answered, "That one is of no use to me. Find the centurion named Longinus and bring me the one he carries. You will know the difference. Trust me."

Khalid thought a moment and spoke, "Agreed, with one more request."

"And that is?" asked the Apprentice.

Khalid pointed to his dog and said, "Vitali gets ten pieces of gold as well."

The Apprentice smiled, "I said you were a shrewd bounty hunter, you have proven me correct. Vitali shall receive ten gold coins as well."

"When I get the spear, where shall you have me bring it?"

"I will know when you have it and shall come to you."

"With the gold?" inquired Khalid.

"With the gold," answered the Apprentice as he turned and left.

Khalid looked toward the palace and then down at Vitali. "First, we answer to Pilate, then we find the centurion, then we get the spear."

IN THE NEGEV

Longinus and Mary had continued South of Jerusalem and found themselves entering an uninhabitable stretch of rugged terrain. Approaching a very shallow water hole, Longinus stopped his horse and said, "We stop here and gather as much water as we can hold." They dismounted, and Longinus handed Mary a goat skin flask. He looked through the haversack and found several other containers that could be used to carry water. "These will do," he said.

Longinus shielded his eye as he looked up into the blinding sun. He pulled off the wrap that he had been wearing to cover his face and eye. He threw it on the ground and declared, "I don't need this anymore."

He focused his eyes on the horizon line and scanned the wasteland to the far left and to the far right. He said to Mary, "The Negev is ahead. If we keep heading in this direction, there will be nothing for us but the heat of the sun and brackish water."

Mary began to fill the flask and asked, "Where are we to go?"

Longinus moved to the water hole; he cupped his huge hand and took a drink. "We head for Beersheba, by way of the spice route. That way," he said as he pointed to a vast, rugged, stretch of desolate wilderness. "We will only have about a day or so journey in the Negev."

"I hear the spice route is full of nomads and thieves," said Mary.

Longinus ignored Mary's comment and busied himself with filling containers with water.

"Drink all you can now. This water will have to last us until we get to the other side of this stretch of Hades," he said. "If we are lucky, we may find a caravan and get more supplies."

"Beersheba is the home of Abraham, Isaac, and Jacob," smiled Mary as she filled the flask.

Longinus looked at Mary and said, "It is a place of people you know? This will be good."

"Oh, they are no longer upon the earth. They are today with my Lord."

"Woman, you confuse me."

Longinus led his horse to the water. As the horse drank his fill he looked up at the sun. It was about to set. "We travel at dusk and into the night. That is the only way to make it through this desert. We rest by day."

Although Mary was very tired, she nodded in agreement.

Longinus mounted his horse and reached out his hand. Mary grabbed hold of it, and he pulled her up onto the back of the saddle.

As they headed out, the sun set in the West. It blazed in a beautiful array of red and gold, lighting the barren wasteland with an amber glow.

"God's creation is all so beautiful," Mary said as she looked at the heavenly wisps of color in the sky. "He waves his hand and glorifies even the most barren of places."

Longinus looked over at the sun setting as he listened to Mary and wondered at her words.

ALIBIS AND LIES

Khalid arrived at the palace of Pilate, and Octavian had already entered in. He did not wait to meet him as he had said.

"Fair enough," said Khalid to Vitali. "Now we are even. He didn't do what he said, so he shouldn't mind if I didn't do what I said." Vitali looked at Khalid and nodded her head in agreement.

Khalid was escorted into the palace by a sentry. He was told to wait outside the chamber door as usual until he was announced. As he waited, he overheard Octavian speaking to Pilate.

"From what I have told you, Prefect, I am sure you can see that the bounty hunter went on a wild chase that bore no fruit for Rome."

"So, Octavian, what do you suggest?" said Pilate.

"You heard the woman bear witness to her husband helping to steal the body of the Nazarene and of the sorcerer's magic."

"Indeed."

"That arrest was the work of a senior centurion. Not a bounty hunter. I say, let the bounty hunter hunt down the sorcerer and leave the hunting of the deserter to my cohort. Give me leave to go with him to Rome to ensure that this matter is dealt with properly. For even though he has methods, he cannot be trusted to act with good judgment."

"Octavian, I will consider what you have said," stated Pilate as he motioned to the sentry to speak.

"Khalid the bounty hunter has arrived, Prefect."

"Let him in."

The sentry opened the door and Khalid entered with Vitali. He took a cold look at Octavian, and then nodded in a half bow to Pilate.

"Well, Khalid, what is your account? Have you captured the centurion?" Pilate asked as though he had not heard a thing from

Octavian. Khalid was well seasoned in the deceitful tactics of liars, thieves, merchants, and now centurions; he decided to answer in a cunning manner.

"Prefect, I can only answer in truth. It seems Octavian was too busy making deals with a sorcerer's apprentice than to have any time to chase the deserter. I chased him with Vitali through the streets, the alleys, the open field, and into the forest. Had we had the company of the soldiers of Rome, they could have rode ahead and encircled him. He would now be in your prison. But Octavian took the guard, all but a few, and went to the Western outskirts of the city."

Octavian squirmed and glared his eyes at Khalid.

"Is that your full account?" queried Pilate.

"One more thing."

"Speak," said Pilate, granting permission.

Khalid looked directly into Octavian's eyes and said, "His woman witness—"

Octavian feared his plot to devise the woman's confession was about to be exposed and gave Khalid a threatening stare,

"—was the only fruit he bared for Rome."

In hearing that phrase, Octavian knew Khalid had overheard his words to Pilate. He was relieved that Khalid held his tongue, yet concerned as to how Pilate would respond to Khalid's account. Pilot looked at Octavian, then he looked at Khalid. He stood up and walked into the middle of his court between the two of them.

"I have heard enough," quipped Pilate.

"Octavian, you are a senior centurion of Rome, however, I have hired Khalid for his extraordinary skill and success in capturing those that seem to slip through the fingers of Roman soldiers. There is a widespread revolt at hand, and I will implement all of my options. Regardless of how unorthodox Khalid's methods may appear to you, Octavian, you will work together with Khalid to complete the assignment.

"It does appear that if you and your men had stayed on task with the bounty hunter, the deserter would be in the prison cell at this moment. I want it understood that pompous rivalry will not be tolerated when it comes to the task at hand. Do you understand?"

"Yes Prefect."

"Now, lastly, you will not be departing for Rome until you complete this task . That is a more pressing matter at this time. You will take the bounty hunter and your soldiers and find Longinus. Bring him to me alive. If he has conspired with the woman, he will know much about the conspiracy the followers have devised. Go now."

"Yes Prefect."

A Meeting of the Mind

Octavian and Khalid no sooner left the presence of Pilate and they began to vent their displeasure trying to out glare one another as they left the palace. Once outside it escalated.

"Ahh," Octavian taunted, "Rome owns you now. You answer to Rome."

"I am not a Roman soldier! I answer to no one but me," growled Khalid.

"It is clear that when you accepted this assignment, you became Pilate's prize bull."

The two stared eye to eye and moved around in a circle. Khalid lunged into the side of Octavian, thrusting his body into his. Khalid grabbed Octavian in a neck hold. "I am no man's prize."

Octavian, choking, managed to say some words, "Your freedom that you cherish will belong to Rome if you do not stop this madness now."

Khalid loosened his grip and sneered, "I will stop when you know this bounty hunter will not be stabbed in the back with lies and deceit."

"I hear you," gasped Octavian reluctantly.

Khalid held his grip and said, "I don't want Roman command. I want to earn my bounty without you in my way."

Fighting for breath, Octavian wheezed out, "I can't breathe."

"I will let you go, but know this, the next time you lie of me, I will not relent."

At that, Khalid released his hold. Octavian puffed and panted struggling for air. He rubbed at his throat, finally catching enough breath to utter out, "Be glad that I will keep this between us."

"You have no choice," snarled Khalid. "Or Pilate will hear more truth of your deceitful ways."

Octavian dusted off his armor and placed his centurion's helmet on his head. He stroked the crest to make sure it was straight. He looked at Khalid as though nothing had happened and stated, "I trust that matter is settled. Now let us proceed."

Khalid wondered at his nice behavior especially after nearly choking him to death. "Proceed?"

"Yes. Get your gear ready, we leave at dawn. I hope your Vitali docs better this time. I want to get this over with. As soon as we arrest him, we head to Rome. Now where would he be hiding?" Octavian placed his forefinger at his chin and thought.

Khalid answered, "There is only one place."

"And where might that be?" asked Octavian, very cockish.

"Beyond the western outskirts, he went south from Jerusalem. That leads to rugged terrain and blasting heat of the Negev. To survive he'd have to pass that. He could only be heading for Beersheba."

Octavian thought and answered, "Yes. You just may be right. We travel south. Now go, we leave at dawn."

As they departed, a shadowy figure stepped forth from a dark, secluded area. It was the Apprentice. Remaining unseen, he said under his breath, "Beersheba? Of course."

A BLESSED OMEN
IN THE NEGEV

Dawn was approaching and Longinus and Mary had traveled all through the night. Longinus was weary from all the events of the past few days and was trying hard not to nod off. He looked behind at Mary, and her head was bent over like she was dozing.

"We stop here," he said. "We bed down under that cleft in the rock. We will be shielded from the sun and out of sight from any Bedouins." They dismounted and walked to the cleft in the rock.

Mary could hardly stay awake as they made some sort of camp. She was so hungry. Longinus watched as she sat down and pulled the jerky from her pocket and pulled off a small bit. She said a prayer of thanks and placed it in her mouth. She chewed it and lay her head down. She was soon fast asleep.

Longinus bedded down and looked over at Mary still holding a small piece of jerky in her hand. He noticed how beautiful she was, even though the desert dust had now covered parts of her face. Taking a quick look around the cave he reached over and grabbed his spear, carefully placing it over his chest. Too tired to think any more he lay his head down and fell asleep

Longinus began to dream.

In his dream a lion was seen coming from the hills of Judea. The lion kept coming, approaching with great speed.

Longinus was unarmed and felt a fear that he had never felt before. In his dream, Longinus thought the feeling of fear was strange. He connected the fear with his life and knew it was the fear of death. Death was something he had never feared until that moment in his dream.

Suddenly, the lion came to an abrupt stop, just five feet from him. Longinus lifted up his arms and yelled to scare the lion away. The lion remained still. In the dream, Longinus had no way to defend himself and feared what the lion might do to him. But the lion remained still and crouched down starring at Longinus kindly.

Instantly, his spear appeared, lying in front of him on the ground. Longinus picked it up. It glowed as he looked at it. In the midst of the glowing beam of light, he saw Romans on horseback. An image of a man with a centurion's crest was leading them. They were approaching the streets to a city; he watched as they entered in. It looked like Beersheba.

There was a man with them that was not a Roman soldier. He had shaggy, unkempt hair with a long dreadlocked braid that hung down his back. A dog that looked like a lion was running beside him.

The lion roared, breaking his concentration. Longinus looked at the lion, and the lion turned and ran north.

Longinus watched as the lion stopped and turned and looked at him. He roared as though he were summoning Longinus to follow.

The lion turned north again and ran. Longinus watched until the lion was out of sight. The dream stopped and he awoke.

Startled by the dream, Longinus jumped up and drew his sword. He ran over to the opening in the cleft and looked out to see if anyone was there. The dream had been very lucid, and he felt it was a warning omen to a foreboding attack. He saw nothing but bright light from the afternoon sun. As he peered out from the opening in the cleft, he felt the piercing rays of the heat. His eyes carefully scanned the surrounding land, from the left to the right. Nothing was there but the rugged terrain.

Just a dream, he thought. He returned to his makeshift bed and lay down. This time half asleep and half awake. He lay with his spear in one hand and his sword in the other. He could not sleep. After a little while, he got up and started to gather up the camp.

"Mary. We go now," he said in a loud voice.

Mary opened her eyes and lifted her head from her makeshift bed. It took a few moments for her to fully wake up, but when she did she nodded in agreement.

Longinus quickly gathered his belongings and was packing them back in the haversack. "I had an omen."

"An omen?" questioned Mary.

"In a dream. We must leave this place and head north."

"But north is away from Beersheba," she said.

"I dreamed a lion came from the hills of Judea and showed me that we are being followed. We are to go north."

Mary gasped. "He has spoken to you."

"The lion did not speak, he showed me," answered Longinus. "Now make haste."

Mary quickly gathered her things, packed them on the horse, and waited for Longinus to mount first.

Longinus mounted, then reached out his hand. Mary grabbed hold. She was no sooner lifted up onto the saddle and Longinus shouted, "Yaa!" The horse bolted out toward the north.

THE PURSUIT

Octavian was heading south of Jerusalem, with a detachment of his best soldiers, along with Khalid the bounty hunter and his dog, of which he had come to despise. The assignment was to arrest Longinus, who was now officially documented as a deserter and an enemy of Rome, and a woman follower, Mary Magdalene. In the process, they needed to find where the two had hidden the Nazarene's dead body and return it to Pilot. Khalid was now unsure whether any of what he had been told by Octavian held any bearing of truth at all. On the other hand Octavian had told so many lies and deceitfully deceived so many that he had come to believe his own lies as the truth. He had his own agenda and that was to find out how to use the power of the spear at any cost. It was definitely a pursuit of confusion with a mad man at the helm.

"It has been a long day in this sun, and now the Negev is in our path," grumbled Octavian.

Khalid overheard his complaining and laughed, "You would not make a good bounty hunter. Keep your command as centurion."

Octavian fumed at the comment. "You are blind to the power of a senior centurion? Lose your freedom and your eyes will open!"

They rode along for several hours more and the sun was starting to set. Khalid discovered tracks in the grit and the dirt that had not been sand swept. He leaned over and took a closer look.

"Just as I suspected. They are headed to the Negev." He took a drink from his goat skin flask and noticed it was dwindling. He shouted to the others, "Save your water. You will need every drop."

As they continued on their journey a soldier who had been traveling ahead to scout was returning quickly. He shouted to Octavian as he pointed, "Sir, there is a water hole over the ridge, that way." Octavian looked toward the ridge and saw the heat form a haze over the land in the direction the soldier had pointed.

THE SPEAR OF DESTINY

"The gods have provided us with water. We go and replenish our supply."

Khalid looked down at Vitali and smiled, "Let's get us some water."

Vitali barked and they took off toward the ridge. In no time at all they were followed by the entire Roman detachment cheering as their horses caught up and passed Khalid one by one. He shouted out to Vitali,

"That's what I get for waiting for you! Meet you at the water!" He kicked his horse and yelled, "Ya!" and one by one, he passed the soldiers and beat them all to the water hole. He rode his horse right into the water, jumped off, waded around and splashed it everywhere then cupped his hands and drank.

Another soldier dismounted and jumped in the water splashing and drinking.

Octavian shook his head in disgust and hollered out to Khalid and the soldiers, "We will have none of that! This water will not be fit to clean our sandals if you all jump in and bath your filth off in it!"

Octavian dismounted and gazed at the soldiers lapping up water. "Men, you may rest for a few minutes and fill your goat skins and anything you have that will carry water. No romping!"

While Khalid was enjoying the water, Vitali was sniffing around on the other side of the water hole. She found something. It was a dirty cloth. Vitali picked it up with her teeth and took it directly to Khalid.

"What you got there, Vitali?" he said as he took the cloth from her. Khalid sniffed the air and smelled something familiar. He put the cloth to his nose and smelled it. It was a floral scent, with a hint of jasmine. "I know this scent, Vitali," he said as he tried to think of where he had smelled it before. He remembered.

"Vitali, when you lost the scent…is this what you smelled?"

Vitali sniffed again and nodded yes as she sounded a deep yawnish yelp.

Octavian looked over and saw Khalid holding the cloth up and examining it. Recognizing what it was, he hurried over to Khalid and grabbed the cloth from his hands. "Where did you get this?" he demanded.

"Vitali found it over there," answered Khalid as he pointed to the far side of the water hole.

Khalid asked, "What is it?"

"He was here. It belongs to Longinus."

"What is it?" Khalid asked again.

"It is his wrap for his blind eye," he said as he studied it. "But why would he leave it here?"

Octavian put the cloth up to his nostrils and smelled it. "He was with the woman. They are together."

"How do you know?" asked Khalid.

"It has the scent of jasmine."

Octavian looked up at the sky to determine how much farther they could travel before it got dark. "We can travel half a stadia if we go now. Then we pitch camp."

"We can gain more ground by night with the stars in place of the sun," suggested Khalid.

"The land is to rugged for night travel. We camp soon," ordered Octavian. He placed the cloth under his armor and went to fill his water flask.

Khalid looked at Vitali and said, "He would never earn a bounty... not a one." Vitali nodded in agreement.

NEW HOPE AND A PLACE OF REFUGE

Longinus had been running his horse rampantly, heading north, as though he were being chased by a ghost. Mary had not said a word; she had only held on tight as the horse weaved around jutting clefts and narrow passageways in the rocks.

The sun was just beginning to ease its searing heat, and Longinus knew his horse had been driven hard. He slowed the horse's gate down to a trot and assessed the distance they had come. He wondered where he was going. He only knew the omen in the dream told him to go north.

"Ahead, up there," he said to Mary. "We will stop for a while, the horse must rest."

The terrain had become less barren and was showing signs of vegetation other than desert flowers. Mary had been observing all things along the way. She said to Longinus, "I know this place."

Longinus asked, "How so?"

Mary answered, "I have never come from this direction before, but I believe this is the way to Hebron. I traveled there with my Master. We visited the burial sites of Abraham, Isaac, Jacob, and Adam."

Longinus remembered all the names but Adam; he wondered and asked, "Are these the same men you knew from Beersheba?"

"I never knew them. I knew of them. Yes, they are the same," answered Mary.

"Tell me about this place called Hebron."

Mary answered, "It is said to be a city of refuge. We should be safe there."

"Refuge? I don't understand."

"It is a place of my people. And a place for others to find a friend to help them in need. It is hard to explain to one who knows nothing of my people."

Longinus responded, "I don't want to know about your people. I want to know what to look for so I know when we are getting close to the city. Are there land marks?"

"Oh," said Mary in a surprised tone. "The city sits in a narrow valley surrounded by rocky hills. It can be hard to find."

"What direction does the valley run?" asked Longinus.

"It runs to the north and to the south."

"Now that is what I need to know," he answered.

"We stop here." Longinus let Mary down and then dismounted.

He took a drink from the water flask and handed it to Mary. She took a drink. He then took a tin from the haversack and poured water into it for the horse.

He grubbed around in the haversack and pulled out some stale bread. He held it out to Mary. "It is stale, but I think you will like it better than the jerky."

Mary took the bread and said, "Thank you for your kindness." She said a silent prayer and ate the stale bread.

Longinus shook his head and looked out over the horizon and assessed where they were. There was no haze from the searing heat showing on the horizon.

"That is a good sign," he said. "I believe we are out of the Negev. How far was this Hebron from Jerusalem?"

Mary thought and then answered, "We traveled on foot. The road was very rugged. It took us two days."

"Then, we are almost there!" smiled Longinus. "I say we are less than a stadia away."

"But we are not traveling from Jerusalem?" Mary asked as though she were puzzled.

"I know how far we traveled south, how far we went east, and how far we have traveled north. We are almost there."

Mary smiled, " When we get there, I will get you some fresh bread in the bazaar!"

Longinus returned the smile, "I can taste it now."

Meanwhile on the way to Beersheba...

Octavian and his men had pitched their tents in a rocky canyon. Sentry's were strategically placed to keep guard against any nomad thieves that might dare to enter a Roman encampment.

"We have made good time," boasted Octavian. "By midday tomorrow, we will be entering Beersheba."

Khalid was not so sure. "We have not seen the spice route yet. Are you sure we are so close?"

Octavian, tired of the heat and inconvenience of the rugged terrain, was not in the mood to be questioned. "Beersheba is ahead!" he shouted. "Did I make myself clear?"

"Yes, sir," mocked Khalid as he took his bedding and made a spot for him and Vitali to sleep.

"We will do well to ration our water," he said to Vitali. "This doesn't feel right." Vitali nodded and lay down beside Khalid for the night. "Sleep, Vitali, we deal with this at dawn."

Longinus and Mary continue their journey to Hebron...

The closer Longinus and Mary came to Hebron, the more eager they both were. The mountains of Judah were a welcome sight. It was a blessing to get out of the wilderness. At Hebron, they would have food and fresh water. Mary knew they would find kind people there who would lend their generosity and help them.

As for Longinus, he was unsure of his destiny and still had unanswered questions. The rugged terrain of the wilderness had kept his attention on surviving, but now, with Hebron a short distance away, his thoughts were turned back to his dream and to the vision in the spear. Both seemed so vivid, so real. He wondered if the two were connected? He wondered at Mary's words. Could she be right? Was he actually chosen for something?

Soon they came upon a babbling brook. "Water!" declared Longinus. "We drink." He let Mary down from the horse, and then he dismounted. Longinus led his thirsty steed to the water.

"We have come to the brook of Eshcol," smiled Mary. "They call it, 'the torrent of the cluster.'"

"It tastes as sweet as wine," said Longinus as he filled his goat skinned flask.

"The Lord has led us here," said Mary. "I remember, this place was southwest of Hebron. There should be vineyards nearby." "Vineyards?" asked Longinus. Excited at the thought of mouthwatering grapes, he scanned the view of the valley with its sloping hills. The sun had set, but he could still see the images and silhouettes. "Over there," he shouted in glee. "The land is covered with vineyards!"

Mary looked up and praised her God for such a blessing. They made their way to the vineyard and ate.

"These are the biggest grapes I have ever seen!" exclaimed Longinus. "And the sweetest I have ever tasted."

"My Lord has answered my prayer to give us nourishment for our bodies."

Longinus looked at Mary. His mouth was stuffed with as many grapes as he could fit into it. He swallowed partly. Still chewing, he said, with his words muffled by grapes, "Keep praying, I like what happens when you do!"

Now rested and fed, Longinus and Mary gathered grapes and placed them in the haversack. The horse had fed on sweet grass and was also renewed.

"On to Hebron," declared Longinus as he mounted the horse and extended his hand out for Mary.

Mary grabbed hold and shouted, "To Hebron!"

Longinus smiled at her enthusiasm and they rode onward.

BEDOUIN THIEVES

All was still at the Roman encampment. The soldiers were sound asleep. Suddenly, Vitali heard a shuffling sound. She sniffed the air, then nudged Khalid to awake. Khalid grabbed hold of his sword and drew it out. He slowly got up. He saw a shadow of a man with a Bedouin turban on his head. He waited at the ready as the man came closer.

"Where there is one, there are more", he thought as he prepared for a fight.

The Bedouin bent over to steal a soldier's haversack. Khalid quietly pulled a dagger from a harness on his side. He continued to watch. As the Bedouin picked up the haversack, Khalid hurled his dagger, piercing the Bedouin in the heart. He keeled over and slumped to the ground.

A soldier awakened and seeing the dead Bedouin he shouted, "Thieves!"

"Damn fool," shouted Khalid as he ran to the edge of the camp. He saw two figures in dark cloaks and turbans running down the narrowing canyon. "I could have gotten them all!"

Octavian came running out of his tent. He looked at the dead Bedouin, then at Khalid. "Why is a Bedouin thief so close to Beersheba?" he eyed the camp, "They must have come from the spice route."

Khalid paid no attention to Octavian. He was to busy pulling his dagger out from the dead man's chest.

Octavian watched as Khalid cleaned his dagger, "You have good eyes."

"Yes and Vitali has a good nose for thieves." Answered Khalid, as he examined the dead thief, "That silk scarf tied back with his marira, it will bring good money in the marketplace." He bent down and took it off the dead Bedouin. He proceeded to take the man's cloak and search for valuables in his layers of shirts and found a pouch of coins. He smiled and took them.

Octavian watched as Khalid continued to strip the man of anything of value; lastly, Khalid took the rings from the dead Bedouin's boney fingers.

"If you are finished, throw his body out to the vultures." Ordered Octavian, "I don't want flies gathering in the middle of our camp."

Khalid continued on and ignored the remark.

Octavian turned to his head guard, "Bring me the Sentry who were standing guard. They shall answer to me for allowing Bedouin thieves to enter our camp!"

The guard looked out and pointed to the edge of the canyon, "Sir, they approach."

Octavian looked out and saw soldiers coming toward the camp. They were leading several horses loaded with dead sentry's draped over their backs. He was cold to the matter and shouted, "Bury them under the rocks, and bring them no farther. There are enough flies gathering as it is."

He shook his head in disgust and ordered, "Double the guard. Dead soldiers are of no use to Rome."

"Yes, sir," answered the guard.

Khalid locked eyes with Octavian giving him such a stern glare of disfavor that it made Octavian nervous. Remembering what happened the last time he saw such a glare from him, he quickly marched back to his tent.

Khalid heaved the dead Bedouin over his shoulders. "Come Vitali, that man has lost both mind and soul. We bury this one under the rocks."

HEBRON AT LAST

Longinus and Mary came upon the narrow valley, surrounded by rocky hills. It ran north. "This is it," he declared. "Let's see what lies in Hebron." He kicked his horse and headed up the narrow valley.

As they got closer, they could see a shadow of light above in the dark sky. Longinus announced, "The city is there, just as you have said."

They made their way into the city streets. Most of the merchants in the bazaar were shut up for the night, the last few were just closing up.

"You there," shouted Longinus to a merchant.

The merchant looked up from his work and shouted, "My good man, what can I do for you?"

"We have traveled far. Where might we find lodging?"

"Aha," he said, "Welcome to Hebron. There is an inn just past the end of the bazaar. I am sure there will be room for you there."

Longinus nodded and Mary leaned forward, "Thank you, good man."

The merchant smiled at Mary, "You have the face of an angel. May you find what you seek in Hebron."

Longinus rode on to the end of the bazaar and saw the inn that the merchant spoke of. His first thought was to get Mary settled in, and then find a tavern to drink his fill of their best wine. He let Mary down from the horse, then he dismounted. Handing the reins to Mary he said, "Wait here, I will see what they have for us."

Mary took the reins and nodded.

As she waited outside the inn, she bowed her head and said a prayer of thanks.

It wasn't long and Longinus came out of the inn accompanied by a short man. The man took the reins from Mary and said,

"Welcome, my friend. I will bed down your horse and give him some fine oats."

Longinus pulled his spear and haversack from the horse, then he motioned for Mary to follow him. The man took the horse to the stables and Longinus led Mary to a quaint room, just inside the inn's entrance.

They entered the room and Longinus remarked, "This is a very friendly place, just as you have said. You settle in. I will be back."

"Where are you going?" Mary asked.

He hesitated, then answered, "To taste the fine wine of Hebron. It has been a long while since I have had strong wine."

Mary answered, "Strong wine is good. It is only when one does not know how to stop enjoying it that it leads to troubles. I trust you will know how to enjoy it and return in good spirit."

Longinus looked at Mary and said, "I will be back."

Longinus hurried to the tavern; as he entered, it was half full of men drinking and conversing, telling stories and enjoying their night.

Longinus went up to the barkeep and ordered, "Wine, your best!" The barkeep handed him a jug and a cup. Longinus took the jug and sat at a table. He quickly poured a cup and put it to his lips, then he hesitated. Mary's words rang in his ears, *"Strong wine is good. It is only when one does not know how to stop enjoying it that it leads to troubles."*

He put the cup down and reasoned in his thoughts, *"If I have this cup, I will have another and another and consume the entire jug. Then I will ask for another jug, and when that is empty, another."*

"Ahh, just crazy thoughts," he mumbled as he raised the cup to his mouth, then suddenly halted. His mind began to race fast again with more thoughts.

"I will not remember any of the foolish acts I might have done and be left with a reeling head in the morning. With Romans

hunting me down, this is not a good time to tempt Fortune who favors me."

Longinus looked at the wine in the cup. He longed to taste it. He lifted it to his lips again, then suddenly he slammed the cup down on the table. *"Not now,"* he thought.

He got up from the table and picked up his jug of wine. He walked over to a couple of men and placed his jug on their table and said, "Enjoy the night." The men looked up with surprise and happily thanked Longinus for the wine. "Will you join us for drink?" asked one of the men.

Longinus looked at them and said, "I wish I could. But I must go." The men quickly filled their cups as Longinus left to return to the inn.

Longinus had only been gone a short while and Mary was surprised to see him back so quickly.

"You are back so soon? Did you not find a tavern open?" she asked.

"I choose to get a good night's rest instead. There will be time for strong wine later."

Mary smiled.

Longinus pointed, "You take the bed, I'll take the floor. We sleep and tomorrow we find the best food in Hebron." Mary lay down and rested her head on the bed as Longinus pulled his bedding from the haversack and laid it out upon the floor.

Mary noticed that he was having a hard time getting his head comfortable. She threw down a straw-filled pillow." Here, take this for under your head. That is the least I can offer you as you have given me the bed."

Longinus took the straw-filled pillow and found himself looking deep into her eyes. They radiated such warmth. "Thank you," he said and placed it under his head. He then reached over and held his spear over his chest and stared at the spear, waiting to see if it might glow. It did nothing. He carefully wrapped the spear in a fresh cloth.

Thinking that if he were to carry it with him in Hebron, it would look less threatening covered. After a few minutes, Longinus closed his eyes. From his memory, he recalled his vision.

How the bloody red crosses on the spear's head began to glow and the bloody face of the dying Nazarene was seen, with the crown of thorns and how the image continue to zoom out until the entire man on the cross was shown. He recalled the blood and water bursting forth from the Nazarene's side. He remembered the golden bronze city bursting upward out of the ground and the gate with the face of a bronzed lion.

He recalled how the image zoomed farther out into the distance until the ground broke open and coming up in the front of the most beautiful kingdom was fire and molten lava. He recalled that it was the most horrid-looking place, full of darkness with multiple layers of dungeon-like prisons, guarded by the most hideous of creatures. That smell of putrefactive pools of evil pus was all so real, so hauntingly real, but how?

At the end of the memory, Longinus dozed off into a deep sleep.

LOST IN THE NEGEV

Octavian and his detachment awoke at dawn and were now marching in what Octavian believed to be the direction of Beersheba. With the canyon long behind them, they were feeling the searing heat of the Negev. Beersheba was not in their sight.

Khalid took a drink from his almost empty goat-skinned flask. He shouted to Octavian, "We need to find water."

Octavian shouted back at him, "We need to find Longinus. Return to Pilate if you don't have the strength to carry on. Plead for water to him."

Khalid ignored Octavian's rant and looked at the horizons all around, trying to get a bearing on where they were. Frustrated, he shouted out, "Half of a stadia away. Those were the words of our illustrious centurion last night. Were they not, Vitali?"

Octavian glared at Khalid then kicked his horse, "Yaa!" he shouted as he galloped fast past the soldiers up to the front lead.

"And now he exhausts the last breath of his horse. He shall not exhaust ours. Vitali, we rest." Khalid stopped his horse and sat on the ground, looking over to study the horizon.

"Vitali, he leads us deep into the worst part of the Negev. If there is any water found, it will be brackish, nothing but salt."

Khalid arose to his feet. "We must stop the centurion fool before he marches every one of us farther into the jaws of Hades." Vitali looked at Khalid and nodded in agreement. "First, we turn the fool around, then we find the spice route, then we find a caravan."

Khalid looked out to access the soldiers who had not advanced very far since they had rested. Most were on foot, leading their horses. He and Vitali got up and walked toward them; little by little, they caught up with the troops. Now within hearing range, he shouted out to Octavian, "How long since you've any tracks?"

Octavian stopped his horse. He turned his head toward Khalid and shouted "They had to go this way."

Khalid yelled out, "You've lost their track. We have to go back."

Octavian shouted, "How far back?"

"Not sure, but Vitali's nose says this way." Khalid pointed southeast.

Octavian hesitated as he looked at the searing heat. He knew he was lost but was too pompous to admit it. He hollered back to Khalid, "I do not trust my life to a dog!"

"And I do not trust mine to a fool," muttered Khalid under his breath. He thought of what to say to convince Octavian, then he shouted, "Vitali is never wrong about these things. She has only lost the scent once in her life, and in that, she was tricked."

Octavian reconsidered then shouted back, "Very well, we shall follow that mangy animal's nose."

Octavian raised his hand ordering the soldiers to halt. Acting as though this was all of his own planning he addressed the soldiers. "We go this way!" He pointed southeast and turned his horse around. The detachment turned their horses and followed Octavian southeast.

Khalid looked down at Vitali and shook his head. "Guess we shouldn't care how he goes about it as long as it gets done, hey girl?"

Vitali growled.

"Don't worry girl, I'm not forgetting that one either. Your coat is beautiful."

Vitali held her head up and proudly pranced alongside Khalid's horse.

THE MAN WITH FEW RICHES

Longinus and Mary awoke from a good night's sleep by the sound of someone knocking on the door. "Who is it?" Longinus asked loudly.

"It is I, Timmeon, the innkeeper."

Longinus opened the door and the innkeeper smiled and stepped inside the room. "I trust you and your sister rested well?" he said. In his hands, he held a large bowl, an urn of water, and a small decorated flask. A towel was draped over his arm. "I bring you fresh water to clean with," he said as he hurried over to the table and placed the objects. "And some scented oil. Good food is waiting. Come and eat once you have washed."

"Indeed," smiled Longinus.

Mary looked at the man and said, "Timmeon, you are so gracious to us. May the Lord bless you."

Timmeon bowed his head to Mary and said, "Oh, my dear woman, he has. He watches over me all the day long."

Timmeon looked down on the floor at the makeshift bed, then over to Longinus smiling. He left the room and whistled happily as he went down the hall.

Longinus and Mary looked at each other. Mary commented very cunningly, "You and your sister?" Longinus smiled and Mary giggled.

They quickly got ready and eagerly made their way down the hall, following the sounds of clanging pots and plates. The bustling of people laughing and talking led them right to a large room with two long rows of tables. They watched as two women were bringing food to the table and cleaning up dirty plates.

"Come, come and eat," motioned Timmeon. "There is plenty of room," he said as he pointed to an empty area in the middle of one of the long tables. Mary and Longinus seated themselves and looked around at the food on the table. Longinus placed his spear at his feet under the table, awkwardly trying to fit it so it would not bother anyone's feet.

A woman seated next to Mary handed her a plate of flat bread. "It is the best in all of Hebron," she said. Mary took a piece from the plate, "Thank you." She took a bite. "Oh, you are so right. It is delicious."

Longinus wasted no time in filling his plate with some of everything on the table. "A feast fit for Tiberius," he said.

Suddenly, the room quieted. Mary spoke up, "He is Roman. That is his way of saying it is all very good." The people nodded and smiled as they resumed their laughter and talk.

An older gentleman, dressed very meticulous in a garment of fine cloth, looked at Longinus and said, "From what part of Rome do you hail?"

Longinus thought a moment, remembering that there was now a bounty on his head, he answered, "I hail from the hall of a Roman soldier's barrack, and now, I have no place to lay my head."

"Ahh, I see," answered the older gentleman." I know of another of whom it was said had no place to lay his head."

Longinus continued eating in a ravenous manner, paying no attention to the man. The older gentleman continued, "That one is now at his Father's throne. He has inherited a kingdom that has no end." Longinus did not understand a word he was saying, but Mary did.

"You know of my Lord?" she asked.

The older gentleman looked over at Mary and smiled, "Indeed I do. You look familiar. What is your name?"

"I am Mary of Magdalene."

The older gentlemen looked delighted at hearing this. "Ahh, the fishing village. Now I remember you. Do you remember who I am?"

Mary looked at him closely and said, "I am sorry, sir, I do not remember who you are. Who are you?"

"I am the one that asked your Lord what I must do to inherit the kingdom."

Mary looked and said, "I am sorry, there have been so many."

"Fortunately for me, I sold all I had, or almost all and left Jerusalem not so many days before the quake. I hear my property is little more than rubble now. A man of modest means can live better in Hebron than in Jerusalem, and so I am here."

Mary politely nodded her head to acknowledge she was listening.

"I hear there is great confusion in Jerusalem and people are fleeing."

"I have fled as well," she answered. "With the help of this brave Centurion."

The older gentlemen looked startled, "Centurion?"

"He has saved my life and given up his own. Now we are being chased by Roman soldiers."

The older gentlemen put his forefinger to his lips as though to warn Mary to say nothing more. In a very low voice, he said, "I am an honest man, one who is well trusted. For some reason, I believe we have met for a divine purpose. I must talk with you more, but not here. Can you and your friend meet with me later? There is much to discuss."

Softly and in a low whisper, Mary answered, "I cannot answer for my friend. But I can speak with you."

"That will be god...perhaps after the evening supper?"

Mary nodded.

" See if you can persuade your friend. After the supper hour, I will linger at the front of the inn. From there, we can go to my room or yours and talk of many things."

Mary answered, ""If it be my Lord's will, we shall meet."

The older gentlemen smiled.

OCTAVIAN AND KHALID AT ODDS

The day was passing and the boiling heat of the Negev was unforgiving. The soldiers were weak, and their tongues were dry and parched. Little water was left, and those that had some were silent about the fact that they did, for Octavian had ordered all the water to be placed in a community water draw. One he had possession of and doled out as he pleased.

Suddenly, a pool of water was seen on the horizon. Was it real or a mirage? Somehow, it didn't matter, the soldiers saw it and it gave them hope as they took their last ounces of strength to near it.

Approaching the oasis, Khalid saw that it indeed did exist and was not a devil's trick being played on his mind. He slid down his horse in a very awkward dismount, for he was dehydrated and wasted from hunger as well as thirst. "Vitali, come," he said as he staggered toward the water hole. He fell forward and began to splash the liquid at his mouth; as it was so dry, he had no control over his lips.

The heat had been unforgiving as well on Vitali, especially with her thick coat of hair. Yet that thick coat was what had shielded her from the blistering sun. Vitali drank.

Octavian lagged behind as the men drank from the oasis. He appeared to be allowing his soldiers the first turn at the water. He dismounted and stood at the far side of his horse. Making sure that he was unseen by any of the men, he removed a goat-skinned flask from his haversack and began to drink. He looked around to make sure the men were all at the water hole and paying no attention to him, then quietly returned his flask to the haversack.

Sauntering down to the water hole Octavian watched his men lavishing up the water. He bent down to take a drink and as he did he spied a rotting carcass of a mountain goat floating in the water. He lifted up and said nothing. The men were busy drinking and too faint to notice anything.

Octavian grabbed his spear and imbedded it into the carcass and quickly pulled it over to him.

He quietly leaned against the spear and pushed it to the bottom. Watching the men as they drank, he thought to himself, "They will be sick from the sheer thought of this carcass. What they do not know will not hurt them."

Octavian watched on and announced from his stance at the water's edge, with his spear holding down the dead goat's carcass, "Rest a bit, and drink 'til you are full. Be sure and fill your flasks, for there is no more water for you from the community water draw."

Octavian stood there, leaning on his spear until all the men had satisfied their thirst and filled their flasks. "Mount up," he ordered.

He waited and watched until all the soldiers had mounted. Then with great stealth, he released his spear from the dead goat's carcass and quickly made his way to his horse. "Onward!" he shouted.

The men rode off as the rotting carcass slowly floated upward in the water.

It was only a matter of hours in the heat until one by one, many of the men were holding their bellies in pain. Octavian ignored their pangs and drove them onward. He was surprised that Khalid was not suffering as the others. He thought to himself, "He has the stomach of a demon."

They rode along, and in a matter of minutes, Octavian's belly begin to wrench within. A sharp pain shot through him as though he were stabbed. He grabbed his belly and keeled forward over his horse, twisting in pain. He had to halt his horse. Khalid saw what was happening to Octavian and rode fast to his side. He helped

Octavian down from his horse and onto the ground. Octavian turned from side to side in the dust as he quivered in pain.

Khalid was surprised at what was taking place. Bending down to help him, he said in a compassionate voice, "What has taken hold of you?" Octavian, writhing in pain, did not answer.

Khalid quickly looked around at the others. Just as he did, a soldier fell from his horse. "What is wrong with him?" he hollered to a soldier who was next to the one who had fallen.

The soldier answered, "He has been sick since we left from Jerusalem."

"What was his sickness, and why did he not tell that he was too ill to march with the detachment?" demanded Khalid.

"He dared not tell any he was so, except for me, as he had only one month left in service of Rome. He planned to do this mission and then retire from Rome's legion. He desired only to receive his land and start a farm."

Khalid asked, "Why would he tell you of such things and no one else?" The soldier answered, "Because he is my brother."

Khalid assessed the soldiers and rode up and down. He looked over at Octavian who was still writhing in pain on the ground.

Khalid announced to the soldiers, "Octavian is in need of a physician's care and unable to lead. We were sent by Pilate to do this task together, I will now take command."

The soldiers shouted, "Yes, sir!"

Khalid continued, "How many of you drank from the community well once Octavian established it?" None of the healthy men raised their hands. Khalid watched as many soldiers who were keeling over tried to raise theirs.

"As I suspected," he declared as he looked to the man's brother. "Tell me what manner of plague did he suffer from?"

The brother shook his head and declared, "I know not."

Khalid glared at him and yelled, "Tell now, for as these good men drop like flies, your lies will follow you!"

The soldier looked at Khalid and said, "May Zeus forgive, it was a plague I nor he knew little of. All I know is that he wore onions under his armor to ward off the effects. For a time, this helped him. In the desert, his onions went dry, and there were no more for him to use. He died. I swear on my honor to Rome, this is a true account."

Khalid looked around. He declared, "We shall not have an entire legion of Rome die from a dead man. You who drank from the common well, separate yourselves from those who did not."

Immediately, the men made a division. Khalid watched on as they did so. He announced, "Those of you who drank from the community well, carry Octavian. Tarry behind. Rome shall not be obliged to bow to Hades for an unfortunate act."

The men followed Khalid's command and the detachment was now divided into two. Those that drank from the community well rode a distance behind, and those who did not drink from it led the way.

Khalid shouted back at the men, "If Zeus has mercy on your souls, you shall recover. If not, Rome bids you honor."

He no sooner said those words and he looked down at Vitali as he led the men, "I sound like a Roman centurion. Dang where did that come from?"

DO UNTO OTHERS...
A LEARNED RESPECT

Back in the breakfast hall, Mary had finished eating and was having a conversation with two women who were sitting by her. She enjoyed the easy discussion back and forth. It had been a long time since life felt so simple. Longinus was still busy filling up his stomach and satisfying his ravenous appetite. Mary would look at him from time to time and wonder where he was stuffing all the food from the pots. She had no understanding of one with such an insatiable desire for food.

Longinus finally reached his fill and turned and ordered Mary. "We go now, and we see Hebron." He picked up his spear and motioned for her to follow.

Mary bid the ladies farewell and followed behind Longinus. Outside, she confronted him, "Why did you speak to me like your horse or a slave in front of the others?"

Longinus looked at her bewildered. "Like my horse or my slave? You are neither to me."

"Then, that must mean you think I am a woman who must answer to you. I tell you now, this very minute, I am no such woman. You are not bound to me in a marriage nor in an oath. You are not promised to me nor am I promised to you. Your actions are not good. They are arrogant, boastful, and they have belittled me. I am not at all happy with any of them. I will have it no more."

Longinus looked at Mary. His first thought was to reprimand her and cast her aside. But when he looked at her to retaliate, his heart stopped him. All he could see was a good woman, underserving of such action. He considered her argument. He was awkward in understanding the emotions of a woman. He recalled the same burst of temper from his beloved in times past. He remembered it did not bid him well to argue. He thought of what to do and what to say. He remembered from his past that he would lose the argument against the reasoning of a woman. It was one battle that he had never won. He decided to remain silent.

Mary waited to hear what Longinus had to say but he said nothing and turned around with his back to her. At that, she marched quickly down the street. Under her breath, she vented to herself, "I have no reason to continue this journey with him."

In anger, she stomped her feet as she headed down the street toward the bazaar. Then suddenly, as she was venting her displeasure and anger, inside she felt ashamed. She stopped and realized that this was not the doing of her Lord. This was serving the pleasure of the devil. She bowed her head and asked her Lord to forgive her anger and to show her the way.

She had no sooner said her prayer, and Longinus hollered at her, "Woman, forgive me."

The choice of words, "Forgive me," went right to her heart. She turned and watched as he came running up to her. He reached her, then bowed his head and bent down on one knee. He said, "I didn't know what I was saying. Nor how it was hurting you. I only know that what I said to you has hurt me more."

Mary felt her emotions well up. She knew he was sincere and God was touching his heart. She answered, "I forgive you." She then reached out and touched his cheek. "Now, shall we see the wonders of Hebron?"

Longinus looked up, smiled, and said, "Will you show me?"

Mary answered, "As well as I am able. Come." She reached out her hand and helped him rise to his feet and they walked together toward the bazaar.

As they walked along, Longinus was happy that Mary had forgiven him. He began to see a strange thing within himself. He realized he was becoming less Roman stoic and more vulnerable to his humanness. He wasn't sure if it was good or bad. He only knew it made his heart feel warm and his conscience secure. It was a feeling he had never felt.

Mary spied a baker. "Come I will buy you the best bread in Hebron like I promised!"

She added, "You will find room for it later, that I am sure."

Longinus laughed, "It is good that you said later. I really can't eat another bite. Truly."

The mouth-watering aroma from all of the fresh baked loaves and rolls permeated throughout the air. Mary purchased the biggest loaf of bread and handed it to Longinus.

He quickly tore off a big piece and stuffed it in his mouth and chewed.

"I see you found some room." She said coyly.

With his mouth stuffed full, he warbled out, "How could I not?"

They laughed and went on throughout the market place looking at all the wares.

THE CARAVAN

Back in the Negev, Khalid was consulting with Vitali as to what to do next. "We must connect with the spice route soon, Vitali. The men who are sick need fresh water and medicinal herbs. There will be a great chance to barter for some at a caravan. They always buy up what they can."

Vitali followed along and listened.

Like a miracle, when all hope is forsaken, a caravan appeared upon the horizon. Khalid shouted to the men, "Behold, to the right, a caravan. We stop there. We barter and find healing herbs for the centurion and the soldiers!"

The soldiers who could, let out a resounding cheer. They turned to the right and headed for the caravan.

"Spices, herbs, armor, weapons, I have them all," shouted a little old man minding his wares. "You want healing potions? I have the best. Amulets? I have many."

Khalid gave the horse reins to Vitali. She stood quietly holding them between her teeth. He walked over and he said, "I have sick men. Sick from a plague in the water. What will heal them?"

The old man put his finger to his head and thought. "Yes... yes...I know. I have just the thing. Over here," he motioned as he lifted up a canvas uncovering a trunk. He pulled out a ruby red, glass, two-piece container. This will cure all things. Have them take a few drops in a cup of hot water with lemon. This will do the trick."

"I have no lemon. You have lemon?" asked Khalid.

"Yes, yes," smiled the old man. "I have everything you need."

"Give me what I need," demanded Khalid. "I have these for payment."

He pulled out the cloak, the silk scarf attached to the turban with the marira, and the rings from the Bedouin.

"Oh, indeed, indeed," said the man at the caravan. "This will be a fine exchange."

Khalid collected the potions and asked the man, "Is this the spice road or is it elsewhere?"

The man answered, "Follow the worn path over there. It isn't far.
It will connect to the spice road. Which way are you going?"

Khalid answered, "To Beersheba."

"Then follow it due east. It will take you right to the city."

Khalid turned to leave and lifted his hand in thanks and farewell.

The old man yelled out, "Beware not to veer off the path. There are dangerous things lurking in the Negev. Even on the spice road."

Khalid waved his hand as to agree. He then turned to one of the soldiers and ordered, "Tell the soldiers to return as soon as they finish their trading. I go on to Octavian with the potion."

The soldier answered, "Yes Sir."

Khalid mounted his horse and traveled with great speed back to where he had left Octavian and the other sick soldiers.

When he arrived he found Octavian still lying on the ground. His horse was lying sideways
in the gravel and sand. He wasn't well. Khalid asked him, "Did you give your horse
water from the community well?"

Octavian nodded his head yes.

"Figured so," said Khalid. "Drink this up. You will feel better."

Khalid put the potion to Octavian's lips and he drank it down.
Khalid then went over to Octavian's horse and did the same. Then he administered potions to the other sick soldiers. Some had already died. He sat assessing the next move of action as he waited for the soldiers to return from the caravan. He was well pleased in knowing the spice road was just minutes from where he

sat. Especially in knowing that once he got back on that road, it would lead directly to Beersheba.

"Vitali, with the caravan so close, we may be able to take the healthy men and go on to Beersheba. It will depend on what happens with Octavian."

He looked over at the pitiful sight of Octavian wrenching and holding his stomach. "He suffers from his own making." Vitali nodded in agreement.

A POWER GREATER THAN ROME

After a good day in Hebron and seeing the many sights that Mary had remembered, Longinus was very pleased that fate had brought him there. He had learned many things from Mary about a man named Abraham, his son Isaac, and his grandson Jacob. He was astounded at the history of these men. How the entire nation of Israel started with a promise from her living God to Abraham and was birthed through his grandson Jacob when he wrestled with the angel of the Lord and given the blessing of the name Israel.

Longinus was amazed at how all these things were recorded by the prophets and historic records were kept in the Temple by the High Priests of Israel. Even more astounded was he in knowing that these men were the forefathers of the Nazarene on the cross and how they knew the Nazarene would come and he would lay down his life that they might live.

The more he learned, the more he felt free from his own self condemnation. He was beginning to understand that a power greater than all the power of Rome was ruling over all things that have happened or ever will happen upon the earth. Yet he regretted that his part in all of the legacy was that he speared the Nazarene's side and made certain he was dead. That was the part he hated, the part he wrestled with, and the part that made him feel as though he were a walking dead man. It was his shame.

Longinus wanted to learn this thing that Mary called faith. Even more, he wanted to learn how to believe in something he could not see. He had many questions, but did not know how to ask them so he kept those to himself.

At supper, Mary and Longinus enjoyed another great meal and show of hospitality from Timmeon, the owner of the inn. Timmeon approached them. "More? There is plenty more."

Mary answered, "Thank you, Timmeon. The meal was delicious, but I cannot eat another bite."

Timmeon smiled and nodded, then looked at Longinus, "More? There is plenty," he asked.

Longinus nodded and said, "More. I will have more."

Mary patiently waited for Longinus to have his fill. When he was finished, she said to him, "The man at the table this morning. He has asked that we speak with him this night. He is in need of having many questions answered. I told him I would speak with him, but as for you, I could not answer, as you are of your own free will. Will you join us, or shall I tell him you do not wish to speak with him?"

Longinus thought a moment. "I will come," he said as he picked up his spear.

Mary smiled and said, "He should be waiting outside."

They went out from the inn, and there by a post was the older gentleman.

"Oh, you have come," he said. "Thank you. There are many things to talk about. Oh, I forgot to tell you this morning, my name is Matthias."

"Matthias," said Mary. "That means 'gift of God.' It is a very good name."

Longinus looked at the man and said, "My name is Longinus."

Matthias smiled at him and said, "Longinus, what a very interesting name. It means 'long.' Perhaps you are destined for a very long life?" He pondered a moment then said, "I am glad you have come. I have much to tell you. Let us go to my room or do you prefer to speak in the garden?"

Longinus, uncertain of the man, answered, "We will go to the garden."

"Follow this way," said Matthias.

He led them a little way, and the aroma of exotic plants filled the evening air. A row of flowering orchid trees led the way into the garden. Their scent was mingled with the sweetness of the hibiscus and rose of Sharon. The garden was filled with the majestic beauty of many plants that Mary did not know, but she recognized the angel's trumpets, foxtail ferns, and white lilies. It felt to Mary as though she had found the Garden of Eden. "Oh, how the Lord has blessed this garden with his mighty hand," she said.

"It is indeed a place to stop and wonder," answered Matthias as he breathed in the sweetness of the air. "Here, we sit here," he pointed to a green bed of grass surrounded by Hoya bella shrubs filled with big, flowery clusters of delicate little flowers in full bloom.

As they settled down, Mary was so happy that Longinus had chosen to talk in the garden. It reminded her of the many times she had gone to such gardens with her Master and how he would speak of his Father's creation. These were some of her most cherished memories now.

Longinus was not as enthralled with the gardens as Mary was. His curiosity rested more in what Matthias had to say.

Matthias waited for a moment as they all took in the night air and aromatic scents, then he got right to the point of their meeting, "I must tell you, I am compelled to share with you my dream. My heart has told me to do so."

"Your dream?" asked Longinus.

Matthias was now very serious. "Yes, I have had many dreams and visions. Many that led me here to Hebron. I believe such things are a warning from God. An omen. A chance to go to the left or the right, and in so doing change destiny's course."

Longinus was paying close attention and asked most sincerely,

"You speak of destiny. What do you know of destiny?"

Matthias's voice changed to a very low pitch as he leaned in and said, "Nothing is without purpose. All things work together and are reaped in their season. Evil to whom have done evil, and good to whom have done good. Both good and evil have masters. You can never serve both. You will either hate the one and love the other, back and forth, back and forth. There is no inner peace in this. Destiny is waiting on both sides to give you your just due."

"I don't understand," said Longinus.

"Your destiny is determined by which master you choose to serve."

Longinus was still confused. "What do you mean by master?"

"Your master is the one or the thing you cherish and serve above all things."

"And who is your master?" asked Longinus.

Matthias answered in a regretful tone, "I had believed that I followed all the laws of Moses and of the Temple and that in so doing I served my God. My God was my master. Then, one day, I sought out the Nazarene named Jesus who had been teaching the people of the ways of his Father, which was the God I served. He had claimed to be sent by the Father of men, to teach his Father's children meekness, patience, charity, and love. He spoke of his Father's kingdom and how to live in order to enter into it. I was confused at many of the things I heard him say.

"I spoke to him and boasted that I followed all the laws of the Temple and did all the things he had said. I will never forget the way he looked at me, he saw deep into my heart. He said as he stared into my eyes, 'Then go and sell all that you have and follow me.' I was torn at this for I had great wealth. I left and was grieved in my heart. It was at that moment that I understood that I cherished my wealth above all things. My wealth was my real master. It had somehow become the God that I served."

"Rome has great wealth. I hear your Temple has great wealth. What is wrong with having great wealth? It is a sign of authority and power," inquired Longinus.

"It is like I told you, one cannot serve two masters. If you do not serve that which is good, then you serve that which is evil. If you do not know who you serve and deny to serve any, you are left in the hands of evil. Indecision is a cold ray of confusion. To do nothing is to serve evil. I know this for I was tormented with dreams until I could bear it no more. It was then that I sold my properties and gave most all of my profits as alms to the poor in the city streets. In so doing, I became free of the torment and filled with a peace. Then, one day, my Lord saw me in the streets. He came over to me and smiled. He reached out his hand, I took hold of it. He said, 'Now come, follow me. '"

Longinus said, "What is the dream you spoke of?"

Matthias answered, "The dream I must share with you is the one I had last night. I dreamed my Lord, Jesus the Nazarene, came to me and showed me a spear. It had three red crosses of his blood on it. He told me a centurion would come and I was to tell him of destiny. In my dream, I asked, 'How, Lord?' He said, 'Interpret the dream.' I awoke and wondered at the dream."

Matthias turned to Mary and said, "At breakfast, when you told me he was a centurion and you were being chased by Roman soldiers, I believed he was the one whom Jesus spoke of in my dream."

He turned to Longinus and asked, "Have you had a dream?"

Longinus began to tremble a bit, then caught hold of himself and answered, "I have served Rome as my master and my god. Now I am without a master and have no god. I wander with no place to call my home. I am as a walking dead man. A bounty is on my head and the soldiers that guarded my back are ready to slay me. It is their duty and allegiance to follow the orders of Rome, whom they serve. I am left a man who seeks death, yet fears to find it, therefore I strive to live."

"Why do they seek to kill you?" asked Matthias.

"Because I helped the woman, and…I…" Longinus quit talking.

Matthias asked a second time, "Have you had a dream?"

Longinus felt a burning in his stomach; he stood up and removed the cloth from his spear. As he laid his spear in front of Matthias, he said, "A dream and a vision."

Matthias looked at the three blood red crosses and then looked up at Longinus. "This is the blood of my Lord. You must tell me of how you have this spear, then tell me of your dream."

BEERSHEBA IS IN SIGHT

The soldiers returned and Khalid had made the decision to mount up all the soldiers and Octavian to head to Beersheba. Khalid had directed the Roman detachment onto the path the man at the caravan had shown him. Sure enough, it led to the spice road, just as the man had said.

Khalid shouted out, "Men, we now march on to Beersheba!" The men all let out a cheer!

Khalid looked back at Octavian. His head was bent over, bobbing, while his horse trotted along. He looked down at Vitali and said, "It serves him right, Vitali." Vitali barked in agreement.

The Roman detachment continued to ride on, and Khalid had kept it separated into two groups; those that were sick and those that were not.

Finally, as the night was settling in, Khalid shouted out to the men, "There over the ridge lies a beautiful sight, Beersheba!"

The men cheered and those that were ill found new hope. "We are no more than four hours away," he shouted. "We ride on and bed there, yet this night!"

Suddenly, a soldier fell from his horse. Khalid looked at him; he was very ill. "Sentry, help this man." The sentry dismounted and went over to the man; he looked up at Khalid and shouted, "He is too ill to ride."

Khalid thought of the four hours ahead. He wondered what a real centurion would do. A bounty hunter would simply leave the lot and head for the city. He consulted Vitali. "Vitali, should all the men stay behind because some cannot go further, or shall we split our detachment and let those that can ride on?" Vitali looked and lifted her big paw. She drew a line in the sand. She put a paw print on one side and a paw print on the other.

"I knew you would have the answer. Good work, Vitali." He

turned his horse in front of the soldiers and shouted "Those who can ride will ride with me to Beersheba. Those who cannot will make camp here with Centurion Octavian. I need a few Roman soldiers that aren't sick to stay behind and stand watch 'til the morning."

Soldiers cast lots to see who would stay behind with the sick as with Beersheba so close, no one wanted to volunteer. Finally the divisions were made and Khalid shouted a few more commands.

"Post a guard to the front and the back of the canyon. Stay a good distance away from those that are sick. We will find a physician and send him to you as soon as we arrive in Beersheba."

The men were in agreement and detached appropriately. Khalid left them extra supplies and proceeded on with the healthy soldiers to Beersheba.

The soldiers had no sooner left and a dark shadowy figure appeared from out of no- where. The figure lurked about eyeing the moaning lot of sick soldiers. He looked over at Octavian and sneered, "Well, well, how fate does repay double." He then looked over toward Khalid and the soldiers who were riding toward Beersheba. "Now we shall see what my bounty hunter finds."

He took a few steps and stared at the sick men. Then he murmured under his breath,

"It appears Khalid's heart is too good to do much evil, and Octavian is too evil to do me much good. He shook his head, and said, "What to do, what to do?"

LONGINUS LEARNS ABOUT TRUE DESTINY

Back in the garden, not far from the inn, Longinus was pacing while Matthias patiently waited for him to tell his story of how he obtained the spear with the three blood red crosses. Mary saw how hard it was for Longinus to speak of such things and in a soft voice, she pleaded to him,

"Longinus, this man knows nothing of you. He has come to you with his dream. He has been

sent by my Master to help you. Can you not see this? Please tell him what he has asked."

"How can I explain to him what I do not understand myself?" he answered stubbornly.

"You simply begin," she answered.

Longinus looked at Mary and her eyes were so sincere. He looked at Matthias and his eyes were full of understanding and empathy. Longinus had a strange feeling come into his heart, his stubborn pride was beginning to weaken. Something compelled him to speak.

"I am a centurion. I was assigned to escort the Nazarene to Golgotha for his execution. I did what I was ordered to do. Nothing more and nothing less. My senior centurion came with orders to break the legs of the malefactors on the cross. When I took the iron bar to break the Nazarene's legs, I thought he was already dead. For some reason, I know not why, instead of breaking his legs to be sure he was dead, I took my spear and thrust it into his side. His water and blood went everywhere, even onto my face and into my eyes. Later at my barracks, I tried to clean the spear. The blood on the spear would not wash off, no matter how hard I scrubbed it.

"Then, my right eye, which had been blind and clouded over, was healed. I could see and the skin around the eye was smooth again. Aside from the strange healing, the spear has given me nothing but a haunting vision since the day I tried to wipe the blood from it. I cannot understand what it means."

Longinus stopped talking and Matthias asked, "But then, why are you being hunted by Romans?"

Longinus answered, "My senior centurion took the spear from me at the tomb of the dead Nazarene. He ordered me to bring back Mary, who I found inside it and let run away, so he could torture her and find who stole the dead Nazarene's body. I followed her, and for some reason could not arrest her. Instead, I went in secret and stole back my spear from my senior centurion's private quarters. I am now stripped of my rank and hunted down as a thief and a deserter of the Tenth Roman Legion. The penalty of desertion is death. The three red crosses of blood on the spear have cursed me for what I did. It glows and shows me a vision. I must find the way to stop this curse."

Matthias asked, "How is Mary with you now?"

"I returned to the house where I had last spoken to her on the western outskirts of Jerusalem. I sought her to ask of the man on the cross. I had many questions. I had not been there long and the soldiers came with my centurion looking for me, I knew they would torture and then kill her, so I took her with me and we fled."

Matthias had listened very intently to every word. He spoke very calmly, "I understand. Now, what was your dream?"

Longinus paused for a moment, as if to gather his thoughts. He began to tell of his dream in a very somber manner, "In my dream, a lion approached coming from the hills of Judea. The lion kept coming, I was unarmed, and for the first time in my life, I felt the fear of death. The lion came upon me and stopped. I waved my arms to scare him off for I had no weapons to defend myself. The lion crouched down, and suddenly, my spear appeared in front of him. It glowed. As it glowed, I saw Romans on horseback and a centurion was leading them. They were entering Beersheba. That is where we were heading too. There was a strange-looking man with them with a large dog that looked like a lion. He was not a Roman, he had a long dreadlocked braid hanging down his back. The lion roared and headed north. I watched as he ran, then he stopped and roared again as though he were telling me to follow.

"When I awoke something inside me said to quit heading east to Beersheba and head north. We headed north and now we are here in Hebron."

Matthias thought and said, "You have been given mercy. Many are called, but few are chosen. You, Longinus, whose name means long, have been chosen. And now you must fulfill your destiny."

"Destiny? Is destiny waiting to give me my just due?" questioned

Longinus. He reached down and picked up his spear. He looked at it, then shouted angrily, "And what would such just due be for me but my death?" In a rage, he broke the head of the spear off from its shaft.

Matthias and Mary were silent. They both looked down at the broken shaft, lying on the ground. Mary looked at Longinus and asked, "Does this action make you feel better now?"

Longinus stood quietly as he realized what he had just done. Mary's words made him feel like a little boy being scolded by his mother. He wanted to run away from the garden and never have to look at either one of them again. But inside, he knew he had to stay there and answer for his actions.

Matthias felt the tension and prayed for the words to say. He no sooner prayed and Longinus demanded Matthias to explain more.

"Tell me, Matthias, tell me of destiny and interpret my dream. Isn't that what you asked me here to do?"

Matthias answered, "I did Indeed. First, let's look at your dream. The Lord appeared to you in his victorious counterpart as the lion of Judah."

"Lion of Judah? I do not understand," asked Longinus who was now calm again.

Matthias continued, "The Lord Jesus was born in the flesh, it was written by the prophets of Israel that he would first come as a lamb to offer up his flesh and blood as a final atonement for sin, so that all who believe in him might live. It is written that the next time he returns, he shall come as a lion to avenge his Father, who is the living God, for all the needless bloodshed from precious Abel to the very last martyr. He will come with all the power of heaven and earth to pour out the wrath of God and destroy those who love wickedness and serve evil. He will destroy all the children of the devil himself. For you see, there are only two masters that can be served. One is God, the Father in heaven, the other is Satan, ruler of this world and Hades."

"That is a lot to believe," said Longinus, "I find that as much of a fable as Zeus's thunderbolts or Hermes flying."

"Let me speak less figurative and more plainly," offered Matthias.

"In the dream, he warned you that Romans were following and you should leave and travel north. He led you to this city of refuge, Hebron. You heeded the message in the dream and you are here. You have been shown mercy."

"Had you not heeded the dream, your outcome would have been much different. You see, your destiny is in your hands. God has given each one of us free will. We all must choose how to use it. Even Jesus wrestled with his own destiny."

Mary, had now grown tired of hearing the self-woe of Longinus. She boldly interrupted Mathias, raising her voice with deep passion, "Longinus, I was with Jesus at supper the night before he was arrested. He knew he was going to lay down his life, he told us all. I watched him in the garden at Gethsemane as he prayed for the strength to carry out his father's will, to lay down his life that we might live. I saw him pray that his destiny be taken away from him for he feared the pain and the agony he knew he was to face. I saw him sweat great drops of blood as he prayed to the Father and fell on his face weak from fighting for strength to fulfill his destiny. I heard the terrible agony in his voice as he cried out for strength to his Father to be able to face his destiny.

"I saw angels from heaven come down and strengthen him. No one could have killed him if he had not willingly laid down his life for his Father's children. I heard him ask to have this burden taken from him, but not his will be done, but his Father's. He fulfilled his destiny and overcame death. He lives! He is not dead, he has risen, and he has overcome the world!

"So do not cry about your destiny, Longinus, seek God the Father and ask him what you are to do. Quit acting like a curse follows you because you speared the side of my Lord. If you were cursed for piercing my Lord, you would have died the moment you speared his side!"

Longinus was startled by Mary's words and in the tone of voice she delivered them with. He did not know what to say. He had been so concerned for himself he never thought about the man he pierced as anything more than a blood curse.

Mary took a deep breath then boldly yelled, "Your eye, look at it! It is healed! If your destiny is so terrible and troublesome, why did my Lord heal your eye and give your face back its beauty? You know nothing of destiny nor what it takes to fulfill it. Everything I have heard you say is nothing more than fear of curses that rest in the hands of chance.

"My Lord has opened your eyes, Matthias has opened your eyes, I have opened your eyes, and you are still as a blind man shouting you cannot see!"

Every word that Mary spoke went deep to his heart and cut it like a razor. He spoke back to Mary, "I am a good man. I do what is right to do."

Matthias shook his head and said, "Doing good is not enough. Even a sorcerer does what is good in the eyes of his master."

He paused a moment then asked very directly in a serious tone. "What master do you serve? That is the question you must ask."

"How do I serve a master that I cannot see who comes to me in a dream?" wailed Longinus.

Mathias raised his voice speaking with less compassion and more firmness, "Your dream has shown you how the Lord will speak to you. He will show you things through your dreams and through the spear. You must first prepare yourself. You must accept that he has chosen you."

"How?" shouted Longinus.

"By choosing him—you must accept him. When you do, a world you know not of shall open up for you."

At those words, Longinus was mentally and emotionally exhausted. He fell to his knees and moaned in agony. He cried out, "Help my nonbelief."

Mary put her hand on his shoulder as he moaned on his knees. She spoke to him softly, but with much authority, "You were a part of my Lord's destiny. You provided that the scriptures were fulfilled, that he keepeth all his bones and not a one of them is broken. And that they shall look on him who they pierced."

Longinus lifted his head and looked up at Mary. Mary continued to speak, "You brought both the water and the blood out from my Lord's side to justify and sanctify all who believe in him. You were chosen for this purpose."

Longinus let out a wail of heartfelt grief, then he lowered his head and his body went limp. He cried out, "Lord, if you are there, and if you will have me, please hear me. I want to know you like they do. Help me to know you."

Mary and Matthias prayed for Longinus.

Longinus felt his heart open up, he raised his hands in surrender, and he looked up in the evening sky. The stars had come out, filling the heavens. He looked to the west and saw the celestial constellation of Leo the Lion. He shouted out, "Oh, Lion of Judah, take me and use me. I am empty of all I ever desired. Forgive me of all the evil I have ever done. Fill me up with new purpose, use me, Lord, show me the way. For I am a torn man and have no way. Answer me, I beg you."

Mary and Matthias continued to pray, unceasing.

Suddenly, the head of the spear glowed, and Longinus heard a voice, "Longinus. You wrestle not with flesh and blood, but with principalities and powers. Stay close to me and follow."

Mary and Matthias looked at each other and marveled as they witnessed this miracle.

Mary, struck with great awe, spoke, "He has heard your cry and he has answered you."

BEERSHEBA AT LAST

Khalid and the soldiers finally arrived in Beersheba. Khalid was well pleased and looked down from his horse at Vitali. "We first get water, then we get food, then we find the deserter." Vitali barked in agreement.

He immediately sighted a well, "There we drink!" He hollered to the soldiers and to Vitali.

As they quenched their thirst and filled their goat-skin flasks, Khalid remembered the sick soldiers. He turned to a sentry and said, "You, find a physician and take him to Octavian and the others in the canyon."

"Yes, sir," shouted the sentry.

"Now, Vitali, we find food."

At that, Vitali barked and they went into a tavern. He seated himself on a bench in front of a long table where others were eating and drinking. He shouted out to the barkeep, "I will have your best plate of food and one for Vitali!" He pointed to his dog.

The barkeep hollered back, "Does Vitali take her slab of beef raw or cooked?"

"If it is beef, it does not matter to Vitali, whether it is raw or cooked. I will take mine cooked. But not too much. I like to taste the freshness of the meat!" Khalid looked at Vitali, "It has been a long time since we have tasted meat. It will be good."

The Apprentice Confronts Octavian

Back at the canyon, a shadowy figure still lurked about, walking among the sick soldiers. He was wondering about the sense of duty that was within the heart of Khalid. He quickly assessed the situation and moved over to Octavian. Peering down at him, he spoke, "Centurion, why do you lie there writhing in pain?"

Octavian looked up and tried to open his eyes to see who was speaking to him. His eyes could not focus, all he saw was a blurred image, but he recognized the voice. It was the voice of the Apprentice.

"Have you not the spear with you? Use it to heal yourself."

Octavian shut his eyes. He managed to utter a few words, "How...do...I use…its power?"

"My, my, that is a dilemma now, isn't it?"

Octavian, made an angry face, with his eyes still closed.

"You should have went on to Rome and sought the old man when you could. You were a fool to place such a valuable spear into a rotting carcass."

Octavian opened his eyes halfway and tried to speak, "How…" He closed his eyes and winced in pain.

"How did I know? Is that what you ask?"

Octavian groaned out, "Yes."

"A good Apprentice never leaves a valuable exchange in the hands of a fool who does not pay. Did you really believe that I would be such an unwise sage as to give you the real spear?" said the apprentice as he picked up Octavian's spear and looked at the three blood red crosses that were now attracting flies.

"Look, Octavian, the blood red crosses are half gone. And flies eat the blood that is left."

Octavian opened his eyes to look, then shut them tight.

"This is what happens when you poke at a floating dead carcass full of plague. Had this been the real spear, you would have mingled the blood of a kingdom without end, with the blood of death. You would have died from such action or worse. You would have lived with a terrible curse upon you. But alas, you are alive. Now, should I heal you or should I leave you here to die?"

Octavian managed to utter, "Heal me."

"Why should I do that? I only speak to you now so you will die, knowing that by cheating me, you have cheated yourself."

Octavian, wincing, managed to pull a coin pouch from beneath his armor and handed it to the apprentice. He uttered, "Your payment, take it all."

The Apprentice took the pouch and saw it was filled with gold and silver coins. He smiled, "It is enough." He then placed his hands on Octavian's body and mumbled, *"Lord of Darkness and Prince of Hell, remove the demons that came from the well."*

Suddenly, Octavian's body convulsed violently and rolled back and forth on the ground. He choked and gagged as a vile black liquid vomited out of his mouth. He managed to turn to his side as the last bit of black death dripped from his lips. He spit and wiped his tongue with his shaking hands.

Coughing and gagging, he looked up at the apprentice. He took a breath and was no longer in pain.

The Apprentice put his face an inch from Octavian's and scoffed, "Now we must talk of many things."

THE BAPTISM OF LONGINUS

Meanwhile back in the garden, Mary wept for joy in knowing that Longinus had believed upon the Lord and sought to serve him. Longinus felt limp and his body was trembling. He looked at Mary and asked,

"What must I do now?"

Mary answered, "You were forgiven through the power of his blood, now you must be baptized with water, as an act of faith to show that you believe in his death, burial, and resurrection."

"How do I do this?"

Matthias said, "Come, there is a pond over there. We shall baptize
you now."

Longinus and Mary went to the pond with Matthias, and he motioned for Longinus to come to him. At the edge of the water, Matthias took his hand and led him into the water. They waded out into the middle of the pond and Matthias took hold of Longinus. He placed one hand on his back and the other to the front of his forehead. He said, "In the name of our Father God, through the blood of his Holy Son, the Lamb of God. I baptize you unto repentance that by your belief, you may inherit the kingdom of God."

He then thrust Longinus back into the water, cupping his hand in front of his nostrils and mouth, and submerged his entire body. Then, he lifted him up out of the water. Longinus shook the water from his head and looked up to the heavens. He lifted his arms and said out loud, "I am ready to be filled with new life. Fill me up, Lord, so I am no longer an empty vessel."

Mary and Matthias both wept with joy and praised God for such a transformation.

Mary turned to Longinus, his body dripping of water, and gave him a strong hug. Longinus felt a deep anointing in his heart. It was an euphoric feeling that he could not describe; he only knew it was something he had never felt before, and he did not want it to stop.

Something new was filling him up, and in his heart, he knew that it was a gift from the Father. The dreaded feeling of a hopeless deep void was no longer haunting him. He was now eager to serve his Lord and had a longing to tell others that the Lord has risen. But he knew he had so much yet to learn. There was only one thing he knew for certain: whatever power was in the spear, the power that was now in him, was greater.

This night in the garden was one that Longinus would remember forever.

A NEW ACCOMPLICE

The Apprentice was watching Octavian as he continued spitting the last bitter remnants of the blackened poisons from his mouth.

The Apprentice offered him his flask. "Drink," he said.

Octavian rinsed his mouth and spit. Then he drank. He offered it back to the Apprentice and the Apprentice shrugged his hand at him and said, "Keep it."

Octavian took another drink, then rose to his feet." You said we must speak of many things?" The Apprentice smiled and said, "Indeed."

"There is no one, without a sorcerer's powers, that is as selfish, arrogant, devious, or willing to betray as you, Octavian. And that is what I need. You naturally possess the traits that will serve me well. There is only one problem."

Octavian suspiciously asked, "And what problem is that?"

"You serve only yourself as master." The Apprentice picked up a stone and handed it to Octavian. Octavian took the stone.

The Apprentice then asked, "Now what is it that you hold in your hand?"

Octavian answered, "It is a stone."

The sorcerer placed his hand over the top of the stone that Octavian held. He looked into his eyes and he asked, "Are you certain of that?" He then removed his hand from the top of the stone.

Octavian gasped for the stone had turned into gold.

"It is gold!" Octavian declared." How did you do that?"

"Are you curious to seek my powers too? Or are you content to know only of those within the spear? That is my question to you." Octavian did not answer.

The Apprentice turned and began to walk away. Octavian shouted out, "Wait!" The Apprentice turned and said, "I said, 'We must speak of many things.' You have ceased to talk. I am finished here."

Octavian answered, "Yes, I would want to know how you turned the stone into gold. If that is wanting to learn the power of a sorcerer, then, that is what it is."

The Apprentice smiled, "Now, we can continue our talk."

Octavian looked at the flies feasting on his spear. He pointed to it and asked, "Why did you give me that forgery ?"

"You surely know by now. If you do not, you are a bigger fool than I had believed."

Octavian cunningly answered, "Now, you cease to speak of many things."

The Apprentice smiled at Octavian's craftiness and answered, "Well, well, shall I begin with your request from Pilate to kill the Old Man, my great mentor? Or shall I begin with your leaving me to wait and not returning? Or shall I begin with your refusing to give me my pay? Or shall I begin with your arrogance in having the bounty hunter give me my just due? Or shall I begin with the fact that you are a deceitful liar and there is nothing you say that can be trusted?"

In hearing all that the Apprentice knew, Octavian became fearful. The Apprentice enjoyed watching him squirm and walked around him staring into his eyes. He stopped two inches from his face and spoke in a very sinister manner, "Now, your next question must be: why did I heal you?"

Octavian nodded his head yes.

"I had thought of letting you die. Hades is in want of new prisoners. But you can be of better use to both Hades and myself alive. But…" he paused. Then in a seductive voice he said, "Only if you should decide to serve a new master other than yourself. Are you interested?"

"What master is that?" asked Octavian.

"The same master that I serve. If you cooperate, you will have great powers from him and from the spear. You will be given many secrets that will serve you."

"Why would your master do that for me if I serve him?" asked Octavian with caution.

"Because he can only do his bidding in this world through people who are willing to serve him. Are you willing?"

"You mean like Zeus and the gods of Rome?"

"Yes," said the Apprentice smiling. "Exactly. They are one and the same."

"Then I agree," answered Octavian.

The Apprentice grinned and said, "Come, I shall prepare you for your journey."

ANOTHER DREAM

Mary, Mathias and Longinus were getting ready to depart for the evening and out of habit, Longinus went to get his spear. He looked down at the head of the spear and the broken Shaft laying where he had broken it apart. He picked them up and said, "I should not have done this act. Will the Lord forgive me for my temper?"

Mary touched his arm and said, "If the Lord wanted the spear to stay whole, you would not have been able to break it."

Matthias nodded in agreement. He said, "Come let us return to the inn and get some rest."

Mary, Longinus, and Matthias left the garden and made their way back to the inn. They bid each other good night. And Longinus and Mary went to their room to sleep.

Longinus made his makeshift bed and placed the head of the spear under his straw pillow. Then he fluffed it a bit and laid his head down upon it. As he tried to make himself comfortable, he looked over and saw Mary. She was kneeling in prayer. He thought to himself, "Is that something I should do too?" But he did nothing. He closed his eyes and silently thanked the Lord for the inner peace his heart now felt. He fell asleep as he was thanking him and then he began to dream.

In his dream, Longinus was standing at a window in the dining hall at the inn. Mary was eating supper at a long table with others. Timmeon was not there. Longinus looked out the window and saw that Timmeon was outside speaking to Roman soldiers. The soldiers started to enter the inn.

Longinus grabbed Mary and ran out the back. They ran into the garden behind the inn and a lion was waiting there. It was the same lion from his other dream. The lion roared and turned and ran. Mary and Longinus ran behind him following. Suddenly, a port appeared upon the Mediterranean Sea.

The lion stopped at a merchant ship and roared. He then faded away.

Longinus and Mary got on the merchant ship and sailed out into the Mediterranean Sea.

Longinus tossed and turned as he dreamed, then finally he awakened. In a quick reflex, he sat up straight and grabbed the spearhead from under his straw pillow. He stared into it. He got up and started to place his bedding into his haversack. He went over to Mary and nudged her awake. "Hurry, we must go from this place quickly. Our Lord has given me another dream."

Mary woke up quickly and started to get herself ready. As she did, she said, "What was the dream, tell me, I must know, for I too had a dream."

Longinus asked, "What was your dream?"

She answered, "I was eating supper and you grabbed me and pulled me out into the back of the inn and we ran to the garden. The Lion of Judah was there and he roared and ran. We followed him to a port and he disappeared. We set sail upon a merchant ship into the Mediterranean Sea."

"Where was the port?" Longinus asked with great concern.

"It looked like it was the Port at Gaza. At least I think. There were merchants loading their wares."

Longinus fell to his knees and began to pray, "Oh, great Lion of Judah, the one who shall return to avenge all blood from precious Abel to the last that is martyred, please give us the wisdom to know what port you have shown us."

Suddenly, in his heart, he felt an answer. He looked at Mary and said, "It is the Port of Gaza. We must go there quickly. But first, we must speak to Timmeon. For in my dream, which was the same as yours, Timmeon spoke to Roman soldiers."

Mary nodded in agreement. Longinus carefully placed the head of the spear inside his haversack and looked out the window. The sun was just beginning to dawn. "Come, Timmeon is getting the morning breakfast ready I am sure." They gathered their things and left the room.

Mary looked at Longinus, "Remember, we must pay for our stay before we leave."

Longinus was used to free barracks and had forgotten such a detail as paying. "Oh, that is right."

They walked into the room where cooks were preparing food. They looked and Timmeon was not there.

Mary asked, "Where is Timmeon? We must pay and tell him good-bye before we depart."

"Oh, he is outside gathering fresh eggs," said a woman who was kneading bread.

"Thank you," answered Mary. They went out the door from the kitchen and saw Timmeon coming toward them with a basket of eggs.

"Fresh eggs will be ready shortly," smiled Timmeon. "Come we eat."

Mary answered, "Oh, it sounds delicious, but my brother and I are returning home this day and are getting an early start. We have a long way to go back to Magdalene."

"Come then, you must have some fresh bread to take on your journey."

They followed him to the kitchen and Timmeon gave them two loaves. "This will fill you up."

He smiled. "Oh, this is more than gracious of you," said Mary.

"We must settle our account now, how much do we owe you for our stay?" asked Longinus.

Timmeon thought a moment and said, "Oh, for you…let me see…a denarius shall cover the cost."

Mary asked, "Are you sure? We stayed two nights and your food, your water, and scented oils...oh, a denarius is not enough."

"It is more than enough," smiled Timmeon. "Oh, Magdalene, a fine fishing city. And the Roman legion is close at the sea's edge. Is that where your legion is?"

Longinus placed one denarius in Timmeon's hands and said, "Oh, the fishing will keep you busy for days. It has the best catch for a man's net than any place on the coast."

Timmeon smiled, and Mary said, "Thank you for your kindness. We must go now."

"Come again," said Timmeon as he put the denarius in his shirt pocket.

Longinus and Mary quickly made their way to the stables to. "Wait here while I go and get the horse," said Longinus.

Mary nodded. As she waited outside the stables, she inhaled deeply, taking in one long last breath of Hebron. She closed her eyes and enjoyed all the scents from the aromatic mixture of exotic flowers.

She would miss the serenity of this wonderful city of refuge. She thought of how she would miss Matthias and regretted not being able to say farewell.

Longinus broke her concentration with his firm voice, "Let us leave quickly." He said as he lifted himself up onto the saddle. He extended his hand to Mary and she grabbed hold and he lifted her up onto the back of the horse. They made their way out to the edge of the city and then Longinus kicked the horse and yelled, "Yaa!" They galloped away with great speed.

After going a long way, Longinus slowed the horse and then stopped. "The horse needs a rest," he said as he motioned for Mary to dismount. He watched as Mary got down from the horse, then he dismounted, and turned to Mary. In a very curious tone, Longinus asked, "Why did you tell Timmeon that we were going to your town of Magdalene?"

"I did not plan to lie, but it fell upon my heart to tell him so. In my dream, he told the Romans where we went. When the Romans come, he will have to tell them where we are going. He will tell them Magdalene, and the soldiers will travel there."

"My dear Mary, you are very shrewd. I like that," smiled Longinus.

THE INITIATION

Octavian was following the Apprentice through the scattered corpses and sick dying men that lay all around them. As they walked, Octavian looked down in disgust at the sick soldiers.

 As though the Apprentice had eyes in the back of his head, he hollered out, "That's exactly how I felt when I saw your pathetic soul laying there...disgusted."

Octavian was startled.

"It's all part of dealing with principalities and powers. It goes with the territory. I must say, I'm always rather amazed at souls like yours."

"Like mine?" asked Octavian rather proudly. "How so?"

"Your kind are willing to do anything for absolutely nothing."

"I don't understand your point? That description is not of me. I do nothing without gain."

The Apprenticed laughed, "Do you want me to call out your long line of fruitless deceit? The list is long... with little to show for it but sickness and death in the Negev."

Octavian, "That won't be necessary."

"I didn't think it would be. But I was ready to oblige."

The Apprentice led the way to a cave in the cleft of a canyon side, not far from where the sick men lay. As they entered, the apprentice said, "This shall do nicely."

Octavian anticipated what the Apprentice would do in his preparation and stood there quietly in the darkness of the cave. He watched as the Apprentice touched the wall of the cave and made it glow, giving them a dim light. Octavian wondered at his magic and became eager to see what powers he would be given.

The Apprentice pulled a pouch from beneath his cloak and poured out a dusty material, forming a consecrated circle around both Octavian and himself. He then strategically placed precious stones of ruby, emerald, sapphire, jade, onyx, and amethyst around the outside of the circle.

The Apprentice looked at Octavian in a very serious manner and said, "Take my hand."

Octavian took hold of his hand and immediately felt a surge of great energy. The Apprentice warned Octavian of what he was about to experience.

"The elemental powers of darkness are full of fickle. More than one of the underworld will come forth to tempt you to claim them. When this happens, do not fear for none can enter within the circle. You must choose the one who matches your desires and step out and claim that one."

"But," he cautioned, "Choose wisely for you cannot undo what is done." Octavian nodded to the Apprentice as his heart began to beat rapidly and droplets of sweat filled his brow.

"Once you choose, your soul will be sealed and belong to the master that I serve. Do you have any second thoughts?"

Octavian trembled and asked, "Who is your master, this one I will serve?"

The Apprentice answered, "He is the one that possesses all the wealth and power of this world. He anoints kings and tears down kingdoms. He is the one who decides who shall have power and who shall be powerless. Who shall have great wealth and who shall endure poverty. He is the tempter and tormentor of every man's soul. You cannot escape him. You do well in the flesh to serve him. The flesh is a helpless vessel if you are not filled with his power. As you have witnessed when I found you writhing in pain, poisoned from the water."

"Then I desire to serve this ruler of the world. I offer up my soul to receive his seal."

The Apprentice whispered, "Good, very good indeed." He gave Octavian a sinister grin and began to summon the underworld.

"Elements of darkness, space, time, motion, matter, manifest forth as destiny's toll, Octavian's desire in exchange for his soul."

The cave grew dark and black. The floor of the cave rumbled and began to crack open. Octavian held on to the hand of the apprentice with great fear. The crack opened up a great chasm and plasma bolts shot forth swirling in the air, making bloodcurdling shrieking sounds that pierced the ear.

The apprentice commanded, "Show yourselves." His voice echoed throughout the cave.

In an instant, eerie looking plasma bolts shape shifted into orbs and electrical apparitions streaming throughout the cavern. Some took on recognizable forms of various gods and goddesses; whether real or an illusion, it didn't matter as they were all beguiling. Each shouted convincing pleas, doing their best to seduce Octavian.

"I will give you power to rule the world!" shouted one apparition that appeared as a handsome king.

An Arabian djinn towering over the others with his massive size thundered out in a deep resonating voice, "I will give you all the gold one could ever dream of and manifest your every wish!"

"I will give you both gold and the power to rule the world and me!" seduced a most enchanting voice belonging to the apparition of a woman, who appeared to be the Roman goddess Diana.

"Don't listen to her. I will give you wisdom and the cunning to grant your every heart's desire, and lavish you with my obedience to industry. I can teach you everything in the entire world," whispered a female apparition as she stroked the wings of an owl. Her appearance was that of the goddess Minerva.

A powerful image of Neptune holding a trident tempted him saying, "If you desire to rule the seas, and in so doing control the world, then pick me. I will show you how to make the earth tremble and ravage over the land."

Octavian looked at each one as they made their alluring pleas, each promising more and more. As these orbs of electrical energy filled the cave, their voices mingled, getting louder and louder. Their insistent temptations quickly climaxed into a maddening cacophony of the most disharmonious wailing.

Finally, Octavian made his choice. He looked at the Apprentice and said, "I choose Diana."

The Apprentice looked at Octavian and warned, "You can only choose once, there is no undoing what you choose. Are you certain?"

Octavian thought and nervously said, "I am."

"Very well," said the Apprentice as he let loose of Octavian's hand. "You must step out of the circle and go to the one you choose.

Then you must slice your wrist and let the blood drop in front of the one you have chosen." He reached from under his cloak and pulled out a dagger with a skull-shaped handle. He held it out for Octavian to take. The sounds of the tempters voices all pleading at once, with their hands reaching out toward him, were maddening, causing Octavian to hesitate.

He looked at the apprentice and down at the dagger. "Go on, take it," urged the apprentice. Octavian reached over and cautiously took the dagger. He turned and moved slowly toward the edge of the circle and stopped.

The Apprentice warned Octavian, "You must move quickly. If you hesitate when you leave the safety of this circle, strange and awful things will happen. Make haste."

Octavian took a breath and stepped out of the circle as the apparitions continued to entice him with their temptations. With great speed, he stepped in front of Diana and pulled his dagger and sliced his wrist. He watched as droplets of blood fell to the rugged floor of the cave at her feet.

Suddenly, all the other apparitions melted into thin air as they wailed out a most horrifying cry.

As the droplets of blood continued to fall, the apparition of Diana faded away until it could be seen no more. Suddenly, there was a terrifying sound of chattering teeth. It was a horrid noise as though a thousand scarabs were nibbling on a carcass. It was coming from the ground where the blood had fallen. Octavian looked down and gasped in horror as he watched hideous-looking demons forming from each droplet of the blood. Their jagged teeth were chomping in the air. Their bodies were shriveled and leathery and black as black could be.

Octavian dropped his dagger in horror. The demons laughed and cackled as they continued to chatter their teeth. He watched them as they all merged together into one ominous black form.

The form swirled up to the ceiling of the cave. Octavian looked up with his mouth frozen open in fear. The ominous black swarm spiraled downward and entered into Octavian through his mouth. The force knocked Octavian to the ground and he choked for air. His body shook violently as the ominous black form continued to enter his body. When the last piece of blackness entered in, his body jolted, then laid motionless on the cold floor of the cave.

All at once, the room was still and the cave began to glow again. All things returned to the way they were before the apprentice performed his ritual of dark magic.

Octavian carefully scanned the entire cave as he guardedly arose to his feet. He looked at the apprentice and yelled, "Have I chosen wrong?"

The Apprentice looked at him and said, "You chose your heart's greatest desire. And that was to have it all. Time will tell what shall come to pass. You cannot undo what has been done. You are sealed for all eternity. You come away with whatever power you have chosen. You will use this power to serve your new master. Come, let us go now. For there is much to be done."

Octavian trembled and feared, the only thing he could see in his mind's eye was the horrid, hideous-looking, black, shriveled demons with leathery skin, and now, they were within him.

Khalid in Charge

Meanwhile in a tavern in Beersheba, Khalid and Vitali have just finished the finest slab of meat they had ever eaten. They were now having some of the best wine they ever tasted.

"The fruit of this grape is from the gods themselves, or we have been in the desert too long. This wine is as sweet as I've ever tasted, Vitali."

Suddenly, a sentry entered and went over to Khalid. "I have found a physician to send to the sick soldiers and Octavian. He has asked to place them all under quarantine and not to enter the city. He believes they have a plague that will poison others from the water they drank. I suggest that you grant him permission to do so, Khalid, as I fear he is right."

"Tell him to do what he believes is best. Take him there and make sure you stand at a far distance away, so you do not get sick."

"Yes, sir," answered the sentry and then he left.

Khalid looked at Vitali and said, "It looks like I am with authority for a very long while. I say let us all enjoy a good night. Tomorrow, we find the deserter."

Vitali nodded and barked in agreement.

The Demons Find Their True Master

Back in the cave, Octavian was trying to understand what he was to do. He wondered of his new powers. The Apprentice watched on in amusement as Octavian bantered about trying to make magic things happen.

Picking up a stone, Octavian commanded, "Turn yourself into gold." Nothing happened. He picked up another and repeated the

THE SPEAR OF DESTINY

command. "Turn yourself into gold." Again, nothing happened. He touched the cave and demanded, "Glow brighter."

Nothing happened.

The apprentice tried hard not to laugh. He looked at Octavian and mocked, "Now that you have within you the means to achieve your heart's desire, are you ready to seek the spear?"

Octavian looked angrily at the apprentice. "Have you tricked me again?"

"Tricked?" said the apprentice very innocently. "You freely chose, and even if you chose unwisely, you have a power. You must learn how to command it. And that is something the Old Man can show you. Might I suggest that you find him."

"But you are his Apprentice and you have powers. You can teach me," Octavian argued.

"That was not in our agreement," answered the Apprentice.

"Besides, you haven't even called upon your demons. You only command using your own fleshly devices. Try to command them and then banter at me."

"A-hah, yes. Now I shall call upon them. Let me see what shall I ask?"

The Apprentice suggested, "Perhaps ask them where to go to seek the deserter and the spear?"

"Good idea," answered Octavian. "Oh, demons within me, I ask you this, where is the deserter named Longinus and his spear?"

Suddenly, on the wall of the cave, Greek letters appeared. Octavian was excited and ran over to read them. They spelled out Hebron. "Hebron. They are in Hebron!" he shouted.

The Apprentice looked very surprised for he had not expected the demons to answer him. He thought to himself, "I will have a talk with these demons of Diana". He looked at Octavian and said, "Your men have gone to Beersheba. You must get them and go to Hebron. Hurry, quickly before they leave."

Octavian gloated and said, "I have no need for the soldiers now.

I have a great power."

The Apprentice shook his head and said, "Do not be a fool. You must retain your good standing with Rome, and you will need your soldiers. The power you seem to have is in knowing, not in making things happen. If that were the case, you would have a well-lit cave and many rocks of pure gold."

Octavian thought a moment. He looked at the words on the wall of the cave, then he said, "Very well, I will gather my troops in Beersheba. From there, I will lead them to Hebron."

Octavian motioned to the apprentice, "Come, we go to Beersheba."

The Apprentice answered, "You will go without me. My work with you is done for now. I have other matters to attend to. Now go."

Octavian nodded and left the cave. The Apprentice watched from the cave opening until Octavian was out of sight. He turned and began to summon the demons of Diana.

"Oh, legion of demons of Diana whose master you obey, from this moment forth you shall only answer to me, the one who summoned you. For it was I whose power brought you forth, and it was I who received permission from the power of Beelzebub to offer you this man's flesh as a vessel in which to dwell. Your bidding will be done by the conjuring of my voice, and no more of the voice of the vessel in which you reside. I brought you forth, and I can send you back."

Suddenly, a voice echoed in the cave, "Oh, great master, we have heard and willingly obey. Please do not send us back to the captive chains of Hades."

"Do as I command and you may stay. Go against me and you will be thwarted back to the chains that I freed from you."

The voice echoed, "We shall obey."

The Apprentice smiled an evil grin and left the cave.

The Summoning Must Stop

As Octavian made his way along to Hebron on foot, he found it very tiring. *Why am I walking?* he thought. *Why do I take the words of the Apprentice as true that I can only summon the demons of Diana to give me answers to my questions? I can't believe I have been so gullible as to not even try to summon my demons to give me a horse.*

He stopped walking and dropped his haversack onto the ground. Standing erect with his chest out in a pose of authority, he began to summon his demons. He ordered them, saying, "Oh, demons of Diana, bring to me a horse."

The demons trembled and summoned to the Apprentice. "He asks us to bring him a horse. What shall you have us do, oh, master?"

The Apprentice heard the summon from the legion of demons of Diana in his head. Annoyed at being bothered with such a trivial request by Octavian, he answered under his breath, "Give him a horse, but nothing more. No saddle, no bridle. Just a horse. If he summons you for a saddle and bridle, tell him only two summons may be granted in a day. And now he has had his two."

"Yes, master," they answered.

"That shall make him think of what he desires to have, long and hard, before he asks any future requests of his demons. And the demons of Diana will not weary me with asking permission for each whim and desire Octavian thinks of," sneered the Apprentice.

Octavian waited, standing so boldly with his newfound authority of power, awaiting his request to materialize. Finally, a horse appeared. He was delighted, then he looked and there was no saddle to mount and no bridle to grasp the reins from. Disgusted, he shouted to his demons, "Demons of Diana, I summon you to gird this horse with a saddle and a bridle with reins!"

"Do you not know," a voice whispered in his ear, "that only two summons may be granted in a day? And now, this day, we have already granted you two? Ask again tomorrow and we shall gird your horse."

"Curses!" shouted Octavian. He then looked at the horse, took hold of its mane, and struggled to mount. Octavian's small stature made it difficult for him to pull himself up onto the horses back. It was a comical sight to behold as the horse flailed to the left and the right. After several tries, he finally managed to swing himself up, on top of the horse's back. Once mounted, he repositioned his hands onto the horse's mane. With a steady grip and tossing about on the horses back with every trot, he traveled onward toward Beersheba.

PRINCIPALITIES AND POWERS

Mary and Longinus had made good time toward the Ports of Gaza. The sun was now high in the afternoon sky. Longinus was pleased that the terrain was becoming much easier to travel. "We must allow the horse to rest a bit. Let us stop over there under the shade of those olive trees."

"That will be good," answered Mary.

They dismounted and stretched their legs. Longinus looked at Mary and said, "We should be there by tomorrow. If we keep going and only sleep for a few hours, we can be there by noon. Are you able to that?"

"I will do it," answered Mary.

Longinus took a drink from his goat-skinned flask. Then he pulled back the lower lip of his horse and poured some into its mouth.

Mary looked up at the tree and pulled down a branch. She exclaimed to Longinus, "Look, this is full of ripe olives! I shall gather some for us!"

"Indeed!" answered Longinus. "And I shall help." He went over, and together, they gathered olives. They ate their fill, then they put some in the haversack.

"We should move on now," Longinus said. Mary went to the horse and waited as Longinus mounted; he reached down his hand and lifted her up on the back of the horse and they proceeded to head west toward Gaza.

As they road along, Longinus asked Mary, "Tell me, what are principalities and powers?"

Mary answered, "Principalities and powers are evil and malicious spirits who make war against the people of God. They wield their power in the unseen realms to oppose everything and everyone that is of God. Though they cannot be seen, their afflictions and torment can be both seen and felt, like when one has been afflicted with a plague. These demonic spirits cause all manner of illness."

"I am trying to understand this. My Lord told me I wrestle not with flesh and blood, but with principalities and powers. How does one fight what one cannot see?" asked Longinus.

Mary answered, "I have heard demons cry out for mercy when my Lord has cast them out of people. I saw him cure a leper once…"

Mary paused for a moment then added, "He even cast out a legion of demons from two mad men who had the strength of bulls. The demons begged for another body to enter into and not be cast back to hell. My Lord cast them into a herd of swine and the swine went mad from them and ran into the river and drowned."

"So you fight them like a sorcerer?" questioned Longinus.

"Well, there is a realm we cannot see. A realm where principalities and powers are bound, it's a different dimension. Both the heavenly principalities and powers and that of Hades lay within this unseen realm. We are in the flesh and cannot see it. We fight the evil in this realm, in the manner that Jesus taught us to do. We are to call on the Father to intercede for us. He has mighty archangels that protect and defend us, for we are defenseless against this evil in the flesh."

"So this fight we are in, against these things, we cannot fight it ourselves?" asked Longinus.

"We do fight it ourselves, through our faith in God the Father and calling upon him for divine protection and wisdom to discern what is from him, and what is from the evil ones."

"Why then do many who are good die by the hands of evil men?"

"We are a soul that lives in a body that will grow old and one day perish. Our soul will go to the Father we have loved and served while in the flesh. Either to our Father God in heaven or to the Father Satan in hell. To choose to serve our Father, who is in heaven, we will reap the kingdom of God, which is glorious, and eternal life of joy. We will never be alone in our earthly journey, our Father God will always watch over us.

"To serve the father of all evil means a life of uncertainty and sorrow. Fleeting moments of false peace with granted gifts that fade as quickly as they are given. There is no inner peace, only confusion. In the end, there is nothing but eternal torment and punishment. That is all evil has for one's soul. The soul is the part of us to cherish, not the body that will one day perish."

"So it is a war."

"Yes, it is a war," answered Mary.

"A war to overcome our death? Is that the war we fight?"

"The one you speared is the one who won victory of the war over death, he has overcome all evil. He had to die in agony in order to enter into Sheol and overcome the grip of Satan and the chains that bound all souls to Hades. Did you not see the graves open and hear the people testify in the streets of Jerusalem? They were freed from the chains of Hades. My Lord descended there and broke down its gates."

Longinus answered, "I heard talk of the dead rising from the graves in the streets, but I believed it to be a sorcerer's magic. I did not know then what I know now. He truly did fulfill his destiny here in this world. I see it more clearly now."

Mary thought a moment then added, "In the garden, the night they arrested my Lord. He prayed to the Father that all the people he gives to him will be protected and kept. My Lord has promised that when we call on him, he will be there to help us."

"Is that what he meant when he said to me, 'Stay close and follow me?'" asked Longinus.

"Yes, it is," answered Mary.

"I am seeing that the power that is in the spear is not the spear itself, but the blood that is on it. No evil spirit could dare come near it. For it is the blood of the one who broke down the gates of Hades and emptied out all of its prisoners. The prince of hell could not fight him, and all the evil principalities and powers in the world could not hold him, they could not overcome him. In his death, he arose like a phoenix to begin a new kingdom, one that has no end."

"Your eyes have opened wide, Longinus," Mary said with great joy. "You have understood well."

OCTAVIAN RESUMES COMMAND

Octavian was finally entering the streets of Beersheba. Fortunately for him, he had learned a great deal about riding bareback and was no longer a pitiful sight. He spotted a Roman sentry posted at the road leading into the city. He hailed him down,

"Where is Khalid?"

"Octavian? You are all right?"

"Indeed, now where is Khalid? Don't have me repeat myself again," ordered Octavian most impatiently.

"He is somewhere in the city. I think he stayed at the inn by the winepress," answered the sentry as he pointed down the road.

"Very well, as you were," ordered Octavian as he headed toward the winepress. He found the inn that was next to it, just as the sentry had said.

He dismounted and called out to a sentry in the street. "You there, take my horse and mount a saddle and a bridle with a strong rein."

The sentry looked surprised and said, "Yes, sir. Glad to see you are well, sir!" and led the horse away.

Octavian felt the crest on his centurion helmet and rubbed his fingers across it to make sure it was straight. He then walked into the inn. He approached the innkeeper and asked, "A burly man and a big dog, are they here?"

"Ahh, yes down the hall there, the first door on the left."

Octavian went right to the door and thrust it open. There on the cot laid a sleeping Khalid and a growling Vitali.

"What is it, Vitali?" said Khalid as he opened his eyes. He looked and there standing in the doorway was Octavian.

"Is this how you find a deserter and a grave robber?" he shouted angrily.

"The men are searching. You are well, how did you—"

Octavian interrupted him, "I have no time to answer your heartwarming questions regarding my health. While you sleep and have my men search in vain, the deserter and the woman are in Hebron. If you value your life, you and that thing you call Vitali, you will gather the men and supplies. You and my men will meet me in one hour at the north road leading out of the city. We will head to Hebron."

"Yes sir," answered Khalid. "But what about the sick men in the—"

Octavian cut off Khalid while he was speaking and shouted, "Rome has no use for sick and dying soldiers. Get on with your orders."

"Yes sir."

Octavian turned and began to walk away. With his back turned, he said, "I will meet you after I have a decent meal."

Octavian refreshed himself at the water well, then went into the tavern and ate. When he was done, he stepped outside of the tavern, and there waiting for him was a mounted sentry holding the reins of Octavian's horse, now well girded. Octavian smiled and checked the bridle, the reins, and the saddle. He opened the haversack and saw that it was well stocked. He checked the skinned flask of fresh water and said, "I trust this is from a clean well?"

"The water here is as sweet as wine, sir."

Octavian was well pleased and mounted his horse. They proceeded to the north side of the city. Khalid, Vitali, and the soldiers were all waiting. Octavian rode gallantly to the front and ordered,

"We travel Northeast to Hebron. It is a short journey ahead."

THE PORTS OF GAZA

Longinus and Mary had made great time on the way to the Ports of Gaza. They were able to sleep for a few hours in the night and had diligently pursued their goal of reaching Gaza by noon. They were now so close they could smell the Mediterranean Sea in the warm air.

"Look, we are almost there," said Longinus with a smile. "I need to get rid of my centurion armor. I must look like a merchant or a traveler. What should I be?"

Mary thought for a moment, then she answered, "We must appear to be something different than brother and sister."

"Then you shall be my wife," said Longinus. "I shall strip the armor and ride in with my tunic. When we are there, I will buy a robe, or shall I buy a cloak?"

"A robe will be best."

Longinus continued to think. He wondered where they were going once they reached the ports.

"Mary, has the Lord spoken to you of where we are to travel, once we reach the Ports of Gaza?"

"I have not been shown. He will reveal it to us. Do not worry. Have faith that the Lord is leading our way."

"This faith, that is what I struggle to understand. I am a man who makes a plan or follows an order."

"Then, you follow the order of the Lord and continue to the ports."

"Mary, you are very clever with your words to me."

As Longinus and Mary rode along, he continued to think. He asked, "What shall we tell the mariner? Shall we say, take us to wherever the ship will sail us?"

Mary answered, "If that is what the Lord tells us, then that is what we shall say."

They continued to ride on a ways, and as they got closer, Longinus stopped the horse. They dismounted and he stripped off his armor and buried it under the sand. He stood with his arms out, wearing his tunic, and shouted to Mary, "Now, how do I look?"

Mary smiled and said, "Like a perfect fisherman ready for hire by a great fishing boat."

They both laughed. Then Longinus said, "We are almost at the port, come let us mount up and go."

At that, they quickly got up on their horse and rode along, both were busy with their own thoughts. After about an hour's ride,

Longinus saw the outline from the sandy hills that marked the port city of Gaza. "There it is!" he shouted.

They made their way into the port city and dismounted and Longinus led the horse by its' reins, as they entered the market area. He stopped at a merchant's stand and purchased a new tunic and a robe.

"Is there a place I might use to change my tunic?" Asked Longinus.

"In the back there," said the merchant as he pointed, "Don't touch any of the wares." He cautioned.

Longinus nodded and went to the back to change his tunic.

When he came out from the back, he motioned for Mary to follow him and they walked the horse to the outside of the market place and tied him to a post. He reached into his haversack and pulled out the head of the spear. He wrapped it in a piece of heavy cloth and placed it under his girded leather belt at his side. He put on the new robe and that hid it completely.

"We'll leave the horse here." He said as he lifted the haversack from its back side. As they walked closer to the ports, he noticed it was well guarded by Roman soldiers.

He took Mary by her arm and said, "Come, we must find out why there are so many soldiers here?"

He escorted her into an open market. They made their way as though they were buying food to take to their home. Mary was placing fruits and vegetables in a basket she had purchased from another merchant. They made their way watching the Roman soldiers, but acting as though they were only interested in what was for sale.

Mary looked at a merchant and said, "These soldiers, are they hurting your business? I know I am not wanting to stay long in the market with them breathing down our necks like we are some enemy of Rome."

The merchant answered, "Oh, you will soon ignore them. They have been hassling everyone that comes to the ports. Stay in the market area and you will have no trouble."

Mary nodded. Longinus was listening to the clever way Mary was finding information, as he followed along like he was her husband.

Longinus looked over to the ports. He observed seafaring vessels awaiting orders and ready to sail whenever permission was given by Roman soldiers. He watched as they recklessly searched through everyone's person and belongs. Each traveler who wanted to enter the ports were left with their wares and things all in disarray on the ground, causing them great trouble in having to repack everything back the way it was. All the while, the soldiers shouted for them to move along.

Longinus took Mary by the arm and led her from the market and back toward the horse. There, standing by the horse were a centurion and a sentry. He heard them speak.

"Find the owner of this horse, it has the branding of Roman property," ordered the centurion.

Longinus turned Mary around and they quickly moved into the middle of the most crowded part of the market. He spoke to her softly so no one could hear, "We must make a new plan." Mary, in fear that some Roman might be watching, smiled as though he had whispered something nice and nodded yes.

As they continued to blend into the busiest part of the market filled with people, they were at times shoulder to shoulder with others who were shopping. Suddenly, a woman declared, "Mind where you are going!" Mary apologized to the woman, and the woman said, "Is that you, Mary?" Mary was startled, the voice sounded familiar. She looked at the face of the woman; it was Suzanna, an old busybody acquaintance she knew from Jerusalem.

"Suzanna?" Mary asked, "what are you doing here?"

"I believe for the same reason as you," she answered.

Mary, who continued to be very shrewd, answered, "I don't understand?"

"With all the unrest in Jerusalem, we decided to flee before a rebellion broke out. The ports in Ashkelon were so full, there was not any passageway. There won't be for months, unless you are a merchant. But oh my, what they must go through to get on a ship. It is awful the way they search their wares. Just horrible.

"The Romans are guarding every port along the entire Palestinian coast. My husband was about to travel us to Joppa, but other travelers had come from there and told us the passage was all tied up worse than Ashkelon. It is such a busy port, you know, Joppa. People at every port are being searched by soldiers like they are thieves. And if you give them any trouble, they arrest you. It has made travel by ship almost impossible. At some of the ports, there are as much as several weeks wait. So we came here to Gaza. We are waiting for our mariner to get his clearance to leave port. We head to Greece soon."

"Greece?" questioned Mary.

"Oh, I know, what is in Greece for us? Passage for one thing, and Josiah can find work for another. The ships heading to Rome are only taking merchants and their wares. All other travelers are forbidden. I don't know why, but there are lots of rumors."

Mary knew she must guard her words, but had to say something fast. She didn't want to lie, but she didn't want to tell Suzanna the truth either.

"Why, that is where we are going."

"We?" said Suzanna. "Who are you with?"

"My husband," answered Mary.

"Why, you sly woman," exclaimed Suzanna. "You went and married without letting me know of it! Where is he, your husband?"

Longinus looked over and smiled. Suzanna made her way around Mary and looked up and down at Longinus. She smiled and said, "I hope you know you have a good woman." She then looked directly into his eyes and pointed her finger at his face and said, "You must take care of her as such."

Longinus answered, "Oh, indeed. She tells me the same." At those words, they all laughed.

When the laughter stopped, Longinus added, "We have one problem."

Suzanna looked at him with concern and said, "What problem is that?"

"We have not been successful in securing our passage to Greece.

We were told all the ships were filled."

"Why, that is of no problem," said Suzanna with confidence.

"We shall add you to our passage. You know Josiah, he always has them save more passage than we need, just in case he finds someone who wants on after the ship is filled. He finds people that will pay more than he will have to pay. Then he collects their money, secures the passage, and makes his profit. It is only my husband and I that travel. I will tell him to let you have two of his passages at the proper fare. He may haggle the price, but don't you let him. It will be of no problem for you to come with us to Greece."

Mary burst with joy and said, "Oh, thank you, Suzanna. That will be so kind and an answer to my prayer." She then silently thanked the Lord.

"Come," said Suzanna, as she took hold of Mary's hand. "I must introduce your new husband to Josiah."

"Josiah?" asked Longinus cautiously.

"My husband, Josiah." She turned to Mary and said, "Have you not told your husband anything? We are better friends than that. Shame on you, Mary." She teased.

Longinus and Mary followed Suzanna as she led them straight way to a short, stocky, little man who was haggling with a merchant over the price of a slab of smoked fish.

"There you are, Josiah. Quit your haggling and come here." The man responded quickly and came over to Suzanna. "I almost had him down to my price," he complained.

"Never mind, there are always better prices in the market for smoked fish. But look who I have found, it is Mary."

Josiah looked and said with glee, "Mary. It is you! And who might he be?" He smiled as he looked up to the tall Longinus. Mary answered, "Josiah, meet my new husband, Longinus."

"My, my, now how did you ever get this lovely Mary to agree to wed you?"

Longinus answered, "It took some thinking, but eventually, we both agreed that for me to be her husband was the best thing to do."

Mary shook her head at Longinus and said, "You are indeed very lucky that I agreed to such a thing."

At that, Josiah let out a deep laugh. "Oh, Mary, you still have your great wit."

While Suzanna explained the situation to Josiah, Mary gave Longinus a daring look and whispered to him, "You will do good to mind what you say." Longinus nodded.

After hearing all the dilemma of Mary and her new husband,

Josiah considered and said,
"Indeed, we can help, but the extra fare…?"

Longinus answered quickly, "We will pay. Do not worry about that. We have purse."

Josiah clapped his hands together and declared, "Then I go to the mariner and we secure the passage for four travelers instead of two. Come, we go together."

Longinus and Mary exchanged a nervous glance, and they went with Suzanna and Josiah. Josiah went past the standing guard and hollered out, "Don't detain me, I spent hours with you not to long ago, I have to speak with my mariner about my passage." He ignored the soldiers and motioned for the others to hustle through. The soldier looked and said, "Go on, we haggled with you enough today." They began to pass and another soldier hollered out, "Who goes with them?"

The soldier that okayed his way shouted back, "Leave them to pass, they head to Greece and I will bid them farewell myself when they set sail. The man is nothing but a marketplace haggler."

Josiah looked up at the soldier and shook his finger at him, "Why if I weren't in a hurry to leave this forsaken place…be glad that I am."

The other soldier looked and said, "Oh, now I see," and paid no more attention to them.

Once past the soldiers, they made their way to the ship sailing to Greece. Josiah secured the passage and Longinus paid the coinage. Josiah spoke to the group, "Now, that is done. Shall we go back to the market until it is time to travel. The mariner said we still have about an hour before we sail."

Mary said, "Oh, Josiah, we have everything we need. We will be content to wait here and look out into the beautiful sea."

Suzanna said, "I will wait with them, we have a lot to talk about."

Josiah said, "Very well, I will be back."

Suzanna wasted no time as Josiah had barely turned to leave before she began talking. She had one trivial story after another of her travel with Josiah and how they had one problem after another. As Suzanna was going on and on, Longinus turned and secretly slid the spear out from beneath his clothing and placed it in his haversack for safekeeping.

Suzanna continued to ramble on until her words were nothing more to Mary and Longinus but a dull blur of sounds. They stood there and appeared to be listening, but inside, they were not hearing a word. They were simply keeping an eye on the soldiers until it was time for the ship to sail.

EMPTY-HANDED IN HEBRON

Octavian ordered Khalid to travel in the back of the line of soldiers all the way to Hebron as a form of reprimand. But Khalid actually preferred it that way, and so did Vitali. It gave them more freedom to do as they pleased.

They were fast approaching Hebron after a long climb up a steep rocky hill through the canyon.

Octavian shouted out, "We go in, we get the deserter, and the woman and we head to Jerusalem. I want this over fast. This should be an easy task."

At the entry to the city, Octavian feeling emboldened with his new found powers was becoming power crazed with tyrannical ideas. His orders were getting bolder and bolder. He called out his sentry, "Position the men to take Hebron by force. We may have to flex some muscle to show this peace loving town a thing or two about the commands of Rome."

"Yes Sir," answered the sentry.

They rode into the city and past the bazaar. Octavian saw activity at the inn just up ahead. He ran his horse up to the door. There was a little man standing there with a bucket of water. The man waved and said, "If you are hungry, we have plenty of food. Come inside."

Octavian ignored the man's gesture and stated his purpose, "I am looking for a soldier and a woman. I know they are here in Hebron. Have you seen them?"

The man said, "I am the innkeeper, Timmeon. Yes, I have seen a soldier and his sister. They were here. Nice people."

Octavian questioned, "You said they were here?"

"Oh yes. Let me see now. Was it two or three days ago? People come and they go so often here…let me try and remember."

Octavian demanded, "Where did they go? Did they tell you where were they going?"

"A-hah… yes. They went back to their home on the coastline. Magdalene. Do you know of Magdalene…it is a nice fishing village. Good people are there."

Octavian turned his horse around and Timmeon shouted out, "When you are hungry, I have plenty of food."

Octavian paid no attention to the man. He ordered his sentry to gather the men and get supplies and meet at the northwest side of the city. His new plan was to go to Magdalene.

HAGGLING OVER FISH

Back at the ports of Gaza, time had passed quickly and the mariner was ready to set sail; he rang the ship's bell to alert the people that it was time to board. Suzanna was worried that her hard-headed husband would not hear the bell and know that their ship was getting ready to leave.

"He is off haggling, and if I do not go to get him, I fear he will not hear the bell. What shall I do?"

"I am sure he will be here shortly," comforted Mary.

Suzanna was a very determined woman and very forthright. She did not mince words. She looked at Longinus and asked, very commanding,

"You must go and get him. He must be at the merchant that is selling smoked fish. I know him, he had to finish haggling for his price."

Longinus did not know what to say; he looked at Mary, and Mary just made a wide eye and shrugged her shoulders in bewilderment. She too did not know what to say.

Suzanna persisted, "Go and get him, that is the least you can do to repay the kindness we have shown you."

Mary looked at Longinus and said, "She is right, the Lord will give you his speed."

Longinus took off in a run, then slowed down when he passed the soldiers' post. He took off to the middle of ·the marketplace. Sure enough, he was haggling with the same merchant just like Suzanna had said. Longinus ran up to him and said, "We must go quickly the ship is ready to sail, and it will sail without us if we do not hurry."

Josiah looked and said, "Just when I had my price."

Longinus urged him, "Come now, there is not a moment to spare. There is no time to settle for a fish."

Reluctantly, Josiah looked at the merchant and put both of his arms up and said, "What can I say, I must go."

Longinus started to run, and Josiah with his short legs could not keep up. Longinus slowed down, but he did not like doing that at all. Josiah kept walking fast and yelled, "Let me board first." Longinus stopped and let Josiah pass, and a caravan of donkey full of wares blocked his path. With the market at his back and the port ahead, Longinus could do nothing but wait for them to pass. As soon as they did, he took off running. A soldier saw him running and hollered out, "You there. Halt." Longinus kept running as the bell of the ship was sounding for the last time. The soldier ran after him in pursuit.

Longinus was unsure as to what to do, but he knew not to stop or he would miss the ship. He shouted out, "My ship is sounding to leave the port. I will miss it if I stop."

The soldier hollered out again, "I said halt."

Longinus was so close but feared what would happen when he ran past the set of soldiers guarding the port with another soldier chasing him. He remembered Josiah's obnoxious attitude and how that helped him pass. He thought to remember how Josiah did it. As he approached the port, his heart spoke to him and he listened to it. He hollered out, "Soldier, hail my ship to not leave without me!"

The soldier looked over at Longinus who was running fast toward the ship. Longinus cried out again, "Soldier, please hail my ship and order it not to leave the port without me!"

The soldier shouted back, "Stop your bantering. If you make it, you make it, if you don't, you don't. I have other matters to attend."

Longinus continued to plead with the soldier to halt his ship as he ran, but inside, he was smiling big. He made it to the ship just in time and leaped up on the deck, just as they were pulling up the last anchor. The sails were set and the smaller boats were just beginning to pull it out to sea to reposition it for the wind.

Longinus looked out at the soldier and waved. Abruptly, he stopped waving when he saw the soldier that had been chasing him stop and talk to the soldier at his post and point to him. Longinus's heart began to pound, then he saw the soldier that had chased him throw his hand in the air and wafted it at the soldier he had waved too. Longinus watched as the soldier turned around and marched off in disgust.

"That was close," burst out Mary. Not knowing what Mary meant, Suzanna said, "Sure was, the ship almost left without you."

Josiah had a parcel and handed it to Suzanna. "The best smoked fish at the best price!"

Longinus looked and said, "But you had no time to purchase that, I saw."

"Oh, let me tell you," said Josiah, "I purchased this one before I haggled the other merchant down to my price."

Longinus shook his head and started to speak. Mary quickly grabbed his arm and said, "I hear Greece is beautiful this time of year."

Longinus looked at Mary and said, "And I hear there is plenty of smoked fish for less a price than all of Gaza."

Josiah looked disappointed and said, "Less a price than all of Gaza?"

A WISE REPORT

Octavian led the troops toward Magdalene and continued to have Khalid and Vitali ride behind the rest of the troops. As he rode along, he was counting the hours until it would be time for him to summon his demons of Diana and get another favor. He was obsessed in his thoughts as to what he would ask them to do. Only two summons in a day. What shall they be? he thought. I must make my requests very clear and very rewarding for myself.

At the back of the line of soldiers, Vitali was sniffing the air. She veered off the path to the northwest. She barked at Khalid.

"What is it, Vitali?"

Vitali barked again. It was a familiar bark, one that she used to signal to Khalid that she was on the scent. Khalid shouted, "Vitali, come." Vitali returned to Khalid. Khalid looked down at Vitali and said, "I know, Vitali, they are going in the wrong direction—again. But I have no desire to warn the fool of his error today."

Vitali made a yawning howl and walked along Khalid, but she kept looking northwest.

They traveled for hours, and Octavian believed enough time had passed and he could summon his demons of Diana. "We stop here and rest our horses," he ordered.

As the men dismounted and tended to their horses, Octavian dismounted and gave his reins to the sentry. "Take and water my horse," he ordered, "And make sure I have no interruptions while I assess the terrain."

"Yes, sir."

Octavian moved away from the men into a secluded area where he could not be seen by them. He then summoned his demons of Diana. "Oh, my demons of Diana, bring to me the deserter named Longinus and his spear with the three blood red crosses upon it and the woman he is with, named Mary." He smiled, believing he had summoned most wisely.

When the demons heard the request, they trembled. Forthright, they summoned the Apprentice. The Apprentice heard them call out to him in his mind's eye and listened.

"Oh, master, he has requested that we...we..." the demon's voice was fearful, "that we bring to him the man named Longinus and his spear that has the three blood red crosses upon it and the woman he is with named Mary. Please, what shall we do? Demons cannot go near the blood on that spear, it will send us back to Hades."

The Apprentice was angered and said under his breath, "What does he think I need him for? If I or my demons could just summon the spear and grab it up, what would I ever need him for? That fool has asked way too much." He thought quickly and said to the demons, "Tell him, indeed, he has asked a very wise request. But he has not proven himself for such a worthy summon. He must first prove himself worthy of such high requests by obtaining the deserter Longinus and his spear on his own. You can help him. But not do it for him."

The demons were relieved and answered, "Yes, Master. That is what we shall do."

The Apprentice added, "Wait a moment." He closed his eyes and an image appeared; he saw Longinus and Mary on a ship. They were in the Mediterranean Sea. He felt the presence of the blood on the spear, but could not see it. He wondered at that, It is hidden, but with him, he thought. He opened his eyes, breaking the vision, then spoke to his demons. "His next question will be, 'Then tell me where they are exactly.' You will tell him they are on a ship in the Mediterranean Sea, bound for Greece. Suggest to him to have you cause a storm that will bring them to the shores. Then he can catch them. Go now and do as I have said."

"Yes, Master."

The demons spoke to Octavian through a whisper in his ear. "Indeed, you have asked very wisely. But you have not proven yourself worthy as of yet to be granted such a high request. You must first prove yourself worthy by obtaining the deserter Longinus and his spear, along with the woman named Mary, on your own. We can help you, but we are not allowed to do it for you."

"Then tell me, where exactly is the man Longinus and his spear with the three blood red crosses and the woman named Mary?" demanded Octavian very angrily.

The demons whispered in his ear, "They are on a ship in the Mediterranean Sea, bound for Greece."

"Does that answer count as one of my summons?" asked Octavian.

"Yes," whispered the demons.

"Curses," he said under his breath.

The demons whispered, "Might we suggest that you have us to cause a great storm that will bring them to the shores?"

Octavian thought, If I agree so quickly, I will not know what part of the shore they will be brought to. The coast is so long and vast. I must not be a fool, for all I know, he could be brought to the shores of Italy. I must put great thought into my last request of the day.

"What would you have us do?" whispered the demons.

Octavian thought, We are halfway to the coasts of Ashdod, yet also close to Ashkelon. Hmm…what would be the wiser choice? But why should I ask to just merely have them brought to shore? I know what I shall ask.

Tempting Octavian to answer, the demons whispered, "Have you nothing more to request of us at this time?"

"Wait," answered Octavian, "I have my request. Cause a storm to bring their boat to the shore, but have them not stop at the shore, have Longinus with his spear and the woman named Mary continue on to Jerusalem. I will wait for them there."

The demons were surprised at his cleverness and answered, "It shall be done."

At those words, Octavian smiled. He felt very good about himself. He returned to the men and ordered them to mount. When they were all in line and ready to proceed, Octavian could not help but to boast. He turned and addressed the soldiers, "The gods have favored me and given me a vision. We ride to Jerusalem. They will be running back to that city to hide. We shall arrest them there. On to Jerusalem." He turned and the men followed him.

Khalid looked at Vitali, "We follow a mad man, Vitali." Vitali shook her head as they followed behind.

TEMPEST STORM AT SEA

On the ship bound for Greece, Mary and Longinus finally found some privacy away from Suzanna and Josiah. Longinus asked Mary, "What is for us in Greece?" Mary answered, "I do not know. But if that is where the Lord leads us, that is where we must go."

Longinus looked at Mary as she sadly looked back at the shoreline.

Mary leaned forward over the bow, watching until the city had faded away in the distance and the last scent of olive trees had long passed. Her eyes had grown weary from gazing upon the waters of the Mediterranean Sea. Longinus stood next to her and wondered at the things they had experienced and how the Lord had shown them their way. He wondered what the Lord would show them next.

Longinus and Mary gazed out upon the waters as the moon cast a shine upon the waves causing them to shimmer as they rippled across the sea. It was a beautiful night.

They watched until their eyes were heavy, and they knew it was time to go to their assigned quarters and get some sleep. Morning would come all too soon.

"We must tell Suzanna and Tobias good night. They have been so gracious to us," said Mary, and Longinus nodded in agreement. They walked over to the other side of the ship and found their friends.

Suzanna and Tobias were busy bickering about a many number of inconveniences one of them was sea travel and only stopped long enough to bid Mary and Longinus good night.

"I can't believe there is nothing to do but look out over this dreadful sea…oh, are you leaving?" asked Suzanna to Mary.

"It has been a long day, we go now to get some sleep."

"Well, if you can…I hope you rest well. Tobias, tell me again why you thought travel by sea would be good, why I haven't the slightest idea how you think such things?"

"Suzanna, have some smoked fish…it was a good price," he said as he tore a piece and put it in his mouth. "It is not fresh," he grumbled.

"The man told me it was fresh."

"Well, that is what you get from believing a merchant in the market."

Mary and Longinus looked at each other and shook their heads. As they walked away, the bickering faded into the distance.

Longinus said, "They love being so." Mary giggled.

"How do you know them?" he asked.

"Oh, I don't really. I met Suzanna a few times in Jerusalem. Each time she talked and talked and told me what she thought of things. I only listened."

"But Josiah seemed to know you?"

"I never met him before today. He was being cordial for Suzanna."

Longinus gave Mary a puzzled look and said, "All I can say is I'm glad he was cordial."

Mary and Longinus nestled into their meager quarters. There was not much room, but it was enough. They had to share the same sleeping space, and Longinus was careful not to touch Mary's body.

Mary was pleased with his respect and thanked him. "Sleep well, and thank you for being so mindful."

"Ah…yes. Sleep well," he said.

The ship continued to sail, and the passengers were fast asleep. A warm, soothing breeze whispered through the air, over the calm waters. The night's serenity was accompanied by the sound of gentle waves, rippling against the side of the ship. All was at peace in the Mediterranean Sea.

Then, halfway through the night, the sky began to darken, and ominous black rolling clouds covered the moon and hid the beautiful constellation of the stars. The peaceful waters began to form slashing waves with foaming white caps.

"There is a storm coming, slacken the sails!" shouted a sailor as he looked at the sky and watched the waves beating at the front of the stern.

"Tighten the rudder rope!" yelled another. "It looks like a tempest. It came out of nowhere!" The sailors worked frantically to prepare the ship for the coming storm. They watched and wondered where this storm came from and how bad it would be. The boat began to rock and heave on the water. The passengers were all sound asleep. Then a bolt of lightning cracked in the sky and a thunderous roar followed in an instant. It is directly over our heads!" shouted the sailor." I've never seen anything so fierce in these waters!"

"Grab hold of the ropes and hold this lady in place!" shouted the ship's captain.

The heavy pounding waves fiercely knocked at the ship's stern with great violence. The captain feared it would soon be broken up.

"Alert the passengers—awaken them!" he shouted. "It looks like it may be every man for himself!"

Many of the people were already awake and coming out onto the deck. They slid as the boat heaved and rocked. Many were not able to get a sure footing for the deck was filling fast with water. Waves kept slashing over the sides and into the ship. Barrels and bins of merchant goods were sliding into the passengers as they waded through the water. They grabbed at anything that looked secure enough to hang on to.

Longinus and Mary awoke. They ran to the steps that led to the top of the deck and were met by a wave of water knocking them backward. They slid in the water. Longinus shouted to Mary,

"Grab my hand!" She took hold and he pulled her toward him and they made their way to the top. "Hang on to this!" he hollered at Mary as he threw her a rope bound to the side of the deck. "No matter what, do not let go!"

"I won't," shouted Mary.

Longinus joined the men who were fighting to hold the rudder in place with ropes. He fixed his strong hands around the rope and pulled with all his weight and might against it. He held it steadfast. The ship was making cracking sounds and the mast was weaving back and forth as though it might break into. "Steady her!" shouted the captain through the sound of the roaring waves and the rolling thunder.

"We have to turn her around!" shouted Longinus. "Toward the shore!" The captain looked over and shouted, "Get her turned around, loosen the rudder ropes, and hold her steady!"

The men fought to get the ship turned; finally, they were able to do so. The captain then shouted, "Hoist the main sail—hoist it now!" They hoisted the sail and the blasting wind pushed into it with such force; the men feared the sail might tear apart. The ship shot toward the shore with lightning speed, without any oarsmen, without any help. Parts of the stern were being knocked apart from the great force of the violent waves hitting it.

Mary was holding on to the rope with all her strength, then suddenly, it snapped. She went sliding backward to the back of the ship slushing through the water, slapping into the wall of the stern. She grabbed hold of a bar and hung on tight.

The captain knew he had to slow the ship down, so he shouted, "Lower the anchors. All of them!"

One of the passengers tried to escape by lowering a lifeboat; he no sooner lowered it down with the rope and the wind caught it, sending it upward, straight out in the air. The rope holding it snapped like a tender twig, sending the boat hurling across the water as though someone had shot it from a sling.

The men fought to keep the ship steady in the storm for hours; somehow, the ship held together as it continued to drive itself with lightning speed toward the shore. The men held on to the sides of the ship and braced themselves. That was all they could do as the ship seemed to have a mind of its own.

The shore was in sight and the ship was getting closer and closer and not slowing down. The captain shouted, "You can't jump, she goes too fast. Shield your heads and hang on for your life."

Longinus looked over at Mary who was clinging to a bar at the stern of the ship. He shouted, "Get down, shield yourself!"

Mary could not hear him. He shouted again, "Get down! Shield yourself, when this hits, the stern will break apart!" Longinus tied a rope around the mast pole, left enough slack to reach the stern, and then took the end and tied it to his waist, leaving a good length. He coiled the extra length of rope around his arm and made his way toward Mary. It was hard to move forward against the force of the wind and the speed of the ship, but he inched his way there. He saw the stern was breaking up. There was but a little window of time to get Mary to the front of the ship.

He threw her the rope and shouted, "Tie this around your waist and take my hand."

Mary struggled to hang on and tie the rope at the same time. She finally did it, then reached out her hand to Longinus. He grabbed it and Mary let go of the bar just as the stern ripped apart, sending the bar flying. Longinus pulled Mary to him.

"Hold on tight to me!" he shouted. Mary clung to him as they fought the strength of the wind and made their way to the mast in the middle. He shouted, "If she hits the shallows at this speed, she could shake apart!" But before he and Mary could do anything more, the ship hit the shallows. Mary clung to Longinus. The ship was vibrating and shaking as it skidded in the shallows. It continued to skid past the sands on the shore, skidding and burying the bow deep into the sand. Pieces of the ship were breaking apart and flying in the air. The ship was slowing, but it was still sliding and burying deeper into the sand.

Longinus looked out and saw a wall of canyon rock just ahead and braced himself and Mary for what he thought was a direct hit. Suddenly, the ship stopped two inches before it hit the wall of rock. The bow was buried so deep in the sand one could just step off it onto the ground.

They looked around; miraculously, no one was seriously hurt. Then, a familiar voice was heard, "I paid good coin for this smoked fish and now it's full of nothing but saltwater. Wasted, it is nothing but wasted!" It was Josiah.

"Oh, stop your squabbling, Josiah, and go see what the captain is going to do about getting us to Greece!"

"Greece? Suzanna, I will see what he will do about returning our coins! We paid for safe passage! This is not safe passage!"

Longinus and Mary looked at each other with surprise. They looked over at Suzanna and Josiah who were safe and well. They seemed very content to stand and bicker. They looked back at each other and laughed. Mary said, "In the middle of the most dangerous life-threatening time, God has given us joy through our friends."

THE APPRENTICE SEEKS KHALID

Octavian and the soldiers were making their way back to Jerusalem. The men were growing weary from traveling and having little time to rest, little to eat, and little to drink. As usual, Octavian had full supplies and cared less about the soldiers' grumblings. There was only one thing on Octavian's mind, and that was what he was going to ask his demons of Diana for next.

Khalid looked at Vitali and said, "We stop and rest." Vitali nodded in agreement. They stopped and dismounted as the soldiers traveled on ahead. "Have some water, girl," he said as he poured some into a cup. Vitali lapped it up. Khalid sat on the ground and leaned back looking up at the sandy hills.

Octavian had no idea that Khalid had stopped and he continued to lead the men.

Khalid was at odds with himself trying to decide whether or not he would continue to follow or depart and go his own way. He looked up at the rise of one of the sandy hills, and his eyes caught hold of a shadowy figure. He watched as the figure made its way down the rise and approached him and Vitali. As he came closer, he saw that it was the Apprentice.

"My, my, so have you decided to abandon your mission?" asked the Apprentice as he came closer. "Do you no longer desire more gold? Is Vitali willing to give up her bounty of gold as well?" "The centurion has gone mad. I believe it was from the poisoned water. He is not the same. I follow no mad man. Vitali and I will find the man and his spear for you."

"Good, good. Might I suggest to stay with the soldiers. I know for a fact that the centurion, Longinus, is on his way to Jerusalem as we speak."

"How do you know this?" asked Khalid very curiously.

"A sorcerer's apprentice has his ways of knowing things. That is all you need to know."

Khalid looked at the apprentice and stood up. "Then Vitali and I go to Jerusalem."

The Apprentice smiled with delight. "Hurry then," he said as he reached out his hand and offered Khalid another gold coin. Khalid took the coin and looked at the apprentice with distrust.

"Why do you pay me another coin so soon?"

"For your troubles in dealing with the arrogant centurion. Now go and catch up with them."

Khalid looked down at Vitali, then over at the Apprentice and said, "What does Vitali get for her trouble?"

The Apprentice smiled and pulled out another gold coin, "My, my, you are a clever bounty hunter now, aren't you. Shall I hand this coin to Vitali or give it to you to keep for her?"

Khalid looked down at Vitali and Vitali gave a bark. "She says I can hold on to it for her."

The Apprentice handed the coin to Khalid and said, "Be on your way."

At that, Khalid mounted his horse and shouted, "Come, Vitali, we first catch up with the soldiers, then we go to Jerusalem, and then we get the centurion and his spear." Vitali barked and they rode off to catch up with the soldiers.

The Apprentice stood and watched until they were well on their way. Under his breath, he said, "I need him to take the spear. Octavian will no longer be able to touch it. Not with the demons of Diana within him. Tsk, tsk. Too bad for him. He does so greatly desire to hold it."

DIVINE INTERVENTION

As the people got off the ship, the captain was trying hard to keep some type of order during the chaos. "We will assess where we are and let you know how we plan to make passage. For now, the ship is buried deep and in need of great repair. Two at a time can come aboard and gather whatever belongings the sea did not take."

Longinus anticipated getting his haversack and hoped it was intact. As he waited for his turn to board ship and seek it, he looked up at the sky and the direction of the sun. He looked at the horizons. Then he looked at Mary and said, "Do you have any idea what shore we are on?"

Mary answered, "I do not know. I only know this is the Lord's doing. He will show us what we need. For last night, an angel of the Lord, whom I serve, stood beside me and said, *'Do not be afraid, Mary. The powers of darkness have sought to sift you as wheat, but God has sent me to intervene. Know that God has taken what the devil meant for evil and has turned it into good. He has called you to return to Jerusalem to receive an anointing of the Holy Spirit. Your ship will be struck by a storm at sea, but God has graciously given you safety, and the lives of all who sail with you.'"*

Longinus was very amazed. He marveled at this thing that Mary told. He thought about it and asked, "So is this how the Lord fights for us against the principalities and powers of evil?"

"Yes," answered Mary.

Several hours later…

It was finally time for Longinus and Mary to take their turn to board the ship and look for any belongings that might still remain. Miraculously, everything they came with was still there. The spear was safe.

"It is all wet, but it will dry out," Longinus stated as he gathered up their things. "We must head for Jerusalem and not tarry with these people."

Mary nodded her head yes. They left the ship and passed the mass of passengers. Everyone was so busy no one noticed they were leaving. "Shall we find Suzanna and Josiah and tell them we are leaving for Jerusalem?" asked Mary.

Longinus looked at her and said, "I say, let them be. Let us get on to Jerusalem. I do not want them to decide to come with us. I could not stand to hear them bicker all along the journey."

Mary nodded, "Oh, I did not think of that. You are right."

They made their way from the wreckage and headed out on foot traveling toward Jerusalem.

The Nabatean

It wasn't long and the heat from the afternoon's sun was making the journey most unbearable.

"I must rest a while," said Mary.

Longinus answered, "If we stop, it will be that much harder to start up again. We must not stop until we can find a place with a bit of shade."

Mary was exhausted, but she continued on. It was a short while and a man on a camel, leading six more with a caravan of wares and two other men walking, was crossing over to their path on the horizon.

Longinus looked at Mary and said, "Over there, that caravan, they are crossing over and heading toward the way we are traveling."

Longinus shouted, "Good man, can you help us!" The man did not hear them. He shouted louder, "Good man, can you help us!"

The man looked behind him and stopped his caravan. He waited until Longinus and Mary came near to him. He then hollered out, "Who are you?"

"Our ship was wrecked at sea, and we travel back to Jerusalem. I am Longinus, and this is my wife Mary."

The man pulled down his scarf that was wrapped around his nose and mouth. "I am Arêtes. I travel from Petra to Jerusalem to sell my spices."

"You are a Nabatean?" asked Mary.

"Yes. And you are an Israelite?"

"Yes," answered Mary.

"Here, drink some water, the sun is very unforgiving." He handed them a flask.

"Thank you, you are most kind," said Mary as she took the flask and drank, then she passed it to Longinus.

Arêtes got down from his camel. He looked at Longinus and said, "Help me to arrange these camel loads so you can ride to Jerusalem, unless you would rather walk?"

Longinus smiled and ran to the camel and helped Arêtes rearrange the loads. Mary called out, "Oh, thank you. God has sent you to us like an angel."

Arêtes said, "I am just a Nabatean who knows not how to watch a young woman suffer in the wilderness."

The other two men got down from their camels and helped; they all quickly rearranged the wares and helped Mary and Longinus mount their camel. They journeyed on toward Jerusalem.

That evening they made camp, and Arêtes introduced the other two men. "This is Akeem, he is skilled in the art of the sword, he is my protector from thieves." Akeem nodded his head, then went back to preparing the food. "This is Burhan. He is skilled in the art of language and coinage, so that we do not get cheated in the different markets."

Longinus asked, "Why did you not sell your wares at the port?"

Arêtes looked very heavy in the face and explained, "For years and years, we have always traveled to the ports at Gaza to trade our wares there. When we arrived, it was full of Roman soldiers. They were making all the merchants open their packs and throw everything out on the sand. If the merchant resisted, they pummeled them and tore open their sacks themselves. I saw the Romans take precious oils and pour them out on the sand to see if anything was in the urns. Spices were opened and thrown on the ground, and what the wind didn't take, the sand ruined. It grieved my heart to see such actions happen to these good merchants. We did not stay, we left to go to the ports at Ashkelon. The Roman soldiers were doing the same disgraceful act there.

"My spices are rare, and my oils will spoil in direct sunlight. We did not allow Roman soldiers to destroy our cargo. Instead, we travel to Jerusalem, the priests will buy our incense, spices, and precious oils. There are many Pharisees that can afford the price of our spices and they know the value of such and will pay. It is a sad thing that is taking place at the ports."

Longinus put his head down. He felt guilty in knowing that all the evil that was taking place at the ports was because the Romans sought to find him.

"What is taking place is a great burden for all the people, from Petra to the ports. I had no idea that so many were suffering needlessly from the hands of Romans," said Longinus very sadly.

Arêtes spoke, "There is evil. And evil will always find a way to harm the innocent."

UNFIT TO LEAD

Khalid and Vitali caught up with Octavian and the soldiers. No one had noticed that they had tarried behind for a while. Octavian was brutally pushing his men with no rest. The horses were lagging as well.

A soldier called out, "My horse is about to buckle her knees from the sun and the journey. We must stop and rest our horses."

Octavian looked back at the soldiers, and with disgust, he said, "Very well, we rest."

Khalid looked at Octavian. There was something about him that was different. He somehow did not look the same. He looked over at Vitali and said, "His eyes, Vitali, they have changed. His pupils are no longer round. They are slit, like a serpent's eyes." Vitali looked at him then growled low and deep. "We must watch him closely. The man has a demon in him."

Some time later…

Traveling gruesomely in the heat by the dictates of Octavian had reached its' toll on Khalid. He was no longer willing to tolerate the brutal mistreatment of the men and the tiring of the horses any longer. It was time to do something, but what? He vented his frustration to his trusted confidant, Vitali. "This man has some sickness. He is not as well in his thinking. I have seen such madness from men lost at sea. We must go to him and talk some sense or we'll all drop from the heat." Vitali barked in agreement.

Khalid rode his horse a little faster than the others and made his way to the front where Octavian was riding. He noticed that Octavian's horse was not labored, nor thirsty. He thought this very strange. He spoke out, "Octavian, why is your horse not affected by this journey as mine and those of the soldiers?"

"Oh, it is you. I knew it would only be a matter of time before you bothered me with questions and insubordination."

"I bother you with good reason. The men are exhausted, hungry, thirsty, and need to rest. The horses are the same. I fear if we do not stop, no one will make it much farther, let alone to Jerusalem."

"What does that matter to me, if only I make it back? The soldiers who are fit to ride with me shall make it. All the unfit can drop by the wayside. That is how it shall be," answered Octavian very coldly.

"Then it will be you, the one with authority that shall answer to Pilate for all the unnecessary waste of good soldiers," said Khalid very smugly. He added, "I am but a bounty hunter, and my punishment for abandoning this mission will only be that I receive no bounty. You, on the other hand, could lose your rank, for your reckless actions will not be considered worthy of a senior centurion of Rome."

He then looked down at Vitali and said, "Come, Vitali, we go and rest. Leave this mad man to his own fate. There are better bounties to be earned." Vitali barked and Khalid turned his horse to the right, and they proceeded away from the soldiers.

Octavian thought a moment, then he commanded, "Men, we stop here. Eat, drink, and rest."

Khalid looked back and smiled at Vitali as he stopped his horse. "Do we go back or do we break ties?" Vitali put her paw in the sand and drew a line. He made one paw print above the line and another paw print to the right side of the first paw print.

"Very wise Vitali. We travel along, in the front with Octavian, but to his right, at a distance. Let him wonder what we plan to do."

IN JERUSALEM

After much traveling with the caravan, Longinus and Mary could see the outline of the city of Jerusalem on the horizon. They were almost there. They had been well treated by Arêtes and the men in his caravan and learned many things about Petra. They had enjoyed long, intriguing conversations of all the history of his land. And now, their company would soon be coming to a part.

Longinus shouted out to Arêtes, "We will part ways at the entrance to the city. If that be fine with you?" Arêtes did not look behind to address Longinus, but instead, he raised his left hand in the air to let him know he had heard him.

Mary said to Longinus, "I must find my friends. They will help us."

Longinus answered, "I do not know if your friends will be as forgiving of me as you have."

"They will be," answered Mary.

It was a short while and they were at the city gates. Arêtes stopped the caravan and helped Mary and Longinus down. He bid them farewell, "It has been a pleasure to have your company to Jerusalem. May you find what you seek."

Mary graciously bowed her head to Arêtes and thanked him.

Arêtes bowed his head in return. Longinus watched how Mary bid farewell and bowed his head to Arêtes and said, "Thank you for all of your help. May you get a good price for your wares." Arêtes bowed his head and smiled.

Mary and Longinus made their way into the city on foot as Arêtes and the caravan went on ahead of them into Jerusalem. Once inside the city, there was a lot of talk from the people testifying that they had seen the Lord, just as Mary had testified that she had seen him. Longinus remembered when they had left there was talk of such, but he had thought it was crazy talk caused by the work of a sorcerer. But now, with all the people still speaking of seeing prophets who had died long ago he wondered. What could account for so many yet saying such things? Why were they all saying they talked to dead people who came forth from their graves? Was it true that all these people had risen from the dead and were showing themselves about the city.

Longinus overheard two men speaking, "I swear on Abraham's soul it was him! He told me all things!" The other man answered, "I believe you, there are so many it is the power of the Lord who has risen them all."

They went a little farther and Longinus heard a woman speaking to several men, "They told me how the great chains of Hades were burst asunder! Come, I will show you where I saw them. They may still be there!"

It appeared to be that those who had risen from the dead were yet wandering about the city testifying of all they had seen. There was a strange looming of confusion among the people. Many were rejoicing, and many were fearful. Longinus desired to find one of those who came up from the dead and ask many questions.

Mary turned to Longinus and said, "I must go and find Peter and John."

"I will go with you."

Mary smiled and said, "Come."

They made their way through the streets and came to a house. It was not the place that Longinus had seen Mary and others come out from. Mary said, "When they took my Lord it was agreed that we would meet with John if they sought to take us. In his house, he has a secret place to hide many under the dirt floors. I am sure that Peter is there. If he is not, John will know where he is."

Mary knocked on the door. A voice said, "Who is it?"

The voice was that of John. Mary answered eagerly, "It is I, Mary."

Immediately, John opened the door and his face shined with great gladness. "Mary, my sweet Mary, we have worried so trying to find you." Mary embraced John and they hugged and John welled up with tears of joy. "Come inside, Mary will be glad to see you. She has worried so."

They went inside and when Mary saw the woman, they embraced and wept together with happiness. Longinus recognized the woman as the one that was with Mary Magdalene at the cross on Golgotha.

Longinus stood just inside the door and listened as they exchanged their stories of all that had been taking place. Mary told them of her journey and the dream to receive the Holy Spirit, the others were not surprised. As Mary was talking, she looked over and remembered that she had not introduced Longinus.

She took the woman by one hand, John by the other and led her over to him, "Come and meet the man who helped me. This is Longinus. Longinus, this is Mary, the mother of Jesus, my Lord, and this is John an apostle of my Lord."

Longinus was unsure how to respond as they welcomed him. He felt a tear in his heart to be with the ones who loved the man he had speared in the side. His perceived sin began to taunt him again.

"Mary, I am sorry for the death of your son."

Mary, the mother of Jesus, looked at Longinus and said, "I knew from before he was in my womb, that this day would come. For it was told to me by an angel. He was never mine to keep, he was only mine to bring into this world that he might fulfill his Father's will. He lives."

As Longinus heard those words, he felt a stirring in his heart. He wanted to fall prostrate on the floor before them. But he held himself strong. He had no words to say. Only emotions that he was fighting back.

Mary felt the stir within Longinus's heart and said to him, "Remember, many are called, but few are chosen. You have been blessed, the same as his mother."

Longinus looked in Mary's eyes and said, "I know."

A MAN OF GREAT WITNESS

After much welcomed conversation in the house of John, there was a knock on the door. A voice was heard from outside, "Open up, it is I, Peter."

Mary ran to the door and swung it open. Peter exclaimed, "Mary! It is you! Where did you go? We searched and searched for you. We were afraid you had been arrested!"

Mary gave Peter a hug and said, "I was on a journey from the Lord. And now, I am back."

Peter said to her, "There is much to tell you, come, let us sit and talk."

Longinus wanted to go into the city and see what was happening in Jerusalem and if there was any talk of him deserting. He did not know if it was safe for him to be in Jerusalem and was unsure of whether he should stay or leave.

He turned to Mary and said, "Mary, you have much to discuss, I must go into the city for a while. I will be back if your friends will have me."

Mary looked at John. John smiled as he looked at Longinus and said, "Of course. Return when you please. You are always welcome here."

Longinus thanked John and left for the city streets. As he made his way into the heart of Jerusalem, he felt safe that no one would know who he was while he was in his robe and tunic. He looked over at Antonia Tower and wondered what Pilate had ordered regarding his capture. His thoughts were interrupted when he saw Claudia Procula, the wife of Pontius Pilate. She was alone talking to several people in a huddle.

That is strange, He thought. Claudia is never without a guard. Longinus made his way closer to try to hear what they were discussing. He made his way within hearing range, then acted as though he were entering a building, but instead, he hid himself in the recess of its doorway. He listened.

"It is true that I saw him. I took with me a centurion and several of the soldiers that were at the crucifixion, they were with me there when he asked me, 'Claudia, do you believe in me? Know that in the covenant that was given by God to my fathers that everyone is given the means through my death to live. And now you see that I, who you crucified, live. Now hear me and believe in my Father-God who is in me, for I loosed the cords of death and broke the gates of Sheol and my coming shall be hereafter.' I fear for my husband's life. For he is not sure if he believes, yet he is haunted by his death. You must go and speak to him, tell him I have asked you to come. Please, James, you were his brother. He will listen to you, the same as he did him."

A man with a cart drawn by a donkey stopped in front of them, and the donkey began to bray, making Longinus unable to hear the rest of the conversation. Frustrated, he left the recess in the doorway and made his way to where Claudia was talking with the men, but Claudia had turned and was quickly hurrying away. The men had done the same. Longinus shook his head and continued on in the streets.

After a short while, he heard someone call to him. "You there, good man." He turned and there was a man with his face glowing bright. "I have need to speak to you."

Longinus looked at him and said, "Speak."

The man said, "I was told by the one who gave me life that I must tell you why I am here."

"The one that gave you life?"

"Yes."

"Who is this one?"

"This one is my Lord and Savior, Jesus the Christ."

Longinus was stunned. He thought, Should I ask this man if he has risen from the dead? No. He is probably a follower. I shall not ask a thing. I shall listen.

"Speak," said Longinus.

"I was bound by a great gulf that no one could pass, and within this great gulf, I was bound by the gates of hell. Within these gates, I was bound by chains. All who had perished were bound the same as I. Yet there were different levels of torment. My torment was in being bound. My hope was in knowing that the chains would be broken and I would be freed by the lamb of God as it was promised to my fathers from Adam to Abraham. And now I am freed."

Longinus was astounded at the man's words. He asked, "How were you freed?"

The witness answered, "I heard Satan speak to the prince of hell saying to get ready to receive the man Jesus. Then, I heard all the legions of demons cry out in horror as they were all seized with great fear. Then I saw the prince of hell—Beelzebub—greet him, saying, 'I suppose you are the man Satan has spoken to me of?'

"Then I saw Jesus in all his glory trampling death and seizing the prince of hell, taking away all of his power. He broke down all the gates and all the prisons from the top to the bottom and released all who were bound. Beelzebub was wroth with Satan, and they argued fiercely over the destruction of hell.

"While the prince of hell was arguing with Satan, Jesus, the king of glory, said to Beelzebub, the prince of hell, 'Satan, the prince, shall be subject to thy dominion forever, in the room where he held Adam and his righteous sons that are mine.' Then he stretched out his arms and said to us, 'Come to me all you saints that were created in my image who were condemned by the forbidden fruit, and by the devil and death; live now by the wood of my cross, the devil and the prince of this world are overcome, and death is conquered.' The Lord has brought up my soul from the grave and instructed me to testify what I have seen and witnessed."

"This is all such a mystery to me. It is so hard to understand," said Longinus.

"There are many mysteries we do not understand. There will come a time and you will understand all things. There is a battle between the will of good and the will of evil. It is a war. And the Lord, through conquering death and Hades, has won that war for all who come to his Father God. It is only the battles that rage on until the time that all who are called have come. It is a time of great tribulations that will only grow worse and worse, for the devil knows he has but a short time left to do his evil and then he shall be cast out forever, bound to eternal fire."

Longinus hesitated and then said, "What lies ahead for me, for I am the one who speared the Lord in his side?"

The man smiled and said, "I know this. You fulfilled a great prophecy. What you have done bears great testimony that the Lord has risen. What lies ahead for you is in the hand of God the Father and in the choices you make with your own free will. The one thing I can tell you for certain is this, you are the one that chooses your path. You will be led by the hand of the one you choose to serve. Choose the Lord and you choose wisely."

"I have so chosen," said Longinus.

"Then, you have nothing to fear."

The man turned to walk away and Longinus called out, "What is your name?"

The man turned around, "Isaiah." He smiled and then he left.

DEMONS OF DIANA FAIL OCTAVIAN AGAIN

Octavian and his soldiers were nearing Jerusalem. Khalid and Vitali were still haunting him, riding at his side, at a distance.

"I wonder what that fool is trying to accomplish with his incessant ridicule of my authority. Is he letting me know he is my equal?

Hmph!" said Octavian under his breath. "I wonder what that fool plans to tell Pilate?"

All of a sudden, Khalid and Vitali veered away from their position. They rode hard toward Jerusalem, leaving Octavian and his soldiers behind. "That fool, he has no idea of my powers." Octavian immediately summoned his demons of Diana.

"You summoned, Master?" whispered the demons into his ear.

"Tell me what is Khalid going to tell Pilate," asked Octavian.

The demons quickly summoned the apprentice as they were ordered by him to do.

The Apprentice answered, "What is it that he wants now?"

"He wants us to tell him what Khalid is going to tell Pilate."

"He wastes a summon on a request as this? Not to mention the bother it takes for me to have to answer!" he said angrily to the demons.

The demons trembled and knew to remain silent. "Tell Octavian that you are demons and not fortune tellers that look into the future. If he then asks you to stop Khalid by causing harm to him, then tell him that you will. Then, do as I say..." he whispered more to them. When the Apprentice was finished, he said, "Now go and do as I said."

"Yes, Master," they answered, then they left.

The Apprentice stood there and said under his breath, "He must not harm Khalid, for he is the one who can hold the spear to do my bidding. For he has no demons in him and cares not about who rules what. Khalid is a bounty hunter and works for bounty of which I have plenty to give him for his service. I need him to do with the spear what must be done."

The demons returned to Octavian and answered his request. "I regret that we cannot tell you this, for we are demons and not fortune tellers that look into the future."

Octavian was angry and frustrated. In his frustration, he yelled, "Then cause his horse to stumble and let him fall to his death on the plain!"

The demons whispered, "Yes, master," and left.

Octavian smiled and felt much better in knowing he would finally be rid of the bounty hunter for good. He took a drink from his goat-skinned flask and thought of how pleasing it will be to sadly tell Pilate of Khalid's tragic accident. Especially when they were all so close to returning to Jerusalem.

Time passed by, and Octavian and his soldiers were entering the gates of Jerusalem. He decided to stop first at his private quarters and get a change of armor. Antonia Tower and the palace of Pilate would have to wait for him, he thought. As he entered through the gates of Antonia Fortress, he could not help but look at the Tower, and when he did, he saw Khalid waiting there with Vitali.

What? he thought. He angrily summoned his demons of Diana.

"Yes, Master."

"Why did you not do as I said and have Khalid's horse stumble and him fall to his death?"

"Oh, master, we feared to tell you, but now we must. We went as you said and caused his horse to stumble. He fell to the ground, hitting his head with a mighty blow. But alas, the demons within him were far greater in number and more powerful. We could not touch him nor do him any harm."

"And I suppose that counted as a valid request even though you failed me."

"Yes, master." they whispered.

"Now I must go directly to Pilate and defend myself against what Khalid might say," he mumbled under his breath." He turned his horse and went directly to Khalid.

"I trust you had time to think of what is best and have me speak to Pilate and not you," stated Octavian.

Khalid answered, "Again, we must both go before Pilate emptyhanded. I will not get my bounty, this is true. But you, Octavian, will be stripped of your rank. That is something I long to watch. And so, that is why I return to go with you before Pilate. Nothing more and nothing less." Vitali barked in agreement.

"You will rue this day, Khalid… both you and your precious Vitali." Octavian turned his horse and dismounted. He handed the reins to a sentry to hold. He walked away and secluded himself so no one could see him. He conjured his demons of Diana. They came.

"Yes, Master."

"I am to go before Pilate and give an account of my travels. Make certain that no matter what, Pilate does not strip me of my rank nor any bad thing take place from him to me. Make sure that he has more on his mind and he has no time to listen to our account."

"Yes, Master."

The demons summoned the Apprentice. "You did that very well, just like I told you." He laughed. "So now what does he want you to do?" They told him of his request, and the Apprentice answered, "Very well, let him have his request."

Octavian walked into Antonia Tower with Khalid and Vitali following behind. They no sooner went before the presence of Pilate and he shouted, "I have no time to hear of any account. Rome has many deserters, I care not of the one you pursue. There are greater things that concern Rome at this hour. I must make an account to Tiberius of greater matters that are of no concern to you. Go now, all of you."

Octavian and Khalid bowed and left. Vitali followed at Khalid's side.

"It is a good thing for you, Octavian, that Pilate had no time. There will be another day," said Khalid.

"Yes, there will be," scoffed Octavian, "There certainly will be."

THE CONTRACT

Khalid was standing by his horse. He had just left the Tower of Antonia and was not happy with the entire outcome of his hire. Khalid looked over to Vitali and said, "It is time to leave this place I have had by belly full of Octavian." Vitali barked in agreement.

"Pilate has no bounty for a deserter, and we have wasted enough time." As Khalid was grumbling, he was interrupted by a familiar voice.

"Well, there you are."

Khalid turned and looked, it was the Apprentice.

"Have you found the centurion and his spear?"

"He is an enigma. How can someone who only baffles the mind be found?" answered Khalid.

The Apprentice had grown tired of constantly having to remind Khalid of his agreement to find the centurion and the spear. He needed him to not only obtain the spear but to wield it as well. He devised a new plan, one he believed would remedy the fickle emotions of the bounty hunter. "He is in Jerusalem, just as I told you before. Now that you are free of following the fool, Octavian, he should not be hard for you to find."

"It is a pity that you have been cheated of your time by the Romans. Tell me, have I not always paid you for your effort?"

Khalid thought and answered, "You have."

The Apprentice smiled and said, "Indeed, I have. Now, I have an offer for you. Tell me, how would you like to earn more gold than you could spend and never have to chase thieves and deserters in the wilderness to earn it?"

"I am listening."

"All you have to do is find the centurion and take his spear. You will keep the spear and wield it for me as I tell you to do. Are you interested?"

"Wield it for you?" asked Khalid.

"Yes, wield it. You will be at my call to do what I ask you to do with the spear. My personal bounty hunter, or shall I say, my partner."

Khalid looked down at Vitali, then at the Apprentice, "We do not partner with any. We work alone and travel with no one."

"Oh, you will not travel with me. I work alone as well. You will simply carry the spear for me and be ready to use it as I say when I need you to use it. When I need you, I will find you. I will reward you for merely guarding the spear for me. It will be a contract, so to speak."

"Contract?" asked Khalid.

"A contract agreement that is no different than any other a bounty hunter would agree too. Only it will ensure that I do not get cheated of your services." The Apprentice pulled a coin pouch from beneath his cloak and held it out to Khalid. "Here are twenty gold coins. Take them and agree to do as I say, then I will tell you where you can find the centurion."

Khalid thought and said, "What about Vitali? We work together. What does she get?"

The Apprentice grinned and said, "Oh yes, Vitali." He pulled another pouch from beneath his cloak and said, "I believe there are twenty in this pouch as well. Shall I have her count them?"

Khalid looked over to Vitali and asked, "Do you want to count them?" Vitali barked. Khalid answered, "She said that I can count them for her."

The Apprentice handed the two pouches to Khalid and asked, "Then if the coins are all there, and if you and Vitali agree, I trust we have a contract?"

Khalid took the coin pouches and counted the gold. There were twenty gold coins in each pouch. He then said, "You have a contract. Now, where is the centurion?"

"He is in the city. He is no longer dressed as a Roman soldier; he now wears a robe and soft clothing. He is with the woman and the followers."

Khalid thought and said, "A man in a robe carrying a spear shall be easy to find."

"Well, there is one more thing," said the Apprentice. "He does not carry it with him. He has placed it somewhere. But a tall man in a robe with a woman should not be difficult to find as most of the people are of shorter stature. Look for a tall man in a robe."

Khalid dug around in his haversack and pulled out the cloth that he had used at the very beginning of his search. He tied it around his hand and reached it down to Vitali and said, "Sniff, Vitali, we go and find this man." Vitali smelled the cloth and barked.

The Apprentice said, "When you have found him, I will know. I will come to you then."

Khalid mounted his horse and he said to Vitali, "Come, first we find the man, then we find the spear, then we collect more gold."

Vitali barked and they rode off. The Apprentice smiled and disappeared in the shadows.

Then out from behind the gate, another figure appeared. It was Octavian. He was seething with anger and jealousy. Under his breath, in a vile evil voice, he said, "So the Apprentice betrays me with a mangy bounty hunter and a mangy dog. We shall just see. Let Khalid get the spear, and I will only take it from him. Then I will take my revenge. It will be most vile. I will get even with them all!"

THE MEETING ON THE ROAD

Mary shared the stories of her travel with Peter, John, and Mary. They were astounded at the way the Lord had worked his marvelous work with the man named Longinus and how the angel had come to her and told her of the storm and of the gift of the Holy Spirit. Peter shared his experience at the tomb and how Mary was right about all she had said. John shared that as many as 500 at a time had seen the Lord and heard him speak to them. Mary was full of spirit as she heard of all these things.

Mary was eager to find the Lord as the others had told her that he continued to appear to many. "I must find him. There is much that I desire to ask him," she said.

Mary, the mother of Jesus, took Mary's hand and said, "He knows when you search, and he knows you desire to see him. This I know in my heart. I believe he will find you and share with you all that you desire to know."

"Oh, my dear mother of Jesus, I believe this too," answered Mary with much happiness.

"Come," said John, "Let us all go to the tomb again. We may see him there."

"Oh yes," answered Mary. "Let us go again to the tomb."

Peter cautioned, "There is still a great guard there. It may not be safe for you to go."

Mary looked at Peter and said, "My Lord will let no harm come to me that is not mine to bear. I am not afraid."

John thought then answered, "We must all go together. We will not be forbidden to go to the tomb and to grieve as mourners do. In numbers, we shall be fine. Come, let us all go together."

Reluctantly, Peter agreed. And they left to see the tomb.

As they left the house and headed down the road, a stranger

came upon them and walked close behind. He heard them speak of the excitement of the chance to see the Lord.

"You, of who do you speak that you wish to see." Mary recognized in her heart the voice. She turned and there stood her Master.

"It is you that I wish to see." She ran to him and fell to his feet.

The man lifted up his head covering and pulled it back. Letting it drape over his shoulders, he put out his arms and Mary stood and embraced him.

"Oh master, my heart leaps inside to hold you again."

Jesus smiled and took his hand gently placing it beneath Mary's chin. He carefully lifted up Mary's face and looked deep into her eyes. He said, "There is much for you to do. The good news must be preached in all the world. You will find the place where I will send you. All in due time, for there is much that must be done here before you go. In a little while, I must ascend to my Father, and after that, you shall receive the Holy Spirit. All of the apostles with you shall receive it. Once you have the gifts that my Father has for you, then each one shall begin their journey. Each one will have their earthly destiny awaiting."

Mary stared into his eyes and did not want that moment to stop.

"Come let us walk together," Jesus said. "Follow me."

JOSEPH OF ARIMATHEA

Longinus was astounded at all he had learned from the witness who had been freed from the chains of Hades. As he walked along, he contemplated all the things the man had spoken to him. Then up ahead, he thought he recognized the man who had asked for the body of Jesus. He tried to remember the name that was on the sealed papers of Pilate. He could not remember it. He called out to the man, "You there?"

The man looked over to Longinus and said, "Yes."

"What is your name?"

"I am Joseph of Arimathea."

That is the name, thought Longinus as he walked toward the man. "I must speak with you."

"We can speak here."

"You are the one who took the body of Jesus at Golgotha to bury him. Are you not?"

Joseph hesitated and then said, "I am."

"I must ask, why did you ask for him?"

"What is your need to know?" asked Joseph.

"I am a friend of the woman named Mary who was with him at the cross," answered Longinus.

"My sister?" asked Joseph.

Longinus was surprised at hearing this, but did not let it show.

He answered, "Yes, your sister."

"What is it that you want?" asked Joseph.

"I want to know why you asked for his body and why you buried him in such a fine tomb?"

"Are you not aware of our customs?"

"No, I am not."

"I see. Well, the immediate family cannot request the body of a man who has been sentenced to death on a cross for a criminal act. It can only be requested by a distant relative. And so, I did what was custom. And what the Lord laid upon my heart to do. There was nowhere to bury him except in the tomb that I had prepared for my own burial."

"Immediate family? I do not understand," asked Longinus.

"Mary, my sister, was his mother," he answered. "Jesus was my nephew."

"Oh. I did not mean that Mary. I am friends with the woman, Mary of Magdalene, who was also at the cross."

Joseph raised his eyebrows and said, "Come, we must speak more, but not here in the streets."

Longinus followed with Joseph and they went to find a more secluded place where they could speak.

KHALID FINDS LONGINUS

Khalid and Vitali were busy going through the streets of Jerusalem in search of a tall man with a woman. Khalid had stopped every tall man he came across, but none of them had the scent that was on the cloth. Vitali continued to sniff the air, and Khalid kept his eyes peeled for a tall man.

Khalid looked at Vitali and said, "We would have a better chance finding a ghost than this enigma." Vitali barked in agreement. Then suddenly, Vitali sniffed the air and growled. She postured straight and pointed toward an alley. "You got the scent girl, don't ya?" he whispered.

Vitali growled low and proceeded toward the alley. Khalid followed. There in the alley were two tall men. Both were dressed in robes. One was much older than the other. It was Longinus and Joseph. Khalid slowly pulled his sword from his sheath. "This will be easy," he whispered to Vitali.

Vitali ran toward the younger tall man, barking fiercely as he ran. Longinus looked, then shouted to Joseph, "Run—it is me they are after!"

Longinus pulled back his robe and pulled his sword from its sheath. He raised it in the air and stood at the ready.

Khalid called to Vitali, "Halt, Vitali, I will take it from here." Khalid whipped his sword through the air in a threatening manner at Longinus and shouted, "Alas, the enigma has shown itself to me and is at the tip of my sword."

Longinus glanced quickly at the surroundings in the alley to access how he could escape. He backed up holding his sword with his eyes on Khalid.

"What trouble do you have with me?" Longinus asked.

"I have no trouble with you. I am a bounty hunter, and you have a big one on your head," said Khalid as he slashed his sword at him. Longinus blocked his swing with his sword and the metals clanged. They parried back and forth.

"Who has placed a bounty on my head?" shouted Longinus.

Khalid slashed his sword at Longinus and missed slicing a piece of stone off the wall of a building in the alley.

"That will be your head if you don't surrender yourself now," shouted Khalid.

"It will be more like your head, bounty hunter!" shouted Longinus as he gave a powerful slash clanging against the metal of Khalid's sword and sending it hurling to the ground.

Longinus lunged at Khalid backing him against the wall with the tip of his sword at his throat.

"Tell me, who has placed a bounty on my head?"

Vitali growled and crept toward Longinus snarling his teeth.

"Call off your dog, or I will thrust you now and then thrust her!"

Khalid was not sure what to do; he decided not to take any foolish chances. "Halt, Vitali." Vitali stopped, but stood growling, ready to attack, keeping her eyes on Longinus.

"There are many who have a bounty on your head," answered Khalid.

"Like who?"

"Pilate for one."

"Who else?"

"You will make this easier for yourself if you give me your spear."

"My spear?" asked Longinus.

"If you slice my throat, my dog will have your arm before you can retrieve your sword," shouted Khalid. "And I will not die fast, I will slice your throat open. You will not save your life, you will only make stupid choices!"

"What do you want with my spear?"

"That is worth more bounty than your head!" answered Khalid.

"Give me the spear and you will never have to see me again."

"I no longer have the spear," said Longinus, "It was taken from me in the Negev by a band of Bedouin thieves."

"I do not believe that," shouted Khalid. "A centurion could swat Bedouin thieves like flies."

"Who has placed a bigger bounty on the spear than that which is on my head?"

"A man who wants it."

"Do not mince words with me, bounty hunter, do you not feel the cold steel at your throat?"

"It is a sorcerer."

"A sorcerer? What is his name?"

"I only know him as the apprentice."

Longinus slowly pulled his sword away from Khalid's throat, but kept it pointed at his chest. "You have until I count to three to grab your dog and run."

"I do not run nor does my dog. You will finish this fight, or give me the spear," shouted Khalid.

"Are you a bounty hunter that can be trusted?"

"I have honor. Yes."

"Perhaps we can come to a reasoning then."

"What kind of reasoning?"

"I will let you and your dog go. I will meet you here tomorrow at the early dawn. I will bring you what you ask for. My spear."

"Why should we trust you?"

"Because I am a man of honor as well as reason."

Khalid looked over to Vitali and said, "Should we live to fight another day and trust this man?"

Vitali growled, then drew in the dirt with her paw. She drew two lines, the one she placed her paw print over, the other she placed her paw print on the side of the line.

"She says, we live to fight another day. If you do not do as you say, we find you. And we no longer listen to your reason."

Longinus withdrew his sword and said, "Now go and come back at the early dawn."

Khalid thought about attacking again, then decided to keep his honor. "Come, Vitali, first we go, then we come back at the early dawn, then we get the spear with the three blood red crosses."

Longinus was caught off guard to hear the bounty hunter say, Three blood red crosses, for he had thought to bring a roman hasta and tell him that was his spear.

Longinus stood guard and watched as they left. Then he ran down the alley as fast as he could. He thought to himself as he ran, *"I must leave Jerusalem. But I must take care of his demand first so he will not bother the others. How can I do that?"*

A PERFECT FORGERY AND A SAD FAREWELL

Longinus was torn with what to do. As he ran, his only comfort was the thing that he always turned to when he was confused. I must find a tavern, he thought. One drink will not hurt me, it will make me steady so I can think clearly. He slowed down and sought a tavern. In a little while, he found what he was looking for. He entered in and ordered a drink.

"Wine, your best," he said.

The barkeep hollered out, "A jug or a cup?"

Longinus answered, "A jug. Your best!"

The barkeep placed a jug before Longinus and said, "You don't look like the type that will drink a jug. Are you expecting friends?" Longinus felt a bit awkward and said, "I always find friends in a good place to share good wine."

The barkeep answered, "There are lots of thirsty in here, that is for sure."

Longinus poured a cup and drank it down. He poured another and did the same. All of a sudden, as though he were watching himself from afar, he stopped and thought, What am I doing? Have I come so far to forget my faith to turn to answers in a jug? He wondered at his thoughts, for this type of thinking was all new to him. Except for, as he recalled, the last time he sat down to drink.

"What has happened to me?" he questioned to himself as he looked at the cup in his hand.

He slowly poured one more cup and watched as the purple liquid fell from the jug. It no longer looked so beautiful and no longer tasted the same. He took a drink anyway. He thought of what good it would do him to be drunk from wine.

He placed the cup on the table and stared at it. He was in deep, serious thought. "I must decide what to do. How will I give the bounty hunter a spear by the morning? I have to leave Jerusalem. My head tells me to go now, but my heart says to tell Mary goodbye and to give the bounty hunter a spear. I feel so doomed. I need help."

He felt the urge to relieve his bladder and got up. As he walked toward the back door, he noticed a row of hastas against the wall. He looked around and saw soldiers were drinking and carrying on. He realized that he had been so consumed with wanting wine that he never noticed who was in the tavern. Now feeling relaxed, he had no fear. He continued on and went out the back to the alley to relieve himself.

As he stood in the back, doing what he needed to be done, he heard the cook holler out to a helper. "Get that chicken dressed out fast. The people are hungry."

He looked over and saw the helper cut off the neck and watched as the blood spurted out, falling to the ground. He saw where there was a lot of old blood from the killing of other chickens. Longinus now had an idea.

He went back into the tavern and casually went up to the row of hastas that leaned against the wall. He waited until everyone was so busy they did not notice him. He grabbed one up quickly and hurried past the busy people in the kitchen and out the back. He waited for a moment to see if anyone had noticed him. No one had. He ran over to the blood on the ground from where the helper had killed the chickens. He reached down and dipped his finger in the fresh blood. He strategically made three red crosses from his memory, exactly as they appeared on his spearhead.

"There," he said, "That will do. Now I will hide it in a safe place to dry."

He looked around and could not find a good place to hide the spear. He left the alley, going along very secretively. He found a place, close to where he was going to meet the bounty hunter. He hid the spear from sight. *There, that will be safe*, he thought to himself.

"Now I must return and let Mary know that I will be leaving at early dawn." He went to the house of John, with great sorrow. He had not known he would feel this sad on the day that he was to part from Mary. It was a feeling he had not experienced, but one time in his life. And one he had sworn to himself he would never allow himself to feel again. And now, here it was, back one more time, tearing at his heart.

It was now evening and the sun had gone down. He made his way to the house of John and knocked on the door. "Who is it?" asked John.

"It is I, Longinus."

"Oh, good, we have wondered of you. Mary will be glad to know you are back," said John as he opened the door, "Mary, Longinus has returned."

Mary ran to the front of the door, and she exclaimed, "I have seen my Lord. We talked of many things. I have so much to tell you."

"And I have much to tell you. I must leave Jerusalem at early dawn. It is for the best and to protect you and your good friends."

Mary's glee turned quickly to surprise and then to sorrow as she understood the words Longinus had just spoken. "But why?" she asked.

"There has been a confrontation today. A bounty hunter wants my spear. I have had to bargain with him, and tomorrow, we meet at early dawn. I must complete my bargain and leave this place. If I stay I will be hunted down, and they will hunt you down as well."

"Has the Lord told you to do this thing?" asked Mary.

"I…I do not understand your question," answered Longinus.

"This thing I must do is for the good of all."

"Is this your idea or is it his?" asked Mary.

"Well, I…I..."

"Have you prayed to him and asked him what he would have you do? Or did you drink strong wine and decide this for yourself?"

Longinus felt embarrassed. For the first time since he could remember, he thought of how a woman could always smell his wine when he drank. "It is what he would have me do," he answered.

Mary looked at him and regretted what she had just said. "I will miss you."

"And I will miss you," answered Longinus.

Mary gave him a strong hug. "Come, we must talk. I must share with you the many things that happened today before you rest. For tomorrow, you will be gone at early dawn and there will be no time."

Longinus's heart sunk to hear Mary reflect that there would be no time after the early dawn. But he knew he had to go. For Mary did not understand the ways of bounty hunters nor did he know if she understood the power of the Roman army. He did not want any harm to come to her or her friends.

They spoke and Mary shared her stories of the Lord, and Longinus shared how he had met Joseph. They talked until it was almost early dawn. Longinus said to her, "Mary, you must get some rest, early dawn is almost here."

Mary answered, "So what if it is. This last time with you is more important to me than a few hours of rest. Unless you are tired. I will wait with you until it is time for you to go."

Longinus was not a man of tears, but in hearing Mary say such a kind thing, he felt as though he might cry. He quickly gained his composure and said, very stoic, "You must rest. I will leave at early dawn. We will meet again. When the Lord wills it to be so."

Mary looked at Longinus and said, "Perhaps you are right." She gave him one last hug, then slowly took a few steps away from him. She turned back around and ran up to him, giving him a strong hug and said, with tears streaming down her cheeks, "You, silly centurion, you take care of yourself. Pray to the Lord and he will guide you."

Longinus could not bear her words for they touched his heart. A tear shot down from both of his eyes as he tried as hard as he could to hold them back. His mouth had become so dry that he could not speak. He swallowed hard to wet his mouth, and taking a deep breath, he said, "I will."

Early Dawn

Longinus could not sleep. He kept reliving the last moments spent with Mary. Finally, early dawn came and he was up and ready to depart. He gathered his haversack and went to where Mary was sleeping. He took one last longing look at her, then he turned and left the house of John.

He made his way to the alley where he had hidden the spear. It was right where he had left it. He picked it up and touched the blood. It had dried and hardened nicely. He will never know this is not the real spear, he thought.

Longinus hid his haversack in a manner he knew it would not be found. He thought, If I do not make it back, may the Lord do what he will with the spearhead in the haversack. He then made his way to the alley where they had fought and waited for the bounty hunter.

Early dawn was just beginning to pass and Longinus was beginning to wonder if the bounty hunter was going to come. He began to think of what he should do, if he did not appear. He wondered if he should leave the spear he had made in the alley or take it and return to the house of John and wait until he heard anything else.

He shrugged his head, for he knew he was only thinking of a way to see Mary one more time. Wait, I must wait, he thought. It was only but a few minutes more, and Longinus sighted Khalid and his dog Vitali coming down the alley.

"I thought you had forgotten," said Longinus.

"Haa. You came. We thought this would be a fool's errand and you would not show. So we took time to have food," shouted Khalid.

Longinus stood erect, holding the spear. He waited for Khalid and Vitali to come closer and he said, "Can I trust that you come for the spear and the spear only? Or shall I have to draw my sword?"

Khalid looked down at Vitali and asked, "What answer do we give the man?"

Vitali growled, then barked. Khalid shouted, "She says if you do as you said. You need not draw your sword. If you do not, then dare to draw it, we are ready."

"Such a wise dog you have. I have never seen such a breed. Tell me, what is she?"

"She is rare, one of a kind. Besides her, there will never be a one as she." Khalid always loved to brag on Vitali and had never denied to answer any one who asked questions of her. She was his pride, his other half, his very soul's mate.

"Here is the spear. Take it and go. You will not find me here after today, for I leave Jerusalem," stated Longinus." If we meet again, I will not be as gracious with my honor, nor my reasoning."

Khalid approached and reached out his hand to take the sword, "There should be no reason to meet again. Not if you have dealt with your honor. Vitali and I do not trust any man's reasoning. You can take that with you."

Khalid then took the spear from Longinus. He examined it closely." It looks like it is the one that was told for me to get."

"Then, we are settled here. I trust on your honor that you shall collect your bounty and not bother me again."

Khalid held up the spear and waved it as he said, "Shew now, shew like a bothersome fly that I need rid of!"

Longinus shook his head and left quickly as Khalid laughed, and Vitali barked a high pitch canine bark that sounded like she was laughing too.

Khalid turned to Vitali and said, "First, we find the apprentice, then we collect our bounty, and then..."

"Not so fast," interrupted Octavian who had been secretly watching and suddenly made his presence known.

"Where did you come from?" asked Khalid.

"I have been following you bounty hunter. And now, I will have that," said Octavian as he grabbed the spear from Khalid's hand.

"I will judge whether this is real or this is a forgery. You are nothing but a foolish bounty grubber and know nothing of fine weaponry."

Vitali growled. Khalid looked down at her and said, "Easy girl, I can take care of this."

Octavian started to walk away and Khalid drew his sword. The sound of steel sleeking across leather, accompanied by a swish of air, caught Octavian's ears. He turned and looked at Khalid, who had just drawn his sword and was holding it ready to battle. Octavian stood and laughed. "Do you really dare to challenge me?" he scoffed.

"You will give me back what is mine. If you do not, then I will take it back from you," shouted Khalid. Vitali growled and gnarled her teeth. She moved closer to Octavian.

"Call that mangy thing back," shouted Octavian.

Khalid stood and watched as Vitali continued to move closer to Octavian.

"This is my last warning. Demand that thing you call a dog to halt. I have powers you know." Khalid watched as Octavian summoned his demons. "Demons of Diana, I summon you to kill the dog."

The demons of Diana summoned the Apprentice regarding Octavian's request. The apprentice was angry at this, for both Khalid and Vitali were now under his contract. He shouted at the demons,

"He shall not have such a request! Tell that fool that you have no power over the breed that Khalid possesses as Vitali has the breeding from the underworld. Let him know that if any evil comes to the dog, strange and awful things will happen!"

"Yes, master," they answered. Then they quickly returned to Octavian and whispered in his ear, "Alas, we would, but we have no power over that animal, for he has the breeding from the underworld. If any evil comes to the dog, strange and awful things will happen."

Khalid watched and thought to himself, Octavian has some strange sickness. It must be from the poisoned water. He has not been the same since he fell ill. He is out of his mind. He thought to call Vitali away from Octavian, but for some reason hesitated. He looked at Octavian's eyes and the whites were all he could see.

Octavian, who appeared to Khalid to be in a trance, finished listening to his demons and glared at Vitali. Livid at the answer from his demons, his hatred and jealousy of Khalid raged inside of him. He looked at Vitali and shouted, "Then I shall do this myself!"

Khalid called out to Vitali, "Come, Vitali, come here!" At the very moment Khalid called out, Octavian thrust the spear into the side of Vitali.

Vitali let out a bloodcurdling yelp and fell on her side. Octavian pulled the spear from her and looked at Khalid as Vitali continued to yelp and wailed.

"No-o-o!" roared Khalid. "No-o-o!" He ran to her side and held on to her.

Octavian glared at Khalid and Vitali and shouted, "You are next." Khalid raged at Octavian, "You are a dead man walking!" At hearing Khalid's words, Octavian seemed to wake out of a mad man's actions and realized the consequences of what he had just done. Fearing that Khalid would kill him, Octavian ran away.

Khalid held on to Vitali as she yelped and whimpered. His tears streamed down his cheeks, falling onto Vitali's head. "Don't die, Vitali!" he wailed. "Hang on, girl! Hang on! I'm here. I will help you girl." He heaved up Vitali, whose size was that of a lion, and carried her through the alley and then aimlessly in the street shouting,

"Help, I need a physician, help."

The Apprentice Avenges Khalid...
As Khalid made his way seeking help for Vitali, he refused to accept that she was dead. The people feared the rugged-looking man, carrying a dead dog and yelling for help, mingled with threats against Octavian.

Khalid fell to the ground and raised his fist in the air and shouted, "I swear by the death of Vitali that I shall avenge her death! Octavian is a dead man walking! May the gods curse him to the end of his days!"

As he was grieving, he saw a set of feet standing before him. He looked up; it was the Apprentice.

"I have been watching you," he said. "I am grieving with you." Khalid collected himself as much as he could and said, "I will kill him for this."

The Apprentice nodded and said, "I do not blame you. I would do the same. However, I have a better idea in mind."

"Take the spear from him, but do not worry of your revenge. I will take care of that. For as I watched you mourn, I decided what I shall do. I will curse him above all walking curses. Death is too good for him. I will make him suffer in the flesh. He is so pompous. I thought of no better way to have him suffer than to have a physical form so hideous that others could not look upon. So hideous that he must hide himself away and fear to even look upon himself.

"And what more can I add to that, but to cause him to suffer physical pain. Death would be too good for him. Don't you agree?"

Khalid answered, "So do it."

The Apprentice answered, "It shall be done," and began to chant an evil curse.

"By the powers of darkness that belong to me, I curse the one who speared Vitali. May his face rot off and his belly fill with worms, I bequeath all my powers, these are my terms. May his stench be so strong, no one comes near, may he cringe with horror when he looks in the mirror. To be cured he shall long for, but for him, it will tarry, for as long as he lives, this curse he shall carry."

There was a strange rumbling and the ground shook for a moment. The Apprentice looked at Khalid and said, "It is done."

He turned to him and said, "When you are ready, go and get the spear. I will know when you do this and come to you. You shall wield it for me and I will give you your gold and the gold for Vitali. For my contract is binding even in her death."

The Apprentice took one last look at Khalid and knew it would take some time for him to recover from Vitali's demise.

"If I could do something more, I would," said the Apprentice and then he left.

KHALID AT THE GARDENS OF CALVARY

It was now past dawn, and Khalid continued to ask for help for Vitali. Those that heard him wailing in the streets, holding his dead dog, were afraid and quickly ran away. "Help, somebody help me please," he called out. No one came.

Khalid carried Vitali through the city for a long while, then in desperation, he left and headed up the long trek to Mt. Calvary to the gardens. He found a place and laid Vitali down. He looked at her and continued to grieve. His heart was wrenched and his soul was cut into. Vitali had been dead for a while, but Khalid refused to see it. His mind wandered without any direction. He was numb and filled beyond any man's capacity with grief.

He pulled his dagger out from a harness on his chest. Looking up to the sky he shouted, "I swear Octavian shall woe the day he did this evil."

Wailing out and grieving his loss, his mind was triggered back to the death of his mother. Khalid had told the story to Vitali many times. Vitali would always listen and offer comfort. Khalid thought back and remembered.

He saw himself a young boy again. He recalled that his father was off in the fields. The Parthians were ravaging his village and his mother called out for him to hide. Reliving the horrible memory of his mother being slain, he envisioned the Parthian wielding his sword at his mother's head, sending it rolling to the ground. Her long braid, severed at the neck lay next to it. He saw himself looking at his dead mother's head and picking up the braid, clenching onto it in grief.

His mind shifted to the day his father tired of seeing him holding the braid. For whatever reason, whether it was his own grieving or just believing it was not good for Khalid to cling to it, he recalled the struggle trying to hold on to the braid as his father tore it from his hands and threw it in the fire. The smell of it burning was still in his nostrils. He remembered his self-comfort in swearing that he would grow a braid and never cut that lock from the back of his head in memory of his mother. Whenever he felt forlorn, he would touch his braid and feel her comfort.

Khalid looked down at his tender Vitali, now dead and lifeless. Grieving so in his heart, he took his dagger and cut his long braid. He held it up as an offering of penitence for not being able to save her life from evil Octavian. He beat his chest in agony. He was just a moment too late, and in that action, he would forever sorrow.

He then placed his braid between her paws. "Remember me," he mourned, then stroking Vitali's long coat he wailed out and lamented over her death.

After a long while, Khalid stood up and looked for a wooden branch suitable for digging. He found one and began to dig into the ground. He dug diligently and then frantically, laboring to make a hole deep enough for a burial.

He grieved and wailed all the while. When it was deep enough, he lifted her up and clung to her cold body, giving her one last embrace. Then he gently lowered her into the freshly dug grave, making sure to secure the braid between her paws.

Slowly he began to rake the dirt over the top of her with his hands; he stopped and howled out her name in great grief, "Vitali, Vitali, Vitali!" He wailed and mourned until he fell faint and passed out on top of her open grave.

THE STABLEMAN

Longinus ran to the alley where he had hidden his haversack and grabbed it up. He ran to where he remembered seeing a stable. He went up to the man outside at an anvil, pounding out a horseshoe.

"I need a horse."

"I have some good ones. How much are you paying?" asked the man.

"Give me what this will buy," said Longinus as he handed the man some coins.

The man added the coins and said, "Roman silver will buy you a strong horse."

He came out with a horse, complete with saddle and a fine bridle. "This one is used to traveling the wilderness as well as the Roman roads . Oh, how rough they are," he complained.

Longinus mounted the horse and got a feel for how it handled, then he said, "Thank you." He wasted no time in leaving. All he wanted was to get out of the city as fast as he could. The man stood and watched and said to himself, "Now he was in a hurry." Then he went back to his work at the anvil.

As Longinus rode, he decided to head for the ports in Joppa. They were the biggest ports and the most busy. He would find it easier to move around in a port where a lot of ships were coming and going. I will find a mariner with a small ship, he thought. It will be easier for me to bargain my passage with one as that. I will go to Rome, no one will think to look for me there.

Longinus traveled quickly toward the ports of Joppa.

MARY MEETS KHALID

Mary was up and helping Mary, the mother of Jesus, prepare bread. They had just finished a fine breakfast and were busy preparing food for the afternoon meal.

"I hope he is safe in his travels," said Mary.

"He is a strong man. He will do just fine. Come, let us finish this and then go to the market and get fresh fruit."

Mary smiled and said, "Oh, that sounds wonderful."

The women finished their preparations and headed to the market. When they were there, they heard the merchant telling a story of a big man and how he had gone mad in the streets holding his dead dog. They said he was a bounty hunter. Mary was nervous in hearing the story. She feared Longinus might have something to do with this.

She asked the merchant, "This bounty hunter, did he say what had happened to the poor dog?"

"No, but he was yelling that the man that did this was a dead man walking, and he called out for the gods to curse him until the end of his days."

Mary gasped. "Did he say who this man was?"

"Let me think…it was a funny name…Tavian? No, that's not it, oh, it was Octavian. Yes, that is it, Octavian. Oh, he kept rambling about his dog. People were afraid and ran from him. It was a pitiful sight."

"Where did this man go?" asked Mary.

"Funny thing, I heard he was seen taking his dead dog toward the gardens on top of the hill."

"Calvary?" questioned Mary.

"That is what I heard," said the merchant.

Mary turned to the mother of Jesus and said, "I must go there. Something inside me has said that I must go there."

"Then go. Always listen to your heart. I will take care of the marketing. Go now."

"Oh, thank you," answered Mary, and she headed off quickly to the gardens.

Mary arrived at the hill, and as she made her way to the gardens, she said a prayer for the grieving man and his dog. She saw a big man starting to awake and watched him look into a freshly dug hole. The man looked so grieved, then suddenly his sad countenance changed to joy.

"You are alive!" he shouted as reached inside the hole and pulled out a huge dog the size of a lion. "You are not gone!" Khalid looked at her side where the spear had entered in, "You are alive!" The blood had formed a scab over the wound. And Vitali was going to live.

Tears of joy streamed down his cheeks and he held Vitali tight.

"I will remember this place forever," he shouted. "This place where my Vitali woke from her grave and returned to me."

Mary walked up to the man, holding his dog, and asked, "Are you the man they call the bounty hunter?"

Khalid answered, "I am. I'm also called Khalid."

"And is this the dog that the people have said was dead? Or have they been mistaken?"

"She is alive. I had thought she was dead, but she was not. I almost buried the poor thing alive, didn't I, Vitali?" Vitali barked.

"What caused such a thing?" asked Mary. "Why did you think she was dead?"

"A centurion meddled in my affairs and speared her side," he answered.

"A centurion?" asked Mary.

"A mad man at that. He was chasing a man for a spear. I got the spear and he grabbed it from me and speared my dog with it."

"I don't understand? Please explain," asked Mary.

"Oh, it's just what happens to bounty hunters," he said, not wanting to explain.

"I do so want to know," pleaded Mary.

"I tracked down a Roman deserter, but now, Pilate has no bounty for his head, but a man offered me a bigger bounty to get his spear. I got the spear from the deserter, and the centurion stole it right out of my hands. I drew my sword to fight to get it back, and my girl Vitali was ready to eat him alive, when the centurion was acting crazy again, and the whites of his eyes were all I could see, and he stabbed my Vitali in the side with the spear. I feared she died, but she lives."

"What was the name of the deserter?" asked Mary.

"Longinus."

"Did he escape?"

"He did not escape, he merely ran away. We had a deal, made with our honor. He followed through with his part and I followed through with mine. He left. It is the senior centurion that I am after now to get my spear back. You see, these are things that make no sense to a woman."

"Oh, it is hard to understand. But the man who gave you the spear, he went on his way?"

"Yes."

Mary smiled and looked at Vitali. She said, "What a beautiful dog, he looks like a lion. And what a noble name, Vitali."

"It is a she," corrected Khalid, "and she is a beauty!"

"It must have been of great sorrow to you to have been through so much," said Mary.

"Yes, it broke my heart. But now, I see she is alive and I am so joyful."

"I understand how that feels," said Mary.

"Oh, I'm not sure that you do. I even dug a grave for her," said Khalid as he pointed over to the grave he had just filled in. He then took the braid and wrapped it around Vitali's collar.

"I hope to see you again," offered Mary and she reached over to pet Vitali. As she stroked her coat, she looked at the long braid that Khalid had just attached to her chain collar. "This is a most unusual decoration," she said.

Khalid looked at Mary and said, "It is a sign of our bond. You would not understand such things."

Mary knew that it was a human haired braid and she wondered. "I would understand such things." She continued petting Vitali and said, "There are many ways to show a bond. You must cherish her so to have given her such a great gift."

Khalid felt a tear well up in his eye. He asked, "Woman, what is your name?"

"Mary," she answered. "Mary of Magdalene."

Khalid looked surprised and said, "So you are the woman?"

Mary looked confused, "What do you mean?"

"Oh, we searched for you as well. No bounty on your head, just orders to arrest you."

"Of that, I am aware," said Mary. She held out her hands and said, "Do you wish to arrest me now?"

Vitali looked at Khalid and growled. Khalid looked at Vitali and said, "Lay off, girl, I will do no such thing." Vitali barked happily.

"Mary, you must be careful. These are tricky times. The crazy centurion means you harm. The same one that tried to kill my Vitali may just do the same to you."

"I am not afraid of Romans."

Khalid smiled at Mary and said, "You have the heart and spirit of my Vitali. She likes you. And I think I do too."

Mary smiled and said, "And I like you and your most beautiful girl Vitali."

Khalid started to leave and shouted to Vitali, "Come, we must find the spear."

Mary watched as they left, then shouted out to them, "Khalid, I hope we will meet again."

Khalid stopped for a moment, looked back at Mary, and smiled. Then he continued on.

Mary Warns the Others

Mary left the gardens of Mt. Calvary and returned to the home of John. She shared with the others what Khalid had told her and that it was the spear they sought.

John spoke, "It is a strange thing that they seek the spear that pierced the side of our Lord. What would Romans want with that? The important thing is that you are safe. Perhaps if Pilate no longer seeks Longinus, he no longer seeks you."

Mary, the mother of Jesus, said, "You will be safe, do not fear. But with all that is taking place in Jerusalem, it may be best to be cautious in public places. At least for now."

"You are right," said Mary. "I will do well to be cautious. I have seen how they do."

OCTAVIAN IS CURSED

Octavian returned to Antonia Fortress and went directly to his private quarters, holding his coveted spear. He opened the door and turned to the sentry standing guard and said, "I do not want any interruptions. Summon me for no one. Not even Pilate, is that understood?"

"Yes, sir."

Once inside, he bolted the door. Like a mad man, he ran over to the lamp and lit the oil. He held the spear close to it and gazed upon it and spoke in a soft eerie voice, "Finally, you are back in my hands."

As he examined the spear under the hot lamp, the whites of his eyes turned yellow. Then red veins speckled through the yellow, they began to bulge and a tiny worm slithered from his tear duct along his lower lash. It slithered along his lash line and then burrowed back under, beneath his eye.

Octavian rubbed his eye, then he continued to examine the spear. He was so engrossed with the spear that he did not know that open sores were forming on his face, here and there on his cheek, nose, forehead, and chin. His lips began to burn, and he pulled away from the hot lamp. He put his finger to his lip and touched it. He pulled it back and looked, there was blood. He touched his lip again and looked at his finger; there was green pus mingled with blood. It had a foul stench.

Suddenly, he dropped the spear. He looked down at his hands, and they were full of oozing sores.

He remembered what the apprentice had said to him about the rotting carcass and the spear, that if it had been the real spear he would have died or brought some awful curse on himself. He wondered of the dog, the demons had told him he was bred from the powers of the underworld.

He thought, What have I done? He tore his breast of armor off and tore open his tunic; his chest and stomach was full of lumps that were moving as though he were full of worms. In a panic, he summoned his demons of Diana.

"Demons of Diana, I summon you to tell me what has happened to me. Am I cursed by the spear or is it something else? What is this horrid thing taking place with my body?"

The demons quickly summoned the Apprentice. The Apprentice answered and said to them, "I knew it was only a matter of time and he would have you summon me. Don't tell me, he wonders what has happened to his wretched body, is that it?"

The demons answered, "Yes, Master."

"Tell Octavian that because he took the spear with three blood red crosses upon it and used it to kill a dog that was bred by the underworld, he has what he has. If he asks you how to cure it, tell him the only way is to return the spear to the one that he stole it from. And that one is Khalid. Then bother me no more with his incessant pleas."

"Yes, Master."

The demons returned to Octavian and said, "You are cursed because you took the spear with three blood red streaks upon it and speared a dog that was bred from the underworld."

"Then heal me, I command you to remove this curse," shouted Octavian as his flesh continued to rot away.

"Alas, we cannot, for the only way you can remove this curse is to return the spear that you stole to the one you stole it from, that one is Khalid."

Octavian ran to a mirror and looked at his face. The skin was rotting and peeling off, some places were already exposing muscle. He shrieked in horror. He could not stand to look at himself. He did not want anyone else to see his hideous appearance.

He went to a chest over by the wall and pulled out a clean tunic; he shredded it in strips. He took the strips and covered his face, wrapping it as he had seen the lepers do. Leaving his eyes exposed and overlapping his nose with a gap, so he could breathe, and an opening for his mouth to speak. *I can't go to Khalid like this*, he thought. But I must.

Octavian picked up the spear and tried to think of what to tell the sentry. He looked at the spear's head and noticed the three red crosses were half gone. He looked closer and the blood was warm and running. The heat from the lit lamp had caused the blood to melt.

"Why, this is not the real spear!" he said in a rage. "The blood is dripping away from the heat." He stood there thinking, then suddenly he said, "Longinus? Or is it the Apprentice? Curses, he's done it again."

Again, he summoned his demons of Diana, "Tell me demons of Diana—what is this spear and where did it come from. Where is the real one? Is it with Longinus? "

The demons answered, "We are sorry, master. You have already had your two requests filled for the day. Summon us tomorrow and we can answer."

"Argh!" screamed Octavian.

JOPPA AND THE FISHING BOAT

Longinus made his way to Joppa. When he arrived, something inside told him to tarry there. He didn't know why, but he was learning to listen to his heart and not just let his head rule him. I must find a way to earn some coin if I am to stay, he thought. I know nothing but how to be a soldier. But I can do labor. Perhaps I can work for a fishing boat. Mary did say once that I looked like a fisherman ready for hire by a great fishing boat.

Longinus made his way into a tavern to look about and see if there were any fishermen looking for crew members. He ordered a cup of wine and looked around.

He asked the barkeep, "Any word on fishing boats looking to hire?"

"Ask the man over there. He buys fish from a lot of them in Joppa."

He looked over and saw a well-dressed man sitting alone and studying a map. Longinus went over and said, "The barkeep said you buy from many of the fishing boats in Joppa."

The man looked up, "I do. Why do you ask?"

"I'm looking for hire. Where can I find one that pays well?"

"None pay well, but there are many who seek strong men who will work hard." He then pointed and said, "Over there, that man, he is a mariner with a great fishing boat."

Longinus looked over and saw a clean-dressed man of African descent, sitting with a man who appeared to be Bedouin. He asked, "What is his name?"

"He likes to be called Mariner. His name is Adolla, but call him Mariner."

"I will, you have been most helpful," said Longinus as he made his way over to the mariner's table.

"I was told you are the Mariner."

The mariner looked up at Longinus curiously and said, "I am."

"I have heard you have the greatest fishing boat in Joppa."

"I do."

"I seek to work for a great mariner as you."

"Have you experience on the open sea?"

"I have survived the greatest tempest the wind and the sea has ever conjured up, a tempest so great even the finest of mariners would try and abandon their ship. I live to go out and weather anything the sea dare bring."

"My, you tell great tales. You will make a fine fisherman." The Mariner thought a moment then said, "I will give you a chance to prove your worth. If you fare as well as you speak, you can join my crew. If you speak tales, you will be dismissed."

"I will fare as well as I say. When do we sail?"

"Tomorrow before dawn. My ship has a red sail with a white dove in the middle. The only one of its kind. You will have no problem finding it at the fishing docks. Meet me there early. Or we sail without you."

The next morning, Longinus found the Mariner's ship. It was strongly built and had a regal look. The sail was down, but he could see the Mariner.

He called out to him, "Where do you want me?"

The Mariner looked and said, "Hang back at the stern for now. Until I know what you can do, my men will take care of getting her out to sea."

Longinus climbed on board and stood at the stern. He watched as the men busied themselves preparing the ship. It was not long and they raised the sail, and it was indeed as the Mariner had said, one of a kind. The depth of red was so deep it made the white dove appear to almost illuminate.

"I am going to like this," Longinus stated with a firm smile.

KHALID FINDS A CURSED OCTAVIAN

Khalid and Vitali walked down the steep hill, looking over to Antonia Fortress. "First, we get the spear, then we wait for the apprentice, then we give it to him and tell him we need no contract. It is time to live a simple life." Vitali barked in agreement. "I have had enough of endless chasing and putting your life in danger. I know when a man must change his direction. We will return home to Syria."

Khalid and Vitali arrived at the gate of Antonia Fortress and went straight to Octavian's private quarters. The sentry standing guard raised his hasta and motioned for them to halt.

"Octavian is seeing no one."

"Did I ask permission?" said Khalid as he knocked the sentry down to the floor and pummeled the back of his neck. "There, permission granted, Vitali."

As he tried to open the door, he found it was bolted shut from the inside. "Stand back, Vitali," he said as he took several paces, back then ran, lunging forward into the door with his massive body, bursting it open.

Octavian stood with his back turned, wearing a robe with a hood covering his head. "Leave!" he demanded.

"Not without the spear!" shouted Khalid.

"Take it and go!" he pointed to it, lying on the floor.

Khalid looked and saw Octavian's hand was full of sores and the bone of his forefinger was exposed between his nail and his knuckle. There was a putrefactive stench coming from his body. He bent down and cautiously picked up the spear and began to leave.

He turned and asked, "Why do you give this up so easy?"

"It is worthless. You were deceived."

Vitali let herself be known by growling at Octavian." Your dog, she is alive?"

"She lives," answered Khalid.

"But I was told she was bred by the underworld and had the power to curse me in her death."

Khalid let out a big laugh. "Now who is deceived?" He took a closer look at the back of Octavian and curiously asked, "Why did you want to kill her?"

"I heard you make your deal with the Apprentice. I had a deal as well. He betrayed me. I knew you couldn't work without her so I killed her. Now go and enjoy your new contract. My hope is that you receive the same reward as I."

"Reward?"

At that moment, Octavian slowly turned around and looked at Khalid. His face was wrapped in strips of cloth. His eyes were being eaten away at the socket, and his lip was eaten away from his face, exposing his gums and teeth at the side. Khalid turned his head and cringed at the sight.

"It was the poison water. You have been struck with a plague."

Octavian shouted, "It is a curse I have been struck with. An evil curse. The only way to rid this is to find the Old Man that is the mentor to the Apprentice. He can override his Apprentice's curse."

Khalid shook his head, "You have gone mad. You are a dead man walking, just as I said when you speared my Vitali. I was going to kill you, but now, I have no need to do anything more."

Khalid and Vitali turned and left.

Octavian went to the mirror. He lifted back his hood and started to unwrap the cloth from his face. As he removed the strips, chunks of skin clung to the cloth. His face was coming off as he pulled away each strip. He could not bear to pull any more away from his face for fear he would have no face left at all. He

THE SPEAR OF DESTINY

screamed in agony in the mirror. "Demons of Diana, bring me the Old Man. He can heal me and lift this curse."

The demons feared Octavian may well die and they would have no host. But, they knew the orders were to summon the Apprentice before doing anything and so they did.

The Apprentice heard them summon and asked, "What is it now?"

"He has summoned us again to bring him the Old Man to heal him and lift his curse."

The Apprentice laughed a devious laugh and said, "Ha! Tell Octavian that the Old Man says that he is busy now, come and ask again tomorrow."

The demons returned to Octavian, "The Old Man is busy and will not be interrupted. We must wait and ask him tomorrow."

"I demand you to ask him now!" roared Octavian.

"We really want to, but we are not allowed."

Hearing that, Octavian screamed out in agony.

The demons shuddered and chattered nervously among each other. "Should we give him some healing?" asked one of them. "NO!" answered another, "If we do we will be cast back to Hades."

"But if we don't", said another, "We will be cast back in his death."

They decided to summon the Old Man again.

"What is it now?" asked the Apprentice.

"We fear if he dies what will happen to us?"

"You summoned me for that? Be gone or I will give you something to fear!"

The demons left.

The Apprentice sneered, "Indeed...I hadn't really thought of that."

NEVER TRUST AN APPRENTICE

Khalid and Vitali waited outside of Antonia Fortress for the apprentice to appear. He looked at the spear and saw the three blood red crosses were now only a few stains of blood.

"Something is not right, Vitali."

Vitali gave a yelp, then growled.

Khalid thought a moment and said, "I believe it is true that a curse was placed on Octavian. I want nothing more to do with the apprentice. Vitali barked in agreement.

"First, we return the spear, then we return the gold, then we return to Syria." Vitali nodded.

Suddenly, the Apprentice appeared. "Your Vitali is well I see. Hmm?" Then he smiled and asked, "So you have the spear?"

"I have the spear that Octavian had. I fear he was deceived. The spear, it does not look right." He handed it to the apprentice.

The Apprentice refused to touch the spear, "Hold it up for me to see."

Khalid held it up, and the Apprentice did not sense any power from it. He cautiously took it from him. He then examined it. "It is a forgery. You must find the deserter named Longinus and bring me the real one."

"We no longer want to bounty hunt. We are done with that. We will return your gold." Khalid reached under his leather harnesses and pulled out the money pouches that were tied to the backs of them, and he held them out to the Apprentice.

"Keep them. They are of no use to me. Your contract is still binding, you know."

"We have no contract if we have no gold. Take your gold."

"I gave you the gold for your effort. Let us reason this."

"I trust no man's reason. And I see you have little honor."

"What are you saying to me?" asked the Apprentice very surprised.

"I saw Octavian. He is rotting with a stench like that of a man in his grave. He said you betrayed him and cursed him with your sorcery. Is this true?"

The Apprentice was angered. "I told you I would curse Octavian for revenge of the death of Vitali when you desired to kill him, that death was too good for him. I would make him suffer in the flesh with a physical form so hideous that others could not look upon. So hideous that he must hide himself away and fear to even look upon himself. And what more can I add to that, but to cause him to suffer physical pain. And you said to me, 'So do it.'"

"If I agreed to such a thing, it was only in my grieving. I would never agree to what I saw."

"You will find the spear for me and do as I say or else."

"Or else what? Will you curse me to rot like Octavian?"

"Octavian has filled your head with lies and confusion."

"We decided to give you the spear and be done before we knew Octavian was cursed. We are done doing bounty hunter work."

Vitali barked in agreement.

"I see. Well then, I will have to find another. It has been most unusual doing business with you. I will take the gold. It will be needed to pay another."

Khalid tossed the pouches of gold to the Apprentice and looked down at Vitali and said, "Come, we go now."

As they walked out of sight, the Apprentice held the pouches of gold and said under his breath, "A man in prison has no need for gold." He then burst out a sinister laugh.

He summoned the demons of Diana.

"Yes, Master," they answered.

"Go to Octavian and tell him there just may be a way to please the old man. Suggest to him that if he has Khalid arrested, he may receive some healing."

"Yes, Master."

The demons hurried to Octavian and whispered in his ear, "Oh, Master, we have summoned the Old Man again for you because we felt pity. He has told us that if you have Khalid arrested, he may give you some healing."

Octavian regained a bit of spirit and said, "Tell the Old Man I will do as he says straight away."

"Yes, Master," whispered the demons.

Octavian quickly moved to the table with writing instruments and parchment, then wrote an order to have Khalid arrested on charges of conspiring against Rome by aiding a deserter named Longinus, for assaulting a sentry at his post, and breaking and entering into the private quarters of a Roman centurion at Antonia Fortress. He then called for a sentry.

"Yes, sir."

Octavian opened the door just enough to pass the order to the sentry. He closed the door, leaving just a crack open, and spoke to the sentry his orders, "Give this order of arrest to my centurion, Gaius. Have him carry it out with haste, and bring me word when this man is in the prison."

"Yes, sir."

Octavian summoned his demons of Diana and said, "Tell the Old Man it is being done."

"Yes, Master."

OCTAVIAN ORDERS KHALID'S ARREST

The sentry guard delivered the arrest order to the centurion named Gaius. He read the order and sent word to Octavian that it would be done.

Gaius and his detachment sent out to find the bounty hunter named Khalid and his dog. They spent several days searching through Jerusalem and he was not to be found. No one knew that he had returned home to Syria.

During this time, Octavian was no longer able to do his duty and word was sent to Pilate of his condition. Pilate feared he had a leper's plague or something worse. But in an act of pity, he allowed Octavian to appoint a successor to replace him of his duty while he recovered.

Octavian appointed the centurion Gaius to act as senior centurion in his sick leave. He briefed him of all his affairs of rank and anticipated that he would continue to do all in his power to make the arrest of Khalid his priority.

Gaius had no sooner been appointed, and Pilate had issued new orders to arrest the followers of the dead Nazarene. The spreading of myths that the man had risen from the grave had created great unrest throughout the region. Especially among those of the Jewish Temple and their people. The fear of rebellion against Rome was great. Octavian's orders to arrest Khalid were no longer a priority.

A short time later…

Three months had passed and Khalid heard of the unrest in Jerusalem and of the arrests and killings of followers. He wondered about the nice woman, Mary Magdalene. He worried that she may be in trouble, for she had been on Pilate's list to arrest. Something inside of him made him decide to return.

"Vitali, I don't know what it is, but we need to go see that woman that came to us on that garden hill. See if she is okay."

Vitali barked in agreement.

As fast as he had decided to check on Mary, Khalid was packed and on his way with Vitali, traveling to Jerusalem. "I never thought I would be doing such a thing as this. How 'bout you Vitali?"

Vitali barked as though she too didn't understand why they were going.

It certainly wasn't like Khalid to have a feeling and go see if someone he didn't really know was okay. But there was something inside his heart leading him to act this way.

After journeying a long ways, Khalid and Vitali finally arrived in Jerusalem. "We are here, Vitali. Now where do we find her?" They went into the city and the markets were full of people. "Let us look here," he said as he dismounted from his horse Khalid now had a very short braid at the back of his neck. He was letting his hair regrow.

"This may be a silly idea," he said to Vitali as they made their way. Then, a voice was heard.

"You there halt." Khalid looked over at the Roman centurion with several soldiers who had demanded him to halt.

"I'll take care of this, Vitali," said Khalid, who had no idea that Octavian had issued his arrest several months back. He boldly answered, "Are there any bounties available for a good hunter?"

"Indeed, there are," shouted the centurion as his men surrounded Khalid and threw a net over Vitali. "There is a big one for you. Take him to the prison," he ordered.

Khalid struggled but the men had their swords at his neck and were binding his hands behind his back. He shouted, "Do not harm her!" as he watched Vitali struggle with the net. The soldiers dragged Khalid away and two others struggled to keep the dog in the net. It only took a few minutes and Vitali bit her way through it. She growled, showing her teeth, and snapped at the soldiers; they began to back away, fearing the stories they had heard of this great dog.

Vitali snapped again and then ran away from the soldiers.

"Leave the dog to go," shouted one of the soldiers. "There are no orders to arrest a dog, and Rome has other more important things to chase."

"Agreed," shouted the other soldier.

Vitali ran and ran, then stopped to sniff the air. She headed toward the outskirts, then stopped again and sniffed the air. She found the scent she had been searching for and thrust forward with the speed of a lion after its prey.

She went straight to the house of John and stood at the door barking vigilantly. John opened the door, then jumped back in fright, closing it, thinking a lion was there. Vitali barked again. Mary saw the frightened look on John's face and asked, "What is it?"

"It is a lion, I think."

Hearing the distinct bark, it sounded familiar. Mary ran to the door and opened it; there stood Vitali. Mary exclaimed, "Vitali!" and reached down and petted her beautiful coat.

"You know this animal?" John asked.

"She is the one I spoke to you of a while back. The beautiful dog that looked like the Lion of Judah. The one on the Hill at Calvary."

"This does look like the Lion of Judah," he said.

Mary asked the dog, "Where is Khalid, your master?" Vitali barked and looked toward Antonia Tower, which stood above in the skyline off in the distance.

"They have arrested him?" she asked.

Vitali barked.

"Why, Vitali? Why did they arrest him?"

Vitali barked and rolled her tongue, forming words. John was astounded at this sight.

"She speaks to you, Mary," he said.

"You must stay with us, Vitali, until we can get some help for Khalid." She motioned for Vitali to come inside.

Vitali leaped across the threshold and into the house.

John closed the door.

KHALID IS IN PRISON AND OCTAVIAN ROTS

It had been three long months, and finally, Octavian received word that Khalid was arrested and now sat in the dungeon within the prison. He summoned his demons of Diana, and they came.

"Yes, Master."

"Go and tell the Old Man that Khalid is arrested and in the prison dungeon. Beg of him now for my healing. Please go quickly."

The demons summoned the apprentice and said, "Octavian has arrested Khalid and he begs for his healing."

The Apprentice thought a moment. "Tell him the Old Man is sorry, but the arrest took too long. He will only have some healing."

"Yes, Master," answered the demons and they returned to Octavian.

"Master, the Old Man has told us to tell you that you took too long to make the arrest, and you may only have some healing."

Octavian's body trembled a bit and then stopped. He ran to the mirror and looked. His eyes were not as eaten away as they had been before and the skin around his teeth was no longer gone, but the new skin was full of sores and black in spots.

"This is not a healing!" he shouted. "Go and tell the Old Man that he has not healed me."

"Master, the Old Man has completed his bargain. For he only promised you *some* healing and not to be healed entirely. He kept his part of your agreement. Be happy for what he has given you and complain no more."

"Complain no more? My curse has only been lifted a small measure. Now I am to complain no more? I summon you to bring me the old man to rid my curse and end my misery! I demand it!"

"Yes, Master."

The demons returned to the Apprentice and told him what Octavian has summoned. The Apprentice laughed. "I will deal with this myself!"

In a flash, the Apprentice appeared to Octavian in his room.

Octavian was startled, for this was not who he has asked to see.

"What are you doing here?"

"So you want to see the Old Man?"

Octavian answered, "Yes."

"And be rid of your curse? Out of your misery?

Octavian looked very worried and slowly nodded yes.

"So you want to have the Old Man come and do this for you?"

Octavian answered, "Yes!"

The Apprentice laughed, then quickly spun around and shapeshifted into the image of the Old Man. Octavian was shocked.

The Apprentice shouted, "You fool! I am the Old Man!"

Suddenly, Octavian's body began to tremor; it convulsed and his rotting flesh slung about the room as he tossed uncontrollably on the floor. His skin peeled apart until there was nothing left but a mass of oozing pus on his bones. Then, his skeletal structure began to break apart until there was nothing left connected. All that remained were rotting pieces of flesh and bones scattered throughout his entire quarters. He was dead. His demons shrieked pleading not to return to Hades as they faded away into nothing.

The Apprentice looked around the room at the after math and in a sinister voice proclaimed, "Now your curse is gone and you are out of your misery."

THE BULL WITH ONE HORN

Longinus had been successful with impressing the Mariner with his skills at sea. He was welcomed as a member of the Mariner's crew. Over time, Longinus was well thought of and respected by all. He could pull a net load of fish onto the ship with his own strength. The sailors called him The Titan more than they called him Longinus.

He had just completed a long fishing voyage at sea with the Mariner and the crew. The ship was docked and there were no plans to travel for at least two weeks. Longinus was tired and headed for his small bunk below the ship, which was now where he stayed. It had been six months since he last saw Mary, yet there was not one night that passed that he had not thought of her.

As he got ready for bed, he had a funny feeling that something was not quite right. He wasn't sure what it was. He had managed to avoid any confrontation with Roman soldiers and the spearhead was secure in his haversack. He shrugged it off and went to sleep.

That night, he had a dream.

In his dream, he was in Jerusalem. He saw a big tree that had grown crooked and bent over. Its branches had intertwined with a wall of iron. Then, a beautiful doe appeared and was trapped between the branches in the tree and the iron wall. The doe's eyes looked warm and tender. As he watched the beautiful doe, a ravenous wolf appeared. The wolf growled, showing his teeth at the doe as though he was ready to devour her. Then he saw a bull with one great horn, his other horn had been broken off. The bull gored the wolf with his great horn. The wolf ran away. Then, with his great horn, the bull gored the tree and the wall of iron, freeing the doe. He watched as the doe and the bull ran off together. Suddenly, the wolf returned with his entire pack. They sniffed the air and ran in the direction that the doe and the bull had run. **The dream ended**.

Longinus jerked awake and sat up. "I must know what this means," he said out loud to himself. He ran to the top of the deck and saw the sun was just beginning to rise. He remembered there was an old fisherman that knew how to interpret dreams. I will go to him and have him tell me of my dream, he thought.

He went back below and quickly got dressed. In a hurry, he returned to the top of the deck and saw the Mariner standing at the prow looking out. "Mariner," he shouted, "where is it that the old fisherman lives, the one that tells of dreams."

"He stays in a cave under a cleft not too far southeast from the docks. What is it that you seek him for?"

"I had a dream and I must know what it means."

Longinus turned and made his way with haste. The Mariner called out, "There are dry fish bones all around his cave. Look for the cave with fish bones."

Longinus held his arm up to let the Mariner know he heard him, but took no time to stop.

After a little while, Longinus saw a pile of fish bones. Some were so large, he could crawl inside them. There were small mounds and large mounds of bones. It was very strange and gave him an uneasy feeling as he walked along looking at them all. What kind of man lives with this many fish bones? he thought.

Longinus followed the bones to the cave in the cleft. On the front of the cave, there were bones that had been shaped and mortared into the rock. As Longinus looked more closely, he saw that the bones on the entrance formed an artistic image of an army of men.

Longinus called out, "'Hello there." He walked a little closer and stuck his head inside the cleft's opening. "Hello, is anybody here?"

"That depends," answered a raspy voice. "What do you want?"

"I have had a dream and heard you can interpret it."

"Can do. Can do. Come in."

Longinus entered and found an old man sitting on a rug on the ground. He had the bones and skulls of fish hung by lines all about the cave. Some were bound together in the shape of men. There was a small staff laying by his side and a bit of bread on a plate. A bucket of water was in front of him; he was holding a ladle and dipping it in the bucket. He took a sip from the ladle and said,

"What is your dream? Just had it I'm sure. Sun's barely up."

Longinus quickly told the old fisherman his dream, and when he finished, he asked, "What does this mean?"

"Depends. Do you want a Greek interpretation or a lucid one?"

"What would be the difference?" he asked, very puzzled.

"Greek answers your allegory with another allegory, lucid will give you what is true."

"Why would I want anything but what is true?"

"Some want me to tell them their dreams, and when I do, they wish I hadn't. So if you are not sure, I will give you a riddle for a riddle. That is the Greek way, hee hee."

"I will hear the truth."

The old fisherman got very serious and said, "So you have a woman who has touched your heart. Her eyes are warm and tender. This is the meaning of the allegory of your doe. She is in trouble. There is a tree grown crooked and bent over whose branches have intertwined with a wall of iron. What is this tree? Hmm," he thought a moment.

"A tree is a religious symbol, it can represent knowledge, like the tree of good and evil. And in your dream, you are in Jerusalem? I say it represents the temple. And it is crooked and bent. That means that the Temple has lost its purpose and lost its way. It intertwines its branches with the wall of iron. Iron represents the strength of Rome. This could only mean that the temple has used the strength of Rome to do its bidding. The woman has found trouble with the Temple of Jerusalem and with Rome who governs it. She is now in prison.

"The wolf represents the one that arrested her. I would say it is a Roman. Perhaps to lure the bull to come for her? You are the bull. You will free her from the prison. The wolf returning with his pack represents that the Roman will return with troops of soldiers. They will chase you down when you free her. You will run and run and run.

"Now, there is one more thing to interpret. Are you sure you want to know the rest?"

Longinus was ready to hear everything and answered, "Yes, tell me all you know. Do not leave anything out."

"Well then," the old fisherman's voice got very low as he said, "let me begin by telling you that horns represent a chieftain or a king. A broken horn means you have fallen from your power that you once had. Your ties have been broken. Now, what is most unusual is that you still have one horn and it is a great horn. This can only represent one thing, a great king. Now, you are not a great king, which leaves only one truth left. You have chosen a great king to serve and he has given you a great horn of power to wield in any battle you may fight. Now, I tell you this, you must go and save the woman and take with you whatever weapon you have been given that represents the great horn."

Longinus looked around the cave at all the bones as he thought of all the fisherman had just said.

The old fisherman smiled and said, "You wonder why an old fisherman has so many bones lying about?"

Longinus nodded.

"The greatest fisherman that ever was, I met him once. These dry bones are my own reminder that one day, mankind shall rise up and bring about the kingdom of heaven that has no end."

"I have heard of this kingdom," said Longinus.

The old fisherman smiled and quoted a verse, "Son of man, can these bones live? So I answered, 'O Lord, you know. Prophecy to these bones and say to them 'O, dry bones, hear the word of the Lord.'"

The old fisherman paused, then lifted up his staff and waved it at all the bones about the cave as he said, "These bones are the whole house of Israel. They are my own reminder that one day, all mankind shall rise up and become a great and powerful army for the Lord."

"I was a dry bone," said Longinus.

"And now?" asked the old fisherman.

"Now I stand a strong bull who has been given a great horn to serve the greatest king of all, who is my Lord."

The old fisherman smiled and nodded. "Go now with God's speed. You have great things to do."

As Longinus left the cave, the old fisherman looked up and said, "My Lord, thank you for letting me live to see this day. May he keep his eyes on you always."

Longinus ran back to the ship, gathered provisions, and opened his haversack. He took the head of the spear and carefully unwrapped it from the cloth. He looked at the three red crosses of blood. He knew he had to find a blacksmith and have it remounted on a strong shaft. It was time to wield the spear for his Great King. He wrapped it back up and placed it in his haversack. He ran to the top of the deck and looked for the Mariner. He was not there. He left the ship, and as he was running to get his horse from the stables, the Mariner was coming, leading it by the reins.

"I knew when you took off like lightning this morning to see the old fisherman, you would be needing your horse."

"Thank you, Mariner," said Longinus as he mounted his horse, "I will return, but do not know when."

"I will welcome your return," said the Mariner. "God's speed!"

Longinus kicked the horse and shouted, "Yaa!"

The Blacksmith

As Longinus made his way from the ports, he entered the outskirts of Joppa. He was heading for the shop of an expert blacksmith who he had met a few months back. The man could forge the strongest and sharpest weapons. Longinus was very impressed with the man's skill and craftsmanship. All he needed was to have his spear remounted on a strong shaft. This shouldn't take a man of his skill and talent long.

Longinus sighted the blacksmith's shop and galloped up to a man pounding out a piece of steel on a hot anvil. He shouted out, "Hello there," and dismounted.

The man looked up. "What brings you here today?"

"I need to get my weapon fixed. It busted when I tried to harpoon a big fish."

"Let me see it."

Longinus walked over to the man and said, "I need it mounted on the strongest shaft. You can make me such a hasta. I have seen your work. It is the best."

"Leave it over there. I'll get to it sometime today or tomorrow."

"But, sir, I need it now. Please if you can find any way to do it now, for I cannot wait."

"It took a good part of the day to get this anvil hot enough to bend this iron. If I stop now, it will cool down."

"I will beat the iron out for you while you fix my hasta."

The blacksmith handed Longinus the hammer and said, "If you keep pounding at the middle, the iron will smooth best."

Longinus tossed him the spearhead still wrapped as he grabbed the hammer and started to pound out the steel.

The man looked at it and said, "Do you want me to clean it up too?"

"No! Do not do that!" shouted Longinus. "I'm superstitious about cleaning my spear. I'm the only one that cleans it. Just mount it on the strongest shaft you have."

The man gave Longinus a funny look and went to work picking out a good shaft. It was no time at all and he had it mounted.

"Here she is. Strong as any hasta can be."

Longinus handed the man the hammer and then tested the shaft for strength and feel. "You have done a fine job. How much do I owe you?"

"A denarius will do."

Longinus tossed the man a denarius and mounted his horse. It felt good to have his spear in his hand again. He looked at the blacksmith and said, "Good man, the day will come when kings will lust for the power that lies in this spear you have remounted!"

The blacksmith laughed and said, "You are too proud of another man's work."

Longinus looked at him and shouted, "Another man's work indeed. It is now my destiny!" He kicked his horse and yelled, "Yaa!" and galloped away.

The blacksmith shook his head and smiled.

MARY IS ARRESTED

The elders of the temple feared the followers would compromise their sovereignty and Rome would no longer allow them to govern themselves. They sought to arrest any who were spreading the stories of the man named Jesus and any who followed his dogma. To make an example for others, Caiaphas had pleaded with Pilate to arrest all followers and kill those who resisted. Rome was more than happy to oblige Caiaphas and his council of elders. It was no longer safe to speak in public of the man named Jesus.

The time also came that the old man (apprentice) had befriended the centurion, Gaius. He had made him a lucrative offer to find the spear and wield it for him. Gaius was eager to wield such a powerful spear and ready to find the deserter named Longinus.

The Old Man also had a plan to arrest the woman follower named Mary of Magdalene. He would use her as bait, for he knew Longinus would come to her rescue with the intent to break her out of prison. Then when he came, the Romans would capture him, and Gaius would possess the spear. Gaius would then wield it for the old man and do his bidding.

Two days later, the soldiers found Mary teaching the good news to a small crowd of people. Roman soldiers approached her. It was all too easy; they simply broke up the group and arrested her while she was talking. With one minor setback, Vitali was there and attacked the soldier who grabbed Mary to bind her.

"Vitali, no!" she shouted. "You must not attack. Go run away, hurry before they harm you!"

Vitali stopped attacking and the soldier held his leg to stop the bleeding. A soldier raised his spear to thrust it at the dog and his arm froze and could not move.

Mary shouted, "Go, Vitali, go now! I will be safe. The Lord is with me!"

Vitali ran away and returned to the house of John. He barked and explained all that took place. John was able to understand that Mary was in trouble. John began to run to the hillside where he knew Mary was teaching. He also had great fear for Mary, the mother of Jesus, for she had went with her that day.

As he ran, Mary, the mother of Jesus, came running toward him. She exclaimed, "They have taken Mary to the prison. We must do something."

John gasped in great distress, "Come, we must tell Joseph. He is on the council of the high court of the Sanhedrin. He can talk to Pilate and explain this is a mistake."

They ran to the house of Joseph and told all that had happened.

Joseph looked worried. "This sounds like the doing of Caiaphas. I will speak with him. If it is the doing of Pilate, I will plead for her release. They are all as mad men now. I am not in good favor with any of them as I once was. But, I will do all that I can do. Do not fear, the Lord is with her."

Joseph went straight to Caiaphas and asked why he had ordered the arrest of Mary. Caiaphas answered, "I have asked for her arrest, but that was some time ago. I was declined by Pilate. His wife Claudia would not allow it. I do not know who did this thing, but I am for it. Leave now."

As Joseph left, Caiaphas thought to himself, He must not make any pleas to Pilate. Mary must not be released. I will order the arrest of that bothersome Joseph. As a follower of Jesus, he has broken the laws of the Sanhedrin and acted against the rule of the Temple. He has aided enemies of both the Temple and of Rome.

Caiaphas called the temple guard and ordered them to arrest Joseph and give him over to the Romans to put into prison. The guards left and did as they were told.

Meanwhile, inside the prison the arresting guard is apologizing to Mary for having to arrest her.

"I am just following orders of Gaius. If it were up to me, you would be free to go."

Mary was not shaken, "I am where I was led to be. Can you do me one honor and put me in a place near the bounty hunter you arrested some months back?"

The soldier asked, "You mean the Syrian? The one that Pilot sent to capture you?"

"Yes. That is the one."

"Woman, you have a crazy idea of what an honor is. But none the less, so be it."

Mary nodded in appreciation as the soldier escorted her down the prison corridor and put her in a cell. He pointed, then spoke very low, "Over there. To the right of you, in the next holding cell. Talk if you must, but keep your hands inside as he may have a long reach and ...no telling what that man will do."

Mary stood in the center of the holding cell as the guard locked the door. She knelt down and began to pray. In a little while her prayers grew louder and in the deafening silence it seemed to echo throughout the chambers. Khalid recognized the soft voice. He ran to his cell door and looked out through the iron cage bars. "Mary...Mary?" he said in a loud voice.

"Khalid is that you?"

"Why have they thrown you in here? I'll get them for this!"

"It's okay Khalid. This is where the Lord would have me be. I have been so worried about you."

"Why are you here?"

"For teaching the way of my Master. Your girl Vitali is safe. We have cared for her ever since you were placed in this dreadful place. We sent pleads to Pilate for your release, but nothing ever came of them."

"You don't get out with a plead for breaking into a Roman centurion's private quarters and knocking a sentry guard out cold. They plan to behead me, the guards say."

"We will get out. I have faith," said Mary in a gutsy manner.

"This way!" shouted a Roman soldier. "In there!"

"Another is joining us," said Khalid.

They both listened as a cell door slammed with a loud clang.

"But I have done nothing wrong," pleaded a voice. "Let me speak to Pilate, I beg of you."

Mary whispered to Khalid who was in the cell next to her,

"That is the voice of Joseph. They have arrested Joseph too."

Khalid had a bewildered look on his face trying to think of who she was talking about. He had no idea who Joseph was.

"Shut up or I will flog you!" shouted the soldier. All became very quiet. Then the echo of soldiers' footsteps was heard leaving down the corridor.

"Joseph," whispered Mary.

"Mary, is that you?" answered Joseph.

"Yes. They arrested me because I was teaching of the Lord. And now you, I am sure because of me."

"Not so. Caiaphas had the temple guards arrest me and give me over to the Romans because I follow the Lord and not their rules. He has wanted to do this for a long time. It is none of your doing, Mary."

She asked, "Is Mary safe?"

"Yes. She is with John and a big dog that looks like a lion."

"Good, I was concerned for her," answered Mary.

"That's my Vitali", Khalid chimed in softly.

"Oh, Joseph this is Khalid. Vitali is his dog. Khalid, this is Joseph."

Joseph, "This is an odd introduction, but good to meet you."

Khalid, "The same."

"I am sure I will be able to see Pilate. If not him, I will seek council with Claudia," said Joseph.

"At least we are together and not alone," offered Mary. "John will know what to do to get us out. He will tell the others. I will pray for our release."

"I will pray as well," said Joseph.

Khalid, "I'm not happy you were arrested, but happy you are here. My heart was breaking alone without Vitali. Now I know she is safe."

"You see, we are where the Lord has sent us to be," said Mary cheerfully.

THE SPEAR OF DESTINY

LONGINUS BREAKS THE PRISONERS FREE

Longinus made his way to Jerusalem and went directly to the house of John. He dismounted and knocked on the door. No one answered. He knocked again and said, "It is I, Longinus." The door opened a little way, and John saw it was Longinus and spoke almost in a whisper, "Take your horse to the back and then come in from there. Romans are everywhere."

Longinus looked all around making sure he had not been followed then took his horse to the back and tied him to a post. He saw John waiting at the back door and went in.

"Mary has been arrested," said John. "Joseph went to plead with

Caiaphas and he was arrested too. We must get them out."

Vitali growled at Longinus, and John spoke up quickly, "It is okay, girl, this is Longinus, he is our friend."

"What has happened since I left? You are now friends with the bounty hunter and his dog?"

"Mary befriended Khalid and his dog. Khalid was arrested three months ago, and Vitali has been with us ever since."

"I see. The Lord has placed this great dog with us for a reason. She will be of great help." Vitali barked in agreement.

"The Lord gave me a dream that told me Mary was in prison. I have come to get her out. When I free her, we must flee Jerusalem. It is not safe here for any of you. We must all go. We will need horses and supplies enough to travel a long distance. Gather only what we will need. We must carry very little. It is the way it must be."

"I will gather things for Mary," said Mary the mother of Jesus. "And food and blankets."

"The Romans will not expect anyone to enter into the prison to help followers escape. The Jews are too afraid of Romans. I know the dungeons well. I know the best way in and the best way out. All that we do must be carefully timed. There will be no second chances once we begin."

John spoke, "I am not skilled at fighting."

"You will not have to." Answered Longinus, "But you will get a fine sword, two daggers, and a spear for Khalid. He will wield them. You will take Mary and an extra horse to the south edge of the city. Go out a little ways, stay mounted, and wait. It is not heavily guarded there. You must make sure that all the supplies are secured tight, for when we leave we shall run the horses hard for a while. Can you ride hard?"

John answered, "If I will have to. The Lord will be with me to do so."

Longinus continued to lay out the plan, "I will take two extra horses with me. That is as many as I can handle and remain unseen. Any more is too much to manage. I will ride double with Mary until we meet up with you. She will have to mount fast. If we are chased, there will be no time to mount, so take off fast and hold on to the reins of the extra horse. If you cannot hold on to them, I will see it and take hold of the reins for you.

"Romans will chase us, but do not look back, and do not fear them. We must keep going as fast as we can. They will not catch up with us if you do as I say. I know how soldiers think. It will be evening and they do not want to waste a night running after followers.

They would rather drink wine and find women.

"We must gain as much space between them and us as we can. In the morning is when the matter will be discussed, and it will be then that Pilate will order a detachment to find us. If we do all that I say, we will not be found."

John asked, "Where will you take us to?"

"We go to the Ports of Joppa. I know a mariner there, he will take us by ship away from Palestine. We will travel across the Mediterranean Sea, perhaps to Europe."

"Wherever the Lord leads us, I will go," said John.

"We go to the nations and preach the good news," said Mary, the mother of Jesus. "Just like my son has said for us to do."

"Now, I will need a few things. John, come and show me where I can find some rope and some rags."

They quickly gathered all the provisions and supplies they needed and set out as planned to free the prisoners from the Antonia prison.

Mary and John proceeded with the packed horses to the south of Jerusalem and went just a little ways past the city and waited, staying mounted as they were told with the extra horse.

Longinus rode his horses up to the spot close to the Temple where he could hide them and tie them up with Vitali running at his side. They sneaked in quietly through the temple and made their way to an open colonnade that adjoined the great wall leading to Antonia Fortress. Longinus knew every secret recess and passage well through his time standing guard. As he and Vitali made their way through the colonnade, he was surprised that there were so few guards at the temple. 'The less to worry with', he thought.

They made their way very easily, but what he could not see was an angel of the Lord guiding their way ahead, ensuring that no one saw nor hindered them. Longinus and Vitali snuck past each of the soldiers guarding the colonnade with great stealth. They swiftly made their way to the prison house. Longinus snuck up behind a guard and covered his mouth with a rag and held it tight so he could not breathe until the guard passed out. He slid the body over to the side where it could not be seen. He gagged his mouth and bound his hands to his feet behind his back with some of his rope. He took the guard's keys and made his way down the corridor.

Another guard was leaning against the wall fiddling with his pilum. Longinus snuck up behind him and hit him in the back of the neck with his fist. The guard fell over. Again, he slid the guard out of sight, took another piece of rope, bound his hands to his feet behind his back, and gagged him with a cloth.

Longinus made his way down a block of cells, looked at Vitali, and whispered, "Find Khalid." Vitali went right to the door that led to Khalid's cell. Longinus took the key and unlocked the door; he motioned for Vitali to stay where she was. Khalid was asleep. He went over and covered his mouth and Khalid woke up and wrestled with Longinus until he saw Vitali behind him. Longinus slowly uncovered his mouth and handed Khalid two daggers and a sword.

"Get ready to use these," said Longinus.

Khalid pointed and said, "Mary is in there and the other man Joseph is over there."

Longinus looked through the opening in the door at Mary and put his forefinger over his lips, motioning her not to speak. Mary was silent as Longinus unlocked the door. She embraced him quickly, then led him over to Joseph's cell. Longinus unlocked the door, letting Joseph out. He then motioned for them all to follow him.

Longinus led them out through the same recesses and passageways he had entered through. They made their way through Antonia Fortress, then they snuck down the colonnade, careful not to be seen by the Roman soldiers. At the end of the colonnade, they entered the temple. Carefully, they made their way past the temple guard and out the gate. Longinus led them a little ways to where he had hidden the horses. He motioned for Khalid and Joseph to mount, then he held out his hand for Mary.

She grabbed hold and he lifted her up onto the back of his horse.

They rode to the south of the city with great haste. As they rode away, the angel of the Lord stood at the gate of the temple and smiled upon them.

Mary, the mother of Jesus, and John were waiting for them, just as they were told.

Mary dismounted and got on her own horse. They headed out as fast as they could and Vitali ran beside Khalid.

They did not look back; they kept galloping as fast as their horses would go. Longinus led them west, and they continued until the horses needed to slow down. The terrain was not meant for galloping horses, but they had made a great distance between them and the city and were well pleased at how it all went so well.

In the morning, it happened just like Longinus had said; the Romans took the matter before Pilate, and Pilate ordered a centurion to send a detachment to bring those who had escaped back as well as to kill any who were involved in their release. The centurion that was ordered to do so, just happened to be Gaius.

Gaius gathered a large detachment of soldiers, and they set out, with great speed, to track down and get the escaped prisoners.

ONWARD TO JOPPA

After hours of riding the horses hard, Longinus slowed his horse and addressed the others, "We have made a good distance, let us stop and rest our horses here."

"You have served us like an angel of the Lord," stated Joseph in a deep, sincere tone as he got down from his horse.

"The Lord has truly sent him to us," said Mary, the mother of Jesus.

"Angel of the Lord or sent, I am impressed!" shouted Khalid.

"You would make a great bounty hunter, but you would need to find a good dog like Vitali," he said as he poured water in a cup for her.

Longinus held the reins of his horse and stretched his legs. He looked back toward Jerusalem and studied the horizon.

Mary went over to him and asked, "What is it that you see?"

"I was thinking of my dream and wondering how long it will be until we see the distant dust from horses' hooves."

Mary looked at the horizon for a moment. Then she turned and went over to Mary, Jesus's mother, who motioned for her to come.

She brought out a loaf of bread from her haversack and said, "Mary, go and give the others some bread. They need to be nourished."

Mary smiled and took the loaf. She pulled apart generous pieces and gave to them all.

It seemed as though they had just stopped to rest, and it was time to mount up and travel some more. No one complained. They were all very thankful.

They traveled until the night was beginning to set in. Longinus knew it was time to find a suitable place to make camp. Both the people and the horses needed to sleep.

"There is a wooded area that I stayed when I came to Jerusalem, not far from here. We should reach it soon. We can camp there."

Now miles ahead of the Roman army, Longinus and the others had made a nice camp, and John had prepared some smoked fish and bread.

Longinus looked at Mary and said, "This is very fresh smoked fish."

"And at a price cheaper than Gaza," said Mary with a giggle.

Longinus was slow in understanding, but as he thought, he broke out in laughter, remembering Josiah.

"They are having fun," John said to Khalid.

"They laugh at things that make no sense. The fish is good. I'll have another," said Khalid.

After a good serving of food, they all rested. They had plans to get up before dawn and make their way to Joppa. It wasn't far. Longinus believed that they would be at the ports by the afternoon as long as they got an early start.

The Missing Mariner

Longinus and the others finally arrived at the ports in Joppa. Longinus led them all to the ship of the Mariner, but the ship was not there. At the dock, he asked a fisherman,

"Where is the Mariner's ship? The man from Aksum?"

"Oh, they sailed out yesterday. Planned to bring in a big catch."

Longinus knew that when they planned for a big catch, it meant at least two weeks at sea. *Now what do we do?* he thought.

Joseph and the others heard the report. They looked at one another. Mary spoke up, "The Lord has not led us here in vain. He will show us what to do."

Longinus was concerned and said, "We have no seaworthy ship. We must go from here."

Then Khalid spoke up, "We can get a boat. We have men enough who can row oars."

Longinus thought and answered, "The old fisherman. He had many of such boats. Khalid, come with me. Mary, you and the others wait here. We will be back as fast as we can."

Mary nodded.

Khalid looked at Vitali and commanded, "You stay here and guard the women." Vitali barked in agreement.

Khalid added, "First, we find the fisherman, then we get the boat, then we sail." Vitali barked again, and Khalid and Longinus galloped away to see the fisherman.

When they came upon the bones, Khalid asked, "What does a fisherman do with so many old bones?"

Longinus answered, "He sees in these the day that the dry bones will awake and become a great and powerful army for the kingdom of heaven."

Khalid shrugged his head and rolled his eyes and decided not to ask any more questions.

As they neared the entrance of the cave, Khalid saw the bones on the outside of it formed the image of soldiers. He wondered at it. Then a voice was heard and they turned and saw the old fisherman coming, pulling a boat on a makeshift cart. It was tied very securely and did not move one little wobble.

"I had expected your arrival a little later, but I see you made good time."

Longinus smiled as he saw the boat and said, "What do I owe you for this?"

The old fisherman said, "There is no coinage due for obeying the word of the Lord. One simply does what they are told. Rewards come later. But for now, it is my pleasure to help in any way. Take the boat and the provisions in it. Go now, you must not tarry here."

Longinus held up his spear and shouted, "Look upon the first of your Lord's great and powerful army!" He then pointed the spear at Khalid and shouted, "And look upon the second!"

The old fisherman smiled and said, "Go now, for the Lord has shown me that the Romans come at you with great speed. They are no longer detained."

Longinus nodded, and Khalid grabbed the ropes of the cart that held the boat and shouted, "I will lead, you follow behind to make sure the cart does not lose the boat." "Agreed!" shouted Longinus, and they rode off as fast as they could, being careful not to topple the boat from the cart.

John and Joseph saw Longinus and Khalid coming with the boat tied to the cart and grabbed some knives to cut the ropes that bound the boat. As they cut away the ropes, Mary, the mother of Jesus, said, "The Lord has blessed us with this boat, may he keep us safe as we sail."

They freed the boat from the cart and together the men lifted it down and carried it out past the shallows of the water. The women waded after them, carrying all the haversacks except for one. Vitali carried Khalid's holding it tight between her teeth.

Once past the shallows, the women, Joseph, and John climbed into the boat, while Longinus and Khalid held it steady. Then they lifted themselves up into it. They grabbed the oars and began to row. They made their way out to sea and the ports of Joppa began to look smaller from the distance.

As they continued out to sea, Longinus tried hard to remember all he had learned in maintaining his direction with the sun. If only I had something to navigate with, he thought.

As they got further out to sea, John decided to rummage through the provisions that were provided by the old fisherman. He came across a strange-looking object. Holding it up, he shouted to Longinus, "Do you know what this is?"

Longinus looked as he oared, then shouted, "An astrolabe!"

"Indeed it is!" exclaimed Joseph, "It's God sent!"

Longinus quit oaring and moved over to John and took it from him.

"That old fisherman has blessed us with an astrolabe. With this, we shall be able to navigate our boat. We will not lose our way."

They continued to row as fast as they could until the only thing that was seen from every side of the boat was the horizon line.

Joseph was skilled in the celestial patterns of the stars and would entertain himself using the astrolabe, both during the day with the sun and at night when the stars filled the sky. He shared his knowledge of the stars and their patterns, with the others, on how they traveled and never lost their course. All of them were now learning how to navigate in the waters through the direction of the sun, the moon, and the stars. Longinus learned so much from Joseph who was a great merchant and traveled the seas a lot. The two of them bonded instantly through their shared fascination with that astrolabe.

Tempest at Sea

After a couple days at sea, in the early dawn, Longinus awoke in the boat and spotted a fleet of ships on the horizon. They were Roman biremes.

"Oar fast as you can!" he shouted to Khalid. Khalid grabbed the oars and began to row. He looked on the horizon and saw the Roman biremes.

"May the Lord protect us," shouted John as he looked and saw the Roman biremes on the horizon.

"The Lord will make us a way," comforted Mary to the others. It seemed that no matter how fast the men rowed, the Roman biremes kept coming closer.

"They are so fast," shouted Longinus. "We must keep going." He looked at Mary and the rest who had their heads bowed in prayer and said, "Pray as you have never prayed in your life for a miracle at sea."

Khalid shouted, "You too, Vitali!" and Vitali bowed her head.

"Well, I'll be," said Khalid with surprise as he watched her pray. For those words he spoke out of nervousness and not with any real intent.

As the Roman biremes continued to gain speed, coming closer and closer, suddenly, out of nowhere, the sky turned dark. A tempest was brewing and the waves began to slash against the small boat, rolling it up and down in the water. The sky grew black, and no one could see beyond the boat. The roar of rolling thunder drummed in their ears continuously, and every few minutes, a flash of lightning cracked in the sky, thrusting a quick burst of light.

The little boat raised up and down, hitting against the pounding waves. Longinus feared the boat would turn over or, worse yet, split apart. After a long length of time, their little boat suddenly became very still. Yet the waves continued to slash out and crash downward all around them. They heard the desperate commands of Roman captains shouting to their sailors ordering them to tighten sails and throw down anchors.

Longinus wondered at the strange calm and stillness of their boat when all around them the storm was raging and showing no mercy to the Roman biremes.

In the darkness, none could see that there was an angel of the Lord, guarding over them. The angel had his legs straddled over the boat, and all the water around his legs was still. His head reached up above the darkened clouds. He was an awesome sight to behold. Yet they could not see him.

Mary and the others continued to pray. Longinus saw the miracle in the stillness of their boat and bowed his head and began to pray.

Khalid said, "I do not know this God of yours, but he has answered your petitions. I will petition to him as well." He bowed his head and began to petition.

The sounds of ships falling apart at sea, amidst the roaring thunders, were deafening to their ears. Through the bellowing storm, they heard the shouts of men drowning, and the fearful cries of Romans shouting to pagan gods for help that did not come.

The darkness continued to loom, then all of a sudden, their boat began to sail with great speed. They all held on to the sides of the boat and continued to pray. The boat sailed and sailed. After a great length of time, the darkness lifted, and they all wondered at what had taken place. They could not see the angel of the Lord bending over and taking his mighty hand and pushing their little boat across the water.

Then suddenly, Longinus looked out over the horizon and saw a faint outline of hills. "Land," he shouted!

Khalid reached for his oars, but they were gone. Longinus looked for his and they too had been torn away in the storm. He feared that they would drift back out to sea and ordered Khalid and the men to row the boat with their arms in the water. They all reached over into the water and used their arms to row the boat, and it eventually came to the shallows. Khalid jumped out and began to push the boat from behind through the shallows; Longinus jumped into the water and helped. Then John and Joseph did the same. They pushed it along through the shallows and onto the shore.

"I do not know where we are," said Longinus, "but it is where the Lord has led us." John and Joseph helped the women out of the boat, and Vitali leaped out and ran to Khalid.

Khalid shouted with joy as he took hold of Vitali's mane and shook her head with his two giant hands. "We made it, girl!" Vitali barked and barked.

"Look!" shouted John. "Crates are drifting ashore!"

Longinus looked, then shouted, "They are supplies from the biremes, come, we must get them." The men followed Longinus and began to pull many crates to shore.

Khalid began to open them to see what was inside. To his surprise, the first one he opened was filled with spices. He opened another and it had a small chest inside. He pried open the chest, and it was filled with coins. "Look!" he shouted. "Great riches!"

Mary exclaimed, "The Lord has provided us means for our travel ahead."

Joseph still had the astrolabe and held it out to study the position of the sun. After a few minutes, he exclaimed, "I believe we have landed on the shores of Gaul!"

At the same time the followers were rejoicing on the shore, the Old Man, known as the Apprentice, appeared walking on the waters of the sea, looking down at the floating bodies of dead Roman soldiers.

He looked as debris from a sunken bireme hit against the lifeless body of his precious Gaius. "There goes that one," he said as he placed his foot upon Gaius's head and shoved it under the water. He watched small air bubbles float upward as the lungs of Gaius filled with water. It wasn't long and his body floated downward into the depths of the sea.

"That cursed Longinus has learned to wield the power of his spear. No one can stop him now. I will think of other ways to counter the goodness of his spear. Great persecution and death of little followers is where I shall start. I go to Rome."

FROM OPPIDUM-RA TO A NEW JOURNEY

As they gathered up the crates and stacked them, Longinus was thinking of a plan. Vitali took off running and Khalid called to her, "Where are you going, girl?" Vitali turned and barked for Khalid to follow. Khalid looked at Longinus and said, "I will see what she has found."

He followed Vitali and she led him northeast from the shore where they had landed. She stood there barking. As Khalid came up from the sandy shore, around a hill, he looked and there in the distance was a fortress. "Vitali!" he shouted. "There are people so close! Come, we must go tell the others."

They ran back and Khalid shouted out as soon as he saw them, "There is a fortress over past the shore, up on high ground just toward the northeast!"

Joseph smiled and said, "It is Oppidum-Ra! A settlement!"

Longinus said, "I have heard of this place."

Joseph said, "I know a few fishermen and some tradesmen who occupy this arm of the delta of the Rhone. Come, Longinus, let us go to the settlement and see if we are welcome there."

Longinus opened the crate that had the small chest of coins and filled his coin pouch full. He said to Joseph, "Come get some coins, we will need them. All of you, fill your pouches." They did as Longinus said. Then he left with Joseph to find the tradesmen.

John and Khalid continued to go through the crates to see what else was in them. "Look," shouted John to Mary. "Writing instruments and parchment and it is not damaged from the water."

"Oh, John, that is wonderful. We can write the words of our Lord."

Khalid pulled out a wad of purple cloth. "Now this is finely woven fit for a king." As they went through the crates they were filled with cloths, spices, merchandise, and trinkets generally sold in the bazaars. There were crates of cooking wares, smoked fish, ground wheat, fine scented oils, and things that are not generally found on a Roman bireme.

"They must have boarded merchant ships for their soldiers. At least, one of the ships had to be that of a merchant. The Lord has truly blessed us with these things," said John.

Mary looked over at the view of the land and said, "The land is so beautiful, and the mountains with all their colors touch sky. It is like the Garden of Eden here. The Lord has led us to this place to teach the people all he has taught us!"

Mary, the mother of Jesus, smiled and said, "And we shall, Mary. This is a new beginning and a new journey. The entire land is so full of green, and the water is so blue. God has blessed this place and brought us to it."

"What do you say we take these crates up to the green by the trees?" said Khalid to John as he heaved a crate over his shoulder.

"That will be good," said John as he lifted one and carried it with his hands in front of him.

Khalid and John worked at moving the crates, and the women gathered the things from the boat. They tied the smaller loads together with bigger ones and made bundles that they could drag through the sand. They made their way to the green by the trees. There were beautiful wildflowers growing everywhere and lots of different colored birds.

The last thing that Khalid and John did was pull the boat through the sand and up to the green. They turned it upside down over the top of a double row of crates.

"There," said Khalid to Vitali. "Now we wait for Longinus and Joseph to return."

Vitali barked.

Mary gave everyone some smoked fish and bread. She made sure Vitali had a little extra. They blessed the food and ate. The sun was starting to go down, and the women and John were becoming concerned.

Khalid stood up and told them all, "A man like Longinus skilled in battle and a man like Joseph full of proper speech and knowledge will make their way just fine."

He had no sooner said those words and Longinus and Joseph were seen in the distance coming down the beach toward the coastal shore with a cart and a mule.

"Vitali, go to them and show them where we have gone. They don't know we left the beach," said Khalid, and he got up to go with her.

Vitali took off running and barking. Khalid ran close behind her.

Longinus heard Vitali barking and looked in her direction. He saw Khalid and waved.

"We are welcome to stay at the settlement!" he shouted, "Joseph was right, it is indeed Oppidum-Ra!"

As they made their way to the others, Joseph shouted from the shore, "Look behind you, out in the sea, there is a ship coming."

They watched as the ship came closer, wondering if more Romans were following and if they had brought trouble to the settlement.

Longinus and Khalid readied their weapons.

"Fill the cart with as much as you can and go to the settlement, hurry," shouted Longinus.

John shouted, "Hand me a sword and I will stand with you." Khalid handed him his sword and said, "Use this, I will wield my daggers."

As the ship came closer, Joseph and the women busied themselves with filling the cart. Longinus watched the ship, and as it got closer, he noticed the sail was the brightest red. He saw a white shape in the middle of the red. *Is it? Could it be?* he thought to himself.

As the ship came closer, he was able to see that the white shape was that of a dove. He shouted to the others, "Wait, it is the Mariner!"

Mary asked curiously, "The Mariner you sought for us to travel with?"

"Indeed! Stay. We must all wait for him to land."

The ship reached the shallows and the Mariner waved from the ship. There were several women with him and some men who were not sailors. Longinus and the others watched as a small boat was lowered into the water and the people were helped into it. The Mariner and the Bedouin man entered last. They rowed through the shallows, and then the Mariner and the Bedouin got out and pulled the boat to the shore. Longinus and Khalid ran and helped them pull the boat.

"You made it through the storm, I see," said the Mariner.

"How did you know to find us here?" asked Longinus.

The Mariner smiled and ignored his question, "I have some friends who heard of the miraculous escape from prison of the woman named Mary and the man named Joseph. They came to join them in the new land."

Mary and the others all recognized the people and praised their Lord and ran to greet them.

"Sarah!" shouted Mary as she ran with her arms wide opened. Sarah shouted, "Mary!" and ran to her. They embraced and cried for joy on the shore.

"Maximin, Sidonius, Lazarus, Martha, and Mary Salome, you have all come!" shouted Joseph.

"How did you know to find us here?" he asked.

Before he could answer, Mary shouted, "Lazarus, my brother,

and Martha, my sister, you are here as well! How did you find us, for not even we knew where the storm would send us!"

Maximim answered, "When the Romans found you had escaped, they came after all followers. We fled for our lives in a small boat."

"How did you find the Mariner?" asked Joseph. "He was not at the ports and out to sea."

The mariner heard Joseph's question and answered it himself, "I found them at sea. Their boat was badly damaged. I brought them aboard, and with a speed this ship has never seen and a mind of its own, we are here."

Longinus looked over at the Mariner. They made eye contact and the Mariner asked, "Will you be returning with us to Joppa?"

Longinus answered, "My journey now lies on land."

The Mariner smiled and said, "I understand."

The Mariner gave Longinus a quick embrace and said to the Bedouin, "Our work is done here. Come let us return to the ship."

Longinus looked over at all the people. They were busy exchanging stories. He knew his journey had just begun and there was much more for him to do, for he was given a great horn to wield for a great purpose.

LONGINUS LEAVES FOR CAPPADOCIA

A month passed by and the people were settled in. Mary had started a gathering place for followers and was busy teaching the ways of the Lord.

Longinus knew it was time for him to move on and establish his own purpose for the followers of the way. He had been having a deep longing to return to his home village in Cappadocia. This day the urge was great that it was time to go. He met with Mary to speak of his plans to leave.

"I have had a vision to begin a new journey. I must return to Cappadocia to protect others."

Mary smiled at him and said, "I too had a vision. Last night I saw you were to go to Cappadocia. You were a great guard for the people of the Lord. Persecutions will come and you will help many."

Mary looked deep into his eyes and said, "I will miss you greatly."

"And I will miss you greatly as well," he said.

Longinus gave Mary a quick embrace, then left to pack his belongings. As he was packing, Khalid approached him.

"Vitali and I have talked. We go with you."

Longinus smiled and said, "I would like that."

The afternoon came, and Longinus and Khalid were ready to journey to Cappadocia. They said their farewells to the people, and

Mary waited to be last to say good-bye. She went first to Khalid. "You have been a blessing to us, and I know you will be a great protector for others."

Then Mary turned to Vitali and smiled.

"You, my lion of Judah, take care of these great men." Vitali barked.

Then Mary turned to Longinus. She embraced him, then said, "I will pray for your safekeeping. God has a great work for you to do. Go now and do well."

Longinus mounted his horse. He looked down at Mary and quickly dismounted and ran over to her and gave her one more embrace. He then got back on his horse and they all rode off. Mary stood watching until they were out of sight.

"I will miss him," she said softly. "Lord guide his way."

Cappadocia

After a very long journey, Longinus, Khalid, and Vitali finally made it to Cappadocia. Khalid had never been there before and was taken aback by the breathtaking landscape of the rose-tinted gorge. It was full of soft volcanic tuff sculpted into fantastic shapes with huge stone mushrooms and fairy chimneys, soft ridges, and deep valleys, all riddled with numerous ancient cave dwellings.

"This is from another world," said Khalid in great awe.

Longinus smiled and said, "Wait until I show you the honeycomb of cities beneath the ground. There are places here to hide followers who are running from their death by the hands of Romans."

"Cities beneath the ground? I have heard such stories. Now my own eyes will see it!"

"There are many rooms connected to each other, some with tunnels so tight, only one person can pass at a time, others are so wide a group of four can walk through them standing side to side," said Longinus.

As they made their way into Cappadocia, Longinus began to remember his beloved Sabena. Oh, how she had loved this place, he thought.

For years, he had not known if he would ever return to Cappadocia, but now he was here. He marveled at how much it had grown in size with people. As he rode in, he looked and saw the very same well and the water trough beside it. It was the one where his beloved had been brutally killed.

Longinus had wondered where her soul went that day. He remembered how in his confusion, he had turned away from anything that was called a god. But now he knew there was but one true God, and that was the one he served. He believed in his heart that his beloved was now with the Lord. Mary had assured him of that.

Longinus took Khalid to a strange-looking chimney rock. "We will be able to stay here," he said. "This belongs to me." He went inside and Khalid followed and began to roar with laughter.

"What is so funny?" asked Longinus.

Khalid could not answer just yet, as he was laughing so hard. He finally gained his composure and said, "You, Longinus, live in a rock that looks like a mushroom! Why I wish Mary were here to see this."

Longinus laughed. He went into the back of his chimney rock dwelling and slid a large dusty chest over to the side, uncovering a board on the floor.

He motioned to Khalid and Vitali, "Come, I will show you a wonder."

Khalid and Vitali went over to Longinus as he lifted up the wooden trap door. He began to step down a narrow ladder and Khalid followed. Khalid looked up at Vitali and he said, "Jump, girl." Vitali jumped and landed on the ground just fine. It was only about eight feet to the ground.

Longinus said, "Now which way shall we go?" Khalid looked and there were four different narrow passageways.

Khalid answered, "I go nowhere, they are too dark."

Longinus smiled and said, "Come," and he took him through a dark passage that after about fifty feet had small beams of light that lit their way.

"Where is this light coming from?" asked Khalid.

Longinus pointed to the top of the passage and said, "Little holes up there. This gives us light and air." They went a little ways farther and Longinus showed Khalid a stone on a roller system. "If you are chased, you hurry to this side and then you roll the stone. It can only be rolled from this side. No one will be able to move it. Remember this, it may save your life and the life of others."

"This is indeed a wonder," said Khalid.

Longinus took them back to the ladder, and on the way, he said,

"We will start a gathering place like Mary has done for followers. We will be able to offer safety and protection. We have much work to do and must prepare provisions in many places under the ground. I was told this in a dream one night as we traveled here."

"We will do it," said Khalid, and Vitali barked. They reached the ladder and went back up. Khalid looked down at Vitali and said, "Get a running start and leap, girl." Vitali only had to take a few steps back and thrust herself up to the top of the opening in the floor then lifted herself out.

"Good girl!" shouted Khalid.

Khalid looked over to Longinus and, in a very serious tone, said, "We must gather a band of men to fight with us."

Longinus nodded his head and said, "Bounty hunters as yourself. They know how to fight with cunning and have methods Romans cannot understand."

Khalid smiled and said, "I go this day and find such men."

DEFENDING THE INNOCENT

Khalid and Longinus soon recruited a large number of bounty hunters who were as well skilled as Khalid. Their methods of fighting were no match for the Romans. They went about the villages in Cappadocia interceding for the followers, killing the Roman soldiers who persecuted and sought to kill them.

As time past, many people sought refuge in Cappadocia in the village that Longinus lived. Disciples came and built a church and took care of the refuges with both bread of wheat and bread of word. Longinus had not realized the numbers of followers who would come and use the underground passages he and Khalid had prepared. Over time, there were hundreds.

The years passed, and it was now Ad 35. Longinus's reputation had grown among the people. He was said to be sent by the angel of the Lord to defend those who believed.

One afternoon, there came many Jews who had fled Jerusalem. They had heard there was safety at a church in Cappadocia. They came to Longinus and told him of a disciple of the Lord named Stephen. How he was stoned on the east side of Jerusalem, looking toward the Mount of Olives, and how it was unsafe there for any who followed the Lord. They spoke of hundreds who were being arrested and killed throughout all of Jerusalem.

Longinus had always fought with principles. "Never start a fight, only defend and protect those who were troubled unjustly." But now, times grew worse and soldiers were now killing followers throughout all the Roman provinces. He called his band of men together to figure out a new strategy.

"Word has come to me that soldiers are on their way to Iconium to search out all followers and kill them. They are still five days out. It is now time to fight aggressively."

A bounty hunter spoke out, "Our methods of fighting are no match for the Romans. We will come at them out of nowhere and fight like Parthians! They will turn and run!"

Longinus shared his plan, "The Romans will be entering the city from the west. We go to the western outskirts of Iconium and lay wait for the soldiers in the canyon. We will make sure they never arrive." Khalid boasted, "Daggers will fly from all directions! They will fall like pigeons and not see one of us!"

Longinus and the band of men mounted up and rode fast to the western outskirts of Iconium. They positioned themselves in a narrow canyon and waited.

As time passed, Khalid was at his watch and saw the Roman soldiers approaching through the canyon. He waited until the soldiers were in the most vulnerable position for the men to attack, and then he released a hawk into the air, signaling the others to attack. A whizzing noise filled the air as daggers were thrown from all directions. Simultaneously, arrows flew over the canyon cliffs and soldiers dropped from their horses with daggers and arrows in their chests and backs. In a matter of minutes, every soldier fell from their horse and lay dead on the ground.

Longinus and his band of bounty hunters then snuck away, leaving the dead bodies in the narrow canyon.

Time went by, and Longinus and the band of bounty hunters made more such raids. Rome had gotten word of the attacks from out of nowhere and doubled the number of soldiers sent throughout the provinces.

Some days were harder than others for Longinus to deal with the cruel reality of life. He would rage inside with each damming report that came to him of followers being persecuted just for their faith. The day came and Longinus needed to vent, as he often die and Khalid was now the one he turned to when he needed to talk.

"Khalid, it seems things are getting worse and not better. With each new Caesar, it grows worse. When will this madness end?"

"Rome never tires of war and death." Answered Khalid.

"No. It's built with sour promises given to men like me that they will have land and a life after they serve Rome in battles to conquer other people's lands. Only to die young, or get charged as a deserter for deciding war is not for them. Now they kill for the sheer madness of it."

"We need more men to join us in fighting," said Khalid.

"Only men skilled in cunning battle, like the bounty hunters," added Longinus. "They can't win a battle against men with both skill of weapons and cunning."

"I go and find more today."

Longinus nodded and watched as Khalid mounted his horse.

"I will be back in a couple of weeks. Come, Vitali, we find more men!"

PERSECUTIONS AND GREAT TRIBULATION

Now, it came to pass that it was no longer just the followers of the Lord who were being persecuted. The Jews who followed the Laws of the Temple had to watch their every move as well. For to proselytize to any religion, other than that of Rome, meant death under the new Caesar, Claudius. It was complete chaos in Jerusalem and throughout Judea.

Followers were fleeing Rome in fear and throughout the area. Many came to Cappadocia. Longinus and Khalid took great precautions to secure their safety. Many were hidden in the underground cities, and many were escorted by Longinus and Khalid to other nearby villages and towns where they would be safe.

One day, two disciples came to share news of the apostles with the church at Cappadocia. When they came, one of them had a letter with him for Longinus. It was from Mary.

"Mary, how is she? I think of her so often," asked Longinus.

"Oh, she has been blessed by the Holy Spirit with such gifts. She has done miraculous healings and even raised a dead child. That great woman has baptized many. Truly there is no end to all that have come to the Lord through her ministry."

The other disciple spoke, "I believe he seeks to know how is Mary in spirit and health."

"Yes. That is what I want to know," Answered Longinus.

"Her mind is sharp and her health good. She sent us to give you the letter in person and ask if any need an escort to Gaul for refuge. She knows of the great persecutions."

"Go to the sanctuary and ask for Phillip. He will help you find those who wish to go to Gaul."

Longinus left the men and went inside to read the letter. It smelled of jasmine. He inhaled the aroma and then broke the seal and began to read.

My Dearest Longinus,

My Lord has truly blessed us in Villalata. Your reputation as a great protector and warrior for the Lord has reached the south of Gaul. Many say you cannot die. Others say your face glows like the angel of the Lord. If there are any there that desire to come to the south of Gaul, they will be welcomed here. Continue to put your trust in the destiny that God has chosen for you to fulfill. I pray for you always.

Mary Magdalene

Longinus read the letter several times. His heart longed to see her again. He finally put it away in the safe place where he kept her other letters. Afterwards, he went back about his business doing what needed to be done in Cappadocia.

As the years had passed, Longinus would receive a letter from Mary every year or two, sometimes he would receive several letters at one time. It all depended on who was traveling from the South of Gaul to Cappadocia and how many letters she had written while waiting. He would always write a letter in return, and that delivery always depended on who was traveling from Cappadocia to the South of Gaul.

One night as he fell asleep after saying his prayers, he had a dream of Mary.

In the dream, he was standing at the water trough cleaning his spear. It was the first time after he had pierced the side of the

Lord. He saw himself as he peered into the bloodstained crosses and began to see a vision. In his dream, he realized he was outside of his body watching himself. He saw himself looking into the spear.

The bloody red crosses on the spear's head began to glow. Suddenly, the bloody face of the dying Nazarene on the cross was seen. The image began to zoom out into the distance and the crown of thorns were visible. The image continued to zoom out until the entire man on the cross was shown.

His blood and water gushed forth from his side. He hung on the cross limp and lifeless. Then he saw a golden bronze city bursting upward out of the ground; it had layers and layers of the most stately buildings one could ever imagine. He watched until a magnificent entry gate formed; it had upon it the majestic face of a bronzed lion. It appeared to be a most fantastic kingdom, one of an architecture he had never seen nor could have ever imagined.

Then the image zoomed further out into the distance, exposing a most barren and ugly wilderness in front of the fantastic kingdom.

The ground broke open and coming up in the front of the most beautiful kingdom was fire and molten lava; from the fire was seen the most horrid-looking place. It was full of darkness and had multiple layers of dungeon like prisons, guarded by the most hideous of creatures. They had black leathery tar-like bodies with sharp fangs that hung down past their jaws like stalactites from a cave. Their teeth chattered hauntingly. On their backs were torn blackened, leathery wings, full of jagged rips and slashes.

He looked and saw inside the dark dungeon-like prisons. They were empty, all but one that bound a horrid and pitiful-looking serpent who was wailing out all manner of evil vengeance in tormenting shouts. He could not understand the language this hideous beast was shouting, but he knew it meant that these dark horrid prisons must be filled up.

Suddenly, the smell of putrefactive pools of evil pus filled his nostrils, and he watched himself drop the spear. The dream faded to nothing and he was still standing there. He tried to wake up, he tried and failed, and tried and failed.

Then Mary came to him and smiled. She was dressed in an illuminating white robe, and she didn't say a word. Suddenly, she faded and disappeared.

Instantly he was standing over his body watching himself sleep. He lay down on top of his body and jolted awake..

Breaking out in a cold sweat, Longinus leaped from his bed touching his body all over. Frightened at what he had just dreamed he sat down on the side of his bed and began talking to himself out loud trying to make sense of it.

"My vision, I dreamed I saw myself watching my own vision. It was so real, and Mary was there." He looked around and it was still very dark; he went to the window and the moon was still shining overhead." *Get some rest*, he thought as he laid back down. Soon he fell back to sleep.

In the morning, Longinus remembered his dream. He had never told his vision to Mary even though it had haunted him. Now she was in it, at least in its' dream form. He felt he must tell her about it now. Maybe she could interpret it for him. He quickly grabbed some parchment and began to write his dream and vision to Mary in a letter. At the end of his letter, he asked her to give him the meaning and eagerly folded the parchment and melted some wax to seal it.

After a few weeks, he found some followers who were going to the south of Gaul and they agreed to take the letter to Mary of Magdalene for him.

A year had passed and Longinus wondered if the letter ever made it to Mary. Then, that very day, a group of disciples came, and with them, they had a letter from Mary. Longinus took the letter and ran inside to the table, and again, it had the sweet smell of jasmine, the same as all of her other letters. He broke the seal and opened the letter and began to read it.

My dearest Longinus,

I have received your letter of your dream and your vision. I have prayed to the Lord for the words to give you. The Holy Spirit has led my heart to tell you these things.

In your dream, you saw yourself out of body looking at yourself, seeing your destiny through a vision in the spear. This shows that you struggle with fulfilling your destiny.

In the vision, you see the glorious kingdom of the Lion of Judah that has no end, then you see the kingdom of darkness trying to overshadow the kingdom of heaven. But the demonic forces and powers cannot free the serpent who is trapped. He shouts out in vain for he shall not be freed. His days are numbered. His mission is to trap as many souls as he can in his chains of darkness. In so doing, he believes he will destroy the Lord's work and his death and resurrection will be in vain. Yet as you know, Longinus, the people stand in their faith and die, looking up to the heavens rather than touch any more of the evil in this world.

The smell you smelled was real to impress upon you that the principalities and powers are real. When you realized they were real, you dropped your spear. You want to abandon your destiny. It is too much for you to bear.

You saw me, smiling. Dressed in a heavenly garment, yet I spoke not. I faded away. This is because only you can decide whether to fulfill your destiny or turn from it. It is up to you.

Now, I ask you, Longinus, what will you do with your destiny if it were to be changed?

The Lord will never give one more than they can bear. The destiny to carry the spear was given to you to carry until the Lord returns. Yet if you believe the burden is too great for you to bear, the Lord will take it from you and show you how to give it to another. You must pray to him for the answers you seek. Now, Longinus, I know you are impatient at times and often hurry off to take care of matters without first waiting for the Lord to answer your prayer.

I will tell you this much, the spear should never be placed in the possession of one who is not pure of heart and who does not know the Lord. But for you to go and give it to another is not yours to do. For the one to carry it in your place must also be chosen. It is the Lord who chooses who will follow in the footsteps of those he has appointed. He is the king. Talk to him, and he will give you your strength. Do not decide things on your own. Seldom does any good come from that.

I will pray, as always, that you fight the good fight until the Lord returns. My Lord has told us all to do this. It is the destiny of each one who comes to believe.

Be well, with all the love of my Lord,

Mary of Magdalene.

Longinus knew Mary was right in all that she said. He did not read the letter a second time. He carefully folded it and placed it with her other letters, which he held dearly.

Meanwhile...

The years passed and it was now 54 A.D. Khalid had aged, yet he continued to fight the good fight with great vigor. Vitali was always by his side. Yet strangely, Vitali did not show any signs of aging. Longinus also appeared the same, except that his countenance had grown bright and his face radiated a glow. His strength had grown to match that of the biblical Samson.

The followers had most all accepted the name given to them by the Romans of Christian, and now most all called one another by the same. Yet, there were still those that continued to call themselves the followers of the way.

Longinus and his band of men continued to fight against the Roman soldiers and do many preemptive attacks. His reputation for being a death-defying warrior continued to grow.

Then one day, there came the news of the death of Claudius Caesar, and Rome was about to announce their new Caesar. A young lad, who was only sixteen years of age, whose name was Nero.

THE OLD MAN FINDS NERO

The Old Man, known as the apprentice, had much delight in stirring
strife for the followers under the past Caesars. But now, he had grown tired of doing things so slowly. He wanted the followers gone, once and for all.

"I need to change my approach. The only way to kill them all is to take charge of the most powerful man in the world and control him totally myself. I must kill every follower that exists. Once that is done, there will be no great myth, and no one to go against the forces of darkness.

Now, let me see, let me see," said the Old Man as he peered into his glass globe. "Ahh, yes, splendid." He watched as the City of Rome celebrated great pomp in the crowning of their new Caesar. "There he is. Now what shall I do to ensure that he does not disobey my commands?"

After pondering for a moment, the old man knew what he would do. He spun around, and instantly, he was in Rome at the festivities.

He secretly watched as the new Caesar named Nero stood before the people of Rome on his platform.

"I shall wait for the proper time, after the celebration," he said in a sinister voice.

The late evening came and a very drunken Nero fell into his bed for the night. He did not even undress from his Roman robe nor did he take the civic crown from his head. The chaplet of common oak leaves woven into a crown lay sideways upon his head. That, along with his fat neck and potbelly, gave Nero the appearance of a foolish court jester. His age did not help the matter at all.

The Old Man suddenly appeared in his room and looked at the foolish sight.

"I just may have second thoughts on what I am about to do," sighed the old man. He walked up to Nero as he lay in his bed and stared at him. "Well, he is fair haired," he said as he took his finger and lifted up Nero's right eyelid. "And he has soft blue eyes. He is only sixteen and will rule a great number of years. I guess I will continue."

The Old Man stood over the drunken Nero, who was passed out cold, and chanted, "By the powers of darkness that are all mine to use, grant me his body to serve as my muse. Let me possess it and call it my own, may Nero obey every thought he is shown."

When he finished, the Old Man's body turned into a dark shadowy apparition; it moved over the body of Nero and lay over him. It began to merge into Nero and sunk into his body until all that was seen was a faint wisp, and then, that submerged as well.

The old man had successfully possessed the body of Nero. And now, every evil thought that the master sorcerer thought would be carried out by the flesh of Nero. The old man, known as the apprentice, would now live inside of Nero's body until Nero's death. There was no undoing what had just been done.

Upon the morning, Nero awoke. The old man felt his new skin and started to think of ways to do the most horrendous and devious of acts. "I am now Nero, the most powerful man in the world."

He no sooner thought this and Nero pompously strutted across the room and straightened out his civic crown. He looked in the mirror to assure it was straight.

The Apprentice gave a second test. This time he thought projected inside of Nero's head. He whispered, *"I shall begin this day by ordering that all Christ followers be hanged by their feet, with their heads downward over a small fire and let the smoke strangle them slowly. They will die in pain and torment."*

Immediately Nero went straight to his door and called his guard, "Guard, I have a proclamation for all of Rome. Any Christ follower found shall be hanged by their feet, with their heads downward over a small fire. The smoke shall strangle them slowly. Let this be done as an example for any others that wish to continue to deny the gods of Rome and follow a myth."

The Old Man was well pleased. He had successfully possessed the body and mind of Nero with his demonic powers of darkness, and now, anything the sorcerer thought would be carried out by Nero.

News came quickly to Cappadocia of the ways Nero was persecuting and killing the followers who were now called Christ followers. The barbarous acts against the Christ followers were far worse than any they had ever endured. Only a Satan-inspired imagination could have thought of so many evil means of torture leading to death.

As the years went by, word continued to come to Longinus of horrendous acts of Nero, taking place in the Circus in Rome. Longinus was beside himself at being helpless to stop the acts of the evil Nero. This weighed heavy on his mind.

LONGINUS GOES TO THE CIRCUS MAXIMUS

It came to be Ad 63, and Nero had been terrorizing and killing the Followers of the way of the Christ ever since he became Caesar. Just a year earlier, Nero had made a series of horrid proclamations that basically sentenced all who did not bow down to him as their god would be put to death. He began to use the arena in the Circus Maximus as a ring of torture. He would have hungry lions tear apart mothers clinging to their babes and children who did not deny their Lord; he would place followers before the crowds and have them ordered to denounce their god and bow to Nero. Those who did this would be branded with searing hot irons in their chests, burning into them the markings of Rome, those who did not would be ripped apart by horrid means. The stories and reports of evil torture and death kept increasing. It wasn't going away.

It was mid-morning and Longinus had just finished tending to the horses. He was headed inside the house and spied Khalid. He motioned for him to come and Khalid nodded.

"It's a hot day," Khalid hollered then spoke softly to Vitali, "Let's see what he needs girl." They both made their way to Longinus. As they got closer, Khalid noticed Longinus looked as though something weighed heavy on his mind.

"What's on your mind?" asked Khalid.

"Khalid, we must stop this mad man, Nero."

Khalid responded, "Longinus, we cannot fight all of Rome. If there's one thing I've learned from this journey, it's vengeance this size belongs to God and God only. We can defend ourselves and protect the innocent. That is our purpose. But to take on the entire empire that governs the world? That is God's purpose to do."

"I do not suggest to destroy all of Rome. Just one man. The same man that goes about in public wearing a dressing gown without a belt, with a scarf tied around his neck, and wears no shoes! He is a

lunatic! A mad man possessed by the demonic realm of darkness!"

Khalid was silent.

Longinus continued to rant, "He tortures people, then throws them half dead into prison where they die a slow death."

Khalid answered, "It is hard, yes. But there is little we can do against..."

Longinus interrupted Khalid, "Have you not heard of his hunger to find Christians and place shirts of wax upon them and tie them to poles, only to burn them alive in his garden?"

Squinting, Khalid closed his eyes and sighed.

Longinus got louder, "This he does at night when his guests arrive, burning them like torches to light his palace. These Romans jeer with sick delight as he tortures innocents!"

Khalid knew Nero was bad and said, "This man is not a man. He is evil, I know this."

Longinus raved on, "He is a vile creature of hell itself, led by the desires of demons! And those that partake in his doings are full of demons as well!"

Suddenly, they were interrupted by a follower who came running to them frantically. "Longinus, Longinus, Peter has been crucified!"

Longinus shouted, "What is this you say?"

The follower gasped to catch his breath as his heart raced, "Upside down, they crucified him upside down...", he gasped, "... in Jerusalem by the hands of Romans by order of the mad Caesar."

Khalid moved fast and caught hold of the man as he started to collapse from exhaustion. Holding onto the fainting man, he looked Longinus in the eyes and said, "Nero."

Khalid slowly lowered the man down to the ground.

Longinus looked down at the follower and questioned, "Peter?" The follower nodded yes.

Longinus turned and looked at Khalid. "It is time to do something, whether you are with me or stay behind, I cannot bear this any longer. The only way to protect the innocent is to rid the source of their problem."

Khalid gave the exhausted man some water and slowly helped him up.

He looked at Longinus. "So what is your plan?"

Longinus answered, "Alert the men, we go to Rome!"

Longinus went inside and began filling up a haversack with supplies.

Khalid followed inside and asked, "What do we do when we get to Rome?"

Longinus kept gathering supplies and ranted, "I will not just sit here and hold my spear and pray into it for patience!"

"So you would rather run into the Palace of Nero and have him fit you with a wax shirt for his next garden show?" snapped Khalid. "Or will you just be content to have him put you on racks and stretch every limb out of its socket, then stretch you out until you are nothing but a limbless body screaming as you slowly bleed to death? That's Nero's favorite torture for men who challenge his authority!"

Longinus stopped and looked at Khalid. "Do you not think I know all these things and more. Because of knowing this, I must go there and stop it?"

"Longinus, you can still help many. If you go to Nero, you will help none."

Longinus turned and paced up and down. He thought of a plan. "We will go to Rome and enter the Circus Maximus dressed as Roman citizens. We will spy on them and find the best way to fight this mad man and stop his murderous games."

Khalid took a deep breath, "I will alert the men."

Rome

Longinus and his band of men arrived at the outskirts of Rome. They dressed as Roman citizens, entered the city, and went straight to the Circus Maximus. They strategically positioned themselves throughout the stadium, each taking different seats. The stadium quickly filled up with people who were eager to watch what Nero called "the games." Longinus and Khalid took seats, next to each other, sitting and watching as Nero entered and the crowds cheered.

Nero stood and raised his hand for the soldiers to begin. The crowd grew noisy and stood as the soldiers brought in a massive number of animal skins that had live people sewn inside them. Erie screams and pleas for help resonated from inside the skins by the innocent people who were sewn inside them as the soldiers paraded them around the circle of the Circus Maximus.

Longinus grew angry at the display.

Meanwhile, ravenous lions were salivating behind iron gates that were strategically placed within the walls surrounding the circumference of the arena. Eager to be released, they jumped at the bars and roared unceasing. It was obvious they had not been fed for days and they knew the skins contained their dinner.

Nero was enthralled with the crowd as they cheered in anticipation of the lion's release. He looked raving mad with the whites of his eyes showing all around as he toyed with the audience making them wait. This seemed to be one of his favorite parts of the event, where all the attention was on him and he had the power to please them by giving the signal to release the lions or displease them by not.

Nero lapped up the false accolades as he bowed and waved, pushing his moment right up to the edge where to stall any longer would result in an angry mob. At that exact moment, right at the edge…he signaled the release of the ravenous beasts and the crowd cheered thunderously loud like savages, salivating more than the lions, even drowning out their bellowing roars.

Khalid turned to Longinus and whispered, "Nero and the people of Rome do just as the refugees have said."

The iron gates were raised up, and the ferocious lions leaped at the animal skins tearing them apart with their huge teeth, devouring and ripping limbs from the live people inside of them. Horrid screams were heard and the crowd cheered so loud, it was deafening.

Longinus jumped to his feet, ready to go into the arena. Khalid grabbed his arm and held him back.

"Not now, Longinus. This is not the time."

"If this is not the time, then when?"

Khalid cautioned, "These savage elites lust for blood, they will eat you before the lions do. Look at them, their eyes, the evil noise they make at seeing death."

One of their men came to them and said, "I can't stomach this, I wait outside." And he made his way to leave the Circus.

Khalid being cautious stood up and motioned to Longinus, "Come we have seen enough."

Longinus could not hide his angry aggravated look of distain, but the crowd was in such a frenzy jumping up and down flailing their arms wildly in the air, they didn't notice him. Their eyes were on the lions jaws tearing flesh and crunching bone, mesmerized by the blood and gore.

Khalid led Longinus cautiously out of the Circus, all the while fearing he may try and fight the Romans and Nero single handed. The band of men saw them leaving, and one by one, they followed suit and left the Circus. They returned to their meeting point in a secluded area outside the city ready to devise a plan.

Khalid spoke first, "The only way to end this is to stop their supply of followers. We must kill the soldiers before they can take their captors to the prisons."

"I say kill Nero," said Longinus.

Khalid responded, "You heard the cheers from the crowds. Rome has many like Nero who love this torture. Cut off the supply of people and they have no games."

Longinus thought about what Khalid said. "Perhaps you are right. Then, we will go to the villages where they hunt for followers. We will kill every soldier Nero sends. Do all agree?"

The men all agreed.

"I will go back into the city and spy to find out where the worst threats to the followers are. Wait for me here. I won't be long."

Longinus entered the city and hid outside the Palace of Caesar. He knew how soldiers complained whenever they received new orders and waited to see if any soldiers leaving the palace said anything.

Suddenly, Nero marched up with an entourage of guards; he was having a tantrum.

"I need more of them! I don't have enough to orchestrate the best performance. It would have been more splendid today had we had a hundred more sewn in skins! I want more now!"

The soldiers answered, "Yes, Prefect."

"Send soldiers to every village in every province of Rome!"

"Yes, Prefect."

Nero went inside the Palace, and in a minute, a centurion came out grumbling about having to help at dawn with a detachment returning with followers at the east of the city. Longinus left and returned to his band of men.

"There is a detachment of soldiers due to return at the east of the city at dawn. They are bringing captured followers to the prisons. We must lay wait for them a ways away from the city and make sure they never arrive."

Longinus and his band of men positioned themselves on the east hillside and waited for the Roman detachment to come. Finally, the detachment was seen approaching. The men saw followers being herded with their mouths gagged and hands tied. They were roped at the waist and bound together one by one, in a long line. The band of men waited for Longinus to give the signal to attack.

Longinus raised his hand, and they attacked with stealth. A whizzing was heard and daggers and arrows flew, hitting their Roman targets with pinpoint accuracy. In minutes, all the soldiers were dead on the ground. Longinus and the band of men freed the followers and took them to safety.

The band of men, led by Longinus, continued to perform raid after raid. They released prisoners and took them to safety. Word of these raids came to Nero, and he was not happy. He called his centurions to his court and demanded an account.

A centurion gave his report, "The army cannot be seen, they are led by an enigma that cannot be killed and does not age. His power is said to lie within his spear."

Nero shouted, "I want him killed! Kill him this very day!"

"That is not possible, Prefect."

Nero looked angrily at the centurion and stormed over to him.

He pulled the centurion's sword from his sheath, swung it at his neck, and severed the centurion's head from his body. He turned to another centurion and shouted, "I want him killed this very day!"

The centurion answered, "Yes, Prefect."

LONGINUS RETURNS TO SEE MARY

Longinus and his band of men returned to Cappadocia and had a large number of new refugees with them. They directed them to the underground passages for safety. A disciple was there, holding a letter.

"It is from Mary," said the disciple, handing Longinus the letter.

"It has been three years since she has written," said Longinus as he took the letter.

Khalid remarked wearily, "And three more years of killing Nero's soldiers and we make not a dent in stopping the killings of followers."

Longinus opened the letter as he answered Khalid, "I too am growing weary in shedding all this blood in vain. There must be another way to stop this evil."

"I tell you this much, I'm not as you. I grow older and more tired each day. Don't know how many more raids I can do."

Longinus ignored Khalid and smelled the letter. He smiled at the pleasant aroma. He read the letter.

My Dearest Longinus,

I have heard of your reputation as a great protector and warrior. Many say you cannot die. Others say you do not age. I smile inside when I hear how you have saved the lives of so many, but there is one important thing I must tell you. Evil principalities and powers cannot be killed with spears and swords. Seek the one who has chosen you, and you will find what you need to fulfill your destiny. With all the love of our Lord,

Mary Magdalene

Longinus read the letter again; he was deeply troubled at the words. He turned to Khalid.

"I must go to see Mary. Lead the band of men until I return. I must ask her many things."

Khalid nodded, and Longinus left to gather supplies for his journey.

Many days later…

Longinus traveled the long journey from Cappadocia to the south of Gaul and finally reached Villalata where Mary lived. He rode along the dirt path on his horse wondering how to find Mary. He saw an old man sweeping the door post of a church and hollered out to him.

"Old man, can you tell me where I can find Mary Magdalene?"

The old man looked up, "Longinus, is that you?"

Longinus looked and did not recognize the old man.

"It is me, Maximim."

Longinus quickly dismounted his horse, walked over to the old man, and gave him a quick embrace.

"So the stories are true, you do not age!" smiled Maximim. "Look at you…the strapping image of brawn you always were. The Lord has blessed you greatly. Your destiny is a great one."

"I don't understand it, but it is what it is."

"You are blessed."

"Where can I find Mary?"

"She has been in Aix for a long time. Yet she never stays in the same place. Always moving to where the Lord leads her. I believe she is at the sanctuary at this time. She has made it her second home," he smiled. "Her love is the Lord and she devotes her time in praise and prayer. When people come to the sanctuary, she teaches. Then, she goes back to Aix and teaches there. She comes here too. She visits Carmague and all the places in between. So you see, she goes where the Lord leads her."

"Where is the sanctuary you speak of?"

"At the grotto at the Mountain of Marseille. It has become her second home."

"How do I find this place?"

"You will ride through the path, be careful to stay on it, for it's not well traveled and may at points be hard to see. You will come to the grove at the foot of the sacred mountain of Marseille. You will have to go the rest of the way on foot. It's not fit for a horse to travel. You will come to a mountain path, it's way hidden in the back to the side. But you know it when you see it. There are rocky steps and smooth spots but the path is not hard to climb, only tiresome."

"Thank you, Maximim, I must go and find her now."

Maximim waved good-bye and praised God for the blessing of seeing Longinus again after all the years that had passed. He marveled at the sight of him galloping away on his horse. He stood in awe watching until Longinus was out of sight, then went back to his sweeping.

Longinus followed the directions that Maximim gave to him and finally made his way to the foot of the grove at the sacred mountain of Marseille.

"This must be it", he said to himself. He dismounted his horse and secured it tight to a tree making sure there was green enough on the ground for the steed to feed on. Giving his horse a drink from his flask, Longinus set off to find the mountain path.

After several trial an error approaches, he finally found the path that led up to the mountain. As started the climb, his heart began to pound with anticipation. He was so close to finally seeing Mary again. Yet, he feared Maximim's caution that she may not be there. He finally made it to the top and saw the grotto. He ran to the opening and entered. It was dark and empty, he was beginning to feel she was not there and started to leave when suddenly in the darkness he heard Mary's voice.

"Longinus! Is that you?"

"Mary!" shouted Longinus. He ran to her with his arms out to embrace and wrapped them around her, holding her tight.

"What is wrong? Why are you holding me so tight?" she asked.

"Oh, forgive me," he said as he let her go. "I have missed you so much. I have many important things to ask of you. I need your help."

"Come," she said. They went farther into the grotto and Mary led him to a little opening. They went through, and she slid a wooden door shut to close the entrance. Longinus looked around and there were all the proper things for cooking and for cleaning preparation, and a smaller section of the cave was set apart with orderly rows of urns full of rolled parchments and scrolls.

At the side of the room was a table, with a parchment laying upon it with words filling half of it. Writing instruments were at the right side of it. There were stacks of parchments drying all about the floor. And others that looked as though they had dried, but had been forgotten about.

"So you scribe?" asked Longinus.

"Oh yes. I scribe the things my Lord has done and of things he has shown me."

Suddenly, Longinus stopped and took a good look at Mary, she had aged. She was no longer the young Mary that he remembered in his mind every time he read her letters. She was much older now. Yet her face glowed with an aura of light. She appeared so angelic. He wondered at this, but said nothing.

"Longinus, you look magnificent," she said. "You have not grown old. Not at all. The Lord has blessed you, not only with your vision, but with youth."

Longinus wondered at what she said.

"Oh, where are my manners," said Mary. "Let me get you something to eat and to drink. I have stew that is still warm. And bread that I made this morning." She quickly went to prepare Longinus some food.

Longinus looked down at the half-written parchment on the table and began to read it.

It came to pass then, when Mary had heard the Savior say these words, that she gazed fixedly into the air for the space of an hour. She said: "My Lord, give commandment to me to speak in openness." And Jesus, the compassionate, answered and said unto Mary: "Mary, thou blessed one, whom I will perfect in all mysteries, of those of the height, discourse in openness, thou, whose heart is raised to the Kingdom of Heaven more than all thy brethren."

"Come and eat, you must be very hungry," Mary called out.

Longinus stopped reading and went to Mary. She had prepared bread, warmed up some stew, and was pouring him a cup of wine.

"That looks so good," said Longinus as he sat down to eat. Mary said the prayer to bless the food and she sat and watched him eat.

"You are not eating?" he asked.

"I had some not long before you came." She smiled and said,

"When you are done, you must tell me the important things that you came to say."

Longinus nodded in agreement as he chewed his bread.

Longinus was now curious with questions. He asked, "Where is Mary, the mother of Jesus, and Sidonius? Are they in Marseilles or Villalata?"

Mary answered, "Sidonius went on up north from here about fifteen years ago, he is still teaching. But he is rather old now and can't get around as well. He sends letters, and I send him letters as well. Mary, the precious mother of Jesus, died two years ago. She is with her son, the Lord, now in paradise, resting until it is time to return with the Lord in all his glory."

"I am sorry," said Longinus.

"Do not be sorry, she is at peace for all eternity now. The angels of heaven greeted her and carried her up into the heavens. I saw this myself. It was a glorious sight. But I do long to see her, and I do miss her. I will see her again soon."

After he was finished eating, Longinus began to speak of Nero and the manner in which he tortured the Christians. Mary cringed at hearing such things. "I have heard he was killing many followers, but no one has told me as horrid a description as you have told. It is most evil."

"Mary, I can no longer bare this thing. I do not understand why the Lord has blessed me with great strength to protect, yet I am only one and cannot be everywhere. I do not understand why the Father has shown himself to the followers and then allows them to be slaughtered like sheep? They are as dry bones. When will they stand up and become a great and powerful army?"

"Longinus, it takes great strength and courage to stand for the kingdom of heaven, knowing you will be tortured and then slain for taking that stand. The sheep you call dry bones are standing! Open your eyes and see it!"

Longinus looked like a deer in the headlights as he was being scolded by her words.

"Longinus, hear me please, there is no weapon nor brawn that can ever surpass such a great and powerful army for the Lord. Those who stand firmly on their faith and choose the living God over the dictates of this world will win for death has no victory over their soul. Jesus gave his life for all who believe. He lives in them."

"If he lives in them, why are they being tortured and killed?"

"Longinus it is an evil war we are in. The principalities and powers of darkness want to overshadow the kingdom of heaven. But their demons of wickedness will not ever be as strong or as powerful as even one who is martyred for their faith and belief in the Lord.

"Their rewards shall be great in heaven. Those that do evil for the darkness will burn for eternity in the fires of Sheol!"

"Mary, I can no longer bare to watch this evil, nor can I bare to fight it. Please can you answer me, what will happen if I abandon my destiny?"

"I do not know."

"But, Mary, you are the one whom the Lord perfected in all mysteries, you are the one whose heart the Lord lifted to the kingdom of heaven more than anyone."

Mary looked surprised at Longinus. She knew immediately he had been reading her parchment. She answered him sternly, "Is it not because I sought him so? Is it not that I wait patiently until my Lord speaks to my heart? There is only one Lord who speaks and then things are so. Seek him for your answers. I am but a servant of the Lord. Not the Lord. It is he you must seek. Not his servant."

Longinus was deeply sorrowed at her words for she was not agreeing with him and his countenance fell. Mary saw this, and then, in a comforting voice, she said to him,

"Longinus, from the day I have met you until this day, you have come to me with the very same question. Each time, I give you the same answer. Yet you come again seeking truth and expect me to change the truth to suit the actions you desire to do. There is no one who can help you except the one who has chosen you. The one who has chosen you is the Lord. And he is the one you must go to and ask what you must do."

"Oh, Mary, forgive me. All that you have said is true."

"Come, Longinus," Mary said as she reached out her hand for him to take it. Longinus took her hand, and she led him into the place in the cave where all of her parchments laid strewn about and in urns. "I have things for you to take to Cappadocia. Things you must read, and I pray it will help you to understand the special bond I have with my Lord. A bond that all can have, they must only be taught how to have it."

Longinus smiled and said, "Oh, Mary, thank you so much."

Mary continued, "I have sought his presence for many years. I have asked him to allow the Holy Spirit to guide me in all that he desires that I should write. Sometimes, it is hard to tell the difference between what he is telling me and what I want to say. It is at these times, I stop writing and seek his council in prayer. Sometimes, I fast and pray for several weeks. Sometimes, it may take months. Often, it is hard to wait. But the joy in hearing an angel tell you that the Lord has heard you, and he has been sent to answer, that joy is something few will ever experience, let alone, understand. The heavenly blessings are worth the small price we must pay in the flesh."

Longinus felt compelled to speak from his heart, "Mary, I tell you the truth. I am a stubborn man, my Lord knows this about me. I fumble about trying to help others, my gifts are brawn and cunning. The only thing the Lord can use of me are those two things. I have asked him to search my heart many times. So many times, I cannot remember the count. He knows my heart is good, but it is easily hurt. It is fragile. I guard it so closely because it grieves and it breaks. When this happens, my brawn and my cunning are of no use. I then am a broken vessel.

"I ask you always what can I do to change my destiny because I fear being a broken vessel, of no use for anyone, save alone the Lord. This truth I am sharing, I have never dared to speak. I have only shared this with you. My Lord already knows my heart and my life, yet he uses me anyway. Why he does is what I do not understand."

"Sometimes, to understand is impossible. The way to follow the Lord is to accept," answered Mary. "For God's ways are not man's ways."

"Indeed. I will do as you say and ask him. As the Lord hath said, "Pass this cup from me, but not my will, but thy will be done,'" he said, very somber.

Mary touched his arm and said, "That is what you must do."

Longinus nodded. Mary got up to gather some parchments, and he noticed she moved slowly as if she were in pain. "Are you all right?" he asked.

"Oh, I am fine. My body gets stiff from time to time, but it is fine. Here, I have found what you must take to Cappadocia."

She had several parchments all rolled together. She handed them to him, then said, "Oh, and I have some more." She went to an urn and pulled out three scrolls.

"These you must have them read in the church, the parchments too, but especially these."

Longinus looked at all the bundles and said, "You have been busy with a great work."

Mary answered, "Many cannot read, but they can listen. These things must be taught. They must be read with the Holy Spirit guiding the one who reads, so that the true meaning is told. The meaning the Lord intended. Many will twist the words, just as they have twisted the words of the prophets. You must tell others to guard that this does not happen."

"Thank you, they will be read."

"Now, come, let me prepare a place for you to rest. You must be very tired. It is late. Tomorrow, we can talk some more."

Longinus nodded and watched as Mary gathered some blankets and prepared a place on the floor for him. When she was finished he smiled at her and said, "You treat me well."

Mary smiled back at him, "You are a good man. Stubborn, but God will use that for his good."

"Indeed." He answered.

"Sleep well," said Mary as she left the room.

Longinus took off his sword belt, and clothing down to his tunic and nuzzled between the blankets Mary had provided for his bedding. As he lay there he thought of the things Mary had spoken to him but quickly grew tired and dozed off.

The morning came fast and Longinus awoke to a delicious smell of hot bread. "Ahh," he smiled, "Bread."

Now motivated by the rich aroma, Longinus dressed quickly and went to the table where Mary had a plate of hot bread, butter and a porridge waiting for him.

"I hope you are hungry," she said, "I've made two loaves."

"Indeed I am."

Longinus devoured the food, as he always does and Mary giggled, "This reminds me of the time at Timmeon's Inn when you ate so fast the people stopped eating just to watch you."

Longinus looked up, his mouth was so full his cheeks poked out and looked like a squirrels when gathering food. "You won't let me forget that," he muffled with his mouth full.

"Don't talk, you will choke and then what will I do?" laughed Mary.

After breakfast, Longinus and Mary talked of many things and the time passed by quickly. Everything he came to say and ask was said, and he knew it was time to leave and return to Cappadocia. He did not know how to say his farewell to Mary. There was but one thing more he wanted to ask but felt it was best if he did not ask it, for she had aged, and he had not. He kept remembering a much younger Mary. It bothered him deeply to watch her struggle to get up when she stooped down doing tasks that should be so simple. He knew she was trying hard to not show the pain and struggle, so he kept silent and continued to act like everything was normal and the way it was all supposed to be. He gathered his things and prepared to leave and stood at the door of the cave.

"Wait, the parchments!" Mary exclaimed as she ran to get them. Returning quickly she handed them to Longinus. He carefully put them in his haversack.

"It would have been bad to forget these", he said, "You always look after me with such things."

"I will pray for your safe return to Cappadocia."

"Thank you, Mary."

As the two walked out of the cave into the morning light and the sun shined down upon Mary, Longinus could see the fine lines on her face now appeared very pronounced. He remembered how the last time he saw her years ago, her flesh was so smooth and taut. Her flawless olive skin, which used to match the color of her hair, was much lighter and a bit ashy now, her auburn hair was grayed as well, yet still very long. He noticed that no matter how time had aged her, she still radiated an outward beauty that matched that which she held in her heart.

Whether it was his longing to see the young Mary he remembered, or concern for the fact he was not aging himself, he could not keep silent any longer. He bent his head down and looked deep into her eyes, "I must ask you one more thing."

Mary smiled and said, "Ask."

"Why is it that I have not aged and you have?"

Mary not sure how to answer him, thought a moment and said, "The only answer I can give to you is that you have been blessed by the Lord. The same power of the blood and water that healed your eye has also blessed you with an ageless body. You must use it to fulfill the destiny that the Lord has placed before you."

Longinus wondered at Mary's words and knew she had told him the truth.

They walked together and stood at the edge of the start of the mountain paths downward trail. Mary was quiet and Longinus was already beginning to miss her. He started down the path, then he turned and looked at Mary and ran back to her and gave her one last long embrace.

Mary spoke softly, "Be safe."

Longinus said, "I will come again."

Mary answered, "I would like that."

As Longinus walked down the mountain path, Mary stood and watched until he was no longer in sight.

RUNNING FROM DESTINY- THE PARCHMENT

Longinus was now on his way back to Cappadocia and had traveled three days. He stopped to make camp before the sun went down. He had planned to read some of the parchments that Mary had given to him. He made his camp in a hurry and grabbed some bread. He nestled into a comfortable spot where the sun was still visible, so he could read.

The only problem he had was in deciding what to read first. He decided to unroll a scroll. He read it and pondered. He went to the last lines and read again.

Then Peter, turning about, saw the disciple whom Jesus loved following; which also leaned on his breast at supper, and said, Lord, which is he that betrayed thee? Peter seeing the disciple said to Jesus, Lord, and what shall this one do? Jesus said unto him, If I will that this one tarry till I come, what is that to thee? Follow thou me. Then went this saying abroad among the brethren, that that disciple should not die: yet Jesus said not unto him, this disciple shall not die; but, If I will that this disciple tarry till I come, what is that to thee?

Longinus pondered for a moment, then continued to read: This is the disciple which testified of these things, and wrote these things: and we know that this testimony is true.

Longinus hurried to see who had scribed these words but there was no name on the scroll.

"Mary," he said under his breath. He thought it had to be Mary for it was in her urn with her other writings, and she gave it to him. His mind raced back to what Mary said about the writings.

"You must study them with the Holy Spirit guiding you, so that you receive the true message within them. Many will twist the words, just as they have the words of the prophets."

"If not her, who?" He questioned out loud.

"Stop it!" He scolded himself as he rolled up the parchment. "You always do such things. It gets you no where."

He returned the parchment to his haversack and grabbed his bedding. "You're too tired to make sense," he mumbled as he arranged his bedding on the ground. He lay down and tried to sleep. All the while he was thinking, If I will that this one tarry till I come, what is that to thee? Follow thou me. Those words haunted him.

Longinus calmed himself down and tried to get some sleep. Yet his mind kept thinking as he remembered other things he had read from the parchment.

"I was there at the cross, it had to be Mary, for his mother would not have been able to have testified to all these things. And her aunt was not there on the walk with them. She could not have testified to these things." He thought, Who was Mary to the Lord? Was she more than a disciple? Can she be the chosen one who can take the spear?

Longinus was obsessed with his thoughts and could not fall asleep. He finally jumped up and pulled up camp muttering under his breath, "What is it to you if this one tarry 'til I come? What does this mean?"

Longinus mounted his horse. As he sat in the saddle, he had second thoughts. "This is silly, Mary would even tell me so. It is her scroll. He dismounted and started to unpack his horse but his mind continued to think. "I am but three days out from Marseille, if I return to Cappadocia now, I may not be able to return for a long time, perhaps never?" He shook his head and mounted his horse and rode fast toward the mountain of Marseille. He was head strong to speak with Mary.

Running From Destiny…

Longinus drove his horse like a mad man, heading to Villalata. Somewhere between his obsession to talk with Mary and his own crazy thoughts, he had found the stamina to ride, but now he was still a days ride away and physically unable to go any further. He had only rested his horse briefly and for himself he had rested less.

He was driven to find an answer, and in his obsession, he had failed to call upon the Lord. His every thought was his own. He did not even pray for direction. Somehow, he had totally lost the way of the Lord. It was as though, he went back to the days of his allegiance with Rome, where the only thing he knew was to go forward with marching orders. And the orders he was obeying now were that of his own making.

Longinus was now feeling faint, the adrenaline that had fueled his obsession had finally diminished.

His horse was waning and wanting of rest, food, and water. He finally gave up, for he too needed the same. He stopped. As he dismounted, he grabbed his spear. He tried to walk to the back of his horse to get his haversack, but his legs buckled beneath him, and he staggered, then fell. As he lay in the dust, he tried to get up. He looked over and watched as his horse did the same, he staggered, then lay down, rolling over on his side from exhaustion. Longinus laid on the ground parallel to his horse, his spear still clutched in his hand. His mind was finally quiet.

He was totally alone, with no thoughts. His horse gave a few thrusts through his nostrils, then fell silent as well. Longinus could not think, not one thought. The world around him was deafened.

He lay there, wanting to get up, but could not move.

As he lay in the dirt and gravel, a deep bellowing voice called to him, "Longinus, why are you running so?"

Longinus looked up. He did not see anyone. He lay his head back down in the dirt and gravel.

"You are very weary," bellowed the voice. "Yet you do not seek me to help you."

"Who are you?" asked Longinus in a feeble voice, unable to even lift his head.

"I am the one whose side you pierced."

"Then have mercy on me and help me, my Lord," he cried out as he laid there in a weakened pitiful state.

"How can I help you, when you do not seek me, nor listen to those I have sent before you?"

"I have sinned in this, yes, I have," admitted Longinus. The voice came no more. Longinus waited to hear it again, but it did not come. He waited, and waited, then fell asleep from exhaustion.

He dreamed.

In the dream, he saw Mary; she was radiant and looked the way she did in her youth. She called to Longinus, "Come, follow the way of the Lord." In the dream, he followed her a little ways trying to catch up with her, and then she disappeared.

When Longinus awoke he remembered the bellowing voice. He wondered if it was a dream or real. His horse was now standing. Longinus got up and gave his horse some water. Then he led his horse over off the road to some green. The horse ate. Longinus drank from his goatskin flask and ate some bread. The same bread that Mary had given him for his journey home.

He felt confused, weak, alone, and broken. He knelt down on his knees and prayed as he had never prayed before. As he prayed, he lost all sense of reality, and he was on his face, crying out to the Lord. He shared all of the things he could only speak to Mary about; he poured out all of his fears, his hopes, and his wrongs. He begged for forgiveness in his arrogant ways and his selfish attitude about the great gift he had been given. He shared his thoughts on how he was undeserving to be chosen and how Mary had said he was deserving to be so. He wept and cried out for help. He shared his disdain for the evil being done to the Christians and how it broke his heart. How he could not be in more than one place and the torment of not being unable to help all who were suffering. He cried out against the evil and how it tore his heart apart. He continued in prayer until he could pray no more and his face fell in the dust. He lay there, crying, and then he exhausted himself and just lay.

"Longinus," a voice bellowed, "get up, I have heard your cry. Go on to where your heart longs. I am with you."

Longinus stood up and his body was refreshed. His horse was waiting in a manner so majestic. He mounted and the horse burst forth running over rocks and debris that should have slowed him down, but he rode like the wind, and his feet barely touched the ground.

The next day, Longinus rounded the bend to the cave. He saw the clearing, and his heart leaped. He continued to gallop all the way to the end of the grove, but as he approached, there was a crowd of people gathered. He dismounted his horse, holding his spear, and marched past the crowd and up the long path to the cave.

There were so many there. No one was happy; they were weeping and mourning.

He went inside. A woman looked at Longinus and sadly asked, "Did you know her?"

Longinus did not know how to answer her. He walked on and into the place where she slept. There were many people there. She was prepared for burial. Longinus was torn apart. He dropped his spear and threw himself over her body and wept. No one came near him. He wailed and wept over Mary uncontrollably.

Time went by, no one can say how long, and a man came to Longinus and said, "It is time to take her to the sepulcher."

Longinus would not leave. He clung to Mary. The man put his hand on Longinus's shoulder and said, "Come, we must place her now."

Longinus looked up and his eyes were blurred from the tears. He could not see who was speaking to him. For he was filled with deep sorrow. Little did he know that the man who placed his hand on his shoulder was Jesus, his Lord.

Several men carefully took her body and lifted it into a wooden box, lined with the finest silk cloth of purple. The women then placed several objects of hers inside of it. They began to close the lid, and Longinus shouted, "Wait!" They all looked at him, and he said, "Give me one moment with her alone, I beg you." The people nodded and left the room.

Longinus looked at his sweet Mary, lying so lifeless, and he said, "I broke my spear once in anger, and now I break it in search of mercy." Then he took his spear and broke the head away from the shaft. "This belongs with one pure of heart and sound in faith, one who is chosen for a special purpose." He carefully placed it next to her heart and covered it with her robe.

"You are the one whom it has been laid upon my heart this day to place it with. I know, for I wrestled with the Lord before I came. He told me to go on where your heart longs, and he would be with me. I am here, and you are gone. Yet I know he is still with me. I must give this to you, for what is it if the Lord has this one tarry until he comes? You, Mary, will be in the hearts of many until the Lord returns. I will be but a ghost."

Some men came in and said, "We must take her now," and closed the lid to the wooden box. Longinus stood up and followed the men out.

The people were all gathered outside and Longinus followed them to her burial site. It was a day full of sadness for him as well as the masses. He wept throughout the entire burial. He was torn and ripped apart inside.

When he left, he rode a small ways and stopped and fell prostrate upon the ground. He begged forgiveness of his past selfishness and begged to be forgiven for all he had fallen short of and begged to know that his giving the spear of his destiny to Mary was what the Holy Spirit had wanted him to do and not an act of his own thinking.

When he arose from his deep prayer, he felt good inside and secure that indeed the Holy Spirit had led him to do as he did. Now, he would head back to Cappadocia and serve the Lord there as a man and not as an enigma.

THE GREAT CONFRONTATION WITH NERO

Grieving beyond anything that Longinus had ever felt, even more than from the loss of his beloved Sabena, he ventured toward Cappadocia. It seemed as though he were dead and marching back toward a place of burial. Perhaps because his heart was torn, or perhaps, because he knew that time was no longer on his side since he had broken the spear and buried it with Mary.

Longinus traveled much less aggressively upon his return than he did upon his leaving. Time was all he seemed to have left, and he didn't care how much time it took to go here or there anymore. All of the questions he had seemed to have died with Mary, none of them mattered anymore.

When Longinus would stop for water and food, he would think of what had taken place, and he would be so struck with grief, he could not bear it. His travel back to Cappadocia was one of loss and of sorrow.

Longinus, tired of traveling alone by horse, longed for his home. He decided to go through Rome and to the ports. From there, he planned to board a ship and sail to Cappadocia.

Longinus rode through Rome and was only halfway in when it began to weigh heavily on him. Seeing and hearing all the berating chatter made him remembered why Rome was such a deep well of trouble. His allegiance was gone, far stripped from him. Some of it tossed down by himself. For one cannot hunt a rabbit that was raised in their cage and then suddenly say it is wild. The same, according to Longinus, applied to himself and Rome.

As Longinus rode along, he found that soldiers had the road

blocked and were redirecting all riders toward the Augusta Archway. Longinus was unaware that this was a baited trap, by order of Nero, to capture followers. He rode on through the archway and heard a woman crying out. He looked and saw two Roman soldiers bullying her. They threw her back and forth between them, like a bag of wheat.

"You can have her, no, you can have her," they taunted. "Pray to Nero to have mercy on you."

The soldier laughed as he slapped her down to the ground.

"Come on, let us hear your prayer to Nero," sneered the other soldier as he kicked her hard in the side. The woman screamed in pain.

Longinus jumped down from his horse and ran to the soldiers and pummeled them mercilessly until they fell to the ground. He helped the woman up and said, "Go, run from here."

He turned to get his horse, and Roman soldiers were holding it. Next to them stood a skinny man, in a white tunic with no belt, no shoes, with a scarf around his fat neck, and a civic crown upon his head. It was Nero. "Thou shalt have no strange gods beside me," squealed Nero in a high pitched nasal tone. "Now bow to me and kiss my feet."

Longinus reached for his sword, and immediately, he was surrounded with Roman hastas one inch from his body in every direction.

Nero smiled and sneered, "Shall I have them lance you like a boil? Or something else? Now kiss my feet."

Longinus stood still and remembered Mary's words: "*Longinus, it takes great strength and courage to stand for the kingdom of heaven, knowing you will be tortured and then slain for taking that stand. The sheep you call dry bones are standing! Open your eyes and see it*"!

Longinus looked at Nero's feet and said, "How can I with all these hastas in my way?"

"Guards, take his sword belt, then oblige him to come forth so he can kiss my feet," said Nero.

A Praetorian Guard removed Longinus's sword belt, then frisked him. Finding no other weapon on him, he ordered the hastas to be lowered, and allowed him to go to Nero.

Longinus moved toward him and looked down at Nero's feet. He then looked up at Nero's face and deep into his eyes. Nero had all the whites showing and a look of hysteria in his face, the same as he had seen when in the Circus Maximus awaiting the death of the innocent followers sewn inside animal skins. Longinus then looked down, bent at the waist, and spat on Nero's feet.

Nero was livid and shouted hysterically, "Crucify him now!" The soldiers began to drag Longinus toward the execution area, and he looked over to his horse. A legionnaire threw his belongings and haversack to the ground. He heard the legionnaire order his horse to be taken to the stables and watched the soldier lead the horse away.

Longinus struggled to get free, and another soldier ran over and pummeled him violently with a club. A centurion ordered the soldier to stop.

"Enough! He is to be crucified, not beaten to death in the streets."

The soldiers dragged Longinus along to the execution area.

Nero shouted impatiently to the soldier washing the spit off his feet, "Hurry up, I don't want to miss a thing!"

Soldiers violently forced Longinus to the ground and placed him over a beam. One soldier held his hand in place, while two others struggled to hold his body fast to the ground.

Nero approached and watched, smiling like a mad man.

A tall man in a dark hooded robe walked over to Longinus's haversack. He opened it and saw the parchments and scrolls. He closed it and picked it up. Walking toward the place where Longinus was being nailed to a beam on the ground. He stood a short distance away and watched. A dog that looked like a lion came up and stood by the hooded man's side.

Longinus looked up to the heavens and shouted, "If this is the destiny I have chosen, then let me fulfill it with courage!"

A soldier placed a nail over Longinus's wrist while another lifted a hammer and brought it down with great force, pounding the top of the nail. The shrill clang of the hammer hitting the nail rang in Longinus's ears. He wailed out a painful scream and looked up to the heavens. Longinus mustered his courage and shouted as loud as he could, so Nero would hear.

"Lord, receive my soul!"

Nero's smile of glee quickly changed to a look of disgust and distain. He ran over to Longinus and spat on him. "Shut up!" he shouted as he grabbed the hammer from the soldier's hand and raised it to pound the nail in deeper.

Nero thrust the hammer down, but not having the strength to control its weight, he lost his balance and toppled over on top of Longinus, totally missing the nail.

Nero shouted, as he clumsily climbed to his feet, "Guard finish this now!"

His Praetorian Guard picked up the hammer, and raised it high to pound the nail, at the same time the man in the hooded robe raised his hand. Suddenly, the soldier fell forward with a dagger in his back, feebly dropping the hammer and gasping as he crashed face down in the dirt.

Instantly daggers whizzed through the air targeting the Roman soldiers, while simultaneously arrows filled the sky like a black cloud coming from over the top of the Augusta Archway. The sound was like a thunderous wind as they rained down on all the soldiers at once striking them with precision.

In the flash of an eye the streets were filled with fallen, bleeding Roman soldiers pierced with arrows and daggers in their backs and chests, including all of Nero's Praetorian Guard.

Nero was terrified at the sight of his best soldiers dropping dead before his eyes and shrieked. "Guards, guards!" Nero looked around, panicked, only to see that none of his Praetorian Guards were left standing. Every one of them lay in a pool of blood.

He shrieked again, this time long and loud like a woman in terror and turned to run. A dagger whizzed through the air barely missing his temple, and sliced off a lock of his hair. Nero flailed his arms frantically, screaming for guards to help him as he ran away.

Meanwhile, the man in the hooded robe ran over to Longinus.

Longinus looked and saw it was Khalid.

Khalid shoved a rag in Longinus's mouth.

"Bite Down!" He instructed.

Longinus bit down as Khalid began to pry the nail from his wrist. As the skin ripped open from the pull, Longinus screamed into the rag. Khalid quickly tied a cloth around it then helped him up.

Another hooded man leading two saddled horses rode up at a steady clip. Khalid and Longinus mounted quickly and rode out of Rome with great speed.

Then, from out of nowhere, a band of bounty hunters on horses appeared from all sides of the city riding out like a storm behind them with several wagons full of Followers of the Way. It was Longinus's band of men. The galloping hooves of the rider's horses and rolling wagons left a haze of dust so thick the sun could not be seen. An ominous darkness filled the air and drifted over the dead soldiers bodies like a black plague.

The Old Man (sorcerer) more angered at the loss of the wagons filled with followers of the way than the Praetorian Guards deaths burst forth in a rage inside Nero's possessed body sending him convulsing uncontrollably in the thick dark haze. "Idiots!" he shouted, "Idiots all of them idiots!"

Meanwhile, Khalid and Longinus rode out with the band of men headed to the foothills of the Apennines mountain range. After a long distance away from Rome they eased their horses down to a trot.

Khalid, "You're lucky more than you know. We were hauling the followers out the other side of the city and Vitali caught your scent way on the other side. We were leaving. Vitali sniffed you out. She led me to your haversack and I alerted the men to take position. Right girl?" Vitali barked as she ran along side of Khalid's horse.

Longinus, "She's good."

"Sure is!" answered Khalid.

Longinus looked over at the many wagons of people. "How did you get them all out?"

"Oh the soldiers had been loading them up all day getting ready to haul them off to the dungeons. We just said we'll take it from here, and we did."

Longinus smiled, "I was ready to die. Now I'm ready to live."

"That's the spirit!" answered Khalid.

"Indeed, the journey has just begun. I am chosen!"

The End.

To continue the epic adventure of Longinus be sure and read the sequel, "The Spear of Destiny II".

CPSIA information can be obtained
at www.ICGtesting.com
Printed in the USA
LVHW022106020221
678131LV00001B/47